COMING UP ROSES

A BEAUFORT SCALES MYSTERY - BOOK 6

KIM M. WATT

BEAUFORT SCALES

For further information contact: www.kmwatt.com

Cover design: Monika McFarland, www.ampersandbookcovers.com

Editor: Lynda Dietz, www.easyreaderediting.com

Logo design by www.imaginarybeast.com

ISBN (PB): 978-1-8383265-9-3

ISBN (ebook): 978-1-8383265-8-6

First Edition: September 2021

10 9 8 7 6 5 4 3 2 1

To all you wonderful readers,
who have assured me that the world does, indeed,
need more tea-drinking, crime-solving dragons.
Thank you.
You're my Toot Hansell.

A BEAUFORT SCALES MYSTERY

CONTENTS

1. Miriam 1
2. DI Adams 13
3. Alice 27
4. Mortimer 39
5. Miriam 51
6. DI Adams 67
7. Alice 81
8. Miriam 97
9. DI Adams 111
10. Alice 127
11. Mortimer 141
12. Miriam 155
13. DI Adams 171
14. Alice 187
15. Mortimer 203
16. Miriam 217
17. DI Adams 233
18. Mortimer 249
19. Alice 265
20. DI Adams 279
21. Miriam 295
22. Alice 309
23. Mortimer 323

Epilogue 337

Thank You 341

Something's Strange in Yorkshire ... 343

Recipes For All Occasions 345

Acknowledgements 347

About the Author 349

Also by Kim M. Watt 351

1
MIRIAM

It was that point in the season when one felt any frosts should have headed off to bother a different hemisphere, but there was a hungry little bite in the early evening air that made Miriam somewhat concerned for the new blossoms on her apple tree, although she knew they weathered the same threat every year. She was collecting logs from the shed in the garden, still partly full of the neat stacks of raw wood she'd put in against the winter cold last autumn. She supposed it might be considered a little indulgent to have a fire at the end of what had been a rather lovely spring day, but the evening seemed to be setting in fast, the edges dull and sad-feeling, and she rather felt a fire chomping away in the log burner was just what she needed to cheer herself up. A fire, a large slice of ginger cake, and a complete excess of tea. That was what the day called for.

It did not call for a wild animal jumping up at her with a roar of delight as she turned to the shed door, making her shriek and drop the log basket. It was only half full (any more and she couldn't carry it), but that was more than enough to make the corner of it landing on her bare toes so spectacularly painful that she could barely see past the involuntary tears as she clutched her injured foot.

She said something fairly unrepeatable, and the monster yelped and fled.

"Are you alright there, Miriam?" someone asked.

"I think I've broken my toe," she said, squeezing it a bit harder. She should have put shoes on, she supposed, but it wasn't *that* cold.

"Let me see." Rose squatted down, swatting Miriam's hand. "Go on, let go!"

Miriam sighed, and let the older woman prod her foot. "Ow!"

"You're being silly. It's absolutely fine."

"It doesn't *feel* absolutely fine."

"You should be wearing shoes."

"You shouldn't be sneaking around people's gardens!" Miriam tried to glare at Rose, but she couldn't make it stick. Rose just folded her arms and looked unimpressed, her short hair dyed a rather vivid shade of violet today. Her Great Dane, Angelus, skulked behind her contritely, not appearing in the least bit monstrous now that Miriam knew who he was.

"I wasn't *sneaking*," Rose said.

"Well, maybe not *deliberately*." Miriam picked up the log basket, and Rose collected a couple of bits of wood that had made a run for it. "Fancy a cuppa?"

"Wouldn't say no."

Miriam led the way into the warmth of her stone-flagged kitchen, the ceiling beams low and heavy above them, the big old AGA cooking range breathing contented heat across the little room. She took the logs through to the living room, and by the time she came back in Rose had already put the kettle on and was clattering about with mugs. The small woman was restless, even for Rose, and Angelus was standing at the table licking the last of the ginger cake crumbs off the plate.

"Angelus!" Miriam said, and he flopped to the floor, his eyes huge.

Rose looked around. "Oh, no. Angelus, you brute!"

He wagged his tail and rolled onto his back, getting one leg caught up in a chair rung and almost knocking it over. Miriam caught it before it could fall and tried to look stern, which was quite hard to do, given the dog's beseeching look.

"It's alright," she said with a sigh. "I've got some custard creams. They're only packet ones, but they'll do. It's not going to make him sick, is it?"

"Just fat," Rose said, swirling hot water in the tea pot to heat it. "And the vet says he's that already anyway."

"How rude." Miriam went to the pantry to find the biscuits. "He looks very handsome to me."

"It's ridiculous," Rose agreed. "It's like beauty standards for dogs. They don't need it."

"No one needs beauty standards at all," Miriam said. "Such a silly concept. As if there's anything standard about beauty. Everyone's beauty is completely unique." She rubbed Angelus' tummy, just to make sure he understood that he was included in this, and handed Rose the milk from the fridge. "Is everything alright, Rose? Not that I'm not very happy to see you, of course—"

"Oh, I know. It's late to be coming around for a cuppa," Rose said, slopping milk into the mugs and onto the worktop. "Sorry."

Miriam handed her a cloth without comment. A little of the dull evening seemed to have crept into the kitchen with them, lovely dog tummies notwithstanding. The lights were a touch dimmer than they should be, the fading sun outside marginally more distant, and the heat of the stove couldn't quite dissipate the chill in her belly. She knew why, but the knowing didn't mean she understood it. Miriam was Sensitive, not in some psychic talking-to-the-other-side thing (she did do Tarot readings, rather successfully, but she drew the line at seances, which were either predatory fakeries or very real unpleasantnesses), but in a way that meant she felt things others didn't, and sometimes it could change the way she saw the world around her.

It also meant, of course, that she had been able to see dragons quite easily, which is a rare ability. Most people can't – or don't – see the magical Folk that inhabit the edges of the world around them, since they simply never believe in anything outside the recommended parameters of human experience. So a dragon appearing in one's garden and stealing a scone is impossible, and therefore never happened. Miriam, however, had been quite sure she was seeing a dragon, and had merely adjusted her understanding of the world to fit that reality. She *had* been slightly startled to discover that the dragon in question (and dragons in general, as it turned out) had rather a taste for baked goods, though. That had never been mentioned in any of the books she'd read. But being Sensitive had a less pleasant side, too, such as knowing when something sad or frightening had happened in the world around her. And that was what the day felt like now. A little grief-stained.

She took her tea from Rose and they sat in the old wooden kitchen chairs with their worn, comfortable cushions, and she offered the older woman a custard cream without asking anything further.

Rose took the biscuit, dunked it in her tea, and took a bite before it could collapse, making a small noise of appreciation. Angelus sat up, a long thread of drool already descending from his chops and his ears cocked hopefully. They drank their tea and ate the first of their biscuits in a companionable sort of silence, then Rose said, "Have you ever forgotten you've done something?"

"Oh, yes," Miriam said. "I forget cakes in the oven all the time. And tea. I found a cup of tea in the greenhouse the other day. I don't know how long it had been there, but there was a snail drinking from it."

Rose nodded. "I'm terrible with tea. It's a good thing I have so many mugs. I can only ever find a few at a time. But what about … *bigger* things? Things you really *should* remember?"

Miriam considered it. Not just the question, but who was asking it. Rose was the sort of small that meant she still shopped in the kids' section of clothes stores, and was full of a matching exuberant energy, but she was over eighty. She was both of the age when forgetting things became commonplace, and where it became more worrying. "Teresa drove into Skipton the other week," Miriam said at last. "Then she took the bus back, and when she got home she thought someone had stolen her car. She was about to report it to the police, but luckily she told Pearl first, and Pearl reminded her she'd driven."

Rose snorted. "That's quite big."

"A car is," Miriam agreed. "And Carlotta forgot her niece was coming to stay, and went to Majorca for the week. Her niece had to stay with Rosemary instead."

Rose scratched Angelus' heavy head, and he flopped his drooling jaw onto her lap. "That makes me feel a bit better."

"Have you been forgetting things?"

Rose gave a funny little shrug. "Yes. Sort of. I mean, I always forget my tea. And sometimes I don't remember where I left the car and have to retrace my steps to find it, or I'll go to the shop for something and not remember what it was, so buy something else entirely and end up with six jars of marmalade but no butter, say."

Miriam made a sympathetic noise. That seemed very normal to her, but that dull shade to the day hadn't gone away. It was like watching an old movie, all the colours a little washed out and not quite as they should be.

Rose took another biscuit, twisting the two halves apart and staring at the pale yellow icing inside. "But there seems to be *more,* lately. Things don't stay where I put them. Or … I don't know.

They're not where I usually put them, and I don't remember putting them where I find them."

Miriam frowned, thinking of their stay in her sister's country house the previous spring. Things hadn't stayed where you put them around there, either, and the explanation had been less forgetfulness and more small creatures with kleptomaniacal tendencies. "Do you think you have bollies, or something like that?" she asked. "There seem to be lots of creatures around that we didn't know about a year ago. Brownies, maybe. They're house spirits, aren't they?"

Rose nodded. "Maybe." She didn't sound convinced.

"Well, we shall ask the dragons," Miriam said. "Mortimer will probably be down tomorrow, so we'll come over and he can have a look around and see if that's the problem."

Rose tapped her fingers on her mug, looking less reassured than Miriam had hoped. "But it was just small things they moved, wasn't it?"

"I don't really know," Miriam admitted. "They *did* move Beaufort, but that was an emergency. Maybe they move bigger things if they can get away with it?"

"Mmm." Rose didn't look up from her mug.

"What is it?" Miriam asked. "What's missing?"

"It's not what's missing," Rose said, looking up finally. "It's what's turned up."

MIRIAM WASN'T QUITE sure what she expected. The dragons had been known to *leave* things before – the High Lord of the Cloverly dragons, Beaufort Scales himself, had actually left Detective Inspector Adams an offering once. It had been a very well-cooked rabbit, presented artfully on a bed of leaves and set outside her car door while she'd been staking out Miriam's house.

As DI Adams had not, at that stage, known about dragons, it had led to some very awkward questions. Still, Miriam hoped that this might be something similar. Perhaps the rather sweary French lizards from Christmas had relocated from Pearl's chimney to Rose's. Or maybe the water sprite had left a goose in the living room, which would be alarming but not *entirely* terrifying. Miriam thought of the geese that periodically invaded the village green, and revised that. It would be *manageably* terrifying. Or maybe one of the dragons' new dragon scale baubles had blown up into something unexpected. There were still glitches at times, no matter how carefully Mortimer designed and tested them. Anything was possible, and she felt she could manage a situation like that rather well. However, Rose's serious face suggested that whatever had turned up might not be quite as pleasant.

They walked to Rose's house, crossing the village green with its reputedly bottomless duck pond (a TV crew calling themselves monster hunters had tried to find the bottom once, but the sprite had set some of the aforementioned geese on them, so that had been the end of that). The grass was damp on Miriam's ankles, and she thought, a little distractedly, that she should have worn her wellies.

Rose's house was perched on a slight rise on one corner of the village green, where the road curved around, giving her a large plot with a neighbour only on one side. The front and opposite side were bounded by the road, where it ran past the village hall and the church. A chunky, sprawling bungalow, the house squatted in an unruly garden that was partly given over to vegetables and fruit trees, and partly a wilderness of mysterious undergrowth sprouting bird boxes and insect habitats and hedgehog huts, with a wildflower meadow instead of a front lawn. The bungalow itself was a rambling sort of place that appeared to have started life as an old stone hut of some description, which various families had slapped extensions onto in a gleefully haphazard manner, and with little regard for the original architecture, such as it was.

"Are you sure we shouldn't call Alice?" Miriam asked, as they crossed the green toward Rose's gate. The more overgrown side of her garden met the village green, and various bushes and low trees crowded together, fighting for space where they hung heavy over the low stone wall. "You know she's very good at dealing with things."

"If I wanted Alice, I'd have gone to Alice's," Rose said. "I don't want someone being logical at me, Miriam. I'm perfectly capable of being logical myself."

"I just... I'm not the best person in a crisis."

"It's hardly a crisis," Rose said, then considered it. "Well, I don't think it is. Not yet, anyway. Besides, you underestimate yourself."

Miriam didn't think she did, but she didn't argue.

Rose opened the little wooden gate and Angelus bolted into the depths of the garden, ears flopping and long legs splaying all over the place.

"Angelus, *no!*" Rose shouted, running after him as he vanished into the undergrowth. *"Angelus! Sit! Sit, dammit!"*

Miriam looked at the gate swinging gently in their wake, sighed, and stepped into the garden, latching the gate behind her. She could hear the older woman still shouting deeper in the undergrowth, and the birds sang to each other with no sign of alarm at the chaos below. She followed the tree-shaded flagstone path through the back garden to the kitchen door, leaving Rose to deal with the Great Dane and listening to the anxious shifts and sighs of her own thoughts. Everything felt a little too dark, a little too sombre, and she wished the dragons were here. Everything was better with dragons.

The door was unlocked, and she pushed it open onto the low-ceilinged, shadowed kitchen, the lights not yet lit against the night. She was about to step inside when something *moved* in the shadows, and she jumped, stumbling back down the single stair into the little covered porch and catching the heel of her flip-flop as she went. She teetered on the edge of her balance, heart pounding, and called, "Hello?"

There was a pause, and she squinted into the dim kitchen, wondering if she'd been mistaken, then someone detached themselves from the shadows and rushed forward. Miriam almost bolted, then remembered she was here to help Rose, and if that meant tackling strangers in her kitchen, she would.

"Stop!" she shouted, the word teetering on a shriek, and the figure stumbled to a halt, revealing themselves to be a woman of about Miriam's height, all bundled up in a big jacket with her long dark hair gathered into a messy bun.

"Ooh, sorry," the woman whispered, pressing her hands to her chest. "I didn't mean to scare you."

Miriam blinked at her. She was familiar yet not, and Miriam wasn't sure if it was just the taut evening confusing her, or if she had met her before. "What are you doing in Rose's kitchen?" she asked.

The woman pressed her hands harder against her chest, licking her lips, and said, "Is Rose with you?"

"Yes, but who are you?"

The woman licked her lips again, and at that moment Rose clattered up behind Miriam with a contrite Angelus following her, his ears drooping.

"Honestly, he's awful," she said. "He found some fox poo at the bottom of the garden the other day, and now he has to go and see if there's more to roll in every time we get home. And I've gone and stepped in a puddle trying to catch him." She looked at Miriam. "Are we going in?"

"There's someone in your kitchen," Miriam said.

Rose flinched, one hand clutching at the front of her jacket, and said, "Who? Who is it?"

"It's me," the woman called from inside. "I was just … I came to see you."

"Bethany." Rose's voice held a mix of relief and annoyance. "I wasn't expecting you today."

Bethany peered out the door past Miriam. "I just wanted to talk some things over with you."

Rose shook her head. "Not tonight. Digitising all my old papers isn't exactly time sensitive." She made a shooing motion at Bethany. "I'll call you later."

"I really wanted to talk," the young woman said, not moving, and Rose frowned at her.

"Miriam and I have some important business. Whatever it is will have to wait, Beth."

For a moment Bethany didn't move, wavering on the doorstep, then her shoulders slumped and she nodded. "Alright. Sorry for scaring you," she added to Miriam.

"That's alright," Miriam said, although she could feel a nasty sweat on her shoulders and across her belly. That might not have been the scare, though. Or even Rose's mention of *important business,* which sounded ominous. It might be entirely unrelated. Of all the things about ageing she could do without, unnecessary sweating ranked very highly on the list.

Rose waved Bethany off, then pushed Angelus ahead of her onto the old stone floor of the kitchen. She kicked her shoes off and followed him inside, her one damp sock leaving darker marks on the flags.

Miriam stepped out of her flip-flops and walked barefoot into the house, her chest tight with the strangeness of the evening. There was a faint whiff of woodsmoke coming from somewhere, mixing with the lingering scents of baked apples and old books, and Rose flicked the lights on, flooding the kitchen with a warm and friendly glow. The big table in the middle of the room was cluttered with opened mail and discarded science magazines and a fruit bowl stacked with apples and tangerines and precariously balanced eggs, but the worktops were clear of everything except a decrepit-looking microwave and a couple of mugs draining by the sink.

Rose led the way to a side door, opening it onto a utility room that looked considerably younger than the kitchen. It smelled a little damp, and when she turned on the lights they gave a couple of reluctant flickers before settling into a cold, fluorescent wash that lit dense mats of spiderwebs in the corners above the crowded shelves.

"Come on," Rose said, as Miriam lingered in the safety of the kitchen, and Miriam followed her reluctantly. The floor in the utility was gritty under her bare feet, and she gazed around at the half-forgotten detritus of life around her. A set of shiny golf clubs with a forest of cobwebs engulfing the bag leaned against one wall, and a harness that looked like the sort of thing one wore for climbing into caves hung above them, a hardhat clipped to the belt. A giant, mouldy kite dived over a torn lampshade, and a chipped porcelain ladybird lay on its back next to a clock with plastic cockroaches on the ends of its hands. There were also the several boxes of empty jars and bottles that seem to be compulsory in every utility room, saved Just In Case.

But Rose ignored all of those, crossing the little room to a big chest freezer that was humming contentedly to itself next to the washing machine. She rested one small hand on the top and looked back at Miriam. Miriam stared at her, a shiver creeping its way up her spine and raising the small hairs at the base of her neck. She couldn't quite read Rose's expression.

"I'm sure I didn't put this here," Rose said. "I'd have remembered."

"The freezer?" Miriam asked hopefully.

"No," Rose said, without even the suggestion that she thought it was a silly question. She lifted the lid.

For one wild moment Miriam considered covering her eyes with both hands and refusing to look, but, she reminded herself, she *was* a grown-up, despite never being quite sure how she felt about that. And it couldn't really be anything too terrible, could it? Not in Rose's freezer. Maybe Rose had discovered some new type of creature that liked living in chest freezers, building a home from blocks of frozen spinach. It was possible. Or perhaps Rose had been given a rabbit by the dragons herself, although that wouldn't be any great mystery.

Miriam stepped next to Rose and stared down into the freezer.

It was not a rabbit. It was certainly a body, though. It wasn't looking at her, which she managed to feel thankful about for one moment before she really did close her eyes. When she opened them again, the body was still there, its pale hair frosted with ice and a packet of frozen peas resting on one hip, as if someone had put it there to soothe a bruise. She looked at Rose.

"I wanted some ice cream," Rose said. "And, well." She waved at the body. "It's on my ice cream."

Miriam thought she might never eat ice cream again.

2
DI ADAMS

DI Adams looked at the body in the freezer, then at the two women. Miriam's hair was standing out in the sort of directions that suggested she'd been spending a lot of time fiddling with it. Rose looked calm but pale, her hands in the pockets of her fleece.

"When did you find it?" DI Adams asked.

"This morning," Rose said. "Around six, I guess?"

"You said you wanted ice cream," Miriam said.

Rose shrugged. "I'm an adult. I can have ice cream for breakfast if I want."

DI Adams didn't disagree with the sentiment, but she said, "It's almost nine. At night. Why didn't you call me earlier? Or call *someone?*"

"I called Miriam."

"You came and had tea," Miriam said. "And it was almost dinner time then." She sounded less accusatory than bemused, and DI Adams felt rather the same way. Although she didn't know why she was surprised. Expecting anyone in Toot Hansell – let alone any member of the Toot Hansell Women's Institute – to act reasonably was, she was starting to suspect, an impossibility along the lines of expecting good weather on a bank holiday weekend.

"You knew it was here all day?" she asked.

Rose scratched her chin. "Well, yes. I wasn't quite sure what to do. I've never found a body in my freezer before."

"I don't think it's a situation you need to have prior experience with to know that calling the police is usually the first step."

"I thought it might go away," Rose admitted.

"You thought ... why?"

"Well, it just appeared on its own, so you never know, do you?"

DI Adams pressed her fingertips under her left eye. The tic hadn't started yet, but it couldn't be far off. This was another issue with Toot Hansell, and the Toot Hansell Women's Institute. Spending any length of time dealing with either (and it was impossible to have one without the other) inevitably set off a tic. And often a headache. And that was before anyone even mentioned dragons, which were a whole other kind of headache.

She looked sideways at the grey, dreadlocked dog sniffing around the golf clubs. Dandy was currently the size of a Labrador, which seemed to be his favoured proportions. Angelus had taken one whiff of him and fled, howling, to the bottom of the garden, but Dandy didn't seem bothered. He just ambled about in all his matted glory, putting his paws up on the edge of the freezer to examine the contents, and giving no indication whatsoever that he was finding anything interesting. He was much less helpful than she'd imagined a magical dog, visible only to herself – or mostly only to herself – might be. She sighed and checked her phone.

"I'll have some officers here soon to secure everything. Forensics are going to have to come out, too. And you'll have to come in to the station and give a statement."

"Not tonight," Miriam said. "You can't drag Rose all the way to Skipton *tonight*. It's late!"

"Both of you," DI Adams said, and Miriam went an interesting shade of pink.

"Me?" she squeaked. "Why me?"

DI Adams looked at the body, then at Miriam, her eyebrows raised, and Miriam went from pink to very pale.

"Are you *arresting* us?"

DI Adams fought the urge to look around for someone else to deal with this. She was first on the scene. It was her responsibility. But she couldn't help wishing DI Colin Collins had been on duty, and not off at some cheese-tasting event. Miriam was his aunt, after all. *And* he was much better at this sort of thing.

"No," she said finally. "You're just giving a statement. The body's in Rose's house, and you were party to discovering it."

"It doesn't feel like a party," Miriam said, almost to herself.

"Can't we do it tomorrow?" Rose asked. "Angelus gets grumpy if he stays up too late."

"You are aware that there's a body in your freezer, right?" DI Adams demanded.

"Well, I'm not *blind*," Rose snapped. "But it's not like he's going anywhere, is it?"

For one moment DI Adams considered arresting both of them, just to make life easier, then someone shouted from the kitchen door, "Adams? You in there?"

"In the utility," she called back, trying not to sound as relieved as she felt.

There was the scuff of worn trainers on the old stone floor, then Collins loomed in the doorway, his round face creased with concern. "Aunty Miriam? Rose? Are you both okay?"

"No," Rose said, folding her arms. "DI Adams wants to take us down to the station and interrogate us. At this hour! And at our age, too."

DI Adams folded her arms too, although part of her wanted to slap a hand to her forehead, and possibly shout. She resisted both urges. "No one said anything about *interrogations.* We're not MI6. I just need to take your statements, and I couldn't do it with just me here."

"Well." Collins put one arm around Miriam's shoulders and gave her a quick hug. "There's two of us now, and Lucas is already securing the scene as well as he can."

"He got here already?"

"He was with me when you called. He's a committed turophile too," Collins said.

DI Adams tilted her head at him, wondering if she should ask.

"Cheese lover," Collins explained. "Besides, he said he didn't want to miss another Toot Hansell drama."

"I'm glad someone's enjoying themselves," she muttered, and scowled at Dandy. He was chewing on something, and she hoped it wasn't evidence. It wouldn't be the first time.

"So we aren't arrested?" Miriam asked, and Collins gave DI Adams an amused look.

"I wasn't *arresting* you," she started, then shook her head. "Look, just wait in the kitchen for a moment, can't you?"

Miriam almost ran for the door, and Rose followed at a more sedate pace. "Do you want a rum?" she asked Miriam as she went. "I need a rum after all that."

"I think I'd rather some cheesy puffs," Miriam said, and DI Adams pushed the door closed behind them.

DI Collins raised his eyebrows and tucked his hands into the pockets of his jeans. It had obviously been a very casual cheese-tasting event. "Trying to get me alone, Adams?"

"I have more than enough alone time with you as it is," she said, pushing Dandy off the freezer. He was trying to steal the frozen peas. "You don't even eat peas, you horrible dog." Although, admittedly, the only thing she was sure he consumed was caffeine. He certainly had no interest in the dog food she'd tried buying him.

Dandy looked at her, his eyes hidden beneath his thicket of

grey hair but disappointment written in every line of his shoulders.

"Dandy helping out again, is he?" Collins asked.

"Less helping out, more ... well, I don't know. Being Dandy."

Collins looked around the garage carefully. "It's very awkward, his being invisible. I never know if I'm going to step on him or not."

"You preferred him visible?"

Collins made a face, and she knew he was remembering Dandy looming over a suspect who'd been threatening DI Adams, the man's arm clamped in the dog's massive jaws. It seemed an angry Dandy was a large Dandy, and being large also made him visible to *everyone.* Which certainly took the threat out of most suspects, being confronted with a furious, dreadlocked dog the size of a Cloverly dragon. Although, as said dragons were no bigger than a small pony, it still didn't make him enormous. The red eyes and large teeth were very effective, though.

"Invisible is fine," Collins said.

"I thought so, too," she said, and stepped back so Collins could peer into the freezer and examine the man occupying most of it.

"Well," he said finally. "Lucas is quite right. Toot Hansell never fails to surprise."

"I'm not sure it surprises me anymore," DI Adams said. "I think I'd be more surprised if we went six months *without* some sort of criminal undertaking in Toot Hansell."

"You've not even been here two years yet," Collins said, as the door opened and Lucas leaned in, a heavy-looking bag in one hand. "That's not long enough for such gross generalisations. And, d'you know, I think it's got worse since you arrived. We barely had any cases out here before that, did we, Lucas?"

"Nope," he said. "Quiet as anything, it was. I mean, it's always been weird, but not exactly crime central."

"Great," DI Adams said. "I feel so lucky."

Lucas threw a roll of police tape to Collins and said, "Can you get your suspects out of the house? The whole place is a crime scene, and they seem to be making cheese and pickle sandwiches."

Dandy jerked his head around and rushed for the door, and DI Adams tried to grab him without making it look as if she were grabbing an invisible dog. Lucas gave her a puzzled look as she snagged a handful of Dandy's hair and pulled him to a halt. "Cramp," she said, then added, "They're not suspects – or I don't think so, anyway. One of them may be an intended victim."

Lucas nodded. "Fine. Then can you get your probably-not-suspects-but-maybe-intended-victim, and her companion, out of my crime scene?"

"We can do that," Collins said.

"We should take them to the station," DI Adams said, without much enthusiasm.

"Like you said, they're not suspects."

"*Probably* not."

He gave her an amused look. "Can you see Rose lifting a full-grown man into that freezer?"

"Miriam might have helped her."

"Yes, because my aunt is quite the criminal mastermind," Collins said, and Lucas glanced behind him, then back at the inspectors.

"Will you go and theorise somewhere else, and take those two with you? The small one's on her second glass of rum already, and the other one's just asked if I take milk."

"We're going," DI Adams said, letting Dandy go as Lucas stepped away from the door. The dog went straight back to peer at the peas hopefully, cheese and pickle sandwiches apparently forgotten. "Let's get a preliminary statement at least, then we can do a full interview tomorrow. Maybe even at the station. That way we might be able to avoid any run-ins with the full might of the Women's Institute."

"Excellent plan," Collins agreed, and waved at the freezer. "All yours, Lucas. We'll have a poke around and see what else we can turn up."

"Please don't poke anything," Lucas said, examining the body. "Or at least make it a hands-off poke." He flicked a hand around his neck, as if to dislodge a fly, and Dandy panted on him happily.

"We shall be visions of discretion," Collins said, and ambled toward the door, a big man with his hands in his pockets and his waxed jacket stretched at the shoulders. DI Adams followed, checking she had gloves in her pocket in case there was a need for poking after all. Dandy stayed behind, apparently in the hope that someone was going to get the peas out of the freezer if he just waited long enough.

In the kitchen, Rose was pouring more rum into a small glass while Miriam held a cheese and pickle sandwich out to her and wondered aloud if anyone was lactose intolerant, and if she should make some tuna sandwiches as well.

"Enough sandwiches, Miriam," DI Adams said, waving for her to put the plate down.

"But I've only made four," she said, staring at the chopping board. "How many people are coming?"

"It's a crime scene, not a picnic," DI Adams said, and Miriam blinked like a startled owl, plucking at the neck of her jumper with her free hand.

"Just come and sit down for a moment, Aunty Miriam," Collins said, pulling out a chair. He was interrupted by a shout from the utility room.

"Not in here!" They turned to look at Lucas, leaning out the door to shake his head at them. DI Adams felt like a rookie DC again, forgetting her shoe coverings or tripping over an evidence marker. "I mean, come on. Crime scene, remember?"

"Sorry," she said, and looked at Collins as Lucas retreated. "Car?"

"We can go to my house," Miriam said. "Rose, you're going to stay with me anyway, aren't you?"

"I suppose," Rose said, eyeing the rum bottle. "If I'm being thrown out of my own home."

"Crime scene," Lucas shouted again from the depths of the utility, and DI Adams watched Dandy walk past with a bag of frozen peas clutched delicately in his jaws. She hoped he hadn't disturbed the body too much. Lucas was sounding upset enough as it was.

"You'll probably have to stay away for a few days," she said to Rose. "I'll accompany you to get your toothbrush, any medication, and a change of clothes now, then we'll sort the rest out later. Is that okay?"

"Well, given that I have a body in my freezer, I can hardly complain about not having my favourite pyjamas," Rose said, and DI Adams caught the faintest quiver at the edge of the words.

Miriam rubbed Rose's arm gently. "I have plenty of T-shirts. They'll do you very well as nighties."

"I don't wear *nighties.* Small children and old ladies wear *nighties.*"

"I quite like nighties," Miriam said, gazing at the teapot in a longing sort of way.

"Let's find you some pyjamas, then," DI Adams said, and Lucas, sounding as if he were deep inside the freezer, shouted, *"Carefully!"*

IT TOOK FAR LONGER than was reasonable to gather Rose's things, mostly because nothing seemed to be in any sort of order. Even DI Adams, who regarded her house merely as a place to sleep and put things, was bewildered when Rose pulled her toothbrush from a vase in the hall.

"What's it doing there?" she asked.

"I have no idea," Rose said, frowning at it. "I'm sure – almost sure – I left it by the sink this morning, but I suppose one never knows."

DI Adams followed her back into the bathroom and watched her remove three preserved scarab beetles in little plastic cases from a toiletries bag so she could put the toothbrush in it. "You keep beetles in there?"

"Not usually," Rose said, her shoulders hunched as she pulled another drawer open, setting a bag of flour next to the sink so she could reach her hairbrush. DI Adams opened her mouth, then closed it again. She kept it closed as she followed Rose around the bedroom, finding her pyjama top stuffed into a shoe and her socks tucked inside her pillowcase. Rose made little annoyed sounds with every discovery, and eventually turned to face DI Adams, clutching a pillow to her.

"I'll take this. I just dyed my hair and the colour always comes out. But that will have to do for the rest. If I have to find anything else we'll be here all night."

"Is this usual, Rose?" DI Adams asked, her voice quiet.

Rose looked around the bedroom, drawers pulled open and the covers of the bed thrown back, a stack of books teetering dangerously on each bedside table and spilled on the floor beneath them. "Sometimes?" she offered. "I seem to have had a bad day."

DI Adams examined her, so small and slight that she felt monstrous in comparison, then said, "How often do you have bad days?"

Rose made a small gesture of dismissal, looking at the books by the bed instead of at the inspector. "A couple of times a week, maybe?"

"Do you forget things easily?"

Rose looked up at her finally, her face pale and drawn in the overhead light. "Not that," she said. "I wouldn't forget *that.* I'm sure of it."

DI Adams thought she didn't sound as sure as she would have

liked, but there was no point in pushing it now. Not if Rose really couldn't remember. "Come on, then. Miriam's going to pass out from tea deprivation soon."

"It wouldn't surprise me," Rose said, handing her bag to the inspector and marching back down the hall to the kitchen, still hugging her pillow. DI Adams looked at the bag for a moment, then sighed and followed her. This is what she got for trying to be approachable.

The kitchen was empty, Miriam and Collins already gone when DI Adams and Rose stepped out into the chill of an early spring night. The stars were a high sweep of luminous dust above them, visible even past the low light seeping from the windows of the bungalow. DI Adams could only see one streetlight, three houses away in the direction of the village centre. All of Toot Hansell seemed to be given over to these quiet, slumbering lanes, the lighting left more to the soft glow of garden solar lamps and the low loom of the houses than to any organised approach. A nightmare for policing, but she had to admit it was wonderful for stargazing.

The shadows among the trees were deep and heavy, full of velvety secrets and whispering nocturnal life. DI Adams glimpsed Dandy drifting soft-footed through the flowerbeds, so he'd obviously dealt with the frozen peas and was on the hunt for something else. Coffee, probably. She clicked her fingers, and he lifted his head to look at her, his eyes gleaming red in the dark for a moment before his hair fell back over them. She shivered slightly, and pulled her coat a little tighter. She wasn't sure she'd ever get used to those eyes.

Everything was still, no breeze to disturb the trees, the roads silent as they rounded the house to the front garden, the wildflower meadow still whispering in the memory of wind. Somewhere she could hear water in one of the becks or streams that ran through Toot Hansell like chattering capillaries, carrying life and secrets and magic, and in the distance a dog barked. Otherwise the only sound was the murmur of Miriam's voice from the car, leaning out of the door to talk to Collins where he stood next to it.

The click of Rose's gate was loud as she opened it, and she almost apologised for breaking the soft evening silence. Then someone coughed, the noise hard and flat, and she wheeled toward it.

A man hurried across the front lawn of the house next door, coughing into his hand as he went.

"Sir," she called. "North Yorkshire Police – *sir!*"

The man didn't hesitate or turn back, just scuttled into the house and pushed the door closed behind him. She frowned, and pointed at the car. "Rose, wait for me there."

"Sure," Rose said, amiably enough. "Good luck getting away once you get him started, though. He can never shut up, that one."

"Adams?" Collins called, as she hurried down the pavement to the house next door.

"Won't be long," she called back, letting herself in the painted gate without pausing. The garden the man had been lurking in was neatly trimmed, the flowerbeds laid out in tidy geometric patterns and stripes mowed into the short grass. There was, inexplicably, a metre-tall lighthouse in the centre of a gravel circle to one side of the path, with a softly glowing light behind the glass at the top. The path to the door was gravel too, edged with stone, and she was raising her fist to knock when the door opened in front of her.

"*Ooh*, hello," the man said, jumping back. He wasn't much taller than her, with a greying goatee and a moustache that curled jauntily at the corners. "You gave me a fright!"

"Detective Inspector Adams," she said. "North Yorkshire Police."

"Dougal Brown." He offered his hand, and she shook it. He was smiling through the beard, an ingratiating little grin that made her want to reclaim her hand as soon as possible.

"So why didn't you stop when I called?" she asked.

"I didn't realise you were talking to me. Why would the police want to stop *me?*" He chuckled, one hand flat on his chest. His words had a softness to them, an accent she couldn't quite place. Welsh, maybe?

She examined him while he beamed the annoying grin at her, then said, "If in doubt, it's best to stop when a police officer calls you."

He nodded vigorously. "Of course, of course. Dreadfully sorry. You must be here to ask if I've seen anything."

DI Adams raised her eyebrows slightly. "Why would you think that?"

"Well, you are police. And while Rose has all sorts in and out her door"—he raised his eyebrows at DI Adams, as if inviting her to make some assumptions, or judgements—"it's not usually *police.*"

"And have you seen anything?"

"Nothing other than her usual parade of visitors. What's happened? She's not hurt herself, has she?"

"Why would you think that?"

He waved a hand vaguely. "She's a little ... Well, she is *old.* One worries."

"Does one?"

"If one's a good neighbour, yes. I always think that a woman of that age, on her own ..." He shook his head sorrowfully. "I try to keep an eye on her."

DI Adams thought that Rose was unlikely to appreciate that. Aloud, she said, "Do you happen to remember what visitors she's had over the past twenty-four hours?"

"I can do better than that," he said. "I have video of everything. I'll get it all together for you."

Of course he did. She wondered if Toot Hansell had a Neighbourhood Watch, or if Dougal was more of a one-man village security system. "That would be very helpful, Mr Brown," she said aloud. "I'll have an officer collect it from you."

"I can bring it to you now, if you want," he said, half-turning to go back inside.

"No, no. That's fine. Someone will be by to pick it up tomorrow. Is there anyone you can think of right now, though? Anything out of the ordinary over the last few days? Disturbances? Strangers?"

He shook his head. "Just her new boyfriend. Rather nice ethnic sort. Only been coming around for a few months, but he's a regular now."

"Ethnic sort, huh?" DI Adams said.

"Is that not right? What do you like being called? I try to keep up, but …" He shrugged helplessly.

"I like being called Detective Inspector," she said. "Anyone else?"

He scratched his chin. "Her ex-husband came around yesterday. He's *French.*" He said the last in a conspiratorial tone, and DI Adams sighed.

"Alright. Thank you for your assistance. A police officer will be by to take your statement and pick up the video footage tomorrow."

"Any time, Detective Inspector," he said. "Do you have a card? I could call if I think of anything else."

"Just call Skipton police station," she said, giving him a quick nod and turning away before he could say anything else. She marched back down the path with her hands in her jacket pockets, frowning at the lighthouse. Dandy stood next to it, his head low between his hulking shoulders, inspecting the house, and she clicked her fingers at him again. He glanced at her briefly, then went back to staring. She didn't blame him. There was something about the precise layout of the flowerbeds and the carefully structured bay trees in pots by the front door that made even a detective inspector want to introduce some rogue dandelions, just for variety.

She left him there and let herself out the gate, not trying to put any pieces together. Not yet. They were all floating, still forming their own shapes in her head, drifting around the dead man in the freezer like moths waiting to settle. And they all involved people. No one seemed to be flinging magic about the place or involving dragons or dryads or goblins or otherwise making things unreasonable. That was nice. She started to smile, but it faded quickly. Because at the centre of everything remained a nagging concern about the toothbrush in the vase and the flour in the bathroom. And it was hard to smile at that.

3
ALICE

Alice had learned that it was always best never to expect certain things, such as snow at Christmas or sunny days for the village fête, or for people to act in a sensible manner. She felt that knowing anything could happen – and usually did – tended to be a sensible approach to life. It made the inevitable unexpectedness of living much more manageable.

However, a phone call at six in the morning from Miriam, in which she only understood every third word – partly because Miriam was talking terribly fast and partly because she was whispering – but from which she gathered that Rose had a dead body in her freezer and no idea how it got there, was unexpected even by Alice's generous standards. She changed out of her pyjamas, took a large smoked salmon quiche from the freezer, and had left the house by seven. Her breath curled in front of her as she walked, letting herself out of the back garden gate onto the well-travelled path in the woodland that skirted the village, listening to the birds arguing with each other and watching squirrels sprinting from one tree to the next, and trying not to make any assumptions about what was happening. It was difficult – a dead body in a freezer did rather invite speculation.

There was smoke climbing from Miriam's chimney as Alice crossed the little footbridge over the stream and walked up the garden path to the kitchen door. There were lights on inside despite the fact that it was a clear morning, and she knocked, then tried the handle. It was locked, which was most unusual, but not unexpected, given a body in the area. Miriam was not terribly good with the unexpected, even though she'd had plenty of practice over the past few years.

Alice waited a moment longer, then knocked again, and a head popped into view through the window over the sink. Miriam, with her hair even bushier than usual and a large orange jumper mis-buttoned at the shoulder. Alice saw rather than heard her say, "Oh!" just as if she'd had no idea Alice was on the way over, then there was the clatter of a key in the lock and a moment later Miriam pulled her into the kitchen. The younger woman peeked warily into the garden, then shut the door and locked it again, pressing her back to it as she stared at Alice.

"Hello, Miriam, dear," Alice said, unbuttoning her coat.

"Oh, Alice, it's awful! Poor Rose!"

"Well, you'd best tell me the whole thing. I couldn't understand you at all on the phone."

"I'm sorry. Rose was still sleeping and I didn't want to wake her."

Alice nodded. She could smell coffee, faintly burned, in the warm air of the kitchen, which didn't bode well. "Have you slept, dear?"

"No. Well, a little." Miriam picked up a mug from the table and slurped it anxiously.

"You could have called me last night."

"Oh, no. It was late by the time we finished up here. Because the police—" Miriam broke off and swallowed hard, looking at her mug. "Colin was off-duty. DI Adams came, but it took her a while to get here, of course, so it was late by the time we got home. And then she and Colin wanted to know exactly how … exactly what we saw, and … Well, it was late. Would you like some coffee?"

"Tea would be better," Alice said, hanging her jacket on one of the hooks by the door. "Is Rose up now?"

"She's still asleep. She brought some rum over." Miriam waved at a bottle on the table, which had a token puddle left in the bottom. "I can't stand the stuff, but it helped her sleep, at least."

"Well, then. We'll let her sleep," Alice said, taking the kettle to the sink to fill it, since Miriam hadn't moved to do so. "Do you want to shower or freshen up, Miriam?"

Miriam touched her hair. "I already have."

"Of course," Alice said, and pointed at her own shoulder. "You might want to fix those, though."

"Oh!" Miriam fumbled with the buttons, squinting and straining her neck as she tried to see what she was doing. Alice put the kettle on, then batted Miriam's hands away gently and redid the buttons, straightening the shoulders of her jumper for her. It really was a most extraordinary orange, and Miriam had paired it with a pink blouse of some sort that was much longer than the jumper and ballooned out the bottom, over her green corduroy skirt. It was enough to give one a headache.

But Alice just smiled and said, "Much better," then went back to making the tea.

By the time the tea was made, Priya was already at the door with a pistachio cake clutched in front of her, her face drawn in worried lines. "What on *earth* is going on?" she asked. "I could barely make out a word you were saying, Miriam!"

Alice put another cup out, and went to the pantry to find the bigger teapot. Evidently they were going to need it.

By eight, Miriam's little kitchen was proving too small for all ten ladies of the Toot Hansell Women's Institute (minus Rose, who was still sleeping), and they packed themselves instead into the slightly larger living room, bringing chairs from the kitchen table with them. The fire was burning lazily against a chill that Alice thought was more in the heart than the air, and Jasmine had been the last to arrive, her face flushed pink and her arms laden with a bowl containing some very doughy-looking croissants.

"What's going on?" she demanded as she handed Alice the pastries. Alice almost dropped them. Baked goods had no call to be quite that heavy. "Ben won't tell me anything! He was out most of the night, and this morning he just said we were all to stay out of it, otherwise he was going to get in real trouble."

Alice thought that Ben was likely a very good policeman when it came to directing traffic or helping small children find their parents, but when it came to women of a certain age he had rather a lot to learn. "I don't think any of us really know exactly what's happened yet," she said, leading the way into the living room. "Rose is still asleep."

"Not for long," Gert pointed out, making room for Jasmine on the sofa. "I don't know how she's slept through all this!"

"It was quite a lot of rum for a very small person," Miriam said. She looked a little more awake now, even though Alice had cut her off from the coffee. Her leg kept bouncing, as if keeping time to unheard music, and the last thing Alice wanted to be dealing with was a jittery Miriam. Well, more jittery than was usual when an investigation presented itself. As it was, the whole room had an air of overexcitement, and Miriam had told the story of Rose showing her the body eight times. Alice suspected there was a little more embellishment in every retelling.

"I can handle my rum very well, thank you," Rose said from the door. She was already dressed in combat trousers and a pale blue jumper with an octopus embroidered on it, her feet bare. Angelus stuck his head around her, his tail wagging enthusiastically. Alice winced as she heard something fall over behind him on Miriam's hall table. "I just have to put Angelus in the garden. I'll pick up after him, though, Miriam."

"That's alright," Miriam said, her face pinker than ever. "Do you want some breakfast?"

"I brought croissants," Jasmine said brightly.

"Um," Rose said.

"We've got blueberry muffins," Pearl said.

"With bran," Teresa added. "Keep you regular."

"Yes," Rose said. "That sounds better. No offence, Jasmine. Cholesterol, you know. Lots of butter in croissants." She pattered into the kitchen, and Alice followed her, watching Angelus lunge out into the garden with an exuberant volley of barking the moment the door opened.

"Are you alright, Rose?" Alice asked, picking up the teapot and emptying the tea leaves into the sieve. Honestly, keeping up with this many people for tea first thing in the morning was a full-time job. But she preferred it to sitting. It allowed one to move from one conversation to the next without getting too caught up.

Rose didn't answer straight away, one arm wrapped around her waist and the other holding the door, her eyes on the garden. "Not so much," she said finally.

"It sounds very upsetting, what happened."

Rose looked at her finally. "It was. Or is, I suppose. I just don't understand, Alice. How did ... *it* get there?"

"Well, someone put it there. The important questions are who and why, I should think."

"I can't even begin to imagine an answer. I've dealt with some very strange things in my life – one does, in entomology – but this really must be the strangest. I can't make sense of it at all."

Alice nodded. "I should think insects make much more sense than humans."

"They do," Rose said. "One knows where one stands with *Chrysolina cerealis* or *Lucanus cervus*."

Alice fixed Rose with a level grey gaze. The smaller woman's eyes were framed with laugh lines, but the eyes themselves were clear and bright. Evidently the rum hadn't had any lingering side effects. "Miriam said you might be having some trouble with remembering things," she said.

Rose shrugged. "I'm eighty-three, Alice. Of course I have some trouble. But I'm quite certain that a body in my freezer isn't something I'd forget."

"Good," Alice said, although she didn't miss the way Rose looked away as she mentioned *the body,* or the fact that her hand was gripping the door hard enough to turn her knuckles white. "I rather thought so, but I supposed we'd best check."

❧

SEATED IN MIRIAM'S BIG, high-backed armchair, her feet not quite reaching the floor, Rose recounted her discovery of the body the previous morning. "I just wanted some ice cream with my muesli," she said. "I had a very nice salted caramel one in the freezer."

"I'm sure there's at least as much cholesterol in ice cream as in a croissant," Jasmine said to no one in particular. The offending pastries were slumping together in the bottom of their bowl, congealing.

"But who could have put it there?" Gert asked. "Moving a body isn't easy, you know." Everyone looked at her, and she shrugged. "I used to be a nurse. We moved plenty of bodies."

Alice supposed that was a reasonable explanation, but given Gert's large and somewhat colourful extended family, she wouldn't have been surprised if there had been a different one. "Who has keys to your house, Rose?" she asked.

"A few people, I suppose," Rose said. "My stepdaughter – well, ex-stepdaughter – because she can't keep her nose out of anything, and is convinced I'm losing my marbles and that she must save me from myself. Bethany, my research assistant. And … I'm not sure. Maybe a couple of other people."

"I have one," Jasmine said. "You gave it to me ages ago."

"Me, too," Miriam said.

"And me," Priya added. "And there's one in your woodshed, too. You told me where it was in case I lost mine. Which I *didn't.*" She said the last bit in a slightly put upon tone. "I just couldn't remember which bag it was in."

Rose waved vaguely. "It's not that relevant, anyway. I don't often bother to lock up."

Alice thought that seemed very careless, but also entirely to be expected in this village. People here seemed to regard locks as decorative features rather than the simple practicalities they really were.

"It's just not necessary to lock up here," Pearl said. "Or it never used to be."

They all considered this. The crime rate really did seem to have gone up over the last year or so, certainly as it related to the W.I. Not that it was their fault, of course. One didn't invite such things, any more than one invited dragons, but they turned up anyway.

"Alright, so who might want to put a body in your freezer?" Teresa asked.

"We should probably ask why, first," Jasmine said. "Ben says that if you have the why, that'll give you the who."

Alice thought Ben might underestimate the sheer unpredictability of the human species, and that it might slow his advancement in his police career somewhat.

"Maybe it was a threat," Carlotta said. "Or a warning."

"I thought that was horse's heads, not whole bodies," Rosemary said. "And in your bed, not in with the ice cream. You know, in the old country. That's right, isn't it, Carlotta?"

Carlotta ignored her pointedly.

"I really fancied that ice cream," Rose said. "I've gone right off even the idea of it now."

"Why put a body in any freezer?" Alice asked, looking around the room. "What's the point of that?"

"To store it," Jasmine said.

"To hide it," Priya said.

"To preserve it," Rose said. "Although it does mess the tissues up. Certainly a domestic one. Different if you have one of those fancy cryogenic things."

No one spoke for a moment, then Gert said, "Are you *sure* you didn't put it in there, Rose?" There was a clamour of protest and she waved it away. "I don't mean that you *did* it. But could it be from work or something?"

Rose frowned at her. "Whole human bodies aren't something you tend to bring home in your specimen box. There'd be forms, at the least."

Gert shrugged. "I remember a few years ago you had all those dead rabbits in your freezer. You completely forgot until you sent me to get ice for the G and Ts. I couldn't even see the ice, there were so many of the damn things."

"That was personal research," Rose said. "I was trying to find out what was killing them. And I guessed it right – it was my awful neighbour. He was putting bleach and vinegar down the holes and gassing the sorry things."

"Imagine doing that to a poor rabbit!" Pearl said.

Rosemary nodded. "Sounds suspicious, if you ask me."

"A rabbit's a bit different to a human corpse," Alice said.

"But isn't that how they start?" Pearl asked. "Serial killers, I mean."

"You have to stop watching all those true crime shows," Teresa said.

"I don't think he's a serial killer," Rose said. "He just didn't like them in his flower beds, the rotten sod."

Miriam leaned forward, twisting her hands together. "What about Bethany? She was there last night. That was a bit strange, I thought. It was late."

"Oh, no," Rose shook her head. "She's there at all hours. She's grasped my paperwork system better than anyone else."

Alice thought that must be quite a feat. The last time she'd been to Rose's she'd found a thesis in the bread bin and a list of half-answered interview questions in with the potatoes. Aloud, she said, "How long has she been working with you?"

"About a year now, I suppose? She started—" Rose stopped as sudden movement in the hallway caught her attention. Alice turned to look, and saw DI Adams folding her arms over her chest as she glared at them. She had an idea that the movement might have been the inspector covering her face with her hands. Miriam's nephew, DI Colin Collins, was peering around the corner of the door, grinning.

"Criminal investigation," DI Adams said, as if she were continuing a conversation that had started earlier. "Not a bloody bake sale!"

"I honestly don't know what else you expected," Colin said. "If you'd been able to contain yourself we might have eavesdropped a bit longer and learned something, but no. Our cover is blown. Hello, Aunty Miriam, ladies."

"I don't know about this sneaking around," Gert said, crossing her heavy arms. "That seems like entrapment."

"I was just hoping for breakfast," Colin said. "I didn't even get a bacon butty before Adams hurried me off this morning."

"You were sneaking," Teresa said, smiling. "I know sneaking when I see it."

"Criminal investigation," DI Adams said to no one in particular, then pointed at Rose. "We need to talk to you privately."

"I don't see the point," Colin said, taking a piece of berry slice delicately topped with golden crumble from Rosemary. "She'll just come back in here and tell everyone what we discuss anyway."

DI Adams pinched the bridge of her nose. Alice thought she looked less exasperated than she might have, though. Perhaps she was adapting to Toot Hansell, albeit reluctantly. Alice had gone through much the same evolution of despair to acceptance herself.

"Coffee?" she offered.

DI Adams dropped her hand and sighed. "I suppose. Rose, can you come into the kitchen at least?"

"Of course." Rose slid off the chair, and Alice led the way down the hall with the older woman and the two inspectors behind her, hearing the scuffling that was the Women's Institute gathering themselves to follow.

"Stay," DI Adams ordered them, and Colin made a sound that was suspiciously like a snort.

In the quiet of the kitchen, Alice rinsed the cafetière and put the kettle on while she found the coffee. DI Adams had closed the door to the hall, but Miriam let herself in and sat down at the table next to Rose, giving DI Adams a very un-Miriam-like glare that clearly said she wasn't going to be turned away. There was a lot of secretive movement going on behind the door, too, and DI Adams gave Colin a despairing look.

He shrugged. "Don't look at me. We can take her in to the station, but we don't need to at this stage, and it'll just delay the inevitable anyway."

"That's true enough," Rose said cheerfully. "We don't do secrets in the W.I."

Alice wondered if that were entirely true. Certainly not on her side. She didn't feel anyone should be privy to all her secrets. Only those she deemed suitable for sharing. What was life without a few precious things held close to one's chest, anyway?

DI Adams slumped into a chair. "Fine." She watched Rose for a moment, then said, "Have you thought any more about if you recognised the body in the freezer? Last night you weren't sure."

"I only really saw the top of his head," Rose said. "I realise it was hardly a scientific approach, but a body in the freezer when you were only expecting ice cream rather puts you on the back foot."

DI Adams nodded, and glanced at Colin, who put a folder on the table and slid it across to Rose.

"When you're ready," he said. "Just tell us if you recognise him."

Rose looked from one inspector to the other, then at Alice. "Take your time," Alice said, and wondered if she should take Rose's hand, or put an arm around her, but to her relief Miriam did so first. She really was much better at such things.

No one spoke for a long moment, then Rose reached out with her free hand and opened the folder. A man stared up at them, his eyes rendered colourless by frost, his eyelashes tiny icicles. He had a long face with indents still worn into the sides of his nose from glasses, the lines around his eyes heavier than the mass of blonde hair that crowned his head. Alice could see grey at the roots, and the tell-tale, uniform lines of hair transplant plugs at the hairline. He wasn't wearing earrings, but there were dimples in one ear where some had been, and a softness to his jaw where the years were catching up.

"Oh," Rose said, the word breathless.

"You recognise him?" DI Adams said, and it was barely a question.

Rose bit her lip, still staring at the man in the photo.

"Rose?" Alice asked, and in the silence that followed someone shouted in the garden.

"*Hey!* What're *you* doing here, then?"

Alice looked up sharply, spotting a flash of movement beyond the window. The inspectors were already moving, Colin's chair smashing to the floor behind him. Miriam gave a little shriek and jumped up, rushing to the window over the sink.

"Stay here," DI Adams snapped to Rose, and ran for the door. She darted outside with Colin close behind her, and the door to the hall burst open under the combined weight of the Women's Institute as everyone hurried in, all talking at once. Rose ignored them, looking from the picture to Alice with her face twisted into an unfamiliar expression, all anxious angles.

"How much can one forget?" she asked, her voice low. "I mean, really?"

Alice squeezed Rose's hand, the movement unfamiliar and awkward. "Nothing this big," she said, and hoped she was right.

4

MORTIMER

Mortimer leaned a little further forward, peering into the grand cavern with its vaulted roof and well-worn perches on the walls, the floor clean but dusty and speckled with the glint of the odd shed scale. The fire that always burned in the centre of the floor was low and red, the smoke rising in lazy plumes to hide in the far reaches of the roof and make its way through natural fissures to the outside world, just as it had for centuries gone, and, Mortimer hoped, as it would for centuries to come.

Shining in the warm light of the fire and incongruous among the lazy expanses of smooth, worn stone sat a large, top-of-the-range Weber barbecue, the sort with multiple burners and fancy racks. It was perched on top of the stone seat of the High Lords, which had until recently held a nest of tarnished armour and rusted swords. It turned out that barbecues were both more comfortable and much, much warmer for old dragons with aching bones than old trophies were, no matter how traditional the latter might be.

Beaufort Scales, High Lord of the Cloverly dragons and owner of the fancy barbecue, didn't look much like he was bothered by aching bones. He didn't even look particularly old, despite the scars from long-ago dragon hunts that pulled his glossy green and gold scales out of alignment in places. He'd already been old in the days of Saint George – although that was a subject best avoided. Somehow, human tales never mentioned that High Lord Catherine had not only been snoozing in a bramble patch at the time of the knight's so-called heroics, but, as a Cloverly dragon, she hadn't been much bigger than his hounds. Mortimer found it best to make sure Beaufort stayed well away from the village around Saint George's Day. He had visions of the High Lord stomping into a pub garden and trying to explain the real story to large groups of red-and-white-clad revellers. Even those who firmly did not believe in the existence of anything outside their own experience might find it hard to explain away an irate dragon interrupting a stirring rendition of *Jerusalem* to lecture them on the truth behind a favourite saint. And it would definitely end in some sort of disaster, possibly involving The Government. And probably tasers.

Right now, Beaufort wasn't lounging on his Weber. He was sitting by the fire, his head low and close to that of an equally old but rather saggier and more threadbare dragon. Lord Walter was holding forth in an indignant grumble that Mortimer could barely make out.

"What's he saying?" Gilbert asked, his snout close enough to Mortimer's ear that the older dragon shook his head violently to stop the tickle of hot, dragonish breath.

"Well, I can't tell with you hissing at me, can I?"

"Shh!" Amelia snapped from Mortimer's other side. "How can we hear anything with you two carrying on?"

"*Shh* yourself," Mortimer muttered, trying to keep his ears out of the way. They'd been having a small disagreement in the workshop, him, Gilbert, and Amelia, Gilbert's older sister. Well, it had *started* as a small disagreement. It had been to do with Gilbert's insistence that they needed to take immediate action in order to save the hedgehogs. Mortimer wasn't against saving the hedgehogs – he rather envied their ability to roll into a spiky ball and ignore the world, and thought it a very sensible way to address matters one would rather not deal with. However, Gilbert's plan seemed to involve stealing or destroying every lawnmower and weed trimmer in the village to stop anyone being able to cut the grass, and that seemed like exactly the sort of thing that would get people asking questions.

Which, problems of The Government and tasers aside, was something he definitely wanted to avoid. Other than the ladies of the Toot Hansell Women's Institute, most people had no idea dragons still existed. Or ever had, for that matter. The Folk – the magical kinds of the world – had encouraged the idea that they were no more than primitive myths for centuries, and had calmly gone on living unseen lives on the edges of the human world mostly undisturbed. Folk might not be invisible, but they were *faint*, and as most humans assumed there were no dragons (or sprites, or trolls, or – ugh – gnomes) to see, they never saw them.

Which was all well and good, but dragons breaking into garden sheds and making off with lawnmowers seemed like the sort of thing that would get the attention of even the most ardent non-believer, just as surely as crashing Saint George's Day. And once someone saw Folk, there was rarely any going back from it. Not unless one knew how to make them forget, which was a job for a cat. Oddly enough, trying to tell someone one didn't exist while standing right in front of them didn't work so well. Cats, on the other hand, were so ubiquitous – and humans were so used to talking to them, even if they never realised cats could talk back – that they got away with anything. And they had a talent for making people not only do what they wanted them to do, but also for making them forget inconvenient truths.

But, as it was best not to have to involve cats, and given

the difficulties of a village-wide cull of garden implements, he had said no. Amelia had also said no, then tried to make her brother promise not to try anything himself. Mortimer had then, rather prudently, taken cover under a workbench. There had been shouting, a basket of broken baubles, some singed walls, a surprisingly large amount of thrown tools, and eventually he had been forced to order both younger dragons out of the workshop. The only solution left was to bring the whole thing to the High Lord, but as soon as they'd entered the grand cavern they'd spotted him in deep conversation with Lord Walter, which was something none of them had any intention of interrupting. Interrupting Walter was likely to earn a young dragon a clip around the ears, at the very least.

Before long, they'd realised that the conversation wasn't to do with Walter's usual objections to fraternising with humans, most of which seemed to revolve around the idea that there would be pitchforks and flaming torches involved at some point. Mortimer had noticed that those objections had eased off somewhat after last Christmas, when the old dragon had discovered Rose's excellent (if highly alcoholic) rum truffles.

"I'm telling you, Beaufort," Walter growled, slamming one heavy paw onto the rocky floor of the cavern. "You think I don't know when there are hunters about? I can feel it in my tail!"

"Dragon hunters, though?" Beaufort asked, his voice a mild rumble. "It seems unlikely."

"I wouldn't be having twinges of the old wound for damn *rabbit* hunters!" Walter patted one gnarled but still muscular shoulder pointedly. His scales generally tended toward the patchy and mismatched, as if they'd given up on trying to line themselves up on his sagging skin anymore, but one could still see where they bundled into snarled scars. Scars that were older than not only Mortimer, but half the houses in the village, even the ones that shared some of Walter's inclination toward sagginess. "We need to do something. We need to be on guard."

"I rather think you're overreacting, Walter. There haven't been dragon hunters for centuries. No one's even *known* about dragons for centuries."

"Well, you've been doing your best to change that, haven't you?"

"I've been very circumspect."

Mortimer almost snorted. *Circumspect* was not a word he'd apply to anything the High Lord did.

"We can't just ignore the risk. You knew messing around with humans would bring trouble to us all."

Beaufort tapped his talons on the floor thoughtfully. "It is a risk, yes, but a calculated one. I really doubt there's anything to worry about, Walter. Maybe it's those monster hunters again. The ones from the television."

Walter growled. "*Television.* All this modern rubbish will be the death of us, Beaufort."

"I quite like the detective shows," Beaufort said, scratching his heavy jaw. "They're very informative."

Walter took a deep breath, his creased chest quivering, and for a moment Mortimer thought he was going to start shouting again, then he just said, "The death of us," and stomped off, shedding a couple of dull, split scales as he went. Beaufort watched him go with a distracted sort of interest, then looked around as Gilbert clattered across the cavern toward him.

"Beaufort! Beaufort, you have to let me save the hedgehogs!"

"Gilbert, stop it!" Amelia shouted, hurrying after him. "And address the High Lord properly, you turnip!"

Beaufort gave the squabbling siblings a bemused look, then looked around for Mortimer. Mortimer considered making himself scarce and letting the younger dragons sort it out themselves, but Beaufort had already spotted him.

"Hello, lad," he called. "What on earth's going on here, then?"

Mortimer sighed, wondering when he'd become responsible for Amelia and Gilbert. They weren't that much younger than him – sixty or so years was nothing to a dragon. And it wasn't even as if they worked *for* him, even though they did help him make the delicate, magic-infused dragon scale baubles that the clan sold (via Miriam, their human partner). They just worked *with* him, and the business had grown admirably, giving them more than enough money to buy (again, through Miriam) some truly excellent barbecues, ones with split levels and rotisserie attachments and hot plates and hooks for hanging fireproof blankets from.

Barbecues, it turned out, not only make excellent dragon beds, once one got used to not rolling over in one's sleep and sliding off the side, but with a steady supply of gas bottles it meant no one had to be out looking for wood for fires anymore. Which meant more time to hunt for food and less risk of being spotted carting logs around the place, while eggs stayed wonderfully warm and old dragons could snooze comfortably even in the coldest of winters.

It also meant more time for arguing about hedgehogs, apparently.

"Hello, sir," Mortimer said. He still had trouble calling Beaufort by his first name. "We seem to be having some trouble regarding hedgehogs."

"Hedgehogs? I hadn't thought they were that problematic," the High Lord said. "What on earth are they up to?"

"No, no, that's not it at all," Gilbert said. "We have to save them!"

Beaufort considered this. "I realise you're a vegetarian dragon, Gilbert, which you are, of course, quite entitled to be. But this means you may not be aware that no sensible dragon eats a hedgehog. They're very spiky, and if you get one lodged in your throat it's most difficult to get out again."

Gilbert stared at him, his orange and russet scales flushing a horrified green at the edges. "How can *anyone* eat them? They're even cuter than rabbits!"

Mortimer took a sideways look at the dead rabbits lined up by the fire. The younger dragons took it in turns to catch rabbits for those who couldn't, or who had more important things to do. He was feeling a bit uncomfortable with it all these days. He really was very busy with the bauble business, and had barely any time to hunt, so he was quite entitled to help himself to the rabbits, and Beaufort had even told him that he must. But Gilbert was right. They were awfully cute, and he was starting to worry that Gilbert was rubbing off on him. He'd never even considered such things as the cuteness of his dinner before.

"Hmm," Beaufort said, apparently pondering the issues of cuteness himself. Eventually he said, "My point is, I don't think hedgehogs need saving from us. Cars are a lot more dangerous to them, and we can't do an awful lot about those."

"I wouldn't mind trying," Gilbert muttered, then said more loudly, "Not us. Lawnmowers. It's that time of year. Everyone in the village is going to be cutting their lawns and trimming their weeds, and they don't even *care* that they're destroying all the wildlife habitats, or that bees and butterflies *like* weeds, and that the dormice will have nowhere to live, and the shrews, and – and there are *robot lawnmowers* these days, which means no one even looking at where they're going! A hedgehog could get run down while it was sleeping!"

"Robot lawnmowers?" Beaufort asked, and Mortimer didn't like the intrigued note in his voice. He'd want to see one now, and Mortimer felt the colour in his scales fading at the idea of the High Lord hunting robots through the gardens of Toot Hansell.

"Yes! But the weed trimmers are the *worst.*"

"Worse than robot lawnmowers?"

"Yes."

"I see."

"He wants to go and steal all the lawnmowers or something," Amelia said. "Like that won't get us noticed!"

"I see," Beaufort said again. His voice was grave, and he folded his front paws on the ground, settling himself more comfortably on the hard floor.

"I tried to talk to the hedgehogs," Gilbert said. "To explain the terrible danger they're in, you know? But they just roll up and scream."

"I think the screaming is also a factor in dragons not eating them," Beaufort said, a little vaguely.

"Sir, you just need to forbid him to go near the lawnmowers," Amelia said. "He won't listen to me."

"Oh dear," Beaufort said. "Gilbert, you should listen to your sister."

"She doesn't care about the hedgehogs! And she still eats *rabbits!*"

"So do I." Beaufort arched his eyebrow ridges at the young dragon, who made a face.

"Well, sure, but you're … I mean, after so many years … that is …"

"I'm old and stuck in my ways?"

"No?" Gilbert offered, his scales starting to fade to a worried grey. There was silence in the grand cavern for a moment, only the sound of Lord Pamela and Wendy arguing about whether the durability of fireproof blankets was a fair trade for the lack of snuggliness drifting to them from the far corner. Cedric was watching the heated discussion with interest, wearing a rather ostentatious silk flower behind one ear. None of them seemed interested in hedgehogs or robot lawnmowers.

"See?" Amelia whispered to her brother. "This is what happens! Now the High Lord's going to scorch your talon polish off!"

Gilbert looked at his talons – painted in stripes of purple and green today – then back at the High Lord. "I just don't think we should abandon the hedgehogs to get chopped up by lawnmowers, is all."

"Quite right," Beaufort said.

"What?" Mortimer and Amelia asked.

"But, sir," Mortimer added, "we can't just go flying about the place rescuing hedgehogs. Someone'll see us!"

"Well, we can't let them be chopped up, either," the High Lord said. "That's very uncaring, Mortimer."

"See?" Gilbert said to his sister, his chest puffed out. "I told you he'd understand!"

She waved a front paw at him. "Whatever. How can we save the hedgehogs without being caught, though, sir?"

"We enlist a little help," Beaufort said, getting to his feet and shaking his wings out. "I'm sure no one wants to chop up hedgehogs. Humans may be a little unthinking, but they're not *nasty*. Not for the most part. We'll just go and have a chat with Miriam. I'm sure the Women's Institute can sort all this out very easily."

Gilbert scratched his ear. "I suppose that might work."

Beaufort ambled toward the tunnel that led to the sheer cliff outside the dragons' mount, shooting the young dragon an amused look as he went. "It may be less spectacular than last-minute rescues, lad, but it'll work very well indeed."

"I should have thought of that," Mortimer said to no one in particular, although the truth was he'd been more concerned with trying to stop the two younger dragons from entirely destroying the workshop than in coming up with solutions.

Amelia huffed and followed Beaufort, and Gilbert looked at Mortimer. "I made baskets," he said. "To carry the hedgehogs in. They've got fluffy linings."

"Oh," Mortimer said. "Well, I'm sure they'll come in handy for something." Then he followed the others, wondering if Miriam might have parkin. He rather liked parkin, and he felt the day was calling for it already, despite it being barely past breakfast.

Then again, he hadn't eaten his breakfast. It had been too cute.

THEY DIDN'T FLY ALL the way to the village, only over the still-wild, green and boulder-strewn land that surrounded the mount until it gave to a stretch of old, tangled woods that separated the fells from the village. They kept low as they flew, not least because Gilbert had some issues with flying and therefore galloped below them, leaping off the occasional rocky outcropping with a whoop and his wings spread joyfully. Amelia muttered to herself about disgraces to dragonkind, but before long they were all on the ground with him, trotting in single file through the hidden ways that wound among the trees, pathless routes known only to the animals and magic Folk of the world.

Eventually the dragons emerged from the woods where the chattering stream that encircled Toot Hansell formed a natural border to the town, and they padded along its edge until they reached a little footbridge that led straight into Miriam's garden. They peered out from among the trees, checking for walkers or people in the other gardens that bordered the stream. All was quiet, just birds shouting to each other over the noise of the fast-running water.

It was a bright morning with a high sky and a cold, sharp wind that tweaked the tips of Mortimer's ears as they hurried across the little footbridge and through the gate into Miriam's garden. His stomach was already rumbling in anticipation of parkin. Or, if not parkin, maybe some plum cake. Plum cake was good, although he felt it lacked the dense intensity of parkin. But parkin was apparently a winter cake, which he felt made little sense. If one liked a cake, shouldn't one eat it all year?

He was still musing on the seasonal qualities of baked goods when Beaufort stopped so suddenly that Mortimer stood on the old dragon's tail.

"Sorry," he whispered, as Beaufort flicked his tail away. The High Lord shook his head, a quick, silencing gesture, and sank to the cropped grass at the side of the path, the gold edges washing from his deep green scales as he took on the lighter, fresher greens of spring growth. Mortimer swallowed a squeak of alarm and pressed himself under the nearest lavender bush, concentrating hard on making himself as *faint* as possible. The younger dragons were silent behind him, and he risked a peek down the path toward the house.

There was a woman crouching under the kitchen windows, a large camera in one hand. Her thick hair was pulled back from her face, and she was examining the ground carefully, drifting one hand through the pansies as if she could divine the future in them. As Mortimer watched, she crept away from the window, keeping low until she could get to the leaning trellis with its new growth of runner beans and put it between her and the house. Then she straightened up and took a quick look about, her gaze still mostly on the ground. There was something unnerving about her focus, as if she were cataloguing everything she saw, filing it away for later reference. She started down the path toward them, her tread slow and deliberate, and Beaufort eased slowly into the shadows of the apple tree. Mortimer tried to think of everything green he could imagine, grass and leaves and the reeds around the tarn by the mount, feeling his scales threatening to give him away with the grey of his anxiety.

The woman was almost to them, scanning the garden carefully as she walked, and Mortimer could smell her, the scent bright and sharp and *interested,* all lemon-yellow and alight with threads of luminous inquisitiveness, like thunder on a library roof. She was going to see them. He was certain of it. She was looking, *really* looking, using deliberate glances that let her catch the world out of the corners of her eyes, in the places where *faint* things were momentarily visible, and she'd spot them, she'd shout *ah-ha!* and that would be it, that would be centuries of hiding gone, there'd be hunts and trophies and scientists and The Government and *tasers*—

"Well, hello," the woman said. "What's this?" The words were less a question than a declaration of triumph. She started to crouch, and Mortimer saw the piercings in Gilbert's tail catching the sun, reflecting it in silver glints. He swallowed something that wanted to become a squawk of horror, and closed his eyes. He couldn't watch. He just couldn't.

5
MIRIAM

"Hey!" A sharp shout rang across the garden. "What're *you* doing here, then?"

Miriam jumped to her feet, as much to get away from the awful photos on the table as to see who was there, and rushed to the window as DI Adams and Colin ran to the door.

"Police!" DI Adams shouted from outside, and Miriam spotted a woman in faded jeans and a khaki jacket with far too many bulky pockets standing halfway down her garden path, looking back at the house.

"*Excuse* me?" Miriam said. "What's she doing in my garden?"

"Who is it?" Alice asked behind her.

"I don't know. There's some woman with a camera— *Oh!* Oh *no!*" Because just beyond the woman Miriam could see the crouched form of Mortimer, his camouflaged greens blotched with grey, and in front of him Beaufort, calmly watching the woman with his old, age-crackled gold eyes half-lidded. "Oh *no!*"

"Oh *what,* Miriam?" Alice asked.

Before Miriam could explain, DI Adams' clear voice rose in the garden, the edges of the words sharp. "Ma'am, I need you to come over here. Right now."

"Why?" the woman called back.

"If a police officer tells you to come here, you come here," DI Adams said, and Miriam was glad that tone wasn't directed at her.

The woman only smiled, though, and said, "I'm not breaking any laws."

Miriam pushed the window open a little wider and shouted, "You're in my garden! I didn't say you could be in my garden!"

The woman started to say something, and a man's voice rose from the corner of the house, where the path wound around to the gate. "Rose! Where's Rose? I want to see her!"

It sounded like the same person who'd asked what someone was doing a moment ago, and Miriam craned around to try and see them through the window, then gave up and hurried to the door. Alice had already made her way past the rest of the W.I., who had pushed into the kitchen, and was standing on the step with her arms folded. Miriam edged past Gert to join her. A tall man with rounded shoulders and dark hair silvering at the temples was trying to get past Colin, which wasn't going well. He was tall, but not as tall as Colin, and only about half the inspector's width. Although Colin was also occupied with holding back a second man, this one a little shorter and stouter and wearing baggy combat trousers under a T-shirt. The T-shirt had a cartoon rat in a chef's hat on it.

"Rose!" the first man shouted again. *"Rose!"*

"Ah, you are like the honking goose," the second man snapped, accents draped casually across the words. "Honk, honk, honk."

"*So?* I'm worried about her. What are you even *doing* here?"

"She is my Rose. I worry too."

"You should go and worry about your *cakes,*" the first man said, evidently feeling this was a dire putdown.

"Gentlemen," Colin said. "Please calm down."

"I am calm," the man in the rat T-shirt said, and waved at Miriam. "'Allo, Miriam, *chérie*."

"Hello, Jean-Claude," she said automatically, and looked back at Rose, who was still sitting at the table staring at the photos. "Jean-Claude's here."

"Okay," Rose said, not getting up.

"Ma'am," DI Adams said. "Come here, now."

Miriam spun back to the garden. She couldn't imagine anyone ignoring DI Adams, but that woman was still standing *right next* to the dragons. She could almost touch them! "What're you doing lurking around my garden?" Miriam shouted. "You better not have stood on my primula!"

The woman smiled at her. "Are you Ms Ellis?"

"I can't hear you," Miriam announced. "You have to come closer." She could see more and more colour washing from Mortimer's scales, and before long he was going to look very much like a stone sculpture of a dragon. She wasn't sure if that would make him easier to spot or not, but she wanted the woman well away from him.

The woman didn't move. "I'm looking for Miriam Ellis," she said. "I thought she might be in the garden."

"Usually you knock on the door first," DI Adams said. "Come here. I'm not telling you again."

"Coming," the woman said, and fished her phone out of her pocket. It tumbled to the ground. "Oops," she said, and crouched to grab it. Miriam clutched both hands in front of her chest, holding her breath and waiting for the woman to scream, or shout *ah-ha!* or … or whatever one did when one saw dragons. Miriam had offered Mortimer cream to go with the scone he'd just stolen from her windowsill, but she supposed that wasn't the usual response to seeing a supposedly mythical creature for the first time.

"Oi!" a new voice shouted, and the woman looked up. "What the hell are you doing here? I told you at Professor Howard's house, there's nothing here for your crappy magazine."

Miriam peered around to see a young man with dishevelled dark hair hurrying past Colin, who couldn't seem to decide if he should let go of the other men to stop him or not.

"*You* don't get to tell me that," the woman snapped, grabbing her phone and straightening up. The young man headed straight for her, and she took a step back, away from the dragons.

"Oh, bloody hell," DI Adams said. "What are you doing here, Mr Giles?"

"Ervin Giles?" Carlotta asked, and Miriam stepped down into the garden before the combined press of the Women's Institute pushed her into it. "That journalist with the dimples?"

"You really do have a thing for his dimples," Rosemary said.

"They're very nice dimples," Carlotta said, straightening the front of her jumper.

"Hello inspectors, ladies," Ervin said, stopping in front of Beaufort and scowling at the woman in the khaki jacket. "She was hanging around Rose's house earlier."

"Ma'am," DI Adams said. "Over here, now."

The woman waved her phone and started up the path toward them. "I just dropped it, is all. Clumsy me."

"Snooping," Ervin said, not moving. "That's what that is. Blatant snooping."

"You stay out of this," DI Adams said to him.

"I was helping," he protested, shoving his hands into his pockets. "*I* was just coming around to knock on the kitchen door, then I spotted her snooping."

"Shut up, Mr Giles."

"Ervin," he said.

DI Adams ignored him, and as the woman stopped in front of her she said, "Who're you, then?"

"Katherine Llewelyn, *Cryptids Today.*" The woman produced a business card from her phone case and handed one to the inspector. "Is Miriam Ellis here?"

"That's me," Miriam said, scowling at her. "You still haven't said what you're doing in my garden."

"I heard you're the local psychic," Katherine said.

DI Adams looked at the sky. "Fantastic," she said, then waved the card at the woman. "Is this a real publication? Seriously?"

"Only the most prominent cryptid news source in the country."

"Bollocks," Rose said next to Miriam, making her jump. "You never verify *anything.* You're still claiming Nessie is a plesiosaur."

"Rose!" the taller man shouted. "Rose, are you okay? There were police at your house, and no one would tell me what happened, and—"

Rose waved impatiently. "I'm *fine,* Campbell."

"My Rose," Jean-Claude said, taking a packet of cigarettes from his pocket. "Other than for me, you have the dreadful taste in men. I leave you for one moment—"

"Do behave yourself, Jean-Claude," Alice said.

"I behave. This *putain* is the problem."

In the press of W.I. ladies gathered in the door, Teresa said, "He sounds like he's been talking to the lizards in your chimney, Pearl."

"Is that a euphemism?" Gert asked, and Jasmine gave a squeak of laughter.

Katherine stared at them all, then looked back at Rose. "Are you a reader of our magazine, then?"

"Only when I fancy a bit of heartburn. You give cryptozoology a bad name, you do."

"And journalism," Ervin put in.

"Only to those with closed minds," Katherine said.

Miriam didn't like the way this was going. Journalists from magazines that specialised in mythical creatures seemed like a very bad thing to have in Toot Hansell. And especially to have so near dragons. "What do you want?" she asked, trying for Alice-like tones but feeling they came off a little wobbly. "Are you looking for a Tarot reading?"

"More wondering about some strange events that seem to be happening around here," Katherine said. "Over Christmas, particularly. It all sounded a little ... *unusual.*"

"I already covered that," Ervin said. "You can read all about it in the back issues of the *Craven Chronicle.* Which is a real newspaper, unlike some."

DI Adams made an impatient gesture. "Never mind that. You're trespassing, Ms Llewelyn."

"I did knock on the front door, but no one answered. I thought you might be back here." She gave Miriam a smile that was probably meant to be encouraging, but it made Miriam uneasy. It felt *knowing.*

"Evidently not," she said. "And you should have tried the kitchen door rather than lurking around someone's garden. It's very rude."

Katherine took another card from her phone case and held it out to Miriam, who took it more on reflex than anything else. "I'll come back at a more convenient time."

"That won't be necessary," DI Adams said, while Miriam stared at the card. "There's nothing to see here."

"The time-honoured homily of the establishment, covering their tracks," Katherine said, and smiled at Miriam. "See you soon, Ms Ellis." She took one last look at the garden, then brushed past Ervin and headed for the road.

"Right, then," Colin said. "I think you two can toddle off, too."

"Yes," Jean-Claude said, and looked at Campbell. "You are trespassing also."

"I'm here for *Rose.* And if I'm trespassing, so are you!"

"No, I know Miriam. See? 'Allo, Miriam!" He waved again, and Miriam lifted her hand automatically. "You see? I am welcome."

"You shouldn't be here! You're *divorced!*"

"Non," Jean-Claude said, lighting his cigarette and puffing smoke at Campbell. "We are not divorced."

"But I'm with her now. You can't be here!"

"But I am."

Colin raised his hands and said, "You gentlemen need to head off now. Rose is in good hands."

"Not till I've talked with her," Campbell said, still trying to get past Colin. He wasn't having an awful lot of success. "She needs my support."

"This is rubbish. Rose needs better things than *support* from a man," Jean-Claude said, making air quotes around *support*.

"What, like *cake?*" Campbell snapped, and the two men stared at each other.

"No," Colin started, and Campbell lunged at Jean-Claude, one arm raised in something that was more flail than punch.

"Merde!" Jean-Claude yelped, jumping back and tripping over the cake box he'd set on the path next to him. *"Non! Mon gâteau! Tu es un monstre!"* He dropped his cigarette and fended the taller man off, driving him away from the cake.

"Hey!" Colin shouted. "That's enough!" He grabbed one of Campbell's arms, then let go again and jumped back to avoid a punch that Jean-Claude evidently intended to be for his rival, but was rather badly aimed. The inspector shook his head and let them stagger away, watching as they crashed into a small juniper bush, slapping wildly at each other and expending a fearsome amount of energy without actually managing to land any blows. They were swearing in an inventive mix of English and French, and Miriam was quite sure she'd never seen such an ineffectual fight. Although, admittedly, her experience of such things was rather limited to what she saw on television.

"Collins?" DI Adams asked.

"Oh, let them wear themselves out," he said, picking up the cake box before anyone could stand on it. "They're hardly going to hurt each other at that rate."

"That is not how we do policing."

Gert pushed past Miriam and marched over to the men. Campbell had fallen over a large half-barrel of mint, and was trying to get up while Jean-Claude poked him with a rake Miriam had forgotten to put away and left leaning against the crab apple.

"Oi!" Gert bellowed, and both men yelped, Campbell rolling away with his hands over his head while Jean-Claude dropped the rake in fright. "What are you, ten? Stand up, the both of you."

Jean-Claude ran a hand back over his short-cropped hair. "I am standing already."

"Shut up, you."

"Okay." He patted his pockets, looking for his cigarettes, as Campbell climbed to his feet. His glasses were hanging off one ear and his hair was standing out at all angles, but otherwise Miriam thought they both looked as if the fight had been just as ineffectual as she'd suspected.

"Apologise to Rose," Gert said. "She has enough to deal with."

"Sorry, Rose."

"I am sorry, *ma chérie.*"

"She's not your—"

"No," Gert said, and both men fell silent again, looking anywhere but at each other. "Now apologise to each other."

"This is too much," Jean-Claude said. "Rose, I am sorry. I bring you a cake, and the police they tell me there is a problem, and—"

"I'm very sorry," Campbell said, holding his hand out to the other man. "This is very silly. Obviously we're both just a bit overwrought."

Jean-Claude stared at his hand, then at him, and for a moment no one spoke, then he grasped Campbell's hand and shook it quickly. *"Putain,"* he muttered, so quietly that Miriam barely heard it.

"Close enough," Gert said.

"*That's* how we do policing," Collins said, grinning at DI Adams.

She shook her head and pointed at the men. "Who're you two?"

"My ex-husband and my toy boy," Rose said.

"Not ex," Jean-Claude said.

"Well, we're not together, are we?"

"Toy boy?" DI Adams said faintly.

"Awesome," Ervin said, grinning.

"Keeps you young," Carlotta said. "For those of us with Mediterranean blood, it's very common."

"Have you told Philip that?" Rosemary asked, and Carlotta looked at the sky.

"I wish you wouldn't call me a toy boy," Campbell said. "It's very demeaning."

"I don't see why," Rose said. "You *are* younger than me."

"So am I," Jean-Claude said, lighting his cigarette. "But I am not a *boy*."

"Well, I mean, I'm not either! Obviously." Campbell waved at himself. His trousers had a grass stain on one knee, and there were twigs stuck to the sleeve of his jacket.

"Oh, *oui*. You are the big man, no?"

"I don't see how you have the energy," Priya said to Rose. "Such hassle!"

"I'm not seeing both of them at once," Rose protested. "Well, not usually, anyway."

"Just one of them seems rather energy-sapping," Alice murmured.

"Enough!" DI Adams said, her voice rising enough that Miriam was fairly sure she was struggling not to shout. "You two, have you got cars here?"

"Yes," the two men said together.

"Then go and wait in them. DI Collins or myself will be with you shortly."

"You can't keep me away from Rose," Campbell insisted.

"Maybe Rose *wants* them to keep you away from her, no?"

"Look, you infuriating little man—"

"*Moi?* Infuriating? I will tell you what you are—"

"Boys," Gert started, and Miriam threw her hands up in exasperation. The orange jumper was scratching her neck unpleasantly, and her arms and shoulders were prickling with the start of a horrible hot flush, and there were photos of a *dead body* on her kitchen table, which was going to put her right off her dinner, and the actual dead body was in poor Rose's freezer, and they were all standing out here watching two silly men argue over Rose, while neither of them even stopped to ask what Rose actually wanted. It was all completely unreasonable, and just so *typical.*

"This is *enough,*" she exclaimed, and everyone looked at her, startled. "This is *my* garden, and *I* get to say who comes in it, and you two haven't even asked, and so you *are* trespassing too."

Jean-Claude gave her a doubtful look. "Miriam, *chérie,* we know each other—"

"No! No, I didn't say you could be here, and you're both being horrible nuisances, so you have to leave. Right now. I … I *rescind* any invitation I ever gave you!" She pointed at the men as she said it, as if she might be able to zap them straight off her property, the way vampires were forced out of a house when one took away their invitation. Or so the books said – Mortimer insisted there were no such things as vampires, but considering it was a dragon doing the telling she had decided to reserve judgement on that.

"Oh, come on," Campbell started, and DI Adams interrupted him.

"Quite right, Miriam," she said. "Do you want to press charges?"

"I can book them right here," Colin said.

Campbell and Jean-Claude fixed him with matching looks of horror.

"Oh, male solidarity is not in my repertoire," the big inspector said. "Aunty Miriam's got a point. And she's my favourite aunt, so off you go now, before I actually do book you."

"Rose," Campbell tried, and she shrugged.

"It's Miriam's house."

"This is a disgrace," Jean-Claude said. "You are a police state."

"We have rights," Campbell agreed, and Miriam thought she'd quite like to shake them both. She'd never shaken anyone before, but her hair was sticking to the nape of her neck and she could feel her face going the colour of a beetroot, and she certainly *felt* like shaking someone.

"Oh, would you just *go away?*" she snapped at the men, and Jean-Claude, who she quite liked but was just being so *annoying* right now, started to say something, then there was the thunder of paws in the garden. Jean-Claude wheeled around as Rose's monstrous Great Dane tore toward them, long legs flying and eyes rolling in alarm, and DI Adams grabbed Miriam, pulling her out of the way as the huge dog arrowed for the kitchen door. Beaufort gave a startled rumble and Angelus changed direction so suddenly he tumbled onto his side, rolling over once then finding his feet and tearing toward the men instead. Colin stepped back smartly, and Jean-Claude yelped, "Angelus, *non!*" then spun and bolted for the front of the house with Campbell sprinting after him. A moment later they heard the clatter of the gate and the twin slam of car doors.

"Oh dear," Rose said, without much enthusiasm. "I think he was just playing, really."

DI Adams let go of Miriam. "It was very effective, whatever he was doing."

"It wasn't—" Ervin started, then stopped as DI Adams glared at him. "Right."

"That was so unpleasant," Miriam said, her voice higher than it should have been. She swallowed and wiped sweat off her forehead. "I hope they're not too upset at me."

"You were well within your rights," Alice said. "It is your garden."

There was a murmur of agreement, then a sudden upheaval from behind Ervin. Mortimer collapsed onto the grass, the colour running out of his scales like wet paint in the rain, and Gilbert shoved Amelia away hard enough that she staggered into the High Lord.

"My *tail,*" the young dragon wailed, grabbing it in his front paws.

"Your silly piercings almost got us caught," his sister snapped.

"Cryptids Today," Beaufort said, starting up the path. "How interesting."

"Terrifying," Mortimer said, more to himself than anyone else. "That's what he means. *Terrifying.*"

"You tore my scales," Gilbert said to Amelia.

"I'll tear your ear off if you keep complaining."

Miriam gave up on worrying about Rose's trespassing admirers and stared at the card in her hand instead. "I really don't like this."

"I wouldn't worry too much," Ervin said, ambling over. "That's got to be a joke publication. I mean, *Cryptids Today?* Really?"

"Its circulation is quite high among the less discerning members of the cryptozoology community," Rose said. "But you're right, it is a joke. No peer review, not a scrap of critical thinking—"

"What're you doing here, Mr Giles?" DI Adams interrupted.

"Scaring cryptid journalists out of Miriam's garden, apparently," he said, using air quotes as he said *journalists,* and grinned at her. "And Ervin, remember? We can't stand on formality like that after we killed Santa together."

Miriam frowned at him. He was awfully sure of himself, which made her rather disinclined to like him, but he had proved very handy with a plum pudding when they'd had some issues with unpleasant faeries and a ravenous Santa over Christmas. "Why are you actually here?"

"It seemed like a reasonable place to find Rose," he said.

"And why are you looking for Professor Howard?" DI Adams asked.

Ervin gave her a dimpled grim. "Word is there's a body in her house. I thought she might like to talk to a friendly face rather than a stranger."

"She doesn't have to talk to *anyone,*" Miriam said, plucking at her jumper. It was proving far too warm, what with multiple journalists lurking around her garden and bodies in freezers. "Least of all any journalists!"

"Oh, come on. I'm basically part of the gang these days." He waved in a vague circle, encompassing the W.I. and the inspectors and Miriam and the dragons. Gilbert was still clutching his tail, and Mortimer was so grey he looked as if he might keel over at any moment.

"You were sneaking!" Miriam insisted to the journalist.

"How was I sneaking? I *shouted!*"

"Should've come to the front door," Colin said, rocking on his heels with his arms crossed over his bulky chest. "Would've seemed much more legitimate."

"Who uses front doors around here? And besides, I wouldn't have interrupted Cryptid Kate, then, would I?"

"That was rather helpful," Beaufort said in a low rumble. "She was terribly close to seeing us."

"That was Gilbert and his ridiculous piercings," Amelia pointed out. "She'd never have spotted us otherwise!"

"They're not ridiculous! You just think *fashion* is sticking some lake reeds behind your ears when Alex is about!"

"As if! Alex is a complete—"

Beaufort cleared his throat warningly, and the two younger dragons subsided, while Ervin stared at them with open fascination.

"Are your claws like that naturally?" he asked Gilbert. "The colours, I mean."

Gilbert looked at Amelia triumphantly. "See? *Some* people get it."

"He would," DI Adams said to no one in particular, then added, "You've done your good deed for the day, then, Mr Giles, so—"

"Ervin."

"For— Fine. *Ervin.* You've done your good deed. Now get off, will you? This is far too early in the investigation for you to be talking to *anyone.* Get your statements from the station, same as anyone else."

"I really think I could get a *little* leeway, all things considered."

DI Adams pointed around the house. "Do we need a repeat of the dog chase?"

Ervin rocked back on his heels with a long-suffering sigh. "Fine, fine. I'll go. Are you sure you don't want to give me a quote, since I'm here? A little titbit for your friendly journalist?"

"Oh, I have so many things I'd like to quote at you," DI Adams said. "Let's go for *no comment,* though."

Ervin gave her a dimpled smile, then ambled for the gate. "I'll wait out here, then. Just in case."

DI Adams watched him go, then said, "Bloody journalists."

"Excuse me?" Mortimer said. He was still a chalky grey. "Did he say something about a body? He did, didn't he? What sort of a body? Not a ... a *person* sort of body, is it?"

"Was it a hedgehog?" Gilbert asked. "I knew it! We should have taken action sooner!"

"I somehow don't think so, lad," Beaufort said, regarding the two inspectors with bright interest. "But I do believe we've arrived at just the right time."

DI Adams made a strange noise, and Miriam looked around to find the younger woman squeezing the bridge of her nose as if she had a bad headache starting. She rather sympathised.

"Come inside," she said to the dragons. "No sense waiting out here when there's a cryptid hunter about."

"A body," Mortimer said mournfully. "Monster hunters and bodies."

"Only one of each, lad," Beaufort said, leading the way into the kitchen. "Let's not get carried away."

6
DI ADAMS

"Alright, everyone inside," DI Adams said. "There's no point standing around out here."

"Certainly not with cryptid hunters and stray husbands all about the place," Teresa agreed.

"Ex-husbands," Rose said. "Well, mostly ex, anyway. And only one of them." She peered around Miriam. "What on earth has got into Angelus? I've never seen him go after anyone like that before, and he knows both of those two."

"Maybe he was fed up with all their squabbling," Miriam said, which DI Adams thought made Angelus one of the more sensible creatures in the garden. Although the truth was she'd seen what had got into Angelus.

"Dandy was chasing him," she said aloud.

"Your magic dog was chasing Angelus?" Rose asked. "Well, call him off at once! You know the poor thing's terrified of that creature!"

"I think Dandy just wanted Angelus to get your men moving," DI Adams started, then caught Rose's glare. "Right. Sorry." She clapped her hands and shouted, "Dandy! Come here, boy!" She stared at the corner of the house expectantly, but there was no response. She hadn't really expected there to be. The only times she'd tried calling Dandy before had been when he was chasing squirrels up trees. He didn't pay much attention then either, so she just left him scrambling around the branches like a weird, oversized cat. As she was the only one who could see him, it hardly mattered. Well, she was *almost* the only one. As she'd discovered over Christmas, a certain journalist could also see him, which she found incredibly irritating. Of all the people she could have shared an invisible dog with, she would not have chosen Ervin. Even Miriam would have been better.

Now she gave Rose an apologetic look. "Sorry. Dandy does what he wants, really."

"That's just poor training," Rose said, and marched off down the path, shouting for Angelus.

"She has a point," Collins said. "Just because he's invisible doesn't mean you shouldn't train him. There are responsibilities with being a pet owner."

DI Adams scowled at him. "I didn't ask for an invisible dog. I didn't ask for *any* dog. And Angelus isn't exactly coming when called, is he?"

"But you still *have* a dog," Pearl said. "So you have to train him. If you don't, he'll turn out like Primrose. Sorry, Jasmine."

"Primrose is very well trained," Jasmine protested. "She's just a little highly strung."

"*Martha* is well trained," Pearl said. "Primrose is a menace."

"Martha's asleep ninety per cent of the time," Jasmine retorted. "You can't even tell if she's trained or not."

DI Adams thought they were both right, and hid a grin as she started after Rose. Her phone rang, and she fished it out of her pocket. *Mum*, the display said, and she groaned, silenced it, and slid it back into her pocket. She had more than enough women of a certain age to deal with right now. She didn't need another one, and especially not one who was going to ask if she'd used the new saucepan set she'd been given at Christmas yet, and if she was seeing anyone, because if not someone's sister's aunt's book club friend knew a nice young man – who probably wore sweater vests and collected stamps – in Yorkshire somewhere.

"Rose!" she shouted. "Come on, we're not finished yet!"

"Where's my dog?" Rose shouted back. "What's your monster done with him?"

"He's not a monster," she protested, jogging to the open gate. Rose was standing in the middle of the little lane, looking up and down the street.

"He's an invisible dog," Rose said. "That puts him in the realm of cryptids, at least."

DI Adams couldn't exactly disagree with that, so she just peered down the lane each way and whistled a couple of times for good measure. There was no movement of either the canine or cryptid variety, but a door cracked open on a car across the street and Jean-Claude checked in both directions before he got out.

"What is happening with Angelus?" he asked. "I do not know what is wrong with him. He likes me!"

"His taste has obviously improved," Campbell called from the safety of his own car.

"You come out here and say this to me, schoolboy."

"*College teacher!* And I'm head of the science department!"

DI Adams held up a hand before they could get started again. "I need both your contact details. If you can't be trusted to stay out here and be civil, you can come down to the station separately later."

"Why?" Jean-Claude asked. "I am not the suspect. Him, *bien sûr*, but—"

"Don't be *ridiculous*, I'm a respected—"

"Evidently *both* of you have temper problems, and no respect for Rose's wishes," DI Adams said. "So you can sit down, calm down, and wait your turn, or you can go away now then come to the station this afternoon to be interviewed."

The men stared at her, then Jean-Claude looked at his watch and said, "I have to work. But I come to the station whenever you say, okay? Anything for Rose."

Campbell scratched his jaw. "I'll wait," he said. "It's Sunday. I don't have any classes."

Jean-Claude glared at him, then pulled out his phone. "I wait too. I have minions."

"Minions?" DI Adams asked, and he waved impatiently.

"Staff, you know."

"Right." She looked at Rose.

Rose shrugged. "Did either of you see where Angelus went?"

"Yes!"

"*Oui, ma chérie!*"

They both spoke at once, pointing at the garden, then scowled at each other.

"Oh, good," Rose said. "He's got no traffic sense at all, the silly thing." She hurried back through the gate, shouting for the dog, and DI Adams regarded the two men for a moment longer.

"Behave yourselves," she said finally, and turned to follow Rose back into Miriam's garden, giving a low whistle for Dandy. There was no response from him, but quick, scuffed steps made her turn to see Ervin hurrying up to her. "What?"

He gave her that same, disarming grin, but he looked wary as he checked Miriam's garden. Looking for Dandy, no doubt. Even if he hadn't been chasing the journalist himself, Dandy was still unnerving. She thought it might be the luminous red eyes that did it. Although, his teeth were pretty alarming, too.

"Sure you won't give me a statement, Inspector?"

"Nothing to say right now, Mr Giles."

He flashed her the dimples. "*Ervin.* Maybe later on the statement? I'll bring coffee?"

"I've got coffee inside," she said. "Enjoy the wait."

"Oh, come *on*. We saved Christmas together, remember? And we share your creepy dog, in a way."

She sighed. "You can share your bed with him, then. He never chooses to sleep in his small form."

Ervin wrinkled his nose. "No, that's okay. I don't fancy him having a nightmare and morphing into eating size on me, or whatever he does."

"Mostly he snores. And drools."

"Lovely. I had a flatmate like that once."

DI Adams couldn't quite hold back a snort of laughter. "Fine," she said. "When, and *only* when, I'm ready to make a statement, I'll call you beforehand, alright?"

She expected him to protest, but instead he just nodded. "That's fair. Watch out for that cryptid hack, though, Inspector. No ethics, some of those crappy papers." And he headed back to his car, throwing her a wave as he went.

She watched him start the engine and pull onto the road, heading for the village, slightly startled that he'd gone so easily and wondering if he was up to something shady. He *was* a journalist, so he probably was.

She gave Dandy another quiet whistle, but he didn't appear, so she headed back into the garden. She rounded the corner of the house to find Angelus trying to climb into Rose's arms (and Priya struggling to hold Rose up), while Gilbert stood in the middle of the path protesting that he was just being friendly and hadn't meant to scare anyone. His sister was talking over him, telling everyone in the vicinity that certain young dragons shouldn't be allowed out until they knew how to behave around different species, and Mortimer was keeping a wary eye on Dandy, who was standing on the top of a rickety trellis arch by Miriam's herb garden, for reasons that escaped DI Adams. The W.I. were discussing, at great volume, the benefits and disadvantages of toy boys, and Beaufort was talking to Alice quietly by the apple tree. That last was a sight that did not fill DI Adams with confidence. They both looked as if they were already far too invested in this investigation.

"Ah, there you are," Collins said, around a mouthful of apple cake. "Looks like we're all here, then."

DI Adams pressed her fingertips against the tic under her eye and wondered if she should go back and take Ervin up on his offer of coffee. It might be easier.

THE KITCHEN SMELLED of fresh coffee and toasting bread and the warm, smoky scent of dragons, and it was far too small for twelve humans, four dragons, and Angelus, who refused to leave Rose. At least Dandy stayed outside, flopped on his back on top of the trellis with his hairy belly exposed to the sun. DI Adams clapped her hands at everyone, much as she'd clapped them for Dandy earlier, and with about as much success.

"Can everyone except Rose go into the living room?" she asked, but was mostly drowned out by Jasmine and Pearl still arguing about dog training, and Teresa trying to tell them that both their dogs were loveable in their own ways, and Carlotta and Rosemary fussing over Collins, and Gert telling them to leave the poor lad alone, just as if Collins wasn't happily taking a tea from one and a sunshine-pale lemon biscuit from the other. She looked at the floor, rubbing her forehead, and found Mortimer looking back up at her, his eyebrow ridges furrowed over his amber eyes.

"I'm so sorry," he almost whispered, and she had to lean down to hear him properly. "We only came about the hedgehogs."

She opened her mouth to ask, decided against it, and struggled her way through the packed kitchen, trying not to stand on anyone's toes or tail. She hooked one arm firmly through Rose's, tipped her head at Collins, and herded the tiny woman out into the hall, which was cool and empty and astonishingly quiet. Her ears were ringing like she'd been at a concert.

She ushered Rose into the living room, and a moment later Collins appeared clutching three mugs, the folder tucked under his arm.

"Coffee," he said, offering one to DI Adams, who took it gratefully. "Tea," he said to Rose, holding another mug out.

"I did fancy something a bit stronger," she said, taking it.

"It's not even ten a.m.," DI Adams pointed out, sniffing the coffee. It smelled strong and rich, like a little dose of normality.

"So?" Rose asked, helping herself to a piece of pistachio cake from a tin on the coffee table. Dried rose petals drifted off it onto her lap.

Collins sat down in one of Miriam's big armchairs and put the folder in front of Rose again. "Do you need to take another look?"

"No," she said, breaking a bit of the cake off. Her voice was level, but DI Adams could see her fingers trembling just slightly. "I'd rather not."

No one spoke for a moment, and there was just the sound of Collins slurping his tea, and the rumble of noise from the kitchen.

Finally Rose said, "His name is— was Eric Latherby. But I have no idea why he was in my freezer."

"How did you know him, Rose?" DI Adams asked.

Rose put the broken bits of cake down uneaten. "We have interests in the same field."

"You were both biologists?"

"I'm an entomologist. And no. He's— *was* a cryptozoologist."

"As in cryptids?" DI Adams asked. "Like that journalist?"

"Anyone who works for *Cryptids Today* is not a journalist," Rose said. "And certainly not a *scientist*."

"But cryptozoology – that's a real field? They study mythological animals?" Collins asked, and Rose nodded.

"Well, a *real* field is pushing things a bit. But it's a field, shall we say. People study it. I've had an interest in it ever since we met the dragons. I wanted to know what else was out there. Most of them are just fantasists, like the lot that read *Cryptids Today,* all speculation and no proper scientific method. But a few of them really put the work in, for all the good it does them."

"And this Eric Latherby? Which was he?" DI Adams asked.

Rose poked her cake uncertainly. "He hosted a podcast, had his own YouTube channel – I never quite worked out if he really believed in any of it, but he didn't fake anything. If he disproved something, he showed people. He didn't mislead anyone."

"When did you see him last?" Collins asked.

Rose shrugged, brushed the crumbs off her hands, reached for her tea, then changed her mind and leaned back on the sofa. "Not since January, I suppose. He gave a talk at the university in York."

"They have cryptozoology at the uni?" Collins asked. "That's not actually a subject, surely."

"Oh, no – it wasn't put on *by* the uni. That was all part of how he did things, you know. He'd go to unis and colleges, and he'd rent halls and give lectures. It made it all seem really legitimate. He was doing very well – he was trying to get a Netflix deal, I think. He'd have been good at that." Her mouth pulled down at the corners.

"So you saw him at the lecture?" DI Adams asked. "Did you speak to him after that?"

"We spent some time together."

DI Adams didn't really want to ask the next question, but she did anyway. "How would you characterise your relationship?"

"Casual. But fun." Rose raised an eyebrow, and DI Adams sighed.

Collins looked at the ceiling, scratched his jaw, then said, "This was before the toy boy, then, I take it."

Rose snorted. "Yes. Monogamy isn't for everyone, but I find anything more just a bit too tiring these days."

"Was your current partner aware of your previous relationship with Mr Latherby?" DI Adams asked.

"Campbell? Yes. But he also knows that Jean-Claude and I still spend time together. He's a grown-up. He can handle it."

DI Adams wasn't sure if she agreed with Rose's evaluation of Campbell as a *grown-up,* not after the fracas in the garden. And she also wished she could hand this interview off to someone else. It was like listening to her gran explain that she and Poppa were going to be embracing swinging. There was nothing *wrong* with it, but it was information she'd just rather not have. "So you didn't have any disagreement with Mr Latherby, then."

"Not personally. I disagreed with his Bigfoot theories, and he insisted on this whole Yorkshire panther nonsense having some basis in reality. We argued about that sort of thing."

"How heated were those arguments, Rose?" DI Adams asked, trying for the gentlest tones she could.

Rose gave her a sharp, almost amused look, and said, "They were more likely to inspire other *urges* than wanting to shove him in my freezer." Her voice faltered on the last words, her half-smile fading.

Collins rubbed his mouth with one hand, raising his eyebrows at DI Adams. She tried not to think about urges and said, "Right. Well, differing views over make-believe animals seem like a poor motive for murder, anyway."

Rose nodded, cleared her throat and sat up a little straighter. "You'd be surprised. Things get very heated in the cryptid world. Although it's nothing like entomology. The arguments over taxonomy – I've seen more than one faculty dinner end in a brawl."

DI Adams looked at Collins expectantly. Let him ask about heated moments in senior entomologists, then. Her questions seemed to keep leading her into areas she'd rather not think about. He shrugged and said, "So it's conceivable someone might have had a grudge against Mr Latherby, then."

"Oh, definitely. You only have to look at the comments section on his videos."

DI Adams tried to imagine getting angry enough about the Loch Ness monster to throw someone in a freezer. It might seem unlikely, but it was possible. If there was one thing she'd learned, it was that anything was possible when it came to people and their passions. "Okay. If you can give us a link for that, I'd appreciate it."

"Of course. I've got his blog, too. He was pretty outspoken about a lot of things."

Collins took a sip of tea and said, "So. Campbell."

"Campbell Jones. Head of Science at Leeds Alive College."

"Leeds Alive College?" DI Adams asked.

Rose nodded. "It used to be called Leeds White Rose, but they felt they were missing out on Lancastrian students."

"Because of the War of the Roses?" DI Adams asked. "Is that a big factor in choosing colleges?"

"They thought so."

DI Adams wondered if they got more or less students now that the name felt like the equivalent of someone's dad crashing a club in a fluorescent headband and roller skates.

"Campbell," Collins said again. "He seemed pretty upset at Jean-Claude."

Rose sighed and retrieved her cake. "Jean-Claude winds him up deliberately. It's like a sport to him. And Jean-Claude and I are just friends now, anyway. Well, mostly. We have been while Campbell and I have been together."

DI Adams stared at her mug, the corner of her mouth twitching. She wasn't going to ask.

"Right," Collins said carefully. "So it sounds like they could *both* have been jealous – of each other *and* of Eric."

Rose popped a bit of cake in her mouth. "Not really," she said indistinctly. "I wasn't in a relationship with Eric. It was just a bit of fun, and it didn't happen more than a couple of times. Both were before Campbell, and Jean-Claude and I split up years ago. We just get together now and then for old time's sake. And Campbell and Jean-Claude are both harmless. I'd be more likely to suspect Angelus than either of them."

"They didn't look too harmless earlier," Collins said. DI Adams took a piece of cake and examined it. She was almost certain he was glaring at her, waiting for her to step in, but she had no intention of doing so.

"*Pah.* Silly boys blowing off steam," Rose said, and DI Adams had to bite the inside of her cheek to stop herself laughing at the thought of the two men, of whom Campbell looked the youngest but still had to be in his sixties, being called *boys.*

"Adams?" Collins asked, and she looked up finally. He was definitely glaring.

"Yes. Do either of those two have a key to your place?"

"Both of them. I didn't change the locks after Jean-Claude moved out, and Campbell insisted on having a key. I barely lock the house, so I didn't see a problem with that. He can be a bit overprotective. He probably thinks I'll lock myself out one day and he'll be able to ride to my rescue, the silly man." She said it with a mix of affection and exasperation.

DI Adams sighed. "You don't lock it? Do people know that?"

"Not many people here bother with locking up."

Of course not. Toot Hansell seemed to have the crime rate of a fair-sized city, but *of course* no one bothered locking up. She took another mouthful of coffee, thinking Rose might have had the right idea with *something stronger.* "So, given that pretty much anyone could have had access to the garage if they wanted, who do you think might have wanted to do this?"

Rose was silent for a while, and when she spoke again her voice was quiet. "I don't know. I mean, Eric could rub people up the wrong way, but he wasn't nasty. He was just a bit loud and flashy and silly."

"Did he have a partner?" Collins asked.

"No idea."

"What about other cryptozoologists?" DI Adams asked. "The whole thing seems pretty fringe. Did that attract some odd people?"

"Odd isn't the same as dangerous," Rose said. "In my experience, it's normally the odd people you *don't* need to worry about."

Collins tapped his pen against his notepad. "Alright. We'll need a list of anyone who might have been in the house over the last few days, so we can rule them out for any fingerprints we find, and we'll chat to Campbell and Jean-Claude a little further. Have a think for us, Rose. Anyone who might have a grudge against you, as well as Latherby. Because his body didn't end up in your freezer by accident. A murderer has been *in your house,* whether they were there for Latherby or … well. Maybe he wasn't actually the target. We're going to be keeping a close eye on you until we find out more."

"We'll get an officer to stay with you," DI Adams said.

"I'm sure I'm safe with the W.I.," Rose said.

"You'll be safer with a police officer," DI Adams said. "No poking around in this, understand?" She took a breath and asked, "Where were you on Friday night?" Lucas had put time of death as Friday night or early Saturday morning, although the freezer made things tricky.

"I was with Campbell," Rose said. "We went to dinner."

DI Adams nodded, trying not to feel relieved. Not that she really suspected Rose, but, well. An alibi made things easier.

Rose ran her hands back over her spiky hair. "I just don't understand why anyone would want to hurt Eric. And why put him in *my* freezer? We collaborated on a couple of articles and podcasts, but nothing since last year."

"We'll need a list of all of those, too," DI Adams said. "And links. See if that gives us any ideas." She got up, watching Angelus snuggling closer to Rose on the sofa, his heavy head taking up her entire lap. "He much of a guard dog?"

Rose scratched his ears. "He's actually very good. I mean, he's scared of every animal going, but humans he's fine with. If he knows you, there's never a problem, but any stranger and he really gives them what for." She stopped, and looked up at them. "So we must've been out when it happened. Or he'd have barked."

"Or he knew who it was," Collins said.

Rose looked from one of them to the other, and hugged the dog a little tighter. DI Adams thought of the flour in the bathroom drawer and the socks in the pillowcase and measured her words carefully before they came out. "When was your last bad day, Rose?"

The older woman looked up at her, the skin of her face looking fragile and pale. "I'm not sure. I don't … I don't *remember* them as bad days. Things just turn up where they shouldn't be."

"What's the biggest thing you've forgotten?"

Rose shook her head slowly. "I … my car was on the village green one day when I got up, and I don't remember parking it there. That was fairly big, I suppose. But I didn't do this." She looked from one inspector to the other. "I *couldn't.*"

"We don't think you did, Rose," Collins said, but he met DI Adams' eyes with a frown pulling at his mouth. "There's no way you could have put him in the freezer on your own."

Rose nodded, looking down at Angelus. He gazed at her with wide, adoring eyes. "Of course. Of course, that'd be impossible, wouldn't it?"

DI Adams watched the anxious lines of the woman's shoulders, and wished the answer could be that simple.

7
ALICE

The kitchen had become excessively hot even with the windows open, although that was hardly surprising. It was crowded with the W.I. and the dragons, and the kettle was going non-stop, and Miriam's ancient AGA was throwing out creaky, insistent heat with no consideration for the sunny day outside. And it all seemed to be making everyone even more excitable than usual, the ladies of the W.I. all talking at once about everything from poor Rose to dog training to the cheekiness of young journalists. Alice opened the door to let a little more fresh air in as Miriam struggled out of her heavy orange jumper. She was flushed a rather alarming shade of red, and Alice said, "Are you alright, Miriam?"

"It's these awful hot flushes," she said. "Always at the worst possible time." She looked around for somewhere to put her jumper, and eventually hung it on a hook behind the door, over her jacket. "And what was I doing buying an orange jumper? I don't even like orange!"

"I'm sure I don't know, dear," Alice said, leaning out into the garden to check for journalists.

"I like orange," Gilbert said. "It's a very nice colour." He looked down at his own orange scales pointedly.

"It's perfectly lovely on dragons," Miriam said, flapping the front of her blouse. "I'm just not sure it's so good for humans. Or this human, anyway."

"Are you sure you're alright, Miriam?" Beaufort asked in his deep, pipe smoke-and-brandy voice. He was tucked as close to the stove as he could manage, the tip of his tail curled under his front paws for safekeeping. "You've gone a most interesting colour, and it's my understanding that humans only change colour with the fiercest of emotions."

She fanned her face with one hand. "Emotions and hormones, Beaufort."

"Ah," he said. "Are you laying?"

Miriam stared at him blankly, and after a moment Alice said, "Rather the opposite, actually."

"The opposite?" he started, and she was thankfully saved from having to explain human reproductive life stages to an ancient dragon by Rose opening the hall door and shouting, "We're done!"

There was a general surge of movement, the W.I. rushing out of the kitchen like froth from a bottle and carrying the dragons with them. A moment later Alice found herself alone in the room with Miriam, who gave her an almost irritated look, still fanning her face.

"Aren't you hot?" Miriam asked.

"A little," Alice said. "That did seem excessive, even for us."

Miriam puffed air over her lower lip. "Are we always so loud? And *crowded?*"

"Yes," Alice said. "But usually with more space and fewer dragons."

Miriam sighed. "I suppose we had better go through. Poor Rose. This is just so awful!"

"Indeed," Alice said, and led the way into the living room,

which was every bit as loud as the kitchen had been, but was at least a little bigger.

"THEY'RE JUST GONE?" Carlotta asked.

"You probably scared poor Colin away," Gert said. "You'd scare me, all that fussing and offering him *tarts*."

"Me?" Carlotta demanded. "Rubbish! You're the one always pinching his bottom!"

"He's got a very nice bottom," Gert said.

"Well, that's true," Carlotta said.

"What did they say, Rose?" Alice asked. She was perched on the arm of the sofa, her legs crossed at the ankles. Everything still felt very hot and crowded, and it was definitely adding to the general feeling of agitation in the room. But there was no point telling anyone to go home. Once the W.I. were involved, there was no going back. Not one of them would have considered that this was Rose's business, not theirs. It was, Alice thought, both their most irritating and most endearing characteristic.

"They think someone might be after me," Rose said. "That they killed poor Eric either by accident, because they were waiting for me, or to frame me."

There was a collective intake of breath around the room, and some dragonish rumbling that sent Angelus into hiding behind the sofa.

"That is *disgraceful*," Beaufort said. "We won't stand for it!"

Priya, sitting next to Rose on the sofa, took her hand and squeezed it. "We really won't. How awful!"

"We'll look after you," Teresa said. "You can come and stay with me and Pearl. We stay over at each other's all the time anyway, so no one'll have any idea where you are."

"Ooh, yes," Pearl said. "It'll be like witness protection. We can put lights on timers in both houses, and then we could be *anywhere.*"

"Anywhere in one of your two houses," Rosemary pointed out.

"Well, it's still not Rose's house, is it?" Teresa said. "And three of us together will be quite safe."

Pearl nodded. "We can have movie nights. The lizards in the chimney get a bit loud, but they're alright, really."

"You're just lucky you don't speak French. They're worse than Jean-Claude."

Beaufort huffed. "We'll keep a dragon with you at all times. It's the best option."

Mortimer gave a very small sigh and picked up one of Jasmine's croissants, almost dropping it.

"I'll call some people," Gert said. "Our Frank's wife's cousin's boys would come up and keep an eye on Rose, no problem. Stay as long as you want. And I can ask my aunt's sister-in-law's second cousin if she wants to bring a few people up, too. They're in the business."

Alice wasn't entirely sure how reassuring being surrounded by Gert's large and questionable family would be, nor what *business* might equip them for guarding small scientists of a certain age, but before she could suggest that the fewer people they involved, the better, Rose flapped her hands at them all. "Honestly, don't make such a fuss. The inspectors are going to keep someone around, and I'm not moving out of my house just for this. How ridiculous!"

"It was a *body,*" Miriam said. "That's not ridiculous, Rose. That's … that's *awful.*"

"You probably won't be able to go home for a while, anyway," Jasmine said. "It'll take them some time to process the scene."

"True," Rose admitted. "But it shouldn't be *that* long, surely. I refuse to be frightened out of my own home."

Miriam shivered. "Well, either way, you can stay here as long as you want. You're very welcome."

Rose smiled at her, and it was almost, *almost* the usual bright Rose smile, but Alice thought it faltered at the edges. "Thank you, Miriam."

"We shall need to go over the evidence," Beaufort said, tapping his talons on the carpet thoughtfully. A large soup mug of tea steamed next to him. "And take a sniff around the place as soon as possible, obviously, to see if we can pick up any clues as to who this nefarious character might be."

"Shouldn't we leave it to the police?" Mortimer asked, taking another croissant.

"Well, I don't think they know much," Rose said. "*I* don't know much, but the whole thing is really very off." She stopped, looking at her hands, then took a deep breath and continued. "*Really* off. Eric was a bit of a silly man—"

"Aren't they all?" Rosemary said to no one in particular, and a murmur of agreement ran around the room from everyone except Jasmine. Alice thought it was rather sweet of her.

"Well, quite," Rose said. "But he was a good person, and he didn't hurt anyone with what he was doing, and he shouldn't be in my freezer!" Her voice rose suddenly on the last word, and she stopped, still looking at her hands. Priya put an arm around her shoulders and hugged her gently.

"Of course he shouldn't be," she said. "No one deserves that."

"Some people do," Carlotta said, and everyone looked at her. "What? They do!"

"He didn't," Rose said.

No one spoke for a moment, then Mortimer swallowed loudly enough that Alice heard it, and said, "Well, I suppose the police don't have dragons, do they?" He was looking rather pasty, but he gave Rose a toothy, encouraging sort of grin, then picked up one of Jasmine's croissants and shoved the whole thing in his mouth. Alice thought that was rather unwise. They were enough to make anyone pasty.

"They've only got a dandy," Amelia said. "And I'm not sure he's that helpful. He's just a bit whiffy."

"So's Alex," Gilbert said, and she poked him in the side.

"That's settled, then," Beaufort said. "As soon as the police are finished, we'll take a look around. Mortimer has an excellent nose for these things."

Mortimer sighed, more deeply this time, and tried for a grin again. It was starting to look a little ghastly.

Beaufort slurped tea, then rubbed his paws together. "Do we have suspects?"

"Beaufort," Alice said, "I'm not sure Rose wants to go through all this again right now. Maybe not at all. This may simply not be a case for us. She may prefer to rely on the police to do their job."

Miriam stared at Alice from where she sat cross-legged on the floor, and Alice rather thought the younger woman might have fallen off her chair if she'd been sitting on one. Mortimer looked as if he wanted to hug her, and everyone else just watched her, waiting.

"Some things may just be a little beyond our abilities," she added, with as much conviction as she could. She actually thought that there was a *lot* they could add to the investigation, through local knowledge and life experience and simply knowing Rose better than the police did, but not everyone was equipped to deal with bodies in their freezer. And everyone was *very* wound up, and the last thing they needed was a lot of overexcitement over the whole thing. That would get them nowhere. Investigations needed cool heads, and no one was going to manage that when Rose might be at risk. "This whole situation seems terribly dangerous for Rose. I think it might be better for her if we listened to the inspectors this time and didn't get involved."

"Oh," Beaufort said, and he managed not to sound disappointed. "Oh, of course. I am sorry, Rose. I was all carried away by the idea of an investigation. It's been months since the last one, but that's really not important."

A murmur of hesitant agreement ran through the assembled ladies, as if no one wanted to be the first to admit they had no appetite for getting involved this time. Priya leaned her head against Rose's, and on her other side Jasmine put a hand on the older woman's, their fingers twining together. Angelus whimpered from behind the sofa, where he seemed to have become stuck.

"And we must consider the cryptid journalist," Alice continued. "It seems an unnecessary risk to have you dragons in the village while she's around."

"That's true," Jasmine said. "She was asking about Christmas as if she knew it was … well. You know. Faeries and so on."

"And she saw Gilbert's tail rings," Amelia said. "She *took* one."

"Only because you ripped it out," Gilbert snapped.

"Oh, did you want to leave it so that she could *grab your tail*, you pixie-brain?"

"Hey—"

Beaufort growled, and Angelus gave an unhappy little howl. The young dragons subsided, and the High Lord said, "We can accept that risk, but if Rose would rather leave things to the police, we shall."

There was a pause, and Alice could see the lovely royal blue and purple colours creeping back into Mortimer's scales, and Miriam's face approaching her normal hues, then Rose said, "Absolute *bollocks*. I'm sorry, ladies, but no. When did you get so soft, Alice?"

Alice smiled at her. "You do remember last summer? I was kidnapped and held at … well, syringe-point."

"And we staged a daring raid to rescue you," Rose said. "Miriam led it!"

Miriam made a strangled sound that suggested she'd rather not have a repeat. Alice nodded gravely, although she thought *rescued* was stretching things a bit.

"And we did save the whole village at Christmas," Teresa pointed out. "Rose was very handy when we were fighting the faeries and those damn holly wreaths. She's not helpless."

Pearl slapped her wrist. "Shush! Alice is right. Rose needs to be careful."

"Sorry," Teresa said, not sounding very sorry. "But you're treating her like a little old lady, and we should all know better."

"Quite right," Rose said. "If I waited around for other people to sort things out, I'd never have got anywhere in life. I'd never have discovered a water mite that eats tadpoles from the inside out."

"Ew," everyone said.

"Oh, that's not even that nasty. Wait till I tell you about—"

"Let's not," Carlotta said.

"Are you queasy? Didn't you have to wring the necks of your own chickens in the old country, or something?" Rosemary asked. Carlotta threw a napkin at her.

"What are you thinking, Rose?" Alice asked, ignoring them.

"Well, it's this parasitic—"

"No," Alice said, while Jasmine covered her ears with both hands. She'd gone very pale. "What are you thinking about *the case?"*

"Oh. Well, it's my freezer. And I liked Eric. If anyone should be investigating, it should be me." She straightened her back and put her hands on her hips as well as she could on the crowded sofa. "You can all help me or not. I'm not going to be scared by some coward sticking bodies in my freezer. It's nothing compared to the feuds I've been in with Cochliomyia."

"Did they put bodies in your freezer?" Gert asked.

Rose sniffed. "Bit difficult, considering they're flesh-eating larvae. But it's just the same old bully tactics people use when they want you to stop talking but are too scared to actually face you."

Alice almost smiled. But there was still a body in a freezer and a murderer on the loose, which were nothing to be smiling about.

"Alright," she said instead. "If anyone doesn't want to be involved, you should go now. For the rest of us, let's go over what we know, and see what suspects we have."

"That's not fair," Miriam said. "It's my house. I can't go even if I want to!"

"Do you want to?" Alice asked her.

"Yes. But I won't, because it's Rose."

Rose smiled at her. "You don't have to be involved, Miriam."

"I'll never sleep if I'm not. I'll just lie there thinking of you all out hunting murderers without me."

"Same," Jasmine said. "I couldn't stand it."

"You shall have to keep this from Ben," Alice said. "This is not something you can share. Not this time."

Jasmine nodded, biting her lower lip. "I know. But *he* wouldn't tell *me* anything about what was going on last night, even though I knew it was to do with Rose. So that's fair."

Alice hoped the younger woman could keep her word. The last thing they needed was Ben running to the inspectors, telling them what they were up to.

"More tea?" Carlotta suggested, pushing herself off the sofa.

"This calls for some of Rose's rum, I think," Gert said.

"I drank it all," Rose said.

Miriam got up, brushing her hair back in some semblance of order. "I've got brandy. Maybe even some whisky."

"Ooh, we could have Irish coffees," Pearl said. "I'll help."

There was a general move toward the door, but not one of the women suggested they were going any further than the kitchen. Alice would have been more surprised if they had. Not when one of their own was in trouble. It just wasn't the way they did things, and not even a murder could change that.

It took a little while for everyone to get settled again, especially when Beaufort gulped his Irish coffee in one mouthful, belched in surprise, and almost set the curtains on fire. But finally they were seated, and Alice said, "So … suspects."

No one answered, and Rose shrugged. "I have no idea."

"Good start," Gert said, to no one in particular.

"What about those two men?" Beaufort asked, sipping his second Irish coffee somewhat more circumspectly.

"Jean-Claude and Campbell?" Rose asked. "No, they're harmless."

"They were both really upset," Amelia said. "I mean, at each other, I suppose, but what if they'd met the victim and had an argument with him?"

"But they wouldn't want to frame me," Rose said.

Beaufort gave a rumbling *hmm.* "They might not have meant to. Maybe it was an accident."

Alice took a sip of her tea – just because there had been a murder was no reason to start drinking before lunch – and said nothing. She thought the dragons were the only ones who could question the motives of Rose's exes without being shouted at, and she was rather pleased they'd come up with it without her saying anything.

Priya frowned. "They weren't exactly very good at fighting."

"True, it was a pretty poor show," Gert said.

"It only takes one good blow." Jasmine's voice was grave, and everyone looked at Rose, who frowned back at them.

"I really can't see it."

"Who else, then?" Alice asked. "Who's been around recently?"

Rose sipped her coffee rather than answer, and made a face. "This is terribly weak."

"What about Bethany?" Miriam asked. "She was there last night. And she was very worried about something."

"Bethany's always worried about something. She couldn't find blue Post-its last month and she was upset for days, because she feels the other colours are too frivolous. She ended up buying off-brand ones and they didn't stick as well, which she was *horrified* by." Rose smiled. "I ordered her some decent ones online just so she'd be able to focus on her work again."

Miriam wrinkled her nose in a manner that suggested she felt worrying about Post-its could be the sign of an unstable mind, but just said, "What about your neighbour, then? He was out in the garden when we left last night, and it was terribly late."

"Oh, you know Dougal. He's such a nosy sod. It doesn't mean he'd *do* anything."

"He was in your garden?" Alice asked.

"No, of course not. His. He's scared of Angelus." Rose grinned. "Every time I see him I throw a dog biscuit at him, so Angelus goes tearing toward him. You've never seen anyone move so fast!"

"That's *terrible,*" Pearl said, and giggled.

"Maybe. But he's far too friendly," Rose said. "He's always popping around with some chickpea salad or hemp smoothie that he thinks I need, in order to boost my brainpower or something, or telling me the house is far too much for me to handle alone and offering to trim the garden. I *like* my garden." She thought about it. "And the dog biscuit thing was a bad idea, actually. Angelus now thinks he's the source of dog biscuits, and won't leave him alone."

"What about poisoning the rabbits?" Miriam asked. "That wasn't very friendly of him."

"*Poison?*" Gilbert spluttered. "I bet he runs hedgehogs down with his mower, too!"

"It's hardly the most important thing right now," Amelia said.

"It says something about his character, though!"

"I second that," Teresa said, and Gilbert grinned at her. Alice considered it a good thing that they were all used to dragon grins. They must be alarmingly toothy to the uninitiated.

"It's just because he has such a thing about his garden," Rose said. "He doesn't even have bird houses, because he thinks the birds will make a mess of his statues. And I suggested he plant pollinator flowers, but he said they don't go with his aesthetic, and he was sure my garden was just fine for all that."

Gert snorted. "Silly man. What's the point of a garden without wildlife?"

"Well, we shall add him to the list," Alice said. "Such as it is. Can you think of anyone else?"

Rose considered it for a moment, then shook her head. "Not really."

"What about someone framing you?" Jasmine asked. "Do you think that's possible?"

"I suppose," Rose said, and Alice caught the flicker of hesitation as she spoke.

"So who would benefit if you were charged with murder?" Jasmine sounded quite officious, and Alice wondered if she'd been watching too many police dramas, or if Ben had been inadvertently giving her tips.

Rose shrugged. "I don't know. But the police won't charge me. They'll be looking for who really did it, won't they?"

"Of course they will," Miriam said.

"Maybe," Alice said, and Miriam glared at her. Alice held up a hand. "If there's evidence of someone else being involved, yes. If it looks very simple to them, they may not look that closely."

"Oh," Rose said, and frowned. "What – you think they'd lock me up just because it was easy?"

Alice spread her hands as protests went up around the room. "I hate to say so, but yes. It's possible." As she had learned in her own experience, an easy suspect could be more appealing than the right one for a time-pressed police force.

"Police," Gert said, glaring at the floor as if it had personally offended her. "The amount of times one of mine's been picked up

for simply being in the wrong place, wrong time. But they just want to close their cases."

"Try being the wrong colour," Teresa said, and Pearl squeezed her knee gently.

"This is Colin and DI Adams, though," Miriam said. "They *know* Rose."

Alice thought that Gert might be overstating the innocence of her extended family, but for the most part she agreed. The police could be very quick to draw conclusions, and very slow to be swayed from them. Although Miriam also had a point. "Of course. But in a case like this, who knows who else might get involved? There could easily be an entirely other officer, one who doesn't know Rose. Or even a different department. DI Adams and Colin might not end up being in charge at all. And how simple an answer for them, especially if there is evidence that points to Rose."

Beaufort growled, and Angelus gave another quavery howl from behind the sofa. "Sorry," the old dragon said, more to Rose than the dog. "But this is just unacceptable. You think the police might actually believe *Rose* did it? *Utterly* unacceptable."

"And what evidence?" Priya asked. "What could possibly point to Rose?"

"We don't know," Alice replied. "But if someone had access to the house to put the body in the freezer, they had access to plant misleading evidence."

Miriam made a horrified noise, and Jasmine clutched Rose as if she were afraid the older woman would run from the room.

"You have to hide," Miriam said, and everyone looked at her. She'd gone very pale. "Not just because of the murderer. The police really might arrest you. But they can't arrest you if they can't find you." She was looking at Rose in a way that made Alice wonder what they had discussed the night before, while they huddled in the kitchen waiting for the police, and the freezer loomed over-large in the utility, rumbling softly around its morbid cargo.

"I can't just run away," Rose said. "And this is all conjecture. We don't *know* anything."

"We know someone put a body in your freezer," Rosemary said. "Isn't that enough?"

"And you wouldn't have to run away," Pearl added. "Just stay with a different one of us all the time. Keep changing houses, and we can honestly say that we don't know exactly where you are if they ask us."

"And meanwhile we'll find the real killer," Alice said, and smiled at the women. Just this morning she'd have said that having the W.I. charging into an investigation was a sure way to derail everything. Now she was starting to wonder if she would ever truly understand just how formidable a force friendship really was. It constantly surprised her in ways not even dragons could.

"I'm still calling some help in," Gert said. "Can't risk the murderer finding you."

"I don't think outside people are a good idea," Carlotta said. "We can deal with this."

Miriam tugged at her hair. "Can we? What if the murderer decides we're getting too close to the truth, and we can't protect Rose?"

"If you let us help, you'd *all* be much safer," Beaufort said, and Mortimer made a small sound of agreement, even though he was the same shade as the grey hearth.

Alice shook her head. "That's not safe for *you*, especially if we do end up with unfamiliar police around. Who knows what they might see? But you're quite right, Miriam. If we could secure Rose someplace else, away from here, then we could carry on with the investigation."

"That wasn't quite my meaning," Miriam said, and looked at Mortimer, who shoved another croissant into his mouth.

"I like it," Priya said. "I have a cousin in London you could stay with, Rose."

Beaufort stomped one paw on the old carpet. "We *have* to help. How can we just sit by when you could be in danger?"

"You can't be involved," Alice said. "Worrying about Rose is bad enough. We can't be worrying about journalists or police officers stumbling over you as well."

"We can be careful," Mortimer said, and Beaufort turned his toothy grin on the younger dragon. "This is too important." Mortimer was still very grey, but he also sounded very determined.

"It absolutely is," Beaufort said. "And if we find a murderer lurking around, we shall deal with them."

"Well, that sounds ominous," Teresa said.

"It sounds perfect," Rose replied, and gave her own delighted grin.

"No," Alice said. "It's far too dangerous. As soon as we know no one who's likely to see you is around, we'll send Thompson with a message. But until then, no dragons. Now, I shall check if the garden's clear, then you really must go. And you mustn't come back until we say it's safe."

Beaufort looked as if he were going to argue, and before he could start Miriam said, "If that journalist really is a monster hunter, she'll see you eventually. She *wants* to see you, even if she doesn't expect to. I think that's why we could all see you so easily. Because we wanted to believe in magical things, even if we didn't ever think we'd see them."

The High Lord regarded her for a moment, then sighed. "You're quite right, of course. We do need to be careful with anyone like that."

Mortimer regained a little colour. "We do," he said.

"Just don't do anything without us," Beaufort said, looking at Alice. "Not when there's a murderer about."

"We shall be very careful," Alice said.

It was only later, as she watched the dragons slip down the garden path, dappled with the colours of the early spring, that she realised Beaufort hadn't actually agreed to stay away.

No more than she had agreed not to tackle any murderers without him.

And that was rather less surprising than anything else had been today.

8
MIRIAM

Miriam wasn't entirely sure how the day had ended with her standing at the bottom of Rose's garden at ten p.m., peering into the undergrowth and trying to decide if the ill-defined shape she could just make out in the shadows was a large and attentive police officer waiting to arrest her, or the trunk of an apple tree. She was fairly certain it was an apple tree, but what if there was a police officer *behind* the apple tree? There could be. It was a murder scene, after all, which brought her back around to wondering how on earth she had agreed to this in the first place.

"Miriam?" Alice said, making her jump.

"Yes?"

"Is there a reason we're waiting here?"

"Um." Miriam examined the apple tree suspiciously, but it hadn't moved. "Is this a good idea, Alice?"

"Well, the police aren't exactly going to let us just walk straight into their crime scene."

"That's because we're *contaminating* their crime scene. Or interfering with it, or whatever they call it." Miriam checked on the apple tree again. It seemed quite tree-like now, but there was a large dog rose bush that looked suspicious.

"We're merely collecting some medication that Rose forgot."

"I'm fairly sure they won't think that's a very good excuse. They're going to ask why we didn't come over while it was still light. Or at least come to the front door rather than sneaking in the back."

"Sneaking is merely a manner of movement," Alice said. "For instance, one might accuse you of *lurking* at the gate if you don't get moving soon."

Miriam frowned at her. Alice was enjoying this far too much. After the dragons had gone, the W.I. had dispersed, Rose accompanying Alice through the woodland path to her house for the night on the theory that it was the last place the inspectors would expect her to stay. Which had left Miriam alone to face a tall and rather friendly police constable who had knocked on her front door once the last of the W.I. had gone. The constable asked if Rose was still there, as she was assigned to keep an eye on her. She might have said *look after her,* but Miriam felt that the meaning had been rather less benign. She had said, as calmly as she could, that Rose was having a nap after such a traumatic night, and she supposed she must have been convincing enough, as the constable had retreated to her car without argument. Miriam had taken her a pork pie she'd been saving for her own dinner, as well as an assortment of W.I. cakes, a packet of cheesy puffs (reluctantly, as she rather thought she might need some stress-eating supplies herself) and a thermos of tea to keep the constable company. Now she was wondering if *that* had seemed suspicious, and as much as she wanted to help Rose, she was regretting having to be quite so proactive about it.

She checked over her shoulder, just in case the constable had heard her tiptoeing out the kitchen door and down the garden path, and had followed her all the way to Rose's house, but there was no one there.

"Miriam," Alice said, and pointed at the garden.

"I really don't want to get arrested."

"We won't get arrested. At the worst, we might get a little caution."

Miriam wished they could use a little caution right now, but that didn't seem to be in Alice's vocabulary. "They're not going to believe we're looking for medication at ten at night."

"They can't prove we're not," Alice said. "And, after all, old ladies do get a little confused and do strange things from time to time. We're well known for it."

Miriam snorted. *Old* was such a relative term, and she didn't feel it applied to either of them. Confused might, but only to her. No one would ever accuse Alice of that.

"Couldn't we just go to the front gate and ask whoever's watching the house if we can go in?"

"No. They almost certainly won't let us in, and even if they did they'd escort us. You know we're looking for clues, not just Rose's antacids. Now do come along. No one's going to arrest you."

Miriam twisted her fingers into the sleeves of her jacket, peering into the darkness and wishing she could feel quite as sure as Alice. And it wasn't just the police she was worried about. Someone had put a body in Rose's freezer. Someone had *killed* the poor man. And who knew what their plans were for Rose? "I don't think we should do this, Alice."

"Nonsense," Alice said, and edged past Miriam to open the little low gate that led into the garden from the village green. "It won't take us any time at all, and we can get Rose some fresh clothes to change into, and her own toiletries to use. She barely packed anything but her pyjamas and a pillow, and she's had to borrow my slippers and a cardigan already. Having one's own familiar items is important when so much is uncertain." And Alice stepped through the gate and started up the path, her back straight and her silver hair catching the light filtering through the trees. She definitely wasn't *sneaking.*

Miriam sighed. Alice was right, of course, and it wasn't as if she hadn't known this would happen. She'd been the one to suggest hiding Rose, after all. She hadn't really thought they were somehow going to avoid an Investigation, but they were always so much more alarming when one was actually in them. She started to sigh again, then realised Alice was about to vanish out of sight in the overgrown garden, leaving her alone on the edge of the green, so she rushed through the gate after her. The shadows seemed much deeper without Alice around.

❧

THE KITCHEN DOOR WAS LOCKED, but Miriam had brought her key, and after jiggling with the stiff lock for a few moments she wrestled it open. They ducked under the tape that crossed the door – it seemed terribly stark and harsh against the old worn stone – and stepped inside, the low light of the garden revealing nothing beyond the threshold but the orange glow of a digital radio screen and the red eye of the fridge. Miriam reached for the lights, and Alice caught her hand.

"I brought torches."

"Really?" Miriam asked, and caught the plaintive note in her own voice.

"Yes," Alice said, and handed her one, the rubber grip smooth and heavy against her palm. "Even if the officer out there is playing on their phone and ignoring their responsibilities, they'd be hard-pressed to miss the lights going on. There's a red filter over the torch lens so it doesn't get too bright, but there's plenty to see by. Just don't shine it at the windows."

Miriam switched the torch on, deeply unsurprised that Alice

would have red filters. She would have been more surprised if Alice *hadn't* been prepared for sneaking around houses undetected.

She had thought the torch wouldn't cast enough light to see by, but after the shadows of the garden she found she could make out the kitchen perfectly clearly. Fingerprint dust bloomed on the worktops and the edges of the cabinets, and all Rose's accumulated detritus on the table had been piled unceremoniously to one end. Some letters had fallen to the floor, and half a dozen pinecones had rolled across the stone flags, scattered like afterthoughts.

"Oh, poor Rose," she said. "They've made a horrible mess."

"We'll get it cleaned up before she moves back," Alice said. She played her light on the floor. "There's Angelus' bed – it's far too big to take. But we may as well take his bowls and some of his food. I'll get that together if you go and pack some clothes and so on. Let's be quick about it, then we'll see if we can spot anything that seems out of the ordinary."

Miriam squeezed the bag she had tucked under her shoulder and said, "This *all* seems out of the ordinary." It did. The whole place felt out of kilter and unfamiliar, as if the procession of police and suspicion had rumpled it almost beyond recognition.

"I know," Alice said, her voice uncharacteristically soft. "But we can help her. We know Rose. We're better placed to be able to tell what's out of place than the police are. What's *not Rose*. The police will just look at all the odd things Rose has and think that anything could belong."

Miriam thought the police could be due a *little* more credit than Alice gave them, and also that, given how eclectic Rose's collections of old specimens and souvenirs from her travels and strange gifts from students were, she wasn't at all sure they were better placed to notice anything odd, but she just said, "I'll start in the bedroom." She didn't move, though. The hall loomed dark and deep beyond the kitchen, and she'd already populated it with murderers and mysterious shifters-of-things.

"Don't be long," Alice said, already collecting the dog bowls.

Miriam shone the torch toward the hall door, but the red light didn't seem to do anything but make the shadows deeper. She turned back to Alice, wanting to suggest that they stick together, but Alice, bowls packed, was pushing through the door into the utility room, and Miriam didn't want to follow her. Not when there had been a body in there just this morning. It wouldn't still be there, of course. Would it? For a panicked moment she imagined the poor man's frost-glazed eyes staring blankly up at her, as they had in the photos, and the way the ice had glistened in his hair, and she had to squeeze her eyes shut against the image. When she opened them again she hurried into the hall, plunging deeper into the house. No, she didn't want to go in the utility with Alice. Not at all.

ROSE'S BEDROOM was at the end of the hall, the curtains still open to the chaotic garden, and Miriam pulled them closed in case anyone saw her torch, reminding herself to open them again before she left. Then she shone the light carefully around the room. There was a big queen bed with an old wooden frame, the whole thing seeming far too large for Rose, but judging by the tatty blanket spread on one side, she shared it with Angelus. Otherwise the room was crowded with two bedside tables, a wardrobe, and two chests of drawers, all in mismatched woods and styles, and some hooks by the door with dressing gowns hanging from them and an ornately carved walking stick resting below. Miriam hesitated, then dropped to her knees to peek under the bed. There was nothing there but big plastic tubs on rollers, a chew toy, and an abandoned hot water bottle. No murderers.

She scrambled up again and picked up Rose's glasses and book from the nightstand, dropping them into her bag, and added a few packets of pills from the nightstand drawer without checking what they were. That seemed simple enough, although the pills were nestled in next to a box of eggs and a spatula, for some reason. She stared at them, then shook her head. Clothes, then. She turned to the two chests of drawers, and tried the closest one. The drawer slid open easily, revealing a collection of shed snake skins and collected skulls that sent her staggering backward, both hands over her mouth to contain a scream. When nothing chased her across the room she crept back and shone the torch cautiously into the drawer, the red light making the scene even ghastlier.

She pushed the drawer shut with a shudder, and opened the next one down more warily. That was full of beetles in little plastic cases, and she decided she didn't need to open the third drawer. She tried the other chest of drawers instead, and this time the worst she found was a family of panicked dormice living in a plastic tub full of chewed up socks. That was fine. She quite liked dormice.

The other drawers were full of clothes, so she grabbed some at random. There were some odd things in here, too – a spray head for a garden hose, a paintbrush still caked with paint, and a mouldering block of cheese. Miriam stared at them, chewing the inside of her cheek. Rose was always a little disorganised, but this was more. She thought of Rose opening the freezer to show her the body, saying, *I'm sure I didn't put this here. I'd have remembered.* And not sounding very sure at all. Could one really forget such a thing? She poked the paintbrush, then shook her head and closed the drawers firmly. Dropping a block of cheese while putting the laundry away was nothing like putting a body in a freezer. *Nothing* like it.

Miriam headed into the bathroom and played the torch over the shelves, frowning. Rose seemed to have six or seven different types of everything, all half-used, including toothpaste. There were also three toothbrushes in assorted colours (although she had said she already had one with her), two hairbrushes, and four different colours of hair dye.

"Well, she won't need that," Miriam mumbled to herself, and as she did she heard a thump and a crash from the direction of the kitchen. She dropped the bag, clutching the torch to her chest with both hands. She wanted to shout for Alice, to ask if she was okay, but what if ... what if ...

She swallowed hard against the memory of the man in the freezer and crept to the bedroom door, listening carefully. There was no other movement from down the hall, no sounds of struggle. Maybe it was nothing. Alice had dropped a sack of potatoes or something. Although Miriam wasn't sure why she'd be moving sacks of potatoes. Or maybe ... maybe Alice had been attacked. Maybe the thump had been the sound of her hitting the floor, and the crash had been her knocking something over as she collapsed. Miriam groped for her phone, but who could she call? It wasn't like she had the phone number for the officer outside. It'd take too long to call 999 and have them pass the information along. She glanced at the curtained windows. Maybe she could climb out and run to the police car? No – the murderer would hear her opening them, and would be in the room before she could make it through. *If* she could make it through. Most windows weren't designed to accommodate a woman of her build. Or of any build, really.

There was another thump from the kitchen, and she fumbled with the torch, switching it off hurriedly. She didn't want them to know she was here. She blinked at the dark, thinking that she shouldn't have drawn the curtains, and, not for the first time, wished the dragons had phones.

She still couldn't see very much, but there was no use standing around. The murderer could be doing *anything* to Alice, and the longer she waited ... well, she couldn't wait. She had to *do* something. She edged out into the hallway, feeling horribly exposed. Could she hear whispered voices from the kitchen? Or was it the breeze in the trees outside? Was she imagining all of it? No, she hadn't made up the awful crash, and surely Alice would have come to tell her not to worry if it had been just a broken plate or something.

Miriam hesitated, then ducked back into the bedroom, kicked her shoes off, and patted her way along the wall by the door until her hand closed on the fancy carved walking stick. It had looked handmade, and probably came from somewhere beautiful and exotic, but it also looked as if it would be just as useful as a cricket bat. And she'd faced down goblins with a cricket bat before, so she felt a little more confident as she tightened her grip on the bottom end of the stick, leaving the heavy handle free for swinging.

The hall was still empty, and she tiptoed down it soundlessly in her bare feet, listening for movement beyond each door before she passed it. But the spare rooms lay silent, as did the living room, and then there was only the kitchen and Rose's office – which had once been the dining room – left to check. She slid up to the office door and leaned against the wall, waiting. Still nothing, and suddenly she was gripped by the idea – no, the *certainty* – that Alice was in the utility room. That the unseen intruder was even now lifting her unconscious body into the freezer and closing the lid. Unconscious, or— No. She couldn't think that.

"Alice," she said, no longer worried about secrecy, and ran the rest of the way down the hall, her makeshift club raised. *"Alice!"*

She burst into the kitchen, still shouting, hoping she might catch the murderer off guard, and charged across the flags toward the utility room door. *"Alice, I'm coming!"*

"Miriam, *stop!*" Alice shouted, and Miriam jerked toward her voice, spotting the older woman straightening up from a crouch by the sink. For one confused moment Miriam thought she must be hiding there, then she glimpsed the utility room door opening and she tried to spin back in its direction as something monstrous hulked into view in the shadows beyond, crouched to leap. She lost her balance and stumbled, a sharp pain lancing through her foot. She gave a strangled yelp, dropped the walking stick, and tried to hop onto her other foot, staggering straight toward the half-glimpsed monster as she did. It gave a rather less restrained squawk, and she tried to stop her helpless forward plunge, but she tripped over the walking stick and tumbled straight through the utility room door, hoping as she fell that she'd at least incapacitate the creature.

She sucked in a deep breath, ready to start screaming, then the heavy, rich scent of smoke and stone washed around her, and a deep voice said, "I say, Miriam. That was most impressive. Is it a war dance of some kind?"

"No," she said, sliding off Mortimer's back and winding up wedged between him and the doorframe. "I'm so sorry. Are you alright, Mortimer?"

"I think so," he said, trying to back out of the doorway. "Are you?"

Miriam considered the question carefully, then said, "My foot hurts."

"You goose," Alice said, appearing above her. "We broke a bowl. I was just about to sweep it up when you came rushing in. What on earth were you doing?"

"I thought something had happened," Miriam said, her cheeks heating up. And Mortimer wasn't helping. He was terribly hot, and he couldn't seem to get out of the doorway. She tried to push herself up, but they were quite firmly wedged together. "Help."

Alice held out her hands, and Miriam grabbed them. There was a moment of struggle, as Mortimer complained that he couldn't go backward because Beaufort was in the way, and he couldn't go forward because Alice was in the way, and what were they *doing* here anyway, then Miriam found herself on her feet. She almost fell again, grabbing Alice for support as painful flares shot up her leg when she tried to put her foot down.

"Ow."

"Let's have a look," Alice said, supporting her as she hobbled to the table. "Beaufort's right, that was very impressive, though. You'd have seen anyone off."

Miriam huffed. She was still feeling far too hot, and she was quite sure Alice was humouring her. She plonked herself unceremoniously in a chair and glared at the dragons. "What are you doing here?"

"Invest— Just looking," Beaufort said, peering around the kitchen with great interest.

"I thought we agreed you would stay away from the village," Alice said.

"I said that," Mortimer said, still not moving from the utility room door.

"And *I* thought you weren't going to do anything without us," Beaufort said, ignoring Mortimer.

"And *I* said *that,*" Miriam said, looking at Mortimer. He huffed steam.

"Well," Alice said. "Since we're all here, we may as well get on with it, hadn't we?" She smiled at the old dragon, and he tilted his head, then showed his teeth in a grin.

"Quite," he said. "No point wasting time. Mortimer, have you found anything on that freezer yet?"

"No," Mortimer said. "There was the plate, and then Miriam came in, and—"

"Let's take a look then, lad. There may still be some traces, even after all the police."

Mortimer groaned, but shuffled back into the utility room.

"I'll pop back into the office briefly," Alice said. "We mustn't be long, though."

"Ow," Miriam said, pointing at her foot.

"Of course," Alice said. "I'm sorry, Miriam." She bent over, shining the torch on Miriam's foot. "Oh dear."

"Oh *dear?* What does that mean?"

"It's just a bit messy, is all," Alice said, and before Miriam could say anything or pull away the older woman grabbed her foot. Sharp, hungry pain roared up Miriam's leg, and she jerked away, finding she knew some words she hadn't even realised she'd heard before.

"*Ow!* What are you *doing?*"

"Done," Alice said, and showed her a large shard of plate. "Where are your shoes?"

"In the bedroom. I was trying to be quiet." The pain had subsided to an insistent throb, and she wiped sweat off her forehead.

"Good thinking," Alice dropped the shard in the bin and came back with a damp cloth from the sink. "Hold that on it while I sweep up, then we can get it bandaged."

Miriam took the cloth obediently and pressed it in place. "Did you find anything?"

"Not yet," Alice said, crouching a little stiffly so she could use the dustpan and broom. "I'd just got into Rose's office when I heard scuffling in the kitchen, so came to have a look."

"You should have called me! It could have been the murderer!"

Alice smiled at her, the red torchlight giving her face ghastly angles. "I should have. I always forget just how capable you are, Miriam."

"I don't feel very capable right now," Miriam said, staring at her foot. She still felt hot, but not for the same reason. There was silence for a moment, only broken by the clink of pottery and the rasp of the brush across the floor, then she said, "You could leave that and finish looking in the office. I'll clean it up as soon as my foot stops bleeding. We don't want to be in here too long, after all. The police officer might come and check the house."

Alice straightened up, smiling, but before she could answer the kitchen was flooded with a bright, warm glow as the overhead lights came on. Miriam squawked and almost pitched head-first off her chair, catching herself with her hands on the floor and finding herself staring at a trail of her own blood that made her foot suddenly hurt rather more than it had been doing.

"Yes," someone said from the kitchen door. "And what a problem that would be."

"Ah," Alice said, as the dragons peered through from the utility.

"Oh, no," Miriam said, and squeezed her eyes shut, as if that would help matters.

"Quite," the newcomer said.

9
DI ADAMS

"I'd say I'm shocked to find you here," DI Adams said, squinting at the two women in the bright light of the kitchen. "But I'd be lying."

Alice set the dustpan and broom down and straightened up, smoothing the front of her cardigan. She smiled, just as if she'd expected the inspector to arrive at any moment, which DI Adams thought she *hadn't*, but it was annoying just how convincing the older woman was.

"I was just about to dress Miriam's foot," Alice said. "She's cut herself."

DI Adams looked at Miriam, who was doubled over in a kitchen chair clutching her foot and trying to look anywhere but at the inspector. There were daubs of blood all over the floor, accompanied by broken pieces of plate, and a walking stick lying amid the debris. With the fingerprint dust still smearing the walls and surfaces, it looked rather more like a genteel and well-staged crime scene than it had earlier, when it had been an actual, *undisturbed* crime scene.

DI Adams sighed. "Is it bad?" she asked Miriam.

"No," Miriam said, then thought about it. "Well, a bit."

"Stitches?" DI Adams asked, directing the question at Alice.

"No, nothing that bad. We'll get it patched up, won't we, Miriam?"

"Yes," Miriam said, still not looking at the inspector. She'd finally stopped giving terrified squeaks whenever DI Adams spoke to her, but she still seemed convinced the inspector was just waiting for a chance to arrest her. DI Adams was entirely aware she had that effect on quite a lot of people, but she didn't know how to change it. Wear floral blouses and straighten her hair and stick a permanent smile on, maybe. Which wasn't going to happen.

Alice handed DI Adams the dustpan and broom. "If you clear up that plate, I'll see to Miriam."

DI Adams looked at the dustpan, then at Alice, then sighed and crouched to finish sweeping up the shards of broken dinnerware. "Beaufort, Mortimer – you may as well come out of the utility. I know you're in there."

"I thought we hid rather well," Beaufort said, peering around the corner.

"I was listening to you from outside," DI Adams said. "You weren't exactly being quiet, were you?"

"We had torches," Miriam blurted. "With red things."

DI Adams blinked at her, and Alice said, "Red filters. Allowed us to see without losing our night vision. And also kept the light levels down a bit, just in case anyone was watching."

"Like me?"

Alice smiled. She'd found a drawer full of gauze and tape and safety pins and ancient-looking tubes of antiseptic cream, and was inspecting Miriam's foot again. "Or like the murderer."

"It's a very silly thing to do, coming here when you think there might be a murderer around," DI Adams said. "And you two coming here when there's some cryptid journalist lurking about the place," she added to the dragons.

"I *said,*" Mortimer muttered. "I said we should stay away."

"And leave Rose to fend for herself?" Beaufort demanded. "That's not cricket, lad. One doesn't abandon one's friends merely because of a small risk of discovery."

"We were being terribly careful," Alice said.

"You were not," DI Adams said sharply, tipping the broken bits of plate into the bin. "You were meddling again, and potentially putting yourselves at risk, *and* getting in the way of a police investigation. You know the police, right? The people who're actually trained to do these things?"

"And can you smell the frozen green of a long-held grudge?" Beaufort asked. "Or the beets-and-dust scent of resentment?"

DI Adams put the dustpan back beneath the sink and leaned against the cabinets, crossing her arms over her chest. "No, Beaufort. You know I can't. But there's a procedure for these sorts of things. We will find who's responsible. We're quite good at it. And you can't just come in here messing up a crime scene. I know you want to help, but—"

"Ex-crime scene," Alice said. "Surely you'd still be working on it now if there was more evidence to be gathered."

"It's a murder scene, Alice," DI Adams said. "We can hold it for quite a while if we feel we may need to come back again to check for further evidence."

Alice *hmm*ed, wrapping some bandage around Miriam's foot to hold the dressing in place. "Well, we visit Rose quite regularly, so I'm sure our fingerprints and DNA would be here already."

Miriam gave a startled gasp and looked at her hands as if they'd betrayed her.

DI Adams shook her head and wondered, not for the first time, if all W.I. chairs were like Alice, or if she just had extraordinarily bad luck. "Quite probably, but you still could have disturbed evidence from the actual murderer. You shouldn't be here. *I* shouldn't be here. I should be at home, waiting on results from the coroner and eating a takeaway curry in my pjs. Instead I'm sitting in my car, guarding a house like a rookie PC and waiting around for you lot to come in breaking the law again."

Miriam made a sound that was very close to a squeak.

"Now," DI Adams said. "What's Rose told you, and what do you think you're looking for here?"

Alice taped the bandage down, admired her handiwork for a moment, then straightened up. "I think I shall put the kettle on. One needs tea for these things."

"*Crime scene,*" DI Adams said, wondering what she had to say to get Alice to pay attention. And also wondering if it really would be more hassle to arrest them both than it currently was just dealing with them.

"As you say, we've already messed it up," Alice said. "Or we can go to my house, if you prefer."

DI Adams pinched the bridge of her nose. "Yes, I would prefer. The judicial system would also prefer. Actually, both I and the judicial system would prefer that you answered my questions right now, without the tea, but I suppose that's asking a bit much, is it?"

"I have had a hip replacement. It's rather unfair of you to expect me to stand while you interview me."

DI Adams scowled at Alice, who simply smiled back, and Miriam said, "I do fancy a cuppa."

"Would there be biscuits, by any chance?" Beaufort asked, finally abandoning the utility room.

"I'm sure that can be arranged," Alice said, and DI Adams looked at the ceiling.

"Oh, good," she said. "That sounds like the most important thing."

"Tea and biscuits are," Beaufort said. "Especially in matters of life and death. Then tea and biscuits are far more important than one might ever imagine."

"Of course they are," the inspector muttered. "Fine. We'll go to Alice's. Now, everyone out."

"I need to get Rose's clothes," Miriam said, and got up, then yelped and sat down abruptly. *"Ow."*

"I'll get them," Alice said, patting her shoulder. "And where exactly are your shoes, dear?"

"Somewhere in the bedroom," Miriam admitted. "I just kicked them off."

"Well, I'm sure I'll find them."

"No, you won't," DI Adams said. "You two will go to my car and wait there. What does Rose need?"

"I already put a bag together," Miriam said. "It's in the bedroom. With my shoes." She stared at her foot doubtfully.

DI Adams followed her gaze and sighed. "Alright. Stay where you are. I'll grab the bag and your shoes, then we'll go to Alice's."

"Are we going in the car?" Beaufort asked. "I rather enjoy a car trip."

"*You* are going straight home from here," the inspector said. "Right now."

"Are you sure we can't—" Beaufort started, and DI Adams interrupted before he could come up with something that would somehow sound reasonable.

"Very sure. Off you go, and *please* stay out of this. I don't want to be explaining stray dragon scales to the coroner's office."

Mortimer checked his tail, his shoulders slumped. "I can't help it. They just keep falling off."

"You should talk to Lydia," Beaufort said, peering at the younger dragon's scales. "She'll know how to fix that."

"She told me to eat more rabbits," Mortimer said. "I don't see how *that's* going to help."

Miriam smiled at him. "I'll get you some more coconut oil. Coconut oil fixes everything."

"You could just stay out of my investigations," DI Adams suggested. "Then you're not going to shed on anything."

"I think I'd shed less in general if we stayed out of investigations," Mortimer said, his tone suggesting that he didn't expect anyone to listen to him.

"I'd certainly sleep better," DI Adams said, and stared at the dragons for a moment. She really *did* want them gone as soon as possible, but ... "Ah – did you find anything?"

"No," Mortimer said, still examining his tail. "There've been too many people through here. Lots of interested people, and some angry people, and even some guilty people, but it's all jumbled up. And Rose's scent's so strong—"

"Honeysuckle in the rain and brook water on a hot day," Beaufort put in. "Most pleasant."

"Yes," Mortimer agreed. "But she's so ... so *Rose* that it rather swamps things."

DI Adams thought that sounded very much like Rose. "But you said angry people? Guilty people?"

"Yes. But there's no telling when. Or why they were angry." Mortimer plucked at a scale that looked a little duller than the others, then added, "They could've been angry because they burned their dinner, or guilty because they were rude to someone. Nothing's clear."

"But there was something," Beaufort said. "I couldn't catch it, but you said, didn't you, lad?"

Mortimer abandoned his tail and scratched his ear instead. "It's not clear. There's something ... calculated. But furtive, too. All built up around the kitchen – maybe even the whole house. It's sort of deep under things, as if the furtiveness is almost an afterthought. If I can check—"

"You can't," DI Adams said.

"That's most unreasonable," Beaufort said. "It might be a lead!"

"You might be wrecking my crime scene." Although she had to admit that it was probably fairly well wrecked already.

"It's just all very confused," Mortimer said. "There's that odd trace, then something that's alarm, but that could be Rose finding the body. I need more time to really sort through them."

"Well, that's not possible." She tried not to feel too disappointed that Mortimer hadn't come up with something more, and wondered what, exactly, she would have done if he *had.* There wasn't exactly a section on the report form for evidence provided by dragons. "Thank you for your help. Now stop it. Go home. Stay away from the village and journalists."

Beaufort gave her a reproachful look. "We're not hatchlings, Detective Inspector."

"No. So I'm trusting you to act like the sensible, mature dragons you are," she said, and shooed them out the door. She watched them vanish into the trees, taking on the muted hues of the night, and had lost sight of them before they'd gone more than a few paces. She shook her head and turned back into the kitchen to examine Alice and Miriam.

"Don't touch anything."

Alice held up a dog bowl. "I'm only picking up Angelus' things, Inspector."

DI Adams gave her a suspicious look as she headed into the hall. *"Don't touch."*

WHEN DI ADAMS came back into the kitchen Alice was holding her phone at arm's length to peer at the screen, and Miriam was still sitting in the chair, frowning at her dangling foot.

"Did you find everything alright, Inspector?" Alice asked, tucking her phone back into her pocket.

"Just fine," DI Adams said, and handed Miriam her flip-flops. "Come on. Everyone out."

Alice picked up a large shopping bag that was sitting by the door, a soft blanket printed with bones spilling over the top. "As you say."

Miriam hobbled down the path, supported by Alice, while DI Adams locked the door with the key she'd commandeered from them. The night was still and quiet, and when she came around to the front of the house she found Dandy standing on the path, watching the women as they let themselves out the gate.

"What're you doing?" she asked him, beeping the car open so that they could get in then reaching down to rub the coarse warm fur between his ears. "Why haven't you caught me a murderer yet?"

He glanced up at her, giving her a glimpse of those luminous red eyes, then looked back at the road. She frowned, following his gaze. He wasn't looking at the car at all, and for a moment she couldn't tell what had caught his interest. Then she spotted the figure standing on the pavement in the shadow of one of Rose's trees. Whoever it was, they *were* watching Alice help Miriam into the car.

"Hello," she said to herself softly, and stepped off the path, walking quick and quiet across the mix of long grass and weeds to the garden wall. "Can I help you, Mr Brown?" she asked, once she was close enough to see the figure clearly in the low light.

He yelped and spun around, one hand going to his heart. "What're you doing, sneaking up on people like that?" His voice had hard edges, the soft lilt gone in his fright.

"What're you doing hanging around my crime scene in the middle of the night?"

He peered at her, and broke into a smile. "Oh, it's you, Detective Inspector. Did you get my videos?"

"I did." From what she'd seen, they hadn't shown anything more interesting than Rose coming and going, but she'd put them in evidence to be examined properly anyway. "What're you doing out here?"

"Moles."

"Moles?"

He nodded. "Rose often has them in her garden. I have sonic repellers, but I also check for any holes too close to the fence. One can't be too careful." He smoothed his moustache. The softness had come back into his voice, but it felt like a front, something put on like a coat against a frost.

"Can't one?" she asked.

"Not with moles."

"Right." DI Adams looked back at her car. Alice was standing next to it watching them while Miriam peered out of the back seat. Dandy stood in front of them, his nose pointed at Dougal. "You check for moles in the middle of the night?"

He hesitated, then said, "Rose doesn't like my using ... preventative measures."

"Like poison?"

"It's not illegal."

DI Adams just watched him.

He shifted, looking at his feet. "They do awful things to the lawn."

She shook her head, then said, "Have you thought more about if you saw anything on Friday night or Saturday morning, Mr Brown?"

"I told the young officer who interviewed me. I was at the pub watching the game."

"All night?"

"As long as it was on, then I came home and went straight to bed." He crossed his arms over his chest. A plastic bag swung from his fingers. "If I knew anything I'd tell you straight away. Is Rose alright? She must be terribly upset. And at her age." He shook his head sorrowfully.

"At her age what?"

"Well, to have to deal with such things. One used to feel safe in this neighbourhood!"

"Have there been other incidents that have made you feel unsafe?"

He thrust the bag at her. "Yes! Look at *this!* Someone's dog messed in my garden. Must've been a monster, too. It's unacceptable!"

DI Adams frowned. "It's hardly threatening."

"Well." He hesitated, then said, "It's a health hazard. There's got to be a law about these sorts of things!"

"One would hope." DI Adams looked at Dandy, who looked up at the sky.

"That's the problem with this country, you know. The rot starts with the little things. No respect!"

She decided to leave before he got started on immigrants. It was feeling inevitable at this stage. "Have a good think about Friday night, Mr Brown. If you had any information at all, it'd be very helpful."

He shook his head. "It's all on the video."

She sighed. "If you change your mind, you know where to find me." She picked her way back to the gate and let herself out, waving Alice into the car. Dougal was gone when she glanced back.

"He's not after the rabbits again, is he?" Miriam asked as DI Adams swung herself into the driver's seat.

"Moles."

"Ugh. Horrible man."

"It seems odd he didn't see anything," Alice said. "He keeps a very close eye on Rose's place."

Miriam nodded. "Rose planted wild privet right along that wall, and he *still* manages to spy on her. Offering to do things around the house, or work in her garden. As if Rose can't cope!"

"He's been very helpful," DI Adams said. "And it's nothing to do with you anyway."

Alice made a noncommittal noise, and Miriam said, "Is there a leak in your car?"

DI Adams looked in the mirror to see Miriam staring at a damp patch on her skirt, and Dandy panting happily next to her. "Dandy, move across," she said.

"Ew," Miriam said. "Why isn't his drool invisible?"

"One of many things I have no answer to," DI Adams said, and pulled away into the quiet dark of the village.

❧

SITTING at Alice's kitchen table with a cup of tea – she'd refused the offer of coffee on the basis that she might, possibly, still get home to sleep at some point tonight – DI Adams wondered if Rose's house was alright left unguarded. There was a PC on the way from Skipton, and she was fairly certain she had her most likely trespassers here, but one never knew.

She sighed, and took a cracker off the board on the table, adding a chunk of softly veined blue cheese and heaping it with some chutney that tasted sweet and tart and smoky all at once. "So, what were you two looking for in there?"

"Rose's clothes," Miriam said immediately, and DI Adams raised her eyebrows at her. "We were!"

"I think the inspector may be onto us, dear," Alice said, daubing chutney on a sliver of cheese delicately.

DI Adams popped the rest of her biscuit in her mouth before she could feel too guilty about the quantity she'd used. "Are you going to tell me, then?" she asked around it.

"I thought I might like a little look at Rose's will," Alice said.

DI Adams regarded her for a moment, then said, "Does Rose

have enough money for that to be a motive?" The state of her house suggested not.

"Rose and I talk investments on occasion," Alice said. "She's rather more astute than one would imagine."

"And did you find anything?"

"No," Alice said. "But I do know she's still married to Jean-Claude, which would indicate that he may still be in the will."

"But Jean-Claude's lovely," Miriam said. "And he adores Rose."

Alice gave her a look DI Adams couldn't quite read. "The restaurant business isn't an easy one."

"He *wouldn't*," Miriam said. "He named his restaurant after her! *After* they split up!"

"But isn't it always the husband?"

"Stop," DI Adams said. "This is not how these things go. You should have told me about the will, not started poking around looking for it yourself."

"It was only a guess," Alice replied. "Besides, I'm sure you'd have followed up on it yourself at some point."

DI Adams frowned at her. "You have *got* to stop this. Someone's been murdered, Alice. This isn't the time for you to play Miss Marple."

"We weren't intending to," Alice said. "We *were* going to get Rose some clothes. Everything else was incidental."

DI Adams wondered what the etiquette was regarding telling ladies of a certain age that you knew they were lying. Not that it'd change anything, as Alice would just smile and nod and do exactly as she liked. She took a sip of tea and said, "Has Rose seemed alright to you?"

"In what respect?" Alice asked. "She's very upset, obviously."

"Not just now. Overall." DI Adams wished she could find an easier way to say it, but she couldn't. It wasn't just the scarab beetles in the bathroom, or the toothbrush in the hall. There had been a pair of trainers in the freezer, too. She'd seen them when the body had been lifted out, and Lucas had photographed them dutifully.

"Be specific, Inspector," Alice said, checking the teapot. DI Adams thought there might have been the smallest tremor in the older woman's hand, but it was impossible to be sure.

She folded her own hands on the table and watched Alice as she said, "Do you think Rose might be experiencing cognitive decline?"

"No," Miriam said immediately. "Of course not!"

Alice twisted her mouth slightly, as if she wasn't as certain. Although anyone would seem disorganised and forgetful when it came to Alice's standards.

"Alice?" DI Adams asked, when she didn't say anything.

Alice added milk to her cup. "I doubt it, Inspector. Rose has always been Rose. Nothing has changed."

"She hasn't mentioned being worried about it to you?"

"Not at all."

"Even though we found letters in her office from a private neurologist regarding appointments that Rose had coming up?"

No one spoke for a moment. Alice topped her cup up, and Miriam just stared at DI Adams. Finally Alice said, "Cognitive issues do not make someone dangerous, Inspector. That's very short-sighted of you."

"I'm not saying she's done anything," DI Adams said. "But if she is having some cognitive issues, that raises other questions. Perhaps she didn't recognise the victim. Perhaps she reacted in a disproportionate manner to finding someone in her house."

"I think the will may indicate other possibilities."

DI Adams frowned at her. "Don't interfere in this investigation, Alice. The sooner we – and by that I mean the police – can get the full story, the sooner Rose can be cleared."

Alice put the milk jug down with exaggerated care. "*If* she's cleared. It all sounds a little tidy, doesn't it? The dotty old lady did it? Case closed?"

"That's not fair, Alice," DI Adams said. "You know I wouldn't do that."

"What if it wasn't Rose who was implicated?" Alice asked. "What if it was someone you didn't know? Would you be so fair then?"

"I don't make it a habit to lock up senior citizens."

Alice started to say something, and Miriam spoke first, her face pink. "This is *Rose*. How *can* you?"

DI Adams leaned back in her chair, taking a mouthful of tea. Rose wasn't exactly her prime suspect. As Collins had said, she couldn't physically have lifted the body into the freezer. Not that it ruled out her having an accomplice, of course, but there was still no motive. She looked from Alice to Miriam, and sighed.

"You need to leave this alone," she said, speaking mostly to Miriam. "You do realise that if something happened and Rose did accidentally kill the victim, you're the first people anyone would be looking at for helping her cover it up?"

Miriam gasped, knocking her mug and sending tea slopping onto the table. She clapped both hands over her mouth, and Alice got up to get a cloth from the sink.

"I mean it," DI Adams said. "You *have* to leave this alone. You could make things much, much worse."

Miriam stared at her, and DI Adams felt a tiny niggle of guilt. But if it stopped them meddling in her case, she'd put up with a little guilt.

Alice gave a small, but very clear chuckle as she came back to the table, and DI Adams shot her a glare. Alice smiled back, although her knuckles were tight on the cloth. "DI Adams, you know quite well that we have nothing to do with it."

"I don't know that," she said.

"Of course you do," Alice said. "Besides, you've already arrested me once simply because my somewhat unsatisfactory husband disappeared. If you continue with that sort of thing, it starts looking like police harassment, don't you think?"

DI Adams scowled. "Are you ever going to tell me what happened when your unsatisfactory husband vanished *again* last year?"

"I don't know what you mean, Inspector. I was a victim, if you recall."

DI Adams thought Alice had never been a victim in her life. Although, technically, she *had* been kidnapped by said unsatisfactory husband. Who had yet to be found. She sighed. "Fine. But I'm following the evidence, alright? Even if it leads to Rose. And I won't stand for you two getting in the way." She pushed back from the table and headed for the door, her face hot.

She didn't think her job had ever made her feel ashamed before.

10
ALICE

Alice stood in her kitchen, frowning at the sink. There was still a daffodil petal in it that she must have missed earlier. Evidently Thompson the cat had been up to something, because she had come home from Miriam's that afternoon with Rose in tow to find her vase of daffodils upended, the water spilled over the worktop and the flowers looking rather sorry for themselves. The scented candle in its glass jar had rolled to the corner of the sill but not fallen, which was a shame. Jasmine had gone through a stage of making scented candles, and Alice had bought one to show support. It was, purportedly, ginger and orange, but whenever she lit it all she could smell was burned popcorn. Still, one couldn't just throw such things away, even if it was a rather ghastly shade of orange that put her in mind of forgotten pumpkins on the turn.

She fished the daffodil petal out of the sink and dropped it in the compost bin, then leaned against the cabinets, her hands gripping the edge of the worktop. Miriam had declared her intention to walk home, but DI Adams had offered her a lift in a manner that had made it clear it wasn't really an offer at all. Alice presumed it was merely the inspector making a point. After all, she could always pick up her phone and call Miriam if she wanted to talk over the day's events. Although she wasn't sure that would be very helpful right now. The day felt crowded with people, after the fraught morning at Miriam's and the evening of mildly criminal activity, and, of course, having an unexpected house guest. It was all faintly claustrophobic, and while she held Rose in the highest affection, she rather wished her house was as still and empty and tranquil as it usually was. One had room to think, then.

But there was no point wishing. One must simply work with the situation at hand, or risk never finding one's way out of it at all. Alice straightened up, tucking her hair behind her ears, and left the kitchen. She switched on the lamp on the hall table and climbed the stairs with one hand pressed gently to her hip, more for comfort than support. It had healed remarkably well after the goblin attack, but it still ached when the weather was sharp and cold, or simply if she stood too long. Small indignities, really. Certainly compared to Rose's issues of memory. The body betraying one was difficult enough. Alice frowned, thinking of Rose leaning over the photos and saying, *How much can one forget?*

Would she have noticed if Rose was getting more ... well, more *Rose?* Although, that was unfair. Rose might be astonishingly disorganised, and incredibly casual when it came to things such as schedules and meeting times, but she was never confused. Alice would have noticed *that,* she was sure. No, it was all too easy for people of DI Adams' generation to assume age was synonymous with decline. And as much as she rather respected the inspector, and felt that with a few more years' practice she'd become pleasingly formidable, everyone had blind spots. And age was a dreadfully common one.

She knocked gently on the door to the spare room, but there

was no response. "Rose?" she called softly. She had sent a text while DI Adams was in the bedroom at Rose's house, telling the older woman to stay hidden until the inspector had left. Now she pushed the door open a smidge and peeked in. "Rose?" she said again. Still no answer. She was suddenly seized by the certainty that Rose was *gone,* that she'd taken Angelus out for a walk and become lost in the familiar streets, her faltering memory rendering the world treacherous and unreliable. That she'd be mired at some small intersection, looking for landmarks she could no longer recognise while the dog whined and pleaded, and she searched for something, anything familiar to clutch hold of.

Alice's breath caught in her throat, and she pushed the door wide. The bedside lamp was on, and it revealed bright violet hair emerging from under a huddle of blankets like a strange sprouting of tussocky grass, glowing softly in the mellow light. Angelus took up the majority of the bed, which Alice had absolutely not given permission for, and his tail thumped on the covers as he looked up expectantly. A small snore emanated from the region of the hair.

Alice let her breath out softly, trying to settle the tightness in her shoulders. She was being ridiculous. These things didn't just happen overnight, like the sudden onset of a cold. Although one could hide it, of course, if one was of a mind to.

She sighed, switching the bedside lamp off and letting herself out, shutting the door quietly behind her. Let Rose sleep. There was no reason for two of them to be awake and worrying as the night crept into the wee small hours. And company was one thing she had no need for right now.

THE LIGHT in Alice's reading room was low and warm, rendering the crowded spines of the books around her indistinct and hard to read. She poured a small measure of whisky into an old glass and sat down on the chaise longue, setting the bag she'd taken from Rose's house next to her. With Angelus' fluffy blanket, food, dog bowls, and tattered soft duck toy removed, the bag held only the cardboard file she'd quickly grabbed from Rose's kitchen while the inspector was fetching Miriam's shoes. She wasn't even sure what it might contain, just that it had been slid underneath the cans of dog food, hidden from sight. It might hold nothing more than old photos, or it might hold a clue to who would want Rose either dead or framed for murder.

Alice sipped her whisky, rolling it over her tongue and thinking of the two men fighting in the garden, and the one poor soul who would fight no more. She didn't know where Rose got the energy from. One unsatisfactory husband had been more than enough. She couldn't understand why one would want to have multiples, whether by marriage or not. And while she knew there were people who shared their love lives with more than one partner quite comfortably, she did wonder just how happy Jean-Claude and Campbell had been with it all. They had certainly seemed less than enthralled to encounter one another.

It was worth looking into. As was the file sitting next to her, but she wasn't sure if she wanted to read it right now. It had seemed very logical when she picked it up, but with Rose asleep upstairs it felt rather more like snooping than she was comfortable with. She looked at it for a moment longer, then lifted the cover, peeking at the contents. If it looked *too* personal, she'd leave it.

But instead of a will, or bank statements, she found herself looking at a letter printed on heavy paper. The letterhead proclaimed it to be from the office of a property surveyor, and Alice wondered if Rose had been thinking about selling. That would be most unexpected. She skimmed the contents, frowning.

"As detailed in the attached full property survey, we have no reservation in declaring the property safe for habitation," she read aloud to the

silent room. "Well, of course it is. Why wouldn't it be?" Rose's house might be a little lacking in maintenance, but it was certainly more than habitable. She moved the survey to one side and examined the next letter. It was from the council.

After consideration of the survey presented to us by independent surveyors, we accept that the property belonging to Professor Rose Howard, located at 1 Church Lane, Toot Hansell, is suitable for human occupation. We will be taking no further action at this time.

Below that was another letter, also from the council. This one was from the social services department.

Following our interview with you and inspection of your living facilities, we believe you could benefit from regular checks by a caseworker …

Alice shook her head, and moved on to the next letter. It was from the same department.

We have received a query from a concerned party, who believes you may no longer be able to live alone, given the location and condition of your property. We will be sending a caseworker to conduct an interview …

Rose had said nothing about this. Nothing at all. Alice checked the dates. The survey had been done six months ago. The ones from the social services department were more recent, the latest dated only a month ago. Why hadn't she said anything? And what about the cognitive tests DI Adams had mentioned? Alice took another sip of whisky, barely tasting it.

How much can one forget?

She put the letters to one side with stiff fingers, and found a magazine underneath them. It was printed on flimsy paper, the pixelated image on the front page made even grainier by the poor print quality. Alice could just make out a smudgy figure that might have been a large dog (or a Cloverly-sized dragon) that didn't look quite like the surrounding rocky landscape. *Bigfoot stole my lunch at Ben Nevis!* blared the main cover line to go with the photo, and smaller cover lines promised *Pixie attractants tested!* and *Is Sellafield causing mermaid mutations?* Alice wasn't sure if that meant that the magazine thought the Sellafield nuclear power plant was causing mutations that made people *look* like mermaids, or if they felt the power plant was causing mutations *to* mermaids. *Cryptids Today,* read the masthead.

"Of course," she murmured, picking up the magazine.

"Evenin'," someone said from the door, and she jumped.

"*Thompson.* Do stop sneaking up on me, or I shall have to get you a bell."

"I'd like to see you try." He jumped up next to her, a big smoky tabby with scarred ears and a kink in his tail, and she moved the bag out of the way with a sigh of resignation. She never used to have to deal with cat hair on her chaise longue. "Besides," the cat added. "I don't *sneak.* I'm a cat. I'm just naturally stealthy."

"Sneaky."

"*Stealthy.*" They glared at each other until he yawned and said, "What sneaky things are *you* up to, then?"

"Reading about Bigfoot." She showed him the magazine.

"Why?"

"We had an incident with a cryptid journalist today. This is her paper."

"An *incident?* Involving dragons, by any chance?"

"Yes, but she didn't see them. Just."

Thompson squinted at her. "I don't suppose this would be the same journalist who poked her camera in the window and took a photo while I was napping?"

Alice frowned. "Was that what happened to my daffodils?"

"It was. What was she after?"

"She has suspicions about Christmas. I've told the dragons to stay away until she's gone."

"Any chance they'll listen?"

"Well, we also have a case involving Rose and a body in her freezer."

Thompson blinked. “Of course you do.”

“Which you could be rather helpful with, if you fancied putting your sneakiness to good use. I’d rather like to know what direction the police are taking, and what evidence they have.”

“Of course you would.” He peered at the magazine. “*Attracting* pixies? Well, they’re going to regret that, for a start.”

“How worried should we be about the dragons?”

“Eh.” He scratched his jaw with a back leg enthusiastically, sending cat hair cascading over the magazine. “Hard to say. Maybe they do believe in it, in which case yes, we do need to be worried. But plenty of people like to pretend to believe in things, just because it gives them a hold over people who really do believe. Just look at politicians.”

Alice brushed some of the hairs away. “You’re rather astute for a cat.”

“There you go making assumptions based on species again. Lots of people of various kinds keep a close eye on humans. You need careful watching, you lot. You’d blow the world up just to see what happens.”

Alice thought that, while her views aligned uncomfortably closely with Thompson’s, she preferred Beaufort’s rather more optimistic views on humans. “And if it was left to cats, the whole world would be a hairball,” she said aloud.

Thompson snorted. “And there would be a sore lack of salmon. The basic moggy is not known for our ability to fish.”

“Quite.” She stared at the magazine a moment longer. “This is worrying, though, isn’t it?”

“It is. Where did you get it?”

“From Rose’s study.”

“You sneak.” There was a huff of amusement in Thompson’s voice.

“I was merely collecting evidence on her case.”

"Sneaking, you mean." Thompson peered at the magazine again. "Why does she have this, do you think?"

"She said she started exploring the world of cryptids—"

"Folk."

"Sorry?"

He narrowed his eyes at her. "You're talking about us. About Folk. Don't call us cryptids, like we're some sort of crossword."

"That's cryptic," she said, then added, "I'm sorry. I didn't mean to be insensitive."

"We don't care when it's clueless sods like this lot," Thompson said, lifting his nose at the magazine. "But you should know better."

"Quite right. I shall *do* better." She tapped the blurry photo. "Rose was looking into the Folk rumours that are known to other humans, to see if there was any truth in them. I imagine this was part of her research."

Thompson sniffed the paper, then sat back. "How involved was she? How much was she revealing?"

Alice frowned at him. "Do you think someone targeted her for *that?*"

"Anything's possible with you lot," he said, which Alice thought wasn't inaccurate. "But there's also the problem of what certain Folk get up to when they think humans are getting a bit too close to the truth. The Watch are meant to handle such things, but, well. Some Folk get impatient." He curled his crooked tail over his toes. "I'll ask around, see if anyone's been hearing about people getting jumpy."

"Thank you," she said, flicking through the paper. There was a blue Post-it stuck next to an article about vanishing ducks in a village pond down south. Someone thought a kraken was responsible, which Alice felt was a stretch, even for such a paper.

Thompson peered over her arm, then said, "Any of that salmon left?"

"No. I have some chicken, though."

"Breast or leg?"

"I'm quite sure all cats aren't this picky."

"I'm being very helpful, you may have noticed."

"You're also being very picky."

He huffed. "I perform a vital service in this village, keeping dragons and you lot on the down-low with the Watch. I should be suitably rewarded for my hard work. And now you want me to go all extracurricular and snoop on the police, too."

Alice sighed. She still didn't entirely understand the threat posed by the Watch, only that it was some sort of council of cats that ensured the magical Folk of the world went undiscovered by humans. It didn't sound terribly dangerous to her – after all, what could the cats do? Shed on people? – but as the dragons took it seriously she supposed there was more to it than was evident on the surface. As with many things in life.

She put the magazine back in the bag and stood up. "I was going to make a chicken curry tomorrow."

"Don't do that. You'll *ruin* that nice chicken."

"On that we shall have to maintain our differences," she told him, and led the way through to the kitchen.

"Is there cream?" he asked, padding softly behind her.

"I thought you wanted chicken."

"Is there a law against having both?"

Alice shook her head and went to the fridge for the chicken and the cream. Honestly, cats were almost as annoying as unsatisfactory husbands. No wonder she'd never bothered with one before.

❧

THE NEXT DAY dawned bright and clear, the sky scrubbed clean of clouds other than thin, high tendrils that lay across the pale blue in blushing threads as the sun edged up over the far hills. Alice had woken early, and stood in the kitchen door with a cup of tea cradled in her hands against the lingering chill of the night. There was a faint mist rising from the garden as the sun hit it and started to warm the dew from the leaves, and the day felt full of possibility and promise and threat.

She'd call Miriam as soon as seemed reasonable, she decided, and ask her to come over. She wanted to talk to Rose about the letters, and she felt it prudent to have Miriam present. Just in case the situation called for comforting.

Of course, she could also *not* talk to Rose about them, as she had undeniably been snooping, and just ask her about the cryptid magazines and the threat of journalists, but Alice wanted to *know*. Wanted to know if Rose was truly worried about her mind, and what she might be forgetting. Not that she'd have murdered anyone, of course, but … well. She didn't know, and it was an uneasy feeling. The thought that the mind could turn on you as surely as the body.

She rubbed her hip, twinging in the cold, and stepped back inside, shutting the door behind her. This was foolishness. She'd do her exercises, then call Miriam. She was accomplishing no more now than she had last night, tossing and turning and finally getting up to read about the warning signs of a deteriorating intellect. Which had mostly made her suspect that no one was exactly running at their ideal mental capacity, an observation she had not appreciated, and which had not made sleep come any easier.

At least Thompson was still sleeping, sprawled across her bed and taking up far more room than was reasonable for an average-sized cat. That would be all she needed this morning. A smart-mouthed feline demanding cream.

ALICE OPENED the front door to find Miriam standing on the road beyond the gate, a large woven shopping basket clutched to her chest as she glared at a slim, tall woman dressed in what Alice considered to be a rather elegant manner, even if it was also somewhat excessive for Toot Hansell.

"I don't know what you mean," Miriam said. Her face was flushed, and curls were breaking free from the scarf she was using as a headband. "I don't even know who you are!"

"I told you," the woman said. "My name's Meena, I'm Rose's stepdaughter, and I'm looking for her. I was meant to pick her up at her house, but some constable sent me to *your* house. Then *another* police officer said she was inside, but no one answered when I knocked. He said that you'd probably be here. What on earth is going on?"

"You can't be Rose's stepdaughter," Miriam said. "Jean-Claude doesn't have children. He's very proud of it."

"I can see why he got on so well with Rose," Meena said, almost to herself. "I'm her *ex*-stepdaughter. Is that better?"

"I don't know?" Miriam offered, shifting her grip on the basket.

"It seems more truthful," Alice said, coming down the path to the gate and wondering if this was the ex-stepdaughter who couldn't keep her nose out of things, according to Rose. It seemed likely. "Can we help you, Meena?"

Meena examined her, and Alice returned the appraisal, her eyebrows lifted. Finally the younger woman said, "Where is she?"

"Still sleeping at Miriam's, I imagine," Alice said. "Since you met the police officers, I take it you realise she had a rather stressful day yesterday."

"You just left her there?" Meena asked Miriam. "On her own?"

"She's not a child," Alice said, before Miriam could get too flustered and blurt out something awkward.

Meena pinched the smooth skin of her forehead, looking as if she wanted to argue the point. "What happened?" she asked finally.

The edge in her voice was gone, and she looked at Alice with something like appeal. "Is she alright?"

"She is. Merely a misunderstanding, I imagine." Alice didn't move from the gate. She wasn't about to invite Meena in, not until she knew why she was there.

"I'm meant to be meeting her." Meena turned the appealing look on Miriam. "I can give you a lift back. Can you let me in so I can see her?"

"Um," Miriam said, and Alice spoke over her.

"If Rose didn't come to the door, then she's doubtless sleeping. Maybe if you go back and wait there, she'll be up soon."

Meena looked from Miriam to Alice, her forlorn expression fading, and nodded slowly. "I see. She *was* meant to meet me, you know. I'm taking her to an appointment."

"She didn't mention it," Alice said.

"She may have forgotten in all the 'excitement'." Meena didn't put air quotes around the word, but Alice heard them anyway.

"I'm sure it can be rescheduled, in light of recent events."

"What *are* recent events?"

"I'm sure Rose will tell you all about it," Alice said, and beckoned Miriam in. "If you don't mind, we have business to attend to."

Meena crossed her arms, gold rings glowing softly against the dark skin of her fingers. "I have a responsibility to Rose. I need to see her."

"And I'm sure you will, once she wakes up."

Meena scowled at them both. "Is this to do with Rose's memory lapses? Because that's why I'm here. She needs proper care, and she has an appointment to be evaluated. She *knows* this. She's hiding from me, isn't she?"

"Proper care?" Miriam asked. "What do you mean by *that?*"

"It means Rose getting the help she needs," Meena said.

Alice pressed her lips together, then said, "It will just have to wait. Surely you don't begrudge her some sleep after all this?"

"All *what?* Why won't you tell me what happened?"

"It's Rose's place to tell you what she sees fit," Alice said. "We older ladies prefer to respect the autonomy of our peers. Come along, Miriam. We need to get those figures together before the meeting."

"Um, yes?" Miriam said, and fled in the gate and up the path. Alice lingered for a moment, looking at Meena.

"I suppose I'll go back to your friend's place and wait," the younger woman said.

"It seems wise," Alice said.

Meena regarded her for a moment, then took a card from her phone case and held it out to Alice. "In case you need to call me on her behalf," she said. "Because I'm certain she'll have forgotten her phone somewhere."

Alice took the card. *Meena Dewan,* it read. *Solicitor.* The card was plain matte white, the printing black and understated. "Solicitor," Alice said. "I suppose you deal with all Rose's legal matters, then?"

"One would think," Meena said. "But no. She prefers to have her own lawyer."

"How wise," Alice said, and walked up to the house, closing the door firmly without looking back. Miriam was hovering in the hall, still clutching her basket. "Are you alright, dear?"

"What does she mean by proper care? And *evaluating* Rose?"

"I'm sure we shall find out," Alice said, and led the way up the stairs. Rose's bedroom door was open, the bed unmade and her clothes gone from the chair in the corner of the room. Alice frowned at them, then went to check the bathroom. It was empty.

"Maybe she's in the kitchen," Miriam suggested.

"Maybe," Alice agreed, and led the way back downstairs. But she already knew what they'd find. Empty rooms, and the faint trace of small footprints and large paw prints in the dew on the path leading away from the kitchen door. "Well. This complicates things," she said, and Miriam stared at her.

"She's just walking Angelus, isn't she? She'll come back."

"Maybe," Alice replied, and checked the back of the door for the small backpack Rose had arrived with the night before. It was gone. "And maybe not."

The folder would have to wait.

11
MORTIMER

"Can you see Walter from here?" Beaufort asked, peering over the lip of the ledge he and Mortimer were perched on.

Mortimer leaned out further, the wind plucking at his wings. Beaufort had rushed into his workshop a little earlier, insisting Mortimer put down the new dragon scale hats he was working on. The younger dragon had been half-relieved by the distraction, even if he was worried about what the High Lord might be planning. The hats were intended to be rain-activated, blooming into an umbrella in inclement weather and shrinking to a wide-brimmed hat in the sun, but he was having some trouble controlling the sizing. One was currently wedged across the workshop, effectively cutting him off from his favourite tools until he could get it to shrink again, and he hadn't been particularly reluctant to leave it after spending all morning on the silly thing.

"I don't see him," he said now. "Why are we hiding from him?" Beaufort had led him in a climb high up the dragons' mount, well away from both the grand cavern and the various little private caves and crevasses inhabited by the Cloverly dragons, and out of earshot of everyone. Wild land rolled away below them toward the village in the distance, and the tarn beneath the peak was shattered silk in the wind. Mortimer could see Gilbert surfacing from time to time with reeds in his spines before sinking below the surface again. He was inordinately fond of swimming for a land dragon.

"He won't let go of this dragon hunter thing," Beaufort said. "He keeps insisting we need to start patrols, and I'm sure it's just an excuse for him to shout at the young dragons and pound his chest a bit."

"Well, that journalist *was* hunting us."

Beaufort huffed. "A *journalist.* That's not a dragon hunter! She didn't even see us. I'm going to bite him if he asks me about patrols again."

Mortimer blinked at him. "Is that a good idea?"

"No. But I shall feel much better after I've bitten him," the High Lord said, and grinned.

Mortimer gave him a doubtful grin back, and for a moment they sat in silence. Mortimer peered toward the village, the houses merely smudges in the distance, and wondered how Miriam was. How *Rose* was. Were they safe? Had the police caught the murderer yet? DI Adams was terribly efficient, but she'd asked *him* if he'd found anything. And he hadn't. He hadn't been any help at all. He sighed, his breath warm on his front paws.

"This is ridiculous," Beaufort said abruptly, his talons digging into the ledge of old rock beneath him and crumbling the edge. "We can't just sit here. The W.I. could be in terrible trouble, and we wouldn't even know!"

"I know," Mortimer said. "But if that journalist is still around, and she sees us – well, we're not helping anyone then, are we?" The words sounded unconvincing to his own ears. Somehow, the thought of being spotted by some sort of cryptid journalist seemed less disastrous than not knowing what was happening. Someone had put a body in Rose's *freezer,* and they couldn't so much as keep watch over her, let alone hunt the killer. What sort of friends did that make them? And he *knew* he'd smelled something in her house. *Knew* it. If only he'd had more time ...

"I don't like it," the High Lord said, the words a rumble.

Mortimer opened his mouth to say, *I know, but there's nothing we can do, we can't risk it, we have to be careful,* but what came out instead was, "I don't either." He blinked, and looked at Beaufort. The High Lord looked back at him with his old gold eyes wide and interested. "I don't like it either," he repeated. "So how do we do this without being seen by anyone?"

Beaufort blew amused steam, his scales flushing to more intense greens and golds. "You *are* full of surprises, lad."

Mortimer looked at his talons, resting heavy and sharp against the grey rock. "I don't feel full of surprises. I feel terrified, and confused, and my scales are itching. But we can't just leave them when there's a murderer around somewhere."

"Nothing wrong with feeling a little scared. We all do, and more often than not. The trick is to make it useful, not let it freeze us." Beaufort lifted his gaze to the village again, as if he could divine what was happening if he only stared long enough. Mortimer thought the old dragon looked as though he'd never been scared in his life.

"So what do we do? It was so hard to smell anything in that utility. There'd been far too many people stomping through it, but there was *something*. I just don't know if it was one person, or more, or even if I'd recognise it again."

Beaufort considered it, his scales gleaming softly. Mortimer wondered how many summers the old dragon had actually seen, and what it said about him that he still greeted the strengthening spring sun with a cat's uncalculating delight (the only thing about cats that *was* uncalculating, as far as Mortimer could tell). He closed his eyes for a moment and tried not to think of anything but the warmth on his own scales, but it didn't work. His mind kept wandering back to the utility room. He must have missed something. *Must* have.

Finally Beaufort said, "We must take a risk, lad. The journalist may be a threat, or she may not, and she certainly has the potential to be a problem. But the bigger risk is that the murderer remains uncaught because the police are looking in the wrong direction."

"At Rose?"

"At Rose. Did you smell her concern?"

Mortimer nodded. "She's very worried about all of it. Scared, even. I don't quite understand it, but I could smell it."

Beaufort didn't reply straight away, but finally he said, "Age makes one do strange things, Mortimer. One becomes … *quirky*."

"You're not quirky," Mortimer said.

Beaufort raised his eyebrow ridges. "I have tea parties with humans and sleep on a barbecue. I fear I may go down in Cloverly history as High Lord Beaufort the Quirky."

Mortimer wondered how he'd be remembered, if he was. Mortimer the Anxious? Mortimer of the Bald Tail? "But being quirky isn't being a murderer. How can the police suspect her?"

"Perhaps they don't, but they will be running down all reasonable suspects, and she is one. And in the meantime the murderer will remain free." He shook his wings out. "If you're willing, lad, we will resume our investigations. And we'll keep an eye on the W.I., too, although without getting too close – we wouldn't want to get told off again." He tilted his head at Mortimer, who snorted. "And if the murderer turns up, we shall take care of the problem."

Mortimer wondered what he'd personally do if the murderer turned up in front of him. It wasn't like he could *bite* someone. He didn't think. Unless he was really upset. Maybe. And then he thought of Miriam and straightened his wings. He could certainly singe someone. That seemed reasonable. "Alright," he said. "I can't stand not helping."

Beaufort nodded. "You're becoming admirably quirky yourself, lad."

Mortimer wondered if that would be the description on his cage when The Government and all its scientists caught up to him. Or if it'd just go on his tombstone.

THEY DIDN'T CLIMB BACK down the mount past the caverns and the tarn below it. Not only was Beaufort still avoiding Walter, but if Amelia and Gilbert knew they were going to the village they'd want to come too. Four dragons (including one who had a tendency to crash) would be much harder to hide than two. Instead they slipped off their perch, Beaufort leading, their scales fading to blues and greys that were harder to pick out against the sky, and climbed high as they left the craggy refuge behind them. The wind lifted and hurried them, the chill of the high air collecting condensation on Mortimer's scales as he followed the High Lord. The old dragon moved fast and effortless, his wing-beats slow as he caught the updraughts and glided where he could.

The tangled tops of the old woods that curved around the side of the village nearest the mount reached up to meet them, and they dropped lower as the untamed fells gave way to quieter, but no less secret lands. There were no paths here – the magical Folk of the world have ways of making their land impenetrable, so the eye and the will slides away. There was no physical reason for humans not to enter these areas, but they just *didn't*. That was how the old places persisted, quiet and beautiful and always turned protectively inward.

Before long they were on the ground, the sky tones of their scales changing to mottled greens and browns. Everything smelt of the warm musk of old leaves and new growth.

"Are we going to Miriam's?" Mortimer asked, as Beaufort led the way between the old, slowly twisting tree trunks.

"Rose's, I think," Beaufort said. "We might not be able to get you back into the utility, but we can check the garden for scents. We didn't get much of a chance to do that last night. We can easily avoid the police officer at the gate, and DI Adams made it quite clear no one else was meant to be there."

Mortimer nodded. He liked the sound of no one being around. If he was going to singe anyone, he didn't want to do it front of an audience.

Rose's wasn't as easy to get to unnoticed as Miriam's, though. The dragons slipped out of the woods and across Toot Hansell's chattering boundary stream, creeping up to the low stone wall surrounding the vicarage where it nestled in its grounds of haphazardly kept flowerbeds and old, leaning trees. There was no one visible in the gardens, although there were some windows open downstairs. They slipped over the gate and crept quietly along the inside of the wall, trying to keep the trees between them and the house, and Mortimer hoped he didn't lose any scales along the way. Just because he'd agreed to this – alright, all but *suggested* it – didn't mean he was happy with it.

From the vicarage they sneaked through the garden of the village hall, Mortimer trying to imagine himself as an oversized rabbit or something equally innocuous, and then they were teetering on the edge of the road, peering each way anxiously.

"This seems very risky," Mortimer whispered.

"It is," Beaufort replied, then ran across the road with his neck out and his wings down, and dived under a large sweet briar bush on the edge of the village green. Mortimer didn't move. Either his legs had somehow mutinied against his brain, or his sensible brain was overruling whatever other ridiculous part of him had thought this was a good idea. He made a small noise that was alarmingly close to Angelus' whines, and stared at the broad expanse of tarmac. It looked impossibly wide and horribly exposed, and he was somehow convinced that the moment he managed to step onto the road he'd freeze again, and would be utterly unable to move until some car came bearing down on him, probably laden with journalists with cameras and government scientists with needles and ... and *someone* with tasers. Or all of them with tasers.

He made another small, alarmed noise.

"Mortimer!" Beaufort hissed from the other side of the road. "Come on!"

Mortimer stared at him. Somewhere he could hear a car. It was the journalists and scientists with their tasers, he was sure of it. *Bristling* with tasers.

"Come on, lad! Hurry up! You can't stay there!"

Mortimer wondered if he could go backward, since he couldn't seem to go forward. Maybe he could hide in the vicarage garden until it got dark. It'd be easier once it was dark.

"Mortimer!"

His legs didn't want to go backward, either. He stared at them. Yes, they were grey as stone. Maybe he'd *become* stone, and would just be stuck here forever, a dragon statue for small children to climb on. He tried to take a deep breath, but apparently his chest was turning to stone, too. He couldn't seem to get enough air.

"Lad." Beaufort was next to him, warm against the frozen chill of Mortimer's side. Mortimer hadn't even seen him cross back over the road. His eyes were closed, but he couldn't remember closing them. "We can't stay here."

But I can't move, Mortimer tried to say, but the words wouldn't come. He could still hear the car.

Beaufort was leaning on him. "Alright. Follow me. We're going back. You're right, it's too exposed to be here in the daylight. Just listen to my voice, lad. We're going back into the vicarage garden first."

Mortimer managed a strangled breath. Yes. Go back. He took a shaky step backward, small and uneven.

"Well done, Mortimer. And again. Another step."

Mortimer did, finding another breath somewhere. Okay. This was okay, he could do this. Beaufort was still talking, his voice low and deep, and Mortimer followed him, eyes still firmly closed, until they reached the gate that led to the vicarage.

"Up and over, lad," Beaufort said. "We'll have more cover as soon as we're among the trees."

Mortimer opened his eyes, squinting against the light, and found the High Lord crouched next to him, the sun washing over his scales. The big dragon gave a toothy, encouraging grin.

"The murderer," Mortimer said, the word coming out ragged and squeaky.

"Later," Beaufort said. "Once it's dark."

"But what if they come back and try again?"

"We can't help if we're running from journalists ourselves," the old dragon said. "I'm sure everyone will be safe until it's dark and we can move more freely without risking being seen."

Mortimer looked at the gate. Over that, and there'd be trees to hide behind. And then it'd just be a quick run along the wall and over a stile, and they'd be back in the woods, safe and hidden from scientists and journalists and everyone else.

And too far from the W.I. to help if anything went wrong.

He turned and bolted for the road.

"Mortimer!" Beaufort whisper-shouted behind him, and he was dimly aware that he could hear the High Lord chasing him, and even more dimly aware that the sound of the car was still around somewhere. He kept running.

He didn't stop where the lawn met the pavement and the street beyond, didn't even pause. He just scuttled straight across the road with his wings back and his head low and stretched forward, his talons clattering on the tarmac. He didn't stop until he'd plunged straight into the bushes on the other side, and even then he probably would have kept going but his wings got caught up on a low branch and brought him to a staggering stop, his eight-chambered heart going so fast that there were spots in his vision.

Brakes screeched behind him, and he spun around just in time to see Beaufort plunge under the sweet briar as a car slewed to a stop in the middle of the road.

"What the hell was *that?*" someone shouted, and the passenger side door flew open. "Was that a crocodile or something?"

The driver got out, shading her eyes with one hand as she stared toward the dragons' hiding place. "Not crocodiles," she said.

It was the cryptid journalist.

"Go," Beaufort whispered. "Now, lad. *Go.*"

Mortimer went. He slipped out from under the bush and raced across the green, eyes on the gate that led straight into Rose's garden. Beaufort ran with him, neither of them bothering to hide. No one was close by, at least, although Mortimer glimpsed dog walkers closer to the duck pond, and a small boy riding a pink bike with his head down in determination.

"There!" someone shouted behind them, and he ran harder. A moment later he had his paws on Rose's gate, and he scrambled up and over to dive into the undergrowth beyond.

"Hide," Beaufort hissed, slipping away to the left and vanishing among the apple trees. Mortimer went the other way, hunkering down behind the compost bins with his paws sinking into the mulch. The gate clattered, then there was a pause.

"You go left," the journalist said, her voice low. Her name was Katherine, Mortimer remembered. It seemed alarmingly innocuous. Dragons should not be hunted by anyone called *Katherine.*

Unless it was short for Katherine the Terrifying or something similar. "Have you got your camera?" she asked her companion.

"Got it. Are you sure they weren't crocodiles? Or iguanas? They looked kind of like iguanas."

"Common in Yorkshire, are they?"

"I don't know. They could have escaped from a private collection or something."

"Sure. With wings?"

"I didn't see wings," the man said, sounding unsure. "I don't think."

"Then you weren't looking properly."

They stopped speaking, and Mortimer listened to the whisper of a set of slow, deliberate footsteps as they edged toward him. Katherine the Terrifying hadn't seen them in Miriam's garden, he reminded himself. She'd only spotted them on the road because they'd been running. There was every possibility that her gaze would just slide away now he was hidden, his scales collecting the colours around him and imitating them, turning him into nothing more than an extra heap of compost, steaming lightly in the midday sun.

Katherine came into sight around a flower-crowned dogwood tree, scanning the ground with creases dug into her forehead, and Mortimer wished he'd thought to scramble up into the branches somewhere. She wasn't bothering to look up at all. Up would have been sensible. Why hadn't he thought of that? Who'd look for a dragon in a tree? He could have—

His thoughts derailed as he stared up into a plum tree, green with new leaves and puffing out blossom, but nowhere near enough of either to hide the large and saggy form of a very old and distinctly drooly dragon.

Lord Walter glared at the woman below as the thin new branches dipped dangerously under his weight. His broken teeth were bared in a snarl, and despite the gaps he still seemed to have an awful lot of them. He tracked Katherine with glittering green eyes that had somehow lost their usual rheum, his muscles strung taut beneath his patchy scales and a thin thread of drool descending from his chin. Mortimer watched in horror as it lengthened, the light catching it like a spider's web, and the woman stood beneath it staring around the garden with her face twisted in concentration.

"Dammit," she muttered. "I *know* they weren't iguanas. I *know* it."

Walter licked his chops and shifted carefully, his eyes never leaving Katherine. The thread of drool snapped and plunged toward her. It hit her shoulder, and she jumped, wiping it irritably.

"Bloody birds," she started, then stared at her fingers. "What—"

Walter gathered himself to leap, and Mortimer opened his mouth to shout a warning. Secrecy was all very well, but they *definitely* didn't want the world introduced to dragons by way of an attack on a cryptid journalist. But before he could say anything Rose came rushing down the path, her face pale. She skidded to a stop as she spotted Katherine, almost looking as if she were about to run back the way she'd come, then her eyes flicked to Walter.

"What the hell are you doing here?" she demanded, focusing on the journalist.

"Do you have iguanas?" Katherine asked, while Mortimer glared at Walter, shaking his head as hard as he could while also trying not to move too much.

"Ig— ? Angelus! Trespassers!" Rose shouted, and pointed at the journalist as the Great Dane thundered down the path to join her, legs flying. "Sic 'em!"

"Oh, bollocks," Katherine said, and bolted for the gate, yelling as she went, "Lloyd! Lloyd, *dogs!*" There was a distinctly human yelp of fright from somewhere deeper in the garden, and Angelus went surging happily in that direction, his tail going wildly and his deep barks echoing through the trees.

Walter snarled, his gaze tracking the woman as she retreated. *"Hunters,"* he hissed.

"Bloody journalists," Rose said, her hands on her hips, and Walter gave another growl. He was still drooling.

From the direction of the house someone called, "Police! Is anyone out here?"

Rose looked back over her shoulder, her face twisting in a scowl.

Mortimer scrambled out from behind the compost heap, his heart still going too fast. "Walter! What're you *doing?*"

"What are *you* doing?" Rose retorted, looking back at him. "This is just the kind of thing we were hoping to avoid, isn't it?"

Walter dropped to the ground, his legs taking up the shock like springs. "Hunters," he repeated. "I *told* you." And he ran toward the gate faster than Mortimer would have thought his old legs could manage.

"Walter!" Mortimer didn't dare shout, and the old dragon gave no sign of having heard his half-whispered plea. He hesitated, wavering between giving chase and finding Beaufort so that *he* could give chase. Walter wouldn't listen to him, but he might listen to the High Lord. Maybe.

"Oh, leave him be," Rose said. "Why do people insist on thinking they need to herd their elders around like toddlers?"

Mortimer blinked at her. He certainly hadn't been thinking of Walter as a toddler, especially as one seldom suspected toddlers of harbouring desires to nibble on journalists.

"Hello? Police!" someone shouted again. Rose shifted from foot to foot.

"Lad?" Beaufort pushed his way past an overgrown clump of box holly and gave Rose a startled look. "Hello, Rose."

"Hello, Beaufort," she said. "Why are there three dragons hanging around my garden?"

"I can only answer for the two of us," Beaufort said. "We were looking for clues."

Rose rubbed a hand over her face and glanced back at the house. "You're not meant to be here."

"I don't believe you are, either," Beaufort said. "And you shouldn't be on your own."

"Oh, bollocks to that," she said. "I've existed very happily on my own for many years. I can't be doing with this *coddling.*"

"Quite," Beaufort said. "But there is a murderer about."

Rose made a disgusted sound, and they stared at each other while Mortimer peered into the garden. Angelus was still barking, but it didn't sound as if any journalists were under attack. And dragons didn't actually eat people. Not these days. Not for centuries. Even if there *were* rumours about what Walter had got up to in his youth, they were just that. Rumours.

"Hello?" a man shouted, sounding distinctly closer now. "North Yorkshire Police. Anyone there?"

"Bollocks," Rose said again. "Now we've done it." And she vanished softly into the depths of the garden, leaving Mortimer and Beaufort staring at each other.

"Walter's out there somewhere," Mortimer whispered, nodding in the direction Walter had gone. "He really thinks that journalist's a dragon hunter."

"Oh dear," Beaufort said. "That may be a problem." He turned and ran down the path, and Mortimer followed him, wondered what *a problem* meant. Maybe it was a Beaufort having to bite him problem. It couldn't be an eating people problem, surely.

Surely.

12
MIRIAM

Miriam stood in front of Police Sergeant Graham Harrison, holding a fried egg sandwich and a large mug of tea, and peered up at him dubiously. He was excessively tall.

"I thought you might be hungry," she said.

"It is hungry work, keeping an eye on you lot," he said, accepting the sandwich and mug from her. "Where's Professor Howard? I haven't seen her since I came on watch at nine this morning, and Ben Shaw said she hadn't been around before that."

"She's still sleeping."

"Huh. He said some woman came by looking for her, too."

"Oh?" Miriam tried to sound mildly curious.

"She knocked on the door, but no one answered."

"I was at Alice's," Miriam said, which was safe enough, as Ben had seen her when she'd left, taking the road to Alice's rather than the dew-damp path through the woods. He'd sent Meena after her as well, which Miriam still wasn't happy about. Although she hadn't seen Rose's ex-stepdaughter since the woman had left Alice's, which Miriam supposed was a good sign. She hoped. "Rose probably didn't hear."

"I suppose not. That dog of hers will need a walk, though," Graham said, and took a slurp of tea. "Ooh, lovely cuppa."

"I took him out in the woods earlier," Miriam said, the back of her neck hot and prickling. "Rose barely slept last night. I imagine she won't be up for a while."

Graham checked his watch. "It's after ten. She usually lie in this long?"

Miriam wished they hadn't told the inspectors Rose was going to be staying at her house. They should have said Alice's. Alice was *much* better at lying than she was. "I don't really know," she said aloud. "But I'm not going to wake her up just because you haven't seen her."

The sergeant regarded her curiously, and her cheeks started to heat up uncomfortably. Then he just nodded and said, "Thanks for the sandwich."

"Of course," Miriam said, and turned back to the house, trying not to walk too quickly. Then she thought she might be walking suspiciously slowly, so she sped up, but then *that* felt suspicious, so she slowed down again, caught the front of her flip-flop on a rough patch on the path, and stumbled around the corner, quite sure Graham was watching her all the way. But when she looked back, trying for a self-deprecating wave, he was just eating his sandwich and watching a dog walker further down the lane.

"I'm really not very good at this," she mumbled to herself, and hurried straight down the path behind the house, over the little footbridge that crossed the stream, and onto the trail that ran through the woods to the back of Alice's garden.

She wished Rose *was* still asleep in her spare bedroom. Or that they knew where she was, at least. Hopefully somewhere safe, and not running around the village with a murderer still on the loose.

MIRIAM HEARD a clamour of voices before she even reached Alice's kitchen door, which sat open onto the neatly trimmed, flower-crowded garden.

"Primrose, *sit!*"

"Jasmine, I do wish you wouldn't bring that dog," Alice said, her tones cool as they floated into the slowly warming day. "My house really isn't set up for it."

"I can't just leave her at home!"

"Why not?" Priya asked. "You did yesterday."

"That was an emergency! I— Primrose, *no!*"

There was a hiss, a yelp, and a torrent of yapping, then Thompson stepped onto the doorstep, his ears back. He looked at Miriam with flat green eyes. "I question my life choices around you lot sometimes," he said, and loped off around the house like a soft-footed shadow.

Miriam leaned in the open door, the bright kitchen crowded with movement and noise. Alice had called the W.I., telling them that Rose was missing and that they must let her know if she turned up at anyone's house, while Miriam went home to check if she'd gone there, and also to head off the enquiries of nosy police officers. Which she wasn't at all sure she'd managed to do convincingly, and she rather hoped she didn't have to do it again.

Meanwhile, as soon as it became clear that Rose *hadn't* turned up at anyone's house, the W.I. had convened an impromptu emergency meeting, complete with dogs. Priya was currently holding off the still-yapping Primrose with one hand, scuffed skin on her bare calves showing where the dog had been jumping at her, and Gert was topping glasses up with elderflower cordial. Carlotta and Rosemary were peering at identical lemon drizzle cakes with matching expressions of suspicion, and Alice smiled at Miriam as she topped the kettle up.

"Hello everyone," Miriam said, and earned a wave from Pearl.

Pearl's old Labrador, Martha, was asleep on her back in the middle of the floor, utterly ignoring the near-hysterical Primrose.

"That dog's a menace," Teresa said, as Jasmine scooped up Primrose to keep her away from Priya.

"She isn't," Jasmine said, looking like she wanted to cover the dog's ears.

Priya pointed at her shins. "She is, Jasmine."

"She's *not,*" Jasmine insisted. "She's just spirited."

Miriam snorted, and turned it into a cough as Jasmine frowned at her.

"Proper training," Pearl said. "That's what's needed."

"No one's seen Rose, then?" Miriam asked, before the training argument could start again.

"No one," Alice said, taking another cup from the cupboard. She looked tired, Miriam thought. Lines were drawn deeper at the corners of her mouth than usual, but her silver hair still hung sleekly above her shoulders, and her back was straight as she turned to survey the kitchen. "We shall need to come up with a plan."

Miriam was almost certain that meant Alice already had one, and was just going to make everyone else *feel* as though it had been a joint effort. That was reassuring. It made her feel as though things were coming back into some sort of alignment, if Alice had a plan.

She wished the dragons were there, though. Nothing felt right without them, although she wasn't sure how anything about getting caught up in an investigation ever *could* feel right. But dragons certainly helped.

"Ladies," Alice said, raising her voice to be heard over the clink of plates and ongoing argument regarding the training of canines. "Ladies, shall we go through what we know?"

"We don't know anything," Gert said. "You haven't seen Rose since last night." There was no accusation in her voice, but she raised her eyebrows as she spoke, and offered Alice a glass of cordial. Alice waved it away, as did Miriam when Gert offered her one. Gert's cordials had a tendency to be potent, and Miriam thought she might still have to face more curious police officers today. The cordial would be no help whatsoever with that.

"Her footprints were on the back path this morning just after eight," Alice said. "Plus, I've been up since five, so she couldn't have sneaked out past me."

"She must have left when we were talking to that Meena," Miriam said. "I bet Rose heard her and ran off before she could see her!"

"Why would she do that?" Pearl asked. "Who's Meena?"

"Rose's stepdaughter, apparently," Alice said.

"*Ex*-stepdaughter," Miriam pointed out. "She was talking about Rose as if she's going potty! She wanted to take her to be *evaluated for proper care!*"

Jasmine gasped and squeezed Primrose a little tighter. "Proper care? Like a *nursing home?*"

"She couldn't," Teresa said. "Not Rose. She wouldn't stand for it."

Carlotta took a mouthful of cordial, wheezed, then said, "It's disgraceful. Packing people off just because they're getting on a bit. It's not how we do things in the old country."

Rosemary patted her on the back. "Manchester does do some things rather well."

Carlotta scowled at her and took a more judicious sip of her drink.

"It *is* disgraceful," Priya said. "And ridiculous. Rose doesn't need to be in *care.*"

"I think we're jumping to conclusions here," Alice said.

Miriam stared at her. "Meena said it, though. That she was being evaluated."

Alice gave her a level look while the rest of the W.I. waited, the silence tense and expectant. "There's more than one possibility here."

"There aren't *any* possibilities," Jasmine said. "Rose is *fine.* She *is!*"

"I'm not saying she's not," Alice said. "But the fact remains that there was a body in her freezer, and she's misplacing things. You saw her house, Miriam."

Miriam stared at her. "But that's just *stuff.* Glasses and her phone and so on. We know it doesn't mean anything."

"Are we sure?"

"Oh, come *on,*" Gert snapped, slamming her glass onto the kitchen table hard enough to slop elderflower cordial over Priya's crinkled chocolate biscuits, splattering their soft dusting of icing sugar with dark spots. "This is Rose! She's not a danger to anyone!"

"I'm not saying she is," Alice said, taking a sip of tea. She shifted as she did, wincing slightly, and Miriam, for all that she was horrified Alice appeared to be harbouring doubts about Rose's innocence, thought the older woman should be sitting down. Not that she would, of course.

"Then what *are* you saying, Alice?" Teresa asked.

"That Meena may not be the problem here. She may have Rose's best interests at heart. After all, she did say Rose was expecting her."

"I'm sure she *said* that," Jasmine snapped. "But Rose obviously didn't want to see her!"

"Which may indicate that Rose herself is more worried than she may have let on to any of us." She raised one hand as everyone started protesting at once, and spoke over them. "We have to consider all possibilities, ladies. We're no help to Rose if we don't know the truth."

"Maybe Meena's forcing her to go," Miriam said. "And with everything else going on, it's the last thing Rose would want to deal with." She frowned at Alice, and picked up a spare glass of cordial. The conversation had her feeling that she rather needed it, and too bad if it wasn't even lunchtime yet, or if she had to deal with more police officers and their questions. It was *just too bad.*

"You can't really believe there's anything wrong with Rose," Pearl said. "You'll be checking all of us into a care home if that's the case."

Teresa patted her arm. "I won't let them take you away, dear."

"You're older," Pearl said. "They'll come for you first."

"Perhaps Martha will protect us." They both stared at the Labrador, who snored and flopped onto her side, leaving a little drool on Alice's previously immaculate rug. Alice winced.

Miriam looked at Alice. "Do you honestly think Rose is in that bad a way?"

Alice took a sip of tea. "I don't know. However, the fact remains that there have been some ... incidents with regards to her memory. And so far, we have no suspect or reason for a body to turn up in her freezer." She hesitated, then added, "Also she ran as soon as she saw the one person she may have been discussing such things with. It doesn't sound very good."

Miriam took another mouthful of cordial, thinking of DI Adams saying, *If she is having some cognitive issues, that raises other questions.* She shivered, not sure if it was the cordial or the horror of the phrase. Surely they'd have known, though. Wouldn't they? She wondered what Alice had wanted to talk over with Rose this morning, before they had found she was gone. She hadn't said anything more about it, simply sent Miriam home again to check on the police.

"What if this whole thing with Meena is the set up?" Gert asked. "What if she's the one behind it all? It's all very convenient, her turning up the day after the body's found. Does she stand to gain anything from Rose being declared incapable?"

"I don't know," Alice said. "She's a lawyer, but she says she doesn't deal with Rose's affairs."

"Damn lawyers," Rosemary said. "You can't trust them."

"You were one," Carlotta said.

"Yes, that's how I know."

Alice regarded Rosemary for a moment, then said, "Would an ex-stepdaughter have any claim to Rose's funds and property?"

"It all depends on Rose's will. Without one, responsibility would go to a spouse or immediate relative. But if she and Rose are close, then she may be named. Or, if she had access to Rose's papers at any point, it wouldn't be beyond the realms of possibility for her to write herself into a living will. It'd look even more legitimate if everything was held by a different lawyer."

"Rose said Meena has a key, too," Miriam said, gulping her cordial and wincing. "She would've been able to get into the house any time, to plant evidence and so on."

"Or to move things," Jasmine said suddenly, and everyone looked at her. "What if Rose *hasn't* been misplacing things? What if someone else has been moving things around, and trying to convince her she's going dotty?"

"That's *awful,*" Pearl said. "Could someone do that?"

"It'd explain why we haven't noticed any difference in her," Gert said. "Hard to convince a social worker of that, though, if Rose is leaving towels on heaters and things."

"And if someone reported all that, then the murder would just be the final straw. They probably wouldn't even look at anyone else. They'd just take her straight into a residential home." Jasmine had gone very pale.

Alice started to say something, then stopped, frowning at her cup.

"The whole evaluation could be a scam," Priya said, her fingers twisted together on the table. "The doctor could be in on it!"

A murmur of concern ran around the kitchen, and Miriam

pressed a hand to her face to try and cool it. She shouldn't have had the cordial. The whole thing – the whole *situation* was getting so terribly far out of control. They'd lost Rose, and now they didn't even know if they should be more worried about a murderer or her relatives and supposed loved ones – or if they were one and the same. She took a piece of shortbread from the table and nibbled it, thinking she had better soak up the cordial if she was going to have to think about this.

Teresa said, "Well, we have to find out about all this. The doctor, and Meena, and everything. Don't we?"

"We also have to find Rose," Alice said. "That seems the most pressing issue."

"Has anyone tried her phone?" Gert asked.

Alice pointed at the mobile lying on the windowsill, turned face down. "She left it in her room. So far the only people calling have been Meena, Campbell, Bethany, and Jean-Claude, so I haven't answered."

Gert scratched her chin. "Damn. Can you get into it? See if she called anyone?"

"I already tried. I don't know the passcode."

"I can take it to our Lindy's niece's stepson's mate. He's good with that sort of thing."

"I'll keep that in mind," Alice said. "I think we may be rather pressed for time, though."

Miriam lifted the hair off the back of her neck, trying to get a little air in the warmth of the kitchen. "We need the dragons," she said. "They can track her."

"They can't be in the village," Alice said. "It's far too risky, and we can't be worried about them as well as Rose." She looked around. "Where's that cat gone? He may be able to track her down."

"He was outside," Miriam said. "He said he was reconsidering his life choices."

"Wonderful," Alice said. "I often think the same when I deal with him."

Gert folded her arms. "What's the plan, then? We're not just going to sit on our hands, hoping she comes back, are we? And we can't go to the police."

"Definitely not," Teresa said. "That'll give them all they need to lock her up."

Alice nodded and set her cup down. "We *must* find her. Then we can ask her about Meena, and see if that leads us anywhere."

"Do we start going door to door?" Pearl asked. "Because she's probably still in the village, wouldn't you think?"

"It's possible, yes," Alice said. "And I think that's a good plan. However, she may have also contacted someone to collect her, such as—"

"Jean-Claude," Jasmine said. "They're still really close. I think he'd be the first she'd call."

"Not Campbell?" Alice asked.

Jasmine wrinkled her nose. "Maybe?"

"He didn't look like he'd be much in a crisis," Gert said. "Wet rag of a man."

"What about Bethany?" Miriam asked. "If she's around so much, maybe Rose would trust her to hide her."

Alice nodded. "These are all excellent suggestions, ladies. And how about family? Does she have any close by?"

There was a moment's uncertainty, while everyone looked at each other, and Miriam bit her lip. How could they not know? Had none of them ever asked?

"I know she has a sister," Priya said finally. "But she never really talks about her."

Alice nodded. "Then she's unlikely to go there. Jasmine, can you find addresses for the two men and Bethany? I suppose it's not as easy as a phone book these days."

Jasmine rubbed her mouth, and Miriam was almost certain she was trying not to smile. "I can do that."

"Good." Alice looked around the room. "Miriam, Jasmine, and I will cover that. Everyone else, door to door. Does everyone have their phone?" There was a general murmur of agreement, and she smiled at them, almost banishing the shadows under her eyes. "Then let's see what we can find out. Oh, and do try not to call too much attention to yourselves. We don't want the inspectors chasing us down."

Miriam thought that was being a bit optimistic.

THE LADIES of the W.I. left in twos, the better to deal with lawyers and murderers. Gert insisted Jasmine went with her and Priya to take Primrose home, as she said neither of them were intimidating enough to deal with so much as a parking attendant if they ran across one. Jasmine said Primrose was at least as scary as Gert, but Priya just shook her head and led them both out of the house and toward the village.

Miriam looked at the kitchen, the cups already stacked in the dishwasher and the cakes sitting in Tupperware waiting for the ladies to reconvene. The table had been wiped down and the chairs straightened, and the only sign that anyone had been there at all was Martha's drool still drying on the rug. Miriam was still hot, even in the empty room, and she hadn't slept well the night before. Her eyes were gritty and her neck hurt, but she straightened the front of her favourite top – it had large, multicoloured flowers embroidered on the white cloth and she felt it was a rather encouraging sort of thing – and looked at Alice.

"Where do we start?" she asked.

"With a phone call," Alice said. "This feels rather *big,* Miriam.

Our primary focus has to be on finding Rose, but if there's a third party involved, we also need to be thinking about them."

"If? You don't really think Rose did this, do you? You didn't seem to yesterday."

Alice tapped her fingers against her mouth gently. "I don't want to think so. But one must adapt as more evidence becomes clear. Remember, the dragons couldn't find any scents that were out of the ordinary."

"They barely had time," Miriam protested.

"This is true. For now, we shall hunt for Rose, but I want to find out what direction the police are taking."

"Isn't Thompson good at that?"

"I've already asked him, but we shall have more need of him to track Rose, if we can find him." Alice picked up her phone and scrolled through the contacts. "And then we shall collect Jasmine and see about some house calls. But first … there we are." She hit dial, putting the phone on speaker, and Miriam started to ask who she was calling, but Alice held a hand up as the phone connected mid-ring.

"Hello?" a familiar voice said, and Miriam blinked, confused. She couldn't quite place who it might be.

"Mr Giles," Alice said. "This is Alice Martin, Toot Hansell—"

"Alice! What can I do for you? And call me Ervin, please."

Miriam frowned, first at the phone, then at Alice. Involving young, dimpled journalists in such affairs seemed rather risky. Maybe things were more dire than she suspected.

"I suppose I shall, since we don't seem to be standing on ceremony." Alice's tone was mildly reproving.

"Ah. Yes, sorry. Do you prefer Ms Martin or Wing Commander? Or Ms Wing Commander Martin? That's rather a mouthful, though."

Alice smiled slightly and said, "In light of our work together over Christmas, I suppose first-name basis is justified. Did you want that interview with Rose, Ervin? An exclusive one?"

"Yes." He said it immediately. "What do you need?"

"I see we're on the same page."

"Somehow I can't see you calling me up and offering me an interview out of a deep-held belief in the freedom of the press." Miriam could hear the smile in his voice.

"Quite. I need some information."

"It's my stock in trade."

"You would be a poor journalist if it wasn't."

"I'd be working for *Cryptids Today* if it wasn't." The lightness left his tone. "I'll help if I can. This isn't to do with more sleepwalkers or murderous Santas, is it?"

"Plain, old-fashioned greed, I should think," Alice said. "Firstly, I should like to know what direction the police investigation is taking."

"I think you're more likely to get that out of a certain detective inspector than I am."

"Not this time. We're ... keeping our distance."

"I see. Well, I can try. What else?" Miriam could hear the scratch of pen on paper on the other end of the phone, although she thought even she could have remembered this. Maybe Ervin was already thinking about his story.

"Meena Dewan. She's a lawyer. Is she well thought of? Any hint of corruption? You know the sort of thing."

"Do I want to know why?"

"It's all connected. And finally those cryptid journalists. See if they actually know anything."

"That's quite a shopping list, Alice."

"Are you saying you can't do it?" Alice smiled at Miriam as she spoke, and Miriam frowned back.

"No. But this is going to take a little time."

"Then you'd best get started," Alice said, and hung up.

Miriam stared at her. "Why are we getting him involved? He's still a *journalist,* and he's not even from Toot Hansell."

"Because he has proved able to conduct himself with discretion, and we can't be calling attention to ourselves right now. We want the inspectors to believe we're keeping out of things, and to stay well away from us until we at least know where Rose is, if nothing else. And he's better placed to find out about Meena than we are." Alice got up and took a light jacket from behind the door. "One must know when to do the work oneself, and when to delegate, Miriam. It's the very essence of leadership."

"I'm not sure that's something I need to worry about," Miriam said, following Alice out the door and waiting as she locked it. "I have no intention of leading anything."

"Not even daring last minute rescues, such as last summer?"

"Definitely not any of those." She shuddered, and watched Alice gaze around the garden.

"Thompson," Alice called. "Puss, puss, puss!"

"Puss puss yourself," the cat said, sitting up from where he'd been sprawled on a garden bench in the sun. He peered over the back at them. "I don't shout *woman woman* when I'm looking for you, do I?"

"No," Alice said. "You just appear at inopportune moments."

He jumped to the ground and wandered over to them. "I still don't get why you're so bothered about my seeing you in the bath. The human form is of no interest to me whatsoever. You're all hairless and weird."

"Such cheek," Miriam said. "I'm so glad he stays with you and not me, Alice."

"Oh, it's wonderful," she said. "I'm honoured."

"Did you actually call me over just to insult me?" Thompson asked.

"No," Alice said. "Although I would point out that you started it."

Miriam shook her head. "You're both as bad as each other. Thompson, we need to find Rose. Can you try and track her?"

"I'm not a sniffer dog."

"So you can't?"

He looked at the sky and huffed. "I *can.* Or possibly can. But Alice already has me skulking around police stations. And I don't work for you, you know. I have things to do."

"I could tell you were busy," Miriam said, crossing her arms over her chest. "All that sunbathing must be hard work."

"I'm gathering my resources."

Alice sighed. "Did you find anything out last night?"

"Cause of death was a blow to the head," Thompson said. "Happened in the kitchen – they found blood traces on the floor. Weapon unknown, but he was killed night before last, most likely."

Miriam stared at him. "How on earth did you find all that out?"

"Skills."

Alice smiled. "So you listened in on a briefing?"

"Yeah, some skinny guy was telling Big Man about it."

"His name's Colin, not Big Man," Miriam said.

"You know who I'm talking about. What's the issue?"

"Did they say anything else?" Alice asked.

"Nothing that interesting. Wallet was on him, but no car keys."

Alice frowned. "I wonder how he got here, then? With no car keys?"

The cat shrugged. "Bike. Bus. Taxi."

"Seems unlikely."

"Humans are unlikely creatures." Thompson yawned. "Happy now?"

"We still need to find Rose," Miriam said.

"Still gathering my resources."

She scowled at him. "Shall we just call the dragons, then? Get them to run all over the village so you have to answer to your Watch thingy about why you let it happen?" Honestly, she'd almost prefer Primrose. At least she wasn't so sniffy. *And* she didn't shed.

"*No.* Gods. Fine. I'll go and find Rose. You're very careless, losing her like that." Thompson turned and stalked down the garden toward the back gate. "How did you lose her anyway? She's not *that* small. And she's got that bloody great dog."

"Are you sure you don't want a cat?" Alice asked Miriam as they watched him go. "I wouldn't mind."

"I would," Miriam said.

13

DI ADAMS

DI Adams leaned down to examine the macarons in the window more closely. They were perfectly uniform, with soft domes that had the gentle, pearlescent lustre of rose petals, forming a multicoloured pastel landscape across two cake stands and lining an assortment of gift boxes. As she watched, a young woman wearing plastic gloves selected one of the boxes and carried it to the counter inside, leaving a gap that said very clearly, *Get yours before they're gone!*

DI Adams *hmph*ed and straightened up, ignoring the immaculately displayed rows of tarte au citron and opera slices. "I never understood macarons. They're a bit … brief."

"Brief?" Collins asked.

"Two little bites and they're gone. What sort of dessert is that?"

"I think they're more whatchamacallit … petits fours."

"Four would be halfway to a decent dessert."

Collins snorted and pushed the door open, letting them into the cool interior of the shop. It smelled of some rich combination of coffee and chocolate and vanilla, with an undercurrent of fresh-baked bread. A broad entrance to the right let onto a restaurant that was almost full at a bit after eleven in the morning, and a waiter passed them carting four plates of delicately balanced cakes.

DI Adams glanced around for Dandy, but he was outside, licking the display window. That was good. She didn't want him trying to help himself to the coffee grounds bin or anything like that.

"I'll be right with you," the young woman with the gloves said, tying a neat bow on a gift box and easing it into a paper bag emblazoned with the shop's name, *Un Rêve de Rose.*

"No rush," Collins said, rocking back on his heels with his hands in his pockets. He was examining a series of small, framed pencil sketches propped on top of a cabinet full of French jams and biscuits packaged up for sale. "He does dream of Rose, alright."

"What—" DI Adams stood on her tiptoes to see better. "Oh. That portrait's very good." There was a pause as she examined the next sketch along, then she added, "That's far more of Rose than I ever wanted to see."

Collins turned his attention to the young woman at the counter, who was smiling brightly at them. "Did Mr Toussaint paint these?"

"Oh, yes. He's quite multitalented."

"So it seems. Is he about?"

"Well, he's very busy, prepping for lunch—"

"Detective Inspectors Adams and Collins," DI Adams said, showing her ID. "North Yorkshire Police."

The young woman swallowed almost audibly. "Is everything okay?"

"We'd just like a word with Mr Toussaint," Collins said, giving her that big, reassuring smile that DI Adams suspected he didn't even have to practise, unlike her own. And hers never seemed to do much in the way of reassuring even when she did practise.

"Of … of course," the young woman managed, and pushed

through a door to the side of the counter, where the sounds of clattering pans and someone singing off-key drifted back to them.

THEY DIDN'T HAVE long to wait. The young woman barely had time to re-emerge and offer them coffee (which DI Adams gratefully accepted) before Jean-Claude pushed through the door, wiping his hands on a cloth and frowning at them in a way that was concerned rather than irritated.

"Is everything okay?" he asked, peering over the top of his flour-smeared glasses. "Rose is okay?" His accent was softer, his shoulders more rounded than they had been with the agitation of the previous day. He was wearing a T-shirt printed with a cartoon chef in a hat and extravagant facial hair today, the design creased with wear.

"We just have a few questions for you, Mr Toussaint," DI Adams said. "Can we—"

"Jean-Claude, please. And yes, yes. We sit." He shooed them toward the dining room. "Kayleigh, *un café, s'il vous plaît.*"

"Do you have somewhere more private?" DI Adams asked, eyeing a large table that was enjoying a rather loud champagne brunch. The occupants were being glared at by two separate tables of elderly couples, a young woman in headphones, and a man who was trying to corral five cake-smeared children under the age of five. They all seemed to rather resent the level of fun going on around them.

"Private?" Jean-Claude asked, standing still for the first time. "I have no secrets. I tell everything to you yesterday."

True to their word, Jean-Claude and Campbell had both been waiting patiently outside the gate when DI Adams and Collins had left Miriam's house the previous day, and they'd both wanted to be the first to be interviewed. DI Adams had the impression that they'd hoped, if they were cooperative enough, that it'd win them some favour with Rose, but she and Collins had sent them off in their respective cars as soon as they'd asked the usual questions.

That had been before the issue of Rose's will had arisen, though. She hadn't been able to find a copy in the chaos of files at Rose's house. She'd found almost everything else one could think of, though. Invitations to museum exhibition openings tucked in with car insurance notices. Rolls of old raffle tickets and dried flowers flattened between bank statements. Power bills interspersed with students' reports. Someone's wedding announcement next to a half-finished paper on some sort of worm that lived in people's eyes. That had been the point at which she'd given up and embraced the fine art of delegation.

Ben Shaw was watching the house today, and she'd set him the task of hunting through the papers for anything relevant, since they were ridiculously understaffed for this. With officers on shifts watching Rose as well as the house itself, there was no one else to spare. Or no one that DCI Taylor was willing to spare, anyway. When DI Adams had asked, the DCI had just spread her hands and said, "It's a big area, Adams. We're a small station. We've got to make do."

She supposed that, given the size of the other stations in the Craven area, she was lucky to have who she had.

"We just have a few more questions," Collins said now. "But some privacy would be preferable, as they will pertain to your relationship with Rose."

"Ahh …" Jean-Claude looked around, arms and shoulders lifting into a shrug. "The office is too small. Is only really for me. We go outside?"

DI Adams glanced at the outside tables, the cushions straining to fly off in the wind snaking down the street. "Great," she said. "Perfect."

Jean-Claude led them out into the street and chose the table furthest from the door, taking a packet of cigarettes from the pocket of his chef's trousers and offering it to them. They both shook their heads, and he took one from the packet, hunching against the insistent wind. He was still only wearing his T-shirt, and DI Adams shivered in sympathy, although he didn't seem to notice the cold.

She tucked her hands into the pockets of her jacket and said, "We understand you're still married to Rose."

"Yes. It is just paper, you know? We agree it is the hassle to make a divorce."

"Why did you get married in the first place, then?" Collins asked. "If it's just paper."

Jean-Claude shrugged. "We go to Vegas on holiday. Maybe we were a little bit drunk." He grinned. "Rose likes Elvis."

DI Adams had no trouble imagining Rose in a Las Vegas wedding chapel, for some reason. "You're still quite close, then?"

"Yes." Jean-Claude paused as Kayleigh emerged from the shop with a laden tray. She placed a teapot and an empty cup in front of Collins, then set the coffees down while they waited in silence. There was a tiny, pale green macaron resting next to DI Adams' mug, a few flecks of darker green spackling the very top of the dome.

"How would you describe your relationship?" Collins asked, lifting the lid of the teapot to inspect the interior. Whatever he saw evidently satisfied him, as he gave a grunt and turned his attention to adding milk and sugar to his cup.

"It is a good friendship. Sometimes friendship with benefits." He grinned as Collins clinked the cup a little overly hard with his spoon, and DI Adams squinted at her macaron, wishing her imagination was a little less cooperative.

"So it was an amicable split, then," she said, when it became clear Collins wasn't going to follow up. Undoubtedly revenge for the other day, although at least she wasn't having to listen to *Rose* talk about her sex life.

"Yes, it is fine. We are good as friends. Not so good together all the time. Rose is very … strong."

DI Adams nodded, and took a mouthful of coffee. It was already cooling in the wind. "And did you want to split up?"

"*Moi? Pas vraiment.* I like to spend time with Rose. I suggest we have a … wide relationship?"

"Wide?" Collins asked, and DI Adams tried to concentrate on the macaron. She wasn't sure about green for a macaron. It seemed odd. What flavour would green be?

"Wide. You know – with other people."

"Ah. Open."

"Yes, this is it."

"And did you end up agreeing to that?" Collins asked. DI Adams glanced at him. He seemed to have recovered from the friends with benefits idea. He just looked mildly interested, and not at all like they were talking about an octogenarian who served them shortbread at every opportunity.

Jean-Claude shook his head. "No. She says she does not like to make the labels." He shrugged again. "I think she means, she does not want to be tied. I understand."

DI Adams leaned back in her chair, crossing her arms to pull her jacket tight around her. The wind was finding more gaps in her clothing than she'd thought existed, and she was starting to shiver. She examined Jean-Claude, who had turned his attention to trying to light his cigarette again. He adored Rose. It was in the name of the cafe, the drawings, the way he smiled when he said her name. But adoration could have an ugly side.

"Did you resent that Rose wanted to be with other men, and not be tied to you?" she asked.

He puffed smoke from the side of his mouth, waving it away from them, not that the wind gave it a chance to linger. "No. We understand each other, Rose and I. Some relationships are better when they are not always, you see? And we still have fun."

"So you weren't jealous that she was seeing someone else?" DI Adams asked, resolutely not thinking about fun.

Jean-Claude shrugged, his crossed leg swinging. "It is her right."

"What about Campbell Jones? You don't seem to like him very much."

Jean-Claude snorted. "Ah, he is okay. He is not quick enough for Rose. He is smart, but not *smart,* you know? And he treats her like she will break. She does not like to be treated as anything less than – or more than – equal."

"Do you think *he* was jealous?"

Jean-Claude considered it. "Maybe. He is very *English.*" He said it with a wave of his hands, and DI Adams assumed that meant Jean-Claude considered Campbell to be rather more proper and less urbane about such things. She couldn't decide if it was also an insult or not.

"Do you know if she was seeing anyone else?" Collins asked.

"I don't know. That is her business."

"Can you think of anyone who might want to hurt her?" DI Adams asked.

Jean-Claude's leg stopped swinging, and he stared at her with his cigarette burning down toward his fingers. "She is hurt? You do not tell me she is hurt!" He stood up abruptly, the chair toppling to the ground behind him. "I must see her at once!"

"There's no panic," Collins said, standing as well to put a heavy hand on the other man's flour-dusted arm. "She's absolutely fine. These are just routine questions."

"She is okay?" Jean-Claude looked at Collins' hand, then up again, his eyes wide and his eyebrows drawn in hard lines. "You are sure?"

"She's fine," DI Adams said. "But someone *had* been in her house. We understand that you might still have access?" That seemed quite tactful, she thought. Maybe Collins was rubbing off on her.

Jean-Claude sat down again, perching on the edge of his chair and staring at her. His bare arms were bumpy with gooseflesh, but he didn't seem to notice. "*Oui.* I offered to give her key back, but she said, no, is okay, she never locks anyway." He smiled. "I take her new cakes sometimes. She is good, Rose. She has the good palate."

"When were you last there?" Collins asked.

"This week. Saturday. I have been working on a new rhubarb tart, and I wanted her to try it. She was not there, but the back door was open, so I left the tart on the table for her."

The inspectors exchanged glances. "When on Saturday?" DI Adams asked.

"The morning. Saturdays we open a little late, at ten, and the minions prepare most things now. I am the executive." He grinned. "I make the tart on Friday night, so I take it to her maybe at eight on Saturday?"

DI Adams picked up her coffee. The cup was already cold to the touch, and she took a hurried gulp. "Did you see anyone else when you were there?"

Jean-Claude shrugged again. He really put effort into those shrugs, DI Adams thought. It was a whole-body affair. "No, I see no one. Just her *putain* neighbour, spying as always."

"Mr Brown?" DI Adams asked.

"Yes."

"You don't like him?"

"He is the fake friendly. He smiles always, comes to her house without asking. He wants to cut the lawn, or cut the trees. For Rose, he says, but it is because he does not like them." Jean-Claude shook his head, scowling, evidently feeling that this sort of neighbourliness was quite damning.

"He was already living there when you and Rose were together?" Collins asked.

"Yes." Jean-Claude rubbed the grey stubble on his cheek. "He arrives ... maybe seven years ago. So in the last year I live there. He wants to buy the house when I leave, as if it is mine to sell. He says is too much for Rose, he gives me the good price." He made a disgusted noise. "Always when I go back I see him, spying like the cockroach he is."

DI Adams was momentarily distracted by the idea of a spying cockroach. "Has he ever had disagreements with Rose?"

He stared at her. "You think he does this? Goes into her house?"

"We're just asking questions, Jean-Claude."

He picked up his espresso and threw it back in one gulp. DI Adams winced. It had to be completely cold by now. "If that *putain*—"

"There is no evidence that suggests he did anything," DI Adams said. "We just want to know if you ever saw or heard him arguing with Rose."

Jean-Claude found another cigarette, his face pulled into a scowl of concentration. "I do not think so. He does not like her garden, but he does not argue about it. He just makes the small comments, because he is a small man. A coward."

DI Adams almost jumped as Dandy put his head on her knee, and she tried to push him off surreptitiously. She didn't need a drool patch on her trousers. He didn't move, eyeing her macaron, and there was silence for a moment, just the chatter of passing people and the sound of a truck reversing somewhere drifting up to fill the space around them. A couple hurried past, hunched against the wind, and a crisp packet and a crumpled paper bag whipped through the gutter. A pigeon landed on the table next to them, tipping its head as it tried to see if they'd dropped anything interesting.

Finally Collins said, "Where did you go on Saturday, after you found Rose was out?"

"To work. I may have the minions, but I still always work. We are open all the days except Wednesday, and three nights, too." He smiled.

"It sounds like an intense schedule," DI Adams said.

"A restaurant always is."

"You must want to retire soon."

"It is not so easy. Maybe if I sell ..." He rubbed the back of his head. "But then what will I do?"

"It's a tough industry."

"Yes." He said it simply.

DI Adams watched him carefully as she said, "Do you know any details about Rose's will?"

He blinked at her. "No. Why would I know this?"

"It's not something you discussed? What would happen if she was ... unwell?"

"No." He frowned. "Why? You say Rose is okay?"

"She is," DI Adams said. "But we're not sure of the reason behind the break-in."

"You think someone is trying to hurt her?" He was already fumbling his phone out of his pocket. "You think *I* am trying to hurt her?"

"No, Mr—"

"You do not tell me the truth! I must talk to her at once!" He hit dial, his free hand flat on the table. "She's not answering. Why is she not answering! Oh— Rose! Rose, is this you? What is *happening?*" He paused, frowning. "Who? Ah, Jasmine. 'Allo, *chérie.* Where is Rose? What? *What?*"

DI Adams looked at Collins, who shrugged.

"She is not here. Why would she be here? The police—" He stopped as DI Adams waved at him, shaking her head firmly. He frowned, then said, "The police ask me questions about Rose.

What is happening, Jasmine? Do you know— A *body? Merde.*" He looked at the inspectors, his frown deepening. "You do not say there is a body. Or that Rose is *missing.* Why do you not tell me?"

"*Missing?*" DI Adams demanded. "Give me the phone."

"*Non.* Jasmine, explain this," Jean-Claude said, and put the phone on speaker, setting it on the table and trying to shelter it from the wind. "The inspectors are here."

"*Ooh.* Oh no. Alice. Alice! It's the police. You talk to them." There was a muffled response, then Jasmine said, "She's driving. You're on speaker."

DI Adams rubbed her face and looked at Collins, who sighed. She leaned forward. "Where's Rose, Alice?"

"Good morning, Inspectors."

"Morning, Alice," Collins said, and raised his eyebrows at DI Adams.

"Yes, morning. Where's Rose?"

"*Salut,* Alice," Jean-Claude said. "We do not have the time to talk yesterday. You are good?"

"Hello, Jean-Claude. Very good, yes. How's business?"

"*Alice,*" DI Adams said, her hand twitching toward the phone. Jean-Claude kept his own hand protectively over it as he answered.

"*Pah,* I do not care about the business. I care about Rose. She is not there?"

"She's not. You haven't seen her?"

"*Non,* she has not been to the restaurant for a month, maybe?"

"*Alice,*" DI Adams said again. "What the hell's going on?" Jean-Claude clicked his tongue disapprovingly, and she ignored him. "Where's Rose gone?"

Someone said something indistinct, and Alice said distantly, "Yes, good idea." Then, more clearly, she added, "We seem to have lost track of her."

"*Lost track of her?*" DI Adams demanded.

"Yes."

Collins leaned toward the phone. "Can you be more specific, Alice?"

"Not really."

DI Adams checked for the tic, but it hadn't started up yet. Small mercies. "What happened before you *lost track* of her?"

"She was in bed, as far as we knew."

"How is this possible?" Jean-Claude demanded. "How does she go missing *from bed?* She is not a doll!"

"It's that awful Meena!" Jasmine exclaimed. "She turned up, and we think Rose ran away because of her. She's making Rose think she's dotty! She— Oh, no. Oh, I'm sorry, Alice!"

"Oh, Jasmine," Alice said faintly, and DI Adams could actually feel the disapproving look over the phone.

"Meena?" Jean-Claude asked. "But she is not so awful. Why would Rose run away from Meena?"

"She ran away?" DI Adams asked. It felt ridiculous, asking if an eighty-three-year-old had run away, but at the same time it felt like the most natural thing in the world for Toot Hansell.

"Well, we don't know exactly," Alice said. "I'm sure she'll be back in no time."

"I will help look for her," Jean-Claude said. "I am coming up there."

"No," Alice and DI Adams said at the same time. "She may come to you," DI Adams said before Alice could say anything else. "You stay put, and call us if she turns up. This is a police investigation, and we're taking it from here. Alice?"

"I'm dreadfully sorry, Inspector. You seem to be breaking up," Alice said, perfectly clearly.

"*Alice.* Where are you going?"

"I can't hear you at all. Terrible reception."

"Where are you driving to?"

"Oh, there goes the connection." There was a pause, during

which DI Adams could hear Jasmine fumbling for the disconnect button, then the line went dead. They all stared at the phone.

"My Rose," Jean-Claude started, and DI Adams raised a hand, cutting him off.

"Stay here. Call us if she turns up. *Do not* get involved, understand?"

"But—" he started, pointing at the phone.

"*No.* I don't care what they're doing. *You* stay out of it." She felt absurdly like adding, *If all your friends jumped off a cliff, would you do it too?*

"I do not like this."

"I understand." She took a breath. "Who's this Meena, then?"

"She is Rose's stepdaughter from another marriage. She is okay – not very much like Rose, but they are good to each other."

"Do you have contact details for her?" Collins asked.

Jean-Claude shook his head. "No. But she is a lawyer in Manchester. Meena Dewan. You will find her."

DI Adams looked at Collins. He spread his hands, and she nodded, then got up. "Thank you for your time, Mr Toussaint."

Collins took the macaron from DI Adams' saucer and popped it in his mouth, Dandy watching it go with his floppy ears as cocked as they could be. "We'll let you know as soon as we find Rose, Mr Toussaint."

"Please," he said, getting up and offering DI Adams his hand. His grip was cool and smooth. "I wish I could help."

"Just let us know if Rose contacts you," she said. "That's all the help we need. We'll be in touch." She led the way back toward Collins' Audi, parked marginally illegally in a delivery zone with his police permit in the window. She looked back before she got in, seeing Jean-Claude collecting their cups, a cigarette jammed in the corner of his mouth. He looked older than he had, his shoulders slumped and defeated.

Collins started the engine and jammed the heater all the way up as he struggled out of his coat, barely managing not to hit DI Adams in the face with an elbow.

"Hey, watch it. I'll do you for assaulting an officer." She wasn't getting out of her jacket until she could feel her fingers again.

He snorted, and threw the coat in the backseat. "Thoughts, Adams?"

"None of my thoughts regarding the W.I. are fit for public consumption."

"No change there, then. What about Jean-Claude?"

"Eh. He seems genuinely upset, and I don't think there's any way he'd willingly hurt Rose, which framing her for murder would definitely count as."

"Agreed. But a weird situation. He can't be *that* happy about the divorce."

"No. I could believe a fit of jealous rage, but Lucas said our vic only had the one bump to the back of the head. It wasn't like he was in a fight."

Collins checked the road and pulled the car out into the light traffic. "He had time to do it. Maybe he surprised the vic in the house, and reacted without thinking."

"It's possible. But I can't see that he'd let Rose take the blame."

"And now she's missing."

DI Adams rubbed her face with one hand. "Now she's *run away.* Because her stepdaughter thinks she's dotty? Is that what Jasmine said? So she actually did do it, and thinks she's rumbled? Or someone's grabbed her – the same someone who put a body in her freezer?"

"All possible," Collins said. "I'd hate to think she actually *did* do it, but from what you told me about her house ..."

"And Alice was very defensive about the whole thing. As if she maybe thinks it's possible that Rose isn't doing so well." DI Adams rested her hands over the heater vents, considering it. "Where would Rose go if she ran?"

Collins shook her head. "I'd have thought the W.I. would be Rose's first option for keeping her hidden. They'd close ranks faster than the SAS."

"If Rose thought Alice suspected her, she might not think it was so safe anymore."

Collins *hmm*ed. "Leeds, then? Talk to the boyfriend? See if he's got any sort of alibi, and if she might have gone there?"

"Best do. Then at least we've covered that side of things. I'll call the station and get someone up to Toot Hansell to start looking for her, and get someone on the stepdaughter, too." She pulled her phone out of her pocket, wondering if it would be considered a waste of police resources to put an alert out on Alice's car.

It'd be satisfying, if nothing else.

14
ALICE

Before they left to pick up Jasmine, Alice had watched Thompson grumbling his way down the back path toward the woods, following Rose's now-vanished footsteps.

"There's a lot of dew in this grass still," he called, balancing on the gate. "And it's long. I'm going to get a wet belly, never mind paws."

"I shall get some salmon while I'm out," Alice said. "Perhaps that will make a damp belly easier to bear."

"It's possible. Trout might be better. I wouldn't mind some trout from that fish farm place up the road. They've got good trout."

"I shall bear that in mind." Alice turned and headed toward her little SUV, parked at the front gate.

"He's unbearable," Miriam said, following her.

"I know," Alice said. "But useful at times."

"Does that make up for it?"

Alice chuckled, starting the car and pulling smoothly into the road.

They headed straight to Jasmine's to collect her, minus Primrose. Alice had had dragons in her car before, but she drew the line at Primrose. She didn't trust her not to chew the armrests.

The streets were mid-morning quiet, and it didn't take long before they rounded the corner into the little street where Jasmine lived. It was lined with smart modern semi-detached houses, all gazing out of big windows over compact front gardens at their twins. Alice spotted Gert, Priya, and Jasmine evidently in the middle of a heated debate with a slim, dark-haired woman who was already looking far too familiar.

"Oh no," Miriam said. "She's still here."

"Well, I hardly expected her to go away just because we said so," Alice said, and parked behind a sleek BMW. She opened the door and got out, catching Meena's firm, irritated tones as she addressed the other three women.

"You can't just hide her, you know. I'm certain she's not at Miriam's house – the police officer there hasn't seen her, and she never sleeps late."

"It's none of your business," Jasmine insisted, her face red. "She can sleep in if she wants, or just *avoid* you!"

"What on earth is your problem with me? I'm trying to help her!"

"Of course," Priya said. "I always help all my elderly relatives by accusing them of having cognitive issues."

"I'm not—" Meena caught sight of Alice and half raised her hands. "Oh, bloody hell. It's the cavalry. What're you going to do, run me out of town?"

"Wouldn't mind," Gert said, before Alice could respond.

Meena shook her head. "I just need to see her, to be sure she's safe. If you won't help me, I *will* go back to that police officer and tell him she's missing."

"You can't call the police on her," Miriam said, sounding bewildered. "She hasn't done anything wrong!"

"I'm a bloody lawyer. Did you think I wouldn't make some calls? And find out she has a *body in her freezer?*"

"It's not like she put it there," Priya snapped.

"I'm not saying she did. But I need to see her. She could be a risk to herself and others, and all this stress could make her act irrationally."

"You're treating her like a child!" Jasmine snapped. Her hands were clenched into fists at her sides, and Alice could see her shaking slightly.

"I'm treating her rather better than I'd treat anyone else who just found a dead body in their freezer and is now playing hide and bloody seek or something," Meena snapped, then shook her head, taking a breath and smoothing a loose curl of hair into place. She added in a calmer tone, "Why can't you see I'm just trying to do what's right for Rose?"

"I suppose you getting control over her finances if she's deemed unfit has nothing to do with it, then?" Gert demanded.

"How—" She stared around at them. "How the hell do you even know that? I mean, *no,* that has *nothing* to do with it, but that's— Have you been going through her private papers?"

"We haven't seen any papers. We had nothing but suspicions until now," Alice said, smiling faintly, and Meena pressed a hand to her forehead.

"It shouldn't be private when you're trying to lock her up, anyway," Jasmine said. She sounded as if she were about to start crying, and Priya put an arm around her.

"I'm not trying to lock her up." Meena's voice was getting higher by the moment, and she scrubbed her hands over her face, holding them there for a moment before dropping them to stare at each of the women. "What is *wrong* with you people? Can't you see that Rose could seriously be a danger to herself? She's *eighty-three.*"

"That's really neither here nor there," Alice said. "Age is not necessarily any indicator of competence. But what is clear is that

Rose *is* avoiding you, as she evidently feels you do not have her best interests at heart. You're not helping here, Meena."

"So what do you expect me to do?" Meena snapped. "Just walk away and ignore the fact that she has a *body* in her *freezer?*"

"Let us look after her," Alice said. "I'm sure you all think we're desperately old and dotty ourselves, for the most part, but we are rather good at looking after our own."

Meena muttered something about *dotty* not being the descriptor she'd use, and patted her hair as if afraid it was betraying her, but it was still sitting in elegant waves in her clip. She checked her phone, clutched in one hand, and made a frustrated noise. "Fine. *Fine.* I will give you today to get her to call me. If I haven't heard from her by this evening I'm coming back up and bringing some proper bloody police with me."

"This *evening?*" Gert started, but Alice talked over her.

"That won't be necessary. She'll call you."

Meena regarded Alice for a long moment, a cool, evaluating stare, and Alice met it calmly.

Eventually Meena nodded. "Alright. I don't like it, but I take your point that she's more comfortable with you than me. I am only trying to do what's right for her, though. Truly."

Jasmine sniffed and nudged Primrose with her foot. The little dog immediately started growling at Meena. Meena shook her head, and turned to her car. "This evening, ladies. No longer."

Alice raised a hand, her smile still in place, and they waited until the car had rumbled softly away from the kerb and turned the corner before she looked at the other three women, all scowling after the car.

"I rather think we need to speed up our investigations," she said.

NOW ALICE CHECKED the road ahead and swung around a much larger SUV that was staying far too close to the speed limit for reasonable driving. She wasn't at all sure why people bought these things with large engines if they didn't intend to use them.

"I'm so sorry," Jasmine said again. "It just came out! I didn't mean to tell them."

"It's alright, dear," Alice said. "We'd have had to tell them soon enough, anyway."

"What do we do now?" Miriam asked, leaning between the seats from the back. Alice had noticed she tended to prefer the back, and thought it was likely a comment on her driving. But it wasn't her fault that Miriam thought anything over thirty miles an hour was much too fast. "If Jean-Claude hasn't seen her ..."

"He *says* he hasn't seen her," Alice corrected. "But I rather think that's true. The inspectors are there now, which is as it should be. We'll have time to go and talk to Campbell before they get there, and hopefully Bethany too."

"What do you mean, *as it should be?*" Jasmine asked.

"I told DI Adams about Jean-Claude when we were at Rose's," Alice said. "It was a likely guess that he was a beneficiary of Rose's will, so that seemed like something that would interest the inspectors."

Miriam craned further forward, but Alice kept her eyes on the road. "You *wanted* them to go and see him?"

"I do know Jean-Claude, Miriam. I find it highly unlikely that he'd bop someone on the back of the head and put him in a freezer. Unless Rose was being threatened, of course, in which case he'd take out a full-page ad in the local paper proclaiming his bravery. So it makes sense to start with Campbell and Bethany, as we don't know them so well. And the inspectors being off in Harrogate gives us a little head start for our own investigations, especially since Jasmine has found Campbell for us." Jasmine had been busy on her phone since they got in the car, and while she hadn't yet been able to find anything on Bethany, she had found the college Campbell taught at in Leeds. It was even on the Toot Hansell side of the city, closer and easier to get to than Harrogate, so that gave them at least some time before the inspectors turned up.

"A head start on finding Rose, you mean," Jasmine said. "That's the most important thing."

"It is," Alice agreed. "And she could quite conceivably have gone to either her boyfriend or her assistant for help, so this is rather a two birds with one stone situation. The village is quite well-covered, what with the W.I. and Thompson."

Miriam groaned and dropped back in her seat. "What's the penalty for misleading police officers?"

"I think it'd be the same as obstructing a police investigation," Jasmine said.

"Oh, good."

"Only if they can prove we did it," Alice said, and she nudged the accelerator down a little harder. Miriam squeaked and grabbed the door handle, which seemed somewhat dramatic.

ALICE FOUND a parking space in the visitor's section of the college car park and switched the engine off. They'd made good time right up until they'd hit the usual Leeds traffic. It reminded her once again that she was very happy to live somewhere that had more traffic hold-ups due to tractors and caravans than it did lights or rush hour queues.

"Alright," she said, opening her door and climbing out. "Jasmine, where did the office say he'd be?"

Jasmine scrambled out, looking at her watch. "He teaches a biology class in twenty minutes, so in his office or the staff room."

Her eyes were bright as she tugged her jumper into place, pale hair clinging to the collar.

"Miriam, are you joining us?" Alice asked. Miriam was still sitting in the back of the car, clinging to the door handle with both hands.

"I feel a little queasy," she said. "I'll catch up."

Alice bent to peer in at her. "You do look a bit pale. Best sit in the front on the way back, dear. Being in the backseat always makes me feel a little iffy, too."

Miriam made a horrified noise and waved them off.

Alice looked at Jasmine. "Alright, then. Lead the way."

"Right," Jasmine said, and headed for the long stretch of two-story red brick buildings, marooned in their seas of grass and stitched about with flowerbeds. It seemed to be a new sort of place, laid out with thought for common areas and green spaces. It was inviting rather than uptight and austere.

They checked in at the front desk, and the receptionist gave them passes then offered to call Campbell down to meet them. Alice explained that Campbell was her nephew and they were there to surprise him, and that his cousin Jasmine had come all the way from Australia just that morning. The receptionist gave Jasmine a doubtful look, and she said brightly, "I know I look pale, but it's just that I'm very sun-safe. I wear factor 50 and a hat, and one of those mask things if it's the middle of the day."

"That seems a lot," the receptionist said, his hand still on the phone.

Jasmine frowned at him. "You wouldn't say that if you'd been so badly sunburned in your first week that you had to wear an icepack to bed every night, and stay in the shade for the next six months."

Alice patted her arm. "You recovered very well. And it was so brave of you to stay in Australia anyway."

"One can't let such things scare you off," Jasmine said. "And I love the kookaburras. I'd miss them too much if I came back." She looked at the receptionist. "Do you like kookaburras?"

"Straight down the hall, left at the end, up the stairs, through the staff door, and it's the third door on the right," the receptionist said. He still looked doubtful, but also like he had other things to be getting on with and didn't want to think about kookaburras. "Don't wander around."

"We have no intentions of doing so," Alice said, and headed down the hall. "Well done, Jasmine," she added, once they were out of earshot.

"Was the sunburn thing a bit much? I saw it on a documentary. I do wear factor 50, you know."

"It gave just the right touch of authenticity. I should have said Canada, thinking about it now, but you recovered the situation admirably."

"Really?" Jasmine said, and grinned. "Do you think I could be good at this after all?"

"You *are* good at it. You're good at many things," Alice said. "But it's not up to me to say so, you know. People will tell you all sorts of supposed truths that are just their beliefs about you. One mustn't listen to them too closely, or they'll become real. One must make up one's own mind." She pushed through the doors to the stairs and hurried up them. "How long do we have?"

"Just over ten minutes," Jasmine said. "I hope he hasn't gone yet!"

The staff doors were just at the top of the stairs, and a moment later they were standing in front of a smaller door marked *Campbell Jones, Head of Science.* Alice knocked sharply.

"Come in," someone called from inside, and Alice pushed the door open to find Campbell tucking a planner and a textbook into a satchel. He was wearing a knitted vest over a long-sleeved shirt that made him look rather older than his years, his glasses clinging precariously to the end of his long nose. He blinked at them. "Jasmine? And ... Rose's other friend ..."

"Alice Martin," Alice said, extending her hand.

He stared at her. "What's happened? Is it Rose? What's going on?"

She looked at her hand, then back at him, and he made an exasperated noise, then gave her an awkward handshake.

"What's going on?"

"I'd ask you the same thing," she said. "When did you last see Rose?"

"What? Why?"

"We don't have much time, Mr Jones—"

"Just Campbell – what do you mean, not much time?" He was blinking furiously.

"You have a class in ten minutes," Alice said, retrieving her hand. He seemed to have forgotten he was holding it.

"Sod the class! What's happened to Rose? Is this about the police thing? Why are you asking me when I last saw her?"

"She's okay," Jasmine said. "Well, she was when *we* last saw her."

"*What?* She's missing?"

Alice resisted the urge to look at the ceiling. Jasmine was proving good at subterfuge, but she was *not* improving when it came to the need to blurt out information. But it was out there now, so they may as well work with it. "Not exactly," Alice said. "We thought she might have decided to stay with you, since her house is still a crime scene."

"Not exactly? What does that mean?"

"Is she staying with you, Campbell?"

"No. I haven't even talked to her since we were at the house yesterday. I've been trying to call and text, but she never answers." He sagged against the desk, taking his glasses off and rubbing his face with his other hand. "I'm so worried. And now she's *missing?*"

"She doesn't have her phone," Alice said. "She left it at my house."

"She's always doing that," Campbell said. "I told her to put that Find My Phone thing on her computer, but she said she couldn't be bothered being that attached to it. But it's always turning up in the weirdest places."

Alice examined him. His face hung in haggard lines from his skull, and she could see little spots of blood on his jaw where he'd cut himself shaving. There was toothpaste on his collar, too. "When did you last talk to her, then?"

"Other than at Miriam's house yesterday?" He considered it, then fished his phone out of the satchel and put his glasses back on to peer at it. "Friday night," he announced. "We went to some silly lecture that a friend of hers put on in York. We had a late dinner, and she was going to stay over, but she hadn't been sleeping well. She was … well, she was worried about some stuff." He shifted uneasily, not looking up from his phone.

"Things turning up in strange places?" Alice asked. "Forgetting things?"

He rubbed his mouth. "Yes. But I don't think it's a big thing, you know? She never puts things in strange places when she's at my place. And she's so sharp. The questions she asked at that lecture …" He shook his head. "Well, he may have been a friend, but she has no mercy when it comes to science. Her mind's fine, I'm sure of it. But she was unsettled that night, for some reason, so she decided to go home after dinner, even though it was late. And then she messaged me from her tablet, because she couldn't find her phone."

Alice frowned. "What time was that?"

"It would've been around one or so in the morning."

"She had the phone on her when she was with you?"

"No, she thought she must have left it at home, but when she got home she still couldn't find it."

Alice took Rose's phone from her handbag. "Do you know her unlock code?"

He shook his head. "No. We believe in allowing each other our privacy."

Alice sighed and put the phone back. "How about her assistant – Bethany? Do you happen to have her address or number?"

Campbell pushed his glasses up his nose. "Not her number, but I dropped some papers off at her place for Rose at some point. It'll be in my maps." He went back to flicking through his phone, and the room was silent for a moment, then he said, "Shouldn't the police be doing this?"

"The police may be taking a slightly different angle," Alice said, and Campbell raised his eyebrows at her. She didn't clarify, so he just sighed and passed her the phone.

"There it is."

Alice peered at it, then nodded. "Good. We shall see if Rose is there."

Campbell scratched his jaw. "It's possible. They're not that close though. Bethany has lots of ideas about how things should be done, and Rose doesn't hold much with *should*."

"Did they clash?" Alice asked, handing Campbell's phone to Jasmine, who frowned at it for a moment then nodded and copied the address to her own.

"Not exactly. It was more that Bethany got a bit disapproving over anything she felt affected Rose's standing or respectability. Like the lecture on Friday."

"She was there too?"

"Yes, but I don't know why she bothered. She spent the whole time huffing and scowling, and only clapped when Rose pointed out inconsistencies in Eric's method."

"Eric," Alice said, and she saw the photos laid out on the table again, the blond hair dusted with frost, the skin drained blue-white.

"The lecturer, Eric Latherby. He's a cryptozoologist, like *that's* a real field. I agree with Bethany on that much, at least."

"You didn't like him?"

"He thinks a lot of himself. Like he's some sort of Indiana Jones of the cryptozoology world." Campbell snorted. "Oh, he talks a good game, and has all these slides and the glamorously weathered man-of-the-world look, but— wait. Didn't? Not don't?" Alice just looked at him, and he stared at her with his eyes wide above his glasses. "Past tense?"

"Past tense," Alice said, since she was almost certain it didn't matter. Campbell was as likely a suspect as Rose herself, as far as she could tell.

"Ohhhh." Campbell wiped his mouth. "I didn't *not* like him. Not like that. I mean—"

"We're not the police, Campbell." She slipped Rose's phone back into her bag. "I believe you have a class."

"How can I go to class when I know Rose is missing? What if whoever ... whoever did *that* to Eric is after her? What if he was just collateral damage?"

"Which is why we're going to find her." Alice turned to the door.

"I'll help," Campbell said. "I can get a colleague to take my class. I'm coming with you."

"No," Alice said firmly.

"He might be helpful," Jasmine said.

Alice examined Campbell, who had flipped his planner open and was running a finger down a list of names, frowning. He looked sweaty and unkempt and more likely to get in the way than help, in her opinion. "No."

"No?" Campbell asked, looking up at her. "How do you expect me to work *now?*"

"Rose may come to find you," Alice said. "You need to stay here for her."

Campbell frowned. "You're not as convincing as you think you are."

"You're still not coming with us." She looked at her watch. "And you're late for your class already." She turned and made for the door before Campbell could say anything else, Jasmine trailing after her.

"Wait!" he called, and she paused reluctantly, one hand on the door.

"Yes?"

"Call me as soon as you know anything? Please?"

She sighed. "Yes, Campbell. I will." And she pushed back out into the hall.

THEY DROPPED their passes with the receptionist and hurried back out to the car, the wind plucking peevishly at their clothes and ruffling through Alice's hair.

"You could have let him come," Jasmine said. "He was really worried."

"And have him hanging about making a nuisance of himself the next time the dragons come around?"

Jasmine made a disbelieving noise. "You just don't like him. I think he's quite nice."

"He's very *needy*."

"He was just worried about Rose," Jasmine said. "Not all men are entirely useless, you know."

Alice gave a little snort of laughter. "Of course not. But we can't be holding anyone's hands right now. We have too much to do."

Miriam peered at them as they let themselves into the car. "Did you find him?"

"We did," Alice said, settling into her seat. "He hasn't seen her."

"He wanted to help us look, but Alice thinks we'd need to hold his hand," Jasmine said.

"She's probably right," Miriam said. She was looking a little brighter. "Men are no good in a crisis."

"You're both quite mean," Jasmine said.

"Ben excepted," Miriam added.

"*Mmm.* Sometimes," Jasmine said, and both she and Miriam laughed.

"What now?" Miriam asked.

"Well, we have Bethany's address," Alice said. "And we know she was at a lecture given by Eric Latherby on the Friday night. *With* Rose and Campbell. Rose went home alone afterward."

"And he died sometime that night," Miriam whispered. "Do you think Bethany went to Rose's after the lecture for some reason, and thought Eric was an intruder? Maybe that's why she was there on Saturday, when Rose showed me the body. Maybe she was going to tell her about it."

"Apparently she disliked anything that she felt made Rose look less than respectable," Alice said. "Maybe it wasn't such an accident, if she felt he was bringing Rose down somehow."

"But what about the things being moved around?" Jasmine asked. "That doesn't answer that."

Alice tapped her fingers against her lips. "That may be an entirely separate question. But I think the best thing we can do now is talk to Bethany. She's in Skipton, so the closest to home. It would have made sense for Rose to call her if she wanted somewhere to stay."

"You don't think we should call Colin?" Miriam asked. "This sounds like quite a solid lead."

"I think we should make sure of it first," Alice said, looking at Miriam in the rear-view mirror as she started the engine. "You should sit in the front, Miriam. You don't mind, do you, Jasmine?"

"I'm fine here," Miriam said, checking her seatbelt. "Maybe we can go a little more slowly, though."

"Maybe," Alice said brightly, and pulled out of the parking space. They passed a silver Audi as they headed for the gate, and as they drew level with it Alice smiled and raised her hand, waving to the rather familiar driver. DI Adams leaned forward in the passenger seat, both hands in the air, saying something that Alice couldn't make out but that she doubted was complimentary. A moment later her phone rang, and the dashboard display came up with, *DI Adams.*

"Aren't you going to answer that?" Jasmine asked, as it continued to ring.

"No," Alice said, and pulled out into the traffic, heading toward Skipton and the Dales and the wide, wild places where Folk still lived.

15
MORTIMER

Beaufort was standing on Mortimer's toes, and the younger dragon squeezed his eyes shut, trying to remain as still as possible, and also to resist demanding to know how an old dragon could both fly and be heavier than a large heifer. Or than he imagined a large heifer to be. He'd never been stood on by one of them, and he had no intention of allowing it to happen, especially not if they weighed anywhere near as much as Beaufort seemed to. He opened his eyes just enough to squint at the slate tiles below him, then closed them again.

"Hello?" someone called from the garden below, sounding discouraged. "Hell— Oh, *bloody hell.*" This was accompanied by a splash. "Is that a fishpond? Why's there a fishpond in the middle of the bloody rhubarb? Who— Oh, great. *Great.* I've got frog spawn on my boots." There was a pause, followed by some enthusiastic scraping and irritated noises, and Mortimer fervently wished the police officer with his damp boots would go back to the car. He and Beaufort were currently flattened to the roof of one of Rose's garden sheds, and there was the occasional ominous creak coming from beneath them which made him feel the structure was not designed for supporting dragons. Plus, he was losing feeling in the toes Beaufort was currently standing on.

The scraping stopped, and for a moment the only noise in the garden was the raucous chatter of the birds, all going about their business with scant regard for trapped dragons on shed roofs. Then the police officer muttered, "Well, sod this for a game of soldiers. I need a machete to get through this bloody place." He stomped off up the path, still muttering to himself, and a few moments later they heard him try the door to the house.

"Oh, *bollocks,*" he said, and Beaufort slid off the roof of the shed, landing far more lightly on the ground below than Mortimer felt he had any right to.

"Come on, lad," he said quietly. "I think that police officer is about to do a far more thorough search of the garden."

Mortimer scrambled after him, wincing as his abused toes touched the soft earth. "What do you think he's found?"

"I imagine Rose left the house unlocked when she ran out, so the police officer will know someone was definitely in their crime scene. We best make ourselves scarce."

Mortimer nodded vigorously. He'd have liked to make themselves scarce *before,* when Rose had gone racing down the garden, but the police officer, who Mortimer recognised vaguely as being Jasmine's husband, had popped out from behind a thicket of hydrangeas, swearing and waving his arms at cobwebs, and they'd had to hastily scramble onto the shed roof before he stumbled over them. The man was being far too careful for them to risk staying on the ground, but humans rarely looked up. He was much less likely to examine the roof with any care.

Now Mortimer said, "What now? Where did Rose go? And what do we do about Walter and those journalists?" He shuddered, picturing the string of drool falling softly from Walter's jaws. No one drooled like that for no reason.

"I'm sure Walter won't actually *do* anything," Beaufort said, leading the way to the gate at the bottom of the garden. "I'm more worried about Rose."

Mortimer scampered after Beaufort, managing a noncommittal noise that stopped short of an outright contradiction. After all, Beaufort had known Walter far longer than he had. "She definitely went this way," he said aloud. "Her and Angelus both." Her scent had the sharp, sweet tang of sunshine on lemons, but there was an undercurrent of rust-red fright as well.

"But when? Is this how she arrived in the garden, or how she left, or both?" Beaufort stopped at the gate, keeping his head low as he peered over the top at the village green. The small boy on his bike had been joined by two equally small girls, and they were all wobbling in unsteady yet recklessly intersecting circles, each pass a deliciously close dance with disaster. A man and a woman were shouting at each other over a picnic hamper, apparently in disagreement over who had been meant to actually put the sandwiches in it, and Teresa and Pearl were marching across the green with determination written in every line of their bodies. Martha trailed behind them with her gaze fixed on the arguing couple, apparently deeply invested in the issue of sandwiches herself.

Teresa raised her hand and waved to someone on the road beyond the green, and when Mortimer peered around he saw Rosemary and Carlotta striding toward the vicarage. Rosemary was wielding a notebook and a pen, and Carlotta was swinging a walking stick with the air of someone who had no need to use it for its designed purpose, but was rather keen to put it to another use if the opportunity presented itself.

"Interesting," Beaufort said, and deeper in the garden the police officer shouted, his voice sharper than it had been, "North Yorkshire Police. Show yourselves!"

Beaufort slipped up and over the gate, and Mortimer followed him, keeping to the scant cover of the bushes as they skirted the green and headed for the vicarage and the safety of the woods beyond.

"We need to go back to Rose's," Beaufort said.

"We can't," Mortimer said. "That police officer knew *someone* had been in the garden, and he'll be searching it right now. Probably with backup."

"But Rose is missing, and we're just sitting here doing nothing." Beaufort huffed frustrated smoke.

"We lost her scent when we left the garden," Mortimer reminded him.

"We didn't exactly have time to look properly. We need to get back in there."

Mortimer swallowed a whimper of alarm at the thought of the damp-booted police officer as well as over-curious journalists. "We can go back once it's dark. It's just too risky now. Those journalists could be lurking anywhere." If Walter hadn't eaten them, of course.

"*We're* lurking. I don't like lurking. Dragons don't *lurk*." Beaufort shook himself impatiently, his scales whispering against each other.

They were currently lurking in the edge of the woods near Miriam's house, having carefully skirted the ladies of the Women's Institute as they searched the village hall and the vicarage. As Beaufort had said, it wasn't that the dragons were *avoiding* them exactly, but the time spent being told off by Carlotta or gently reproached by Pearl was better spent finding Rose. Which, they'd learned from a little circumspect eavesdropping while the ladies were in the church, was exactly what the W.I. were concentrating on too. Rose was gone, and there was a murderer about. Mortimer developed a strange ringing in his ears every time he thought about it, and he couldn't seem to bring either his colours or his breath under any sort of control. Going back to the mount wasn't an option. They had to find her.

That, however, had not been successful so far. They'd lost the bright thread of her scent as soon as they left the garden and sprinted for the cover of the churchyard, and they had yet to find it again. They'd searched every path she might have left the village by, even the ones known only to rabbits and pixies, but there was nothing. Mortimer *knew* their only chance was to go back to the garden and try to find where she'd left it, but there was no use risking being caught by police officers wielding tasers or journalists wielding their cameras. That would help no one.

So they'd slipped around the edges of the village, out of sight among the trees as they watched the ladies of the Women's Institute going door to door, asking everyone if they'd seen Rose. The dragons periodically spotted a bemused homeowner standing in their back garden while Gert or Carlotta or Priya opened garden sheds and checked behind butterfly bushes and shouted for Rose like she was a lost cat. Pearl had attempted to get Martha to track her, but all Martha had done was dutifully sniff the scarf Pearl offered her, then plodded down the garden to the nearest patch of sun, flopped down and gone to sleep. They had yet to see Miriam or Alice, and that was worrying Mortimer almost as much as not being able to find Rose.

"Where do you think they've gone?" he asked Beaufort.

"To do something useful," Beaufort said. "Unlike us. *Lurking.*"

Mortimer wondered if he could risk sneaking down to the stream for a drink. His throat was awfully dry. "I know. And it's all my fault, because I waited too long to cross the road. If I'd been quicker, the journalists wouldn't have seen us, and—"

"It wasn't at all your fault," Beaufort said firmly. "You were very sensible and quite right to be worried. And Rose was already running from the police officer, so it wouldn't have changed that."

"But we'd have been able to help her if the journalists hadn't followed us."

"Possibly. But you are one small dragon, Mortimer. You don't have responsibility for all the things that happen in the world, or all the things that others do. Only what you do." They were both silent for a moment, while Mortimer tried to work out how to respond to something that *sounded* true but *felt* ... well, not true at all. Then Beaufort added, "And I am being too impatient. I was too impatient when we decided to come to the village in broad daylight, and I'm being too impatient now. They are dragon hunters, after a fashion, and we must be careful."

Mortimer didn't bother holding on to his whimper this time. "*Walter.* I really thought ..."

"He wouldn't," Beaufort said, but he didn't sound quite as reassuring as Mortimer would have liked. "And the journalist left in the car, didn't she?"

"We didn't see. The car left, so she must have. Her friend wouldn't have left without her, would he?"

"It would be very poor form if he did."

Both of them stared at Miriam's empty garden for a while, although Mortimer wasn't really seeing it. He was watching the long thread of drool sliding from Walter's jaws toward the journalist's head, over and over. The drool, and the shine in Walter's eyes.

"I know there's *quirky*," he said finally. "But sometimes dragons get a little ... *odd* with age, don't they?"

"Yes," Beaufort said. "Some of us even listen to young dragons and get into newfangled things like barbecues."

Mortimer swallowed. Never mind the stream, he wanted a cup of tea. He wondered when tea had become a necessity for dragons, and if that had been such a good idea. "Barbecues are helpful, though."

"I'm very fond of mine," Beaufort agreed, and held a paw up, rotating it at the joints with a rather impressive chorus of clicks. "Listen to that! So much better."

Mortimer didn't want to imagine what it had sounded like before. "But what if it's a *different* sort of odd? I mean, we know what happens sometimes, when dragons fade." There was a whole cavern in the mount to house those dragons who had quietly turned away from the world, grown too old or too sad, their fire quenched by years or circumstance. They slept deeper than dreams could reach, their scales faded to the dusty texture of stone, cold to the touch. The young dragons were tasked with keeping a fire burning in there, the same as in the grand cavern, in case the sleepers could still feel it, but Mortimer always felt it was more the sort of flame one burned in a shrine. It was for the past, not the future.

"Walter didn't seem inclined to fall asleep," Beaufort said thoughtfully. "He was moving quite well when I saw him."

"He was," Mortimer said. Walter had been moving *far* too well. And far too fast for a dragon of his age. "But I mean, maybe he might have thought things were … different."

Beaufort looked at him. "Different enough to eat a human?"

"He could've been confused. Maybe he thought it was still back when he was young."

"We didn't eat humans even then." Beaufort wrinkled his snout, peering across the stream as a car went past Miriam's without stopping. "Well. *Some* dragons did. But it wasn't very acceptable. Plus humans weren't so keen on baths in those days."

Mortimer didn't reply, still thinking of that long thread of drool. *Some dragons.*

Then Beaufort said, "We really don't know if the journalist made it to the car?"

"No. But we'd have heard—"

"You've never seen anyone hit with a dragon's tail, have you, lad? Not even a cow has much to say after that."

Mortimer tried not to picture Walter overtaking the fleeing journalist on his creaking wings, the lash of his patchy but still muscular tail, her falling to the ground as he plunged after her—

"Come on," Beaufort said. "I'm sure that's not what happened, but let's just go and talk to Walter anyway. And he might have seen where Rose went. It's worth asking." And he headed off into the woods so quickly that Mortimer had to break into an uneven canter to keep up.

Some dragons.

MORTIMER WAS PANTING by the time they broke clear of the trees. Beaufort leaped into the air, wings snapping wide, pulling for the sky with heavy, powerful beats. Mortimer plunged after him, catching his talons on a low bush and almost crashing back to the ground before recovering. The High Lord already had a good lead on him, climbing fast and arrowing back toward the mount. And Walter would be there, of course, shouting at the younger dragons and not cleaning away bits of journalist that were stuck between his teeth. Hopefully.

By the time they were halfway back to the mount Beaufort had opened his lead up so much that Mortimer had given up trying to catch him. It seemed that old dragons could move far faster than one imagined when it was required. Mortimer supposed it didn't really matter – it wasn't as if he'd exactly be backup if there was a confrontation, anyway. The last fight he'd been in, Amelia had had to save him. He rather wished she were here now.

A flash of light caught his eye, coming from the rocky slopes and folds of the fells below. He squinted at it, seeing movement near one of the becks that ran down toward the village, something sprinting along wildly with two other figures scuttling after it. Not figures. *Dragons.* One large, mottled with greens and greys that almost matched the landscape, the other smaller and flashing with indignant orange among a haphazard attempt at camouflage. Light glinted again from the area of their tail. *Gilbert.*

It had to be – other dragons did have piercings, but he couldn't imagine any of them out here in the middle of the day, running across the fells in pursuit of another dragon and ... a deer, maybe? As he watched, Gilbert tried to charge the lead dragon, and only succeeded in tripping himself up. He was definitely trying to stop the other dragon, who Mortimer supposed was probably Amelia, although they looked too big. Mortimer wondered why they didn't just take off to get rid of Gilbert. The young dragon's flying skills – or, rather, lack thereof – were common knowledge around the mount.

Gilbert tried another charge, and the lead dragon reared up, swiping out with one paw. Gilbert was sent tumbling over the rough ground, and the bigger dragon went back to chasing their quarry. "Ouch," Mortimer mumbled as Gilbert righted himself. The bigger dragon shook their wings out, the shape uneven and raggedy even from this distance, and looked up as if they were searching for something.

And suddenly he knew who it was, and why they weren't flying. "*Beaufort!*" he bellowed. "Beaufort, Beaufort, he's here—" He looked around, but he'd slowed to watch the altercation play out below, and the High Lord was well out of earshot. He'd never catch up to him before he got back to the mount.

Mortimer hesitated, arching his wings to slow himself more. Lord Walter was below him, was *right here.* He wasn't flying because he'd seen Beaufort, and was trying to stay hidden. That could only mean he was up to no good, but what could Mortimer do? Walter might be old, but Gilbert's haphazard attacks weren't even slowing him – as Mortimer dithered he saw the younger dragon sent sprawling again, only to scramble up and take up the chase once more. What *were* they chasing? He strained to see, then realised he was wasting time. Walter and his quarry were heading for the nearest line of the woods, and by the time he fetched Beaufort the old dragon would be gone. He had to go now, on his own, or he'd lose them. And poor Gilbert couldn't carry on like this much longer.

"I'm going to regret this," Mortimer mumbled, and tucked his wings into a dive.

He plunged toward the ground, arrowing to intercept the charging dragons, ignoring whatever they were chasing. Walter looked up and found another burst of speed, racing for the rapidly approaching cover of the trees. Gilbert was leaping from boulders, his neck stretched out in a long line of determination, his wings wobbling about the place and doing more to slow him than to help. Mortimer altered his angle just slightly, the ground roaring toward him, eyes narrowed against the speed of his own passage, and at the last moment twisted his wings into brakes, bringing his hind legs beneath him and slamming to the ground so hard that it knocked a wheeze out of him. He teetered on the edge of balance, forelegs reaching for the earth, and looked up just in time to see Walter barrel into him as if he hadn't even considered slowing.

Mortimer screeched as the old dragon tried to thunder right over him – or *through* him, by the feel of things – and grabbed the nearest limb he could find as they both tumbled across the hard ground in a chaos of clashing wings and flailing tails.

"Bloody young dragons!" Walter roared. "Out of my way, damn you!"

"Mortimer!" Gilbert yelled from somewhere off to the side. "Mortimer, are you okay?"

Mortimer couldn't catch his breath enough to answer, and he was still trying to keep a hold on Walter. Partly because he didn't want the old dragon to rush off chasing whatever he'd been chasing – although at least it hadn't been journalist-shaped – and partly because he was fairly sure that when he did let go he was going to end up with a hefty clip to the ear, at the very least.

"Let *go*, you mangey little rock lizard!" Walter was struggling to haul himself away from Mortimer, his wings battering the younger dragon's sides. "How *dare* you? I'm a *Lord!*"

"Stop," Mortimer gasped, but it came out as such a squeak that he doubted the old dragon could even hear him over his own bellows. He just concentrated on hanging on instead, his back pressed to the ground and stones digging into his scales, his view limited to Walter's scraggly belly. He seemed to be clutching the old dragon's foreleg.

"Let Mortimer go!" Gilbert shouted. "You horrible old carnivore! Let him *go!*"

Mortimer appreciated the sentiment, even if Gilbert didn't quite have a grasp of the situation.

"Get off me!" Walter bellowed. "I should have eaten you both as *eggs!* I'll snap your wings like twigs! I'll— *Ow!*"

"Sorry!" Gilbert yelped. "I'll do it again!"

Walter roared in wordless fury, and Mortimer wondered just how much having his wings snapped was going to hurt, and how long it took to recover from such things.

Then the old dragon squawked. "Stop that!"

"I won't. You let Mortimer go or I'll do it again!"

"*He's* holding *me,* you half-grown swamp turtle."

"I am," Mortimer managed.

"Oh," Gilbert said. Mortimer couldn't see him past Walter's furiously puce belly. "Do you want to let go, Mortimer?"

"Yes," Mortimer said.

"So do it," Walter hissed, trying to shake his leg free. "Before I toast your face off. *Ow!* What are you *doing?*"

"Poking you with a stick," Gilbert said, as if it should be obvious.

"Well, stop it."

"Not until … well, until Mortimer lets go?" He sounded uncertain.

"I'm not letting go until I'm sure my face isn't going to get toasted," Mortimer said.

"I'll do that if you *don't* let go. *Ow! Stop poking me!*"

"Why didn't you stop?" Mortimer asked, still hanging on. "What were you chasing?"

"Nothing," Walter snapped.

"Angelus," Gilbert said at the same time. "He was going to eat him!"

"What's Angelus doing out here?" Mortimer asked.

"It's a damn dog. Who the hell knows why it does anything." Walter shook his foreleg irritably. "You're hurting my arthritis."

Mortimer loosened his grip marginally. "You're not going to toast my face?"

"No."

"Bite me?"

"No."

"Hit me?"

Walter paused, then snarled as Gilbert evidently poked him again. "*No.* But you both need a good clip around the ear. No respect for your elders!"

Mortimer let go, and Walter pulled away from him, sitting up on his hindquarters and rubbing his foreleg while he glared at both young dragons. "Sorry," Mortimer said. "But you did try to trample me."

"You dropped out of the sky right in front of me! It was an *ambush!*"

Mortimer was entirely sure the old dragon had known exactly where he was, but he just said, "Where's the journalist?"

"The what?"

"The woman from Rose's garden."

Walter sniffed. "Two of them went off in a car. And she's no journalist. I know a dragon hunter when I smell one."

"You didn't chase her?"

"I should have." Walter looked at Mortimer for a long moment, his old eyes milky and furious. "We shouldn't be letting people like that just wander around. She was looking too closely. She'll find us, and what then?"

"The W.I. know about us," Gilbert said. "And that's been absolutely wonderful."

"Sure. For silly young dragons with holes in their tails." Walter glared at Gilbert, who did his best to glare back, but the old dragon had far more practise, and before long Gilbert dropped his gaze. "That *journalist* is going to bring trouble. I'm telling you now."

"If you're that worried, you should be staying away, not hanging around in trees in people's gardens," Mortimer said, trying to keep his voice steady. "And definitely not chasing dogs!"

Walter made a dismissive gesture. "You tell the High Lord about keeping out of gardens, then. And keep the damn dog. They're not as tasty as a nice rabbit, anyway."

Gilbert looked at his stick as if he were seriously considering poking the old dragon with it again.

"What about Rose?" Mortimer asked. "Have you seen her?"

"What am I, some sort of human-herder?"

"She was in the garden too. And you're chasing her dog."

"Of course I'm chasing her bloody *dog*. It's out here in the wild just *asking* to be eaten." Walter seemed to be going an even deeper shade of purple-brown, if that was possible.

"You monstrous old meat-eater," Gilbert said, his voice wobbling.

"*I'm a dragon.* We *eat* things. *Meaty* things."

"So you haven't seen Rose *or* the journalists?" Mortimer asked, just to be sure.

"*Gah.* No. Damn young dragons. Damn meddling women.

Damn journalists. Damn *sticks.*" Walter lumbered into the air, still grumbling to himself, pulling toward the mount, and Mortimer and Gilbert watched him go.

"Are you okay?" Gilbert asked eventually.

Mortimer looked down at himself. He didn't seem to have lost any scales, although his back was still aching from crashing over the stony ground. "I think so. Are you alright?"

"Yes – horrible old wyrm. I can't believe he was going to eat Angelus!" They both turned to look toward the trees, where the dog had vanished. Gilbert dropped his stick. "Oh *no* – he'll get lost in there. We have to find him!"

"We'll only scare him," Mortimer said.

"But if we leave him out here Walter'll go after him again."

Mortimer groaned. "But what are we meant to do? He'll run if he sees us."

"We'll herd him," Gilbert said, brushing his paws off. "We can guide him back to the village between us and put him in Miriam's garden."

"We're meant to stay away from the village," Mortimer pointed out.

Gilbert gave him a reproachful look. "He'll get lost. He'll be *scared.*"

Mortimer thought about pointing out that Angelus was going to be more scared by two dragons herding him, but Gilbert did have a point when it came to Walter. The old dragon would be back hunting the dog as soon as he thought the coast was clear. Mortimer gave an exasperated growl. "*Fine.* Come on." And he headed for the woods with the young dragon scampering behind him, piercings flashing in the afternoon sun.

16
MIRIAM

Miriam found that keeping her eyes closed was by far the best way to deal with Alice's driving. And, after all, it wasn't as though she were unfamiliar with the road from Leeds to Skipton. She didn't need to see where they were going. Her hands were starting to cramp up from gripping the door handle, though, which was most uncomfortable.

She felt them slow as they went around a roundabout, and ventured a peek at the surroundings. They weren't there yet. There really were an excess of roundabouts on this route, which she normally found quite nerve-wracking on the occasions when she had to drive them herself (she never trusted anyone to actually turn in the directions they were indicating, nor did she trust her little old Volkswagen Beetle Betsy's ability to pull out in a timely manner), but today she quite liked the fact that they slowed Alice down at least a little.

"Do you think DI Adams is following us?" Jasmine asked, sounding as though she were craning around in her seat.

"I imagine she will interview Campbell first," Alice said. "So we have a little time before she catches up."

"Maybe we should leave Bethany to them," Miriam managed, without much hope. "All this driving around, and we're just interfering. We should be looking for Rose."

"We *are* looking for Rose. But, more than that, we're looking for proof of her mental capacity as well as her innocence. It would be too easy for the police to use that as a reason for the murder."

Miriam couldn't argue with that. It was something she couldn't imagine the police looking too closely at. After all, what did it matter to them if one little old lady was getting a bit dotty? It would just be *guilty* or *innocent* to them. She was sure DI Adams wouldn't *want* Rose taken away, and Colin certainly wouldn't, but, as Alice had said, it might not be up to them.

"Can we at least go a little slower?" she asked.

"I'm barely over the speed limit, Miriam. Do open your eyes. It's most off-putting to have you acting as though we're going to crash at any moment."

Miriam thought it was most off-putting to *feel* as though they were going to crash at any moment, but she didn't share that.

BETHANY LIVED in a flat above a row of shops in one of the back streets of Skipton, the front door sandwiched between a takeaway and a laundrette. Alice managed to find a parking space a little further down the street, in front of a grocery store with racks of flowering plants outside it, and Miriam climbed shakily from the car, stretching her cramped limbs. The buildings stole the sun, and the wind was anxious, tugging at her clothes and spinning rubbish against the shopfronts.

Alice beeped the car locked and led the way to the door, finding Bethany's name on one of four possible bells. She rang it firmly, and after a moment the intercom buzzed and a wary voice said, "Yes?"

"Bethany?" Alice asked. "We're friends of Rose. Can you let us in?"

There was a pause, then Bethany said, "Why?"

"We wanted to ask you a couple of things."

Another pause, then, "Are you the police?"

"No, dear," Alice said, her voice tight. "Friends of Rose. We merely want to talk to you."

"What about?"

Alice looked at the sky, and Jasmine leaned past her. "Bethany? It's Jasmine. We're just really worried about Rose. Can you let us in, please?"

"Jasmine?" The voice on the other end grew a little higher. "Why? Is it about the ... what happened at Rose's?"

"It's really cold out here," Jasmine said.

There was another pause, then the door buzzed and Alice pushed it open, smiling at Jasmine. "I didn't realise you knew her."

"I've met her once or twice. She's just a bit nervous of people, I think."

Miriam thought that quite a lot of people were nervous of Alice, but pointing that out was unlikely to help the situation. So she just followed them up the scuffed but clean stairs inside, to where a landing held four plain white doors. One was partly open, and Miriam recognised the young woman in loose-fitting jeans and bulky cardigan peering out at them. She was clutching the front of her top, her eyebrows drawn in anxious lines.

"Hello, Bethany," Jasmine said, and Miriam gave an encouraging little wave.

"Hi," Bethany said, looking at Alice with something close to alarm.

Alice held her hand out. "Alice Martin," she said, and Miriam could almost see her swallowing the *RAF Wing Commander, retired* which was often attached to the end. It seemed wise.

Bethany shook Alice's hand very lightly, examined all three of them for a moment, then stepped back. "Come in, I suppose."

They followed her into a small front room, hung with a large woven tapestry on one wall and lit by an old sash window toward the front of the building. One corner was taken up with a set of bookshelves with a built-in desk, and a squishy sofa covered with a lilac throw snuggled down on the other wall, below the tapestry. A round table just big enough for four wooden chairs sat at the opposite end of the room, and it all smelled of incense layered over the faint whiff of hot oil from the fish'n'chip shop downstairs.

"Do you want tea?" Bethany asked, twisting her fingers inside the heavy weave of the cardigan.

Miriam opened her mouth to say that she would very much like some tea, but Alice said, "No. We won't take up too much of your time. Have you seen Rose recently?"

Bethany blinked at her, her face pale, then looked at Jasmine. Jasmine smiled and said, "She didn't ask you to pick her up from Toot Hansell this morning, did she?"

"No," Bethany said, still fiddling with her cardigan. "I haven't seen her since before … before. When I saw you." She nodded at Miriam.

"Saturday night," Miriam said, and Bethany nodded.

"Have you heard from her?" Alice asked, her tones measured.

The young woman shook her head, long threads of dark hair falling about her face. "No. I tried to call her, but she didn't answer. Then I went up yesterday and there were police everywhere. What's happening?" Her voice was oddly flat, and Miriam couldn't tell whether it was from weariness or fright.

Miriam stepped over to the slightly raised window, hoping to escape the oily smell. She still felt a little queasy from the car ride. The air coming in was unpleasantly fragrant, but at least it was cool. She stayed there, looking around the room while Alice said,

"It's not really our place to explain. When were you meant to see her next?"

"I … we didn't have a schedule, exactly. The work's flexible. I just go there whenever I have the time and do what I can."

"So sometimes you're there without Rose?"

"Yes." Bethany plucked at something on her heavy cardigan. Just looking at it made Miriam feel hot, and she flapped the wide neck of her top.

"When did you plan to go over there again?" Alice asked.

"This week?" Bethany shot a look at Miriam, as if seeking a sign that it was the right answer. "Why are you asking all this?"

"We're merely trying to get to the bottom of things," Alice said. "You had a key to Rose's, I presume."

Bethany frowned. "Yes. Rose gave it to me. She said it was easier. Why are *you* trying to get to the bottom of things? What about the police? And what *things?*"

"But she didn't often lock the house."

"No. And I didn't either. I mean, I did once, but I accidentally locked Rose out."

"I remember that," Jasmine said. "I had to let her in with my spare. She was mostly worried that her ice cream was melting in the car."

Ice cream. Miriam closed her eyes, wondering if it was the same ice cream Rose had been looking for when she'd found the body. She opened her eyes again and examined the room warily. The day had those same dark shadows to its edges as it had two nights ago, when she'd walked into Rose's house to meet the freezer and its tragic cargo.

"Did you ever see anyone suspicious hanging around?" Alice asked.

Bethany shook her head. "No. Just that Cornish neighbour of hers. He's always coming around for something or other. He told me he had me on camera the first time I went there on my own. He said he was just looking out for Rose, but it was *so* rude." She looked up, colour in her cheeks. "As if I was breaking in!"

"He's such a fusspot," Jasmine said. "He thinks that just because Rose is older, someone has to keep an eye on things for her. *I* think he just likes sticking his nose in things." She sniffed. "I thought Cornish people were meant to be nice."

Miriam blew air over her top lip. "He shouted at me once for going to Rose's too early in the morning. He said it was unreasonable." She thought about it. "I was in Betsy, though. She does backfire sometimes."

"He may have had a point, then," Alice said, and looked back at Bethany. "So you definitely haven't seen her today?"

"No." Bethany chewed the inside of her cheek. "Why? Is she alright?"

"She's sort of missing," Jasmine said, and Alice shot her a sideways look. The younger woman pressed her lips together, then added, "Well, not missing, exactly, we just ... well, we're not sure where she is right now, so—"

"Missing?" Bethany demanded. "How can she be missing?"

"She may just be avoiding certain people," Alice said. "But we're a little worried, of course, given everything."

Bethany ran both hands over her face and into her hair. "But there was ... someone ... I mean, *something* happened at her house. Why wasn't she under police watch?"

The oily smell wasn't dissipating. It really was most unpleasant, and so was the conversation. Miriam's gaze drifted over the abstract weave of the tapestry as she tried to distract herself. The design was nice but too large for the space, rendering it a little claustrophobic, and she shifted her attention to the books packed into the shelves, a jumble of sci-fi and fantasy and tatty-eared classics all pushed in with faded cookbooks and out-of-date travel guides and the fat blue spines of old reference books. Framed pictures leaned against them here and there.

"I'm sure she will be fine," Alice was saying. "But the sooner we can find her, the better. Do you know anywhere else she might have gone?"

"How can you say she'll be *fine?* You don't even know where she is!"

"Well, panicking about it isn't going to help anyone," Alice said, then raised her hand, palm toward Bethany, as if telling her to stop. "I'm sorry. We're all a little on edge."

Miriam exchanged a glance with Jasmine, who had her fingers pressed to her lips. Bethany looked at the floor, then nodded. "Are you sure you don't want a cup of tea?"

"Yes, please," Miriam said, before Alice could say anything. "That would be very nice."

"Alright. Sit anywhere." Bethany headed through a door near the table, and Miriam heard the reassuring clatter of mugs being taken from a cupboard.

Alice frowned at her. "We don't have time, Miriam. The inspectors are right behind us."

"She isn't going to help us if she's upset," Miriam said. "I think she really cares for Rose."

"Campbell did say she was very protective of her," Jasmine said, as Bethany came back in with a packet of what proclaimed themselves to be nuts in protein powder.

"I don't have any biscuits," she said, offering the nuts to Miriam. "Sorry."

Miriam took one dubiously. "These look lovely."

"Sure." Bethany held the packet out to Alice and Jasmine. "Have you checked with Jean-Claude?"

"Him *and* Campbell," Jasmine said. "Nothing."

Bethany stared at Jasmine, and the little colour that had come to her cheeks vanished again. "Nothing at all?"

"The only thing Campbell said was that you were with him and Rose at a lecture on Friday night," Alice said. "What did you do after that?"

"I went home," Bethany said, taking a nut and popping it in her mouth. Miriam was still holding hers, and she examined it doubtfully. It certainly wasn't a custard cream.

"Did you enjoy the lecture?" Alice asked.

"Oh, yes. It was very good." Bethany popped another nut in her mouth, although she was still chewing the first one.

Miriam looked at Alice, waiting for her to say something, but it was Jasmine who yelped, "You're *lying!* Campbell said you hated it!"

Bethany stared at her, taking two nuts this time. "So?" she said, somewhat indistinctly. "It was just a lecture!"

"You know he was the victim! That's why you're lying! How do you know he was the victim?" Jasmine pointed a shaking finger at her.

"I *don't!* And it doesn't mean anything, anyway. I'm not a murderer!"

"How do you know there was a murder?" Jasmine demanded.

"You *said!* You said *victim!*" Bethany was almost shouting, Jasmine matching her volume, and Alice raised her hands.

"Ladies, enough—"

"No! No, Miriam said Bethany was *at Rose's house* the night she found the body, and we know she was at the lecture the night of the murder, and now Rose is *gone.* She did it! She must have!"

"How can *I* be a murderer? And you think I put him in the freezer? I'm no bigger than you!"

"I never said he was in the freezer! How did you know that?"

They stared at each other for a moment, and as Alice started to say something else Miriam dropped her protein-coated nut, pivoting on her heel to stare at the bookshelf. She grabbed one of the framed photos up and held it out to the room.

"You put him there," she said, and Bethany bolted for the door.

Afterward, Miriam would have said that she was the least likely person to tackle a murderer, especially not one capable of lifting a much larger man into a chest freezer. She would have said the same if anyone had asked her that question *before* Bethany rushed past her on her way to the door, too. At the time, however, all she did was launch herself after the younger woman. There was very little thought involved.

They crashed to the ground together, Bethany wailing in fright and Miriam trying to trap her arms down. They were frightfully strong arms under the weight of the heavy cardigan, and the young woman's legs were no less terrifying. The disproportionate, muscular power of her reminded Miriam of trying to contain a furious cat. But Bethany *was* smaller than her, so she just concentrated on not being thrown off.

"Get *off!*" Bethany yelped, twisting furiously in Miriam's grip. "Let me *go!* I haven't done anything!"

Miriam had no intention of letting go. Holding onto the younger woman was feeling more like grappling with a cat than ever, and if she let go she imagined she'd have as much chance of catching her again as she would a cat, as well.

"Why are you running, if you've not done anything?" Jasmine shouted. "We need some rope! Alice, we need rope!"

"Nonsense. We're not tying her up. And it's not as if I carry rope around with me everywhere, anyway. That's just silly."

Miriam's hair was hanging over her eyes and she could feel a terrible hot flush coming on. "Help! I can't hold her!"

"I'm not *doing* anything," Bethany said. "I'm not going to fight a bunch of old ladies."

Miriam blinked, and realised that Bethany had stopped moving. She stayed where she was, though, in case it was a trap.

Jasmine huffed. "I'm *barely* older than you!"

Bethany craned her head around and gave Jasmine a doubtful look.

"No more than ten years. Or maybe fifteen. But you *were* running! Miriam was quite right to jump on you."

"Can you get off?" Bethany asked. "Your elbow is in my ribs."

"Sorry," Miriam said. "Are you going to run again, though?"

Bethany sighed. "No. I don't have anywhere to go, anyway. I just panicked."

"So you should," Jasmine said.

"Jasmine, can you go and finish the tea, please?" Alice asked, holding a hand out to Miriam.

"Are you sure? What if you need help?"

"Miriam seems to have the situation in hand admirably."

Miriam rolled off Bethany and let Alice help her up, thinking that was overstating the situation somewhat. She brushed herself off and stood in front of the door, just in case, and Bethany flopped onto her back, looking up at the ceiling.

"Do you have something to tell us?" Alice asked, and Bethany closed her eyes. Tears were welling at the corners, and as Miriam watched they slid down the smooth skin of her cheeks, into her dark hair. Alice looked at Miriam, eyebrows raised, and Miriam went to the bookshelves, coming back with the framed photo in hand. She handed it to Alice.

It showed Bethany in small pink shorts and a black vest top emblazoned in silver with *Lethal Lass*. Her hair curled wildly down her back and about her broad shoulders, and her face shone with triumphant sweat. Her arms were raised, the muscles looking as if they were carved from pale wood, and she clasped a fat black belt with a gleaming circular buckle above her head. Her smile was luminous, matching the cheering crowd that flanked the wrestling ring.

"I see," Alice said, and Bethany covered her face with one trembling hand.

"Do you want another nut?" Miriam asked, offering the packet to Bethany. She was seated on the sofa, her shoulders hunched forward and a mug of tea clutched in her hands.

"No," she said. "I want some of Rose's shortbread." Her voice hitched on the last word, and Miriam patted her knee.

"We'll find her," she said.

"Unless Bethany's already done away with her," Jasmine said. She was hovering by the door with her arms folded over her chest.

"I *wouldn't,*" Bethany whispered. "I'd never hurt Rose."

"So what happened, dear?" Alice asked. Miriam hadn't missed the fact that she kept checking her watch. She wondered if the inspectors would arrest them at the same time as Bethany, or later. Later, she hoped. She had some salmon in the fridge that was going to spoil.

Bethany sighed. "Alright. I couldn't keep this a secret much longer anyway – I only wanted to talk to Rose before I went to the police. The whole thing's been *awful.*"

"Did you put the body in the freezer?" Alice asked.

Bethany nodded, not looking up.

"But you didn't kill him."

"Of course not!" She did look up then. "I thought he was silly, and I thought Rose was far too good a scientist to be involved in all that cryptozoology nonsense, but I wouldn't *kill* someone over it."

"What happened, then?" Miriam asked, helping herself to a nut finally. It tasted just as bad as she'd imagined it might.

Bethany rubbed her face. "I went home and straight to bed after the lecture, but I woke up at about one and realised I'd left some papers I needed at Rose's. I almost didn't bother, because it was so late, and I had a match on Saturday." She nodded at the photo, lying on the coffee table. "But I knew I wasn't going to sleep again until I had them. I'm just like that. And it – he – was just *there.* On the kitchen floor. Rose wasn't home, and I tried to call her, but she didn't answer. I figured she was staying with Campbell. And I didn't want to just *leave* it there. Imagine coming home to that! I ... the freezer seemed logical, you know?"

Miriam tried to follow that train of thinking and couldn't.

"Why didn't you call the police straight away?" Alice asked.

Bethany licked her lips. "I wasn't sure ... I wanted to see Rose. In case she ... she might have already known about it."

"You can't think she *did it,*" Jasmine said, scowling.

"No. I mean, not deliberately. But she's been ... she's old, you know? And there were always strange things going on in the house, like I'd find tuna sandwiches in the printer tray or potting mix in the fridge. Once I even found a towel left over one of those old electric heaters, and Rose swears she never uses the thing." She shook her head. "I wanted to ask her what to do, but she didn't answer her phone, so I just ..." She raised her hands and let them drop. "I didn't want her to find the body and get scared, and I didn't want to call the police until I knew what had happened. If she had ... you know."

Alice nodded slowly, then said, "Misplaced potting mix and sandwiches don't sound quite the same as a body, Bethany."

"I know. But things escalate, don't they? I know it seems silly now, but I had to check. I went back as soon as I could, but then you were there." She shifted slightly, glancing at Miriam. "And I couldn't exactly say it in front of you." She wiped her face with the sleeve of her cardigan and snuffled. "I panicked, I suppose. And then the next day there were police everywhere, and I knew I was too late, and I just wanted to talk to Rose, but ..." She took a harsh, ragged breath and fell silent, wiping her face again.

No one spoke for a moment, then Alice said, "Well. Did you ever see anyone else around the house? Anyone who shouldn't be there?"

Bethany shook her head. "Just people she knew. Friends.

Colleagues. Her stepdaughter came around sometimes, but Rose used to hide in the garden. She'd make me say she was giving lectures in the Outer Hebrides or something. Although it was Scunthorpe on Monday, for some reason." The corner of her mouth twitched up.

"Were there ever people in the house alone? Without Rose being there?"

"I don't really know. Why?"

Alice tapped her fingers off her chin and said, "It's probably not important. Anything at all you can think of?"

Bethany shook her head. "Not really. But I want to help. What can I do?"

"We have this in hand," Alice said, setting her mug down firmly. "The best thing for you is to stay put in case Rose decides to come here, and if she does, contact us immediately."

"Not the police?" Bethany asked, and Miriam snorted. Everyone turned to look at her, and she felt her cheeks flush.

"Incense smoke," she explained. "I think I still feel a little carsick."

Alice raised one perfectly shaped eyebrow, the corner of her mouth twitching up, then turned back to Bethany. "We're in contact with the detectives in charge of the case, so just call me. Do you have a pen? I'll give you my number."

Bethany looked uncertainly between the three women, then went to her desk and dug out a notepad and a pen. "If you think it's best for Rose. I'd still like to help, though."

"This is the best way to help," Alice said firmly, and took the pen to write her number down.

"What about Rose's phone?" Jasmine asked. She still hadn't sat down. "Do you know how to unlock it?"

"Yes. It's ACGT." Everyone looked at Bethany blankly, and she added, "The four bases of DNA. Two-two-four-eight on the keypad."

"Of course it is," Alice said, smiling, and wrote that down on the paper, too, tearing it in half to give Bethany the piece with her number on it. "Do call if you think of anything."

"Alright." Bethany was back to burying her hands in her cardigan, her mouth twisted. "The police don't actually think Rose did it, do they?"

"Of course not," Miriam said.

Alice made a thoughtful noise. "Only if they suspect her of having an accomplice, I think."

"Right." Bethany hesitated, not looking up. "Do they think she might have had one? An accomplice, I mean?"

"I don't believe so," Alice said. "But it's early days at the moment. I suppose everyone's a suspect until they can narrow it down." She regarded the younger woman for a moment, then added, "You may feel better if you do tell the police, you know."

"I know. I was going to. But then when I didn't go right away, well, that looks bad, doesn't it?"

"Not as bad as not going at all."

Bethany pressed a hand to her mouth as if she were going to be sick, and didn't answer.

Alice got up. "Well. I suppose we'll be off. Thank you, Bethany."

Bethany gave a one-shouldered shrug. "Sure."

Jasmine led the way out, and Miriam lingered for a moment, wanting to reassure the young woman that everything was going to be okay, that Rose was *Rose,* a firm embracer of eccentricity and the beauty of being entirely oneself, but not a *murderer*. But she couldn't seem to. The undercurrent of oiliness in the room mingled with a niggling, cloying doubt, making her feel more nauseous than the car trip had.

Rose had gone home alone the night of the murder.

Rose had been unsettled and jumpy, worried about the way things kept *moving*.

Bethany had found the body that night, and Rose *hadn't* been home.

Rose had waited all day to tell Miriam about it.

She'd waited *all day*.

Miriam followed Alice and Jasmine down the stairs, her hand pressed against her chest as she tried to soothe something that might have been heartburn or indigestion, or even the endless irritations of age, but which she thought was something else. Something full of fright and love and concern.

"Are you alright, Miriam?" Alice asked, one hand on the door to the street.

"Not really," she said.

"No," Alice said, and waited for her so that she could take Miriam's hand and squeeze it. "Me either."

Miriam wasn't sure if that made things better or worse.

17
DI ADAMS

DI Adams stepped out into the long, echoing expanse of the school hallway to answer her phone. The display said *Lucas, Skipton.*

"Lucas? What've you got?"

"Hello to you, too, DI Adams. How's your day going?"

"Delightfully. Our possible intended vic-slash-suspect has done a runner, and no one bothered to tell us."

"That seems very careless, losing your intended vic-slash-suspect. I'd've expected more from an experienced London copper such as yourself."

"I'm sorry to disappoint," she said, and wondered if she'd ever had to have such pointless exchanges with any of the crime techs back in London. She didn't think so, but then she'd never been in charge of cases, and the entire tech department hadn't been made up of one full-time officer and a handful of others who seemed to come and go as they pleased. Everything was different since London. There were dragons, for a start. And the W.I. She shuddered. "Do you have anything for me?"

"Yes, as it happens. And I'm doing double duty, as PC McLeod also has something for you, but he asked that as I was calling anyway, if I could possibly pass it on."

"That seems reasonable."

"He was almost unseemingly pleased that he didn't have to make the call. Unseemly-ly? Un—"

"Lucas."

"Is unseemingly a word?"

"I have no idea, but I've just stepped out of an interview for this, so could you tell me what you and PC McLeod have come up with?"

"You need to work on the fine art of small talk, you know."

"I'll put it on my list, right under *be less terrifying to PC McLeod* and above *learn to love pork pies.*"

Lucas snorted. "Fair enough. Look, we found the vic's car – that's McLeod's info – and—"

"Where was it?"

"I'm getting there, Adams. I thought you'd be more interested to know that we found a few short hairs on the driver's seat that almost certainly aren't the vic's. On first glance they look like a match to some we found at the scene. Can't be sure until I've run some tests, obviously, but colour, texture and length look the same."

"What colour?"

"Pink," Lucas said. "Very, very pink, but the roots are white."

DI Adams tried to ignore a twist in her belly that she couldn't put down to too much coffee. Rose's hair was currently violet. But so freshly so that she'd taken her own pillow to Miriam's. "I certainly never saw any pink hair on the vic."

"He had some white roots, but the rest was dyed blond. Any of the Gateau Gang up there have short pink hair?"

"The Gateau Gang?"

"I was thinking of the Posset Posse, but does anyone really eat posset anymore?"

"I'm not even sure I know what posset *is.*"

"And here I thought you brought with you the cosmopolitan knowledge of the big city cop."

"I'm not sure posset is really classed as cosmopolitan."

"Probably not," Lucas agreed. "Well done, Adams. That was an excellent foray into small talk."

She snorted. "Do you have anything else for me other than more dubious nicknames?"

"Not yet. The car's going to take time to process fully, but thought I'd let you know about the hair, in case you encounter any shedding suspects. Also, we found it in Leeds. Keys still in the ignition, no fuel in the tank. Looked like someone had been joyriding it, so the evidence is going to be a right mess, and the hair could be from whoever nicked it. But I'm running comparisons now against the one from the scene."

"Alright. Anything else?"

"The blow to the head was from the side, with deeper impact toward the face. In other words, the attacker was in front of our vic, but either he was side-on or had his head turned away at the time of the blow. The attacker was also a similar height to the vic, judging by the angle."

"What height are we talking?"

"Around 170 centimetres."

"And the blow killed him?"

"No, the fall did. The blow would've knocked him out or mostly insensible, and when he fell he landed in such a way that his neck broke. Probably hit the worktop or the kitchen table on the way down. The kitchen was pretty well cleaned up – we've not discovered much trace other than on the floor."

"Right." DI Adams rubbed the back of her neck and watched Dandy emerging from a closed door further down the hall, chewing on something. She hoped it wasn't anyone's lunch. "So

Rose is definitely clear on that. She can't be more than 150 centimetres."

"Unless he was bending over. It's possible."

"Any idea on the weapon?"

"Not so far. No debris in the wound, and it was blunt force. Something strong and clean – a golf club, a crowbar – something like that. I'll let you know if I come up with anything else, and once I've had a better look at those hairs."

"Thanks. Did you get anything off those video files from the neighbour?"

Lucas *hmm*ed. "Not so far. Jules was looking at them. I'll check."

"Alright. Cheers, Lucas."

"Sure. Watch out for the Mince Pie Mob."

"I think Gateau Gang has a better ring to it."

"You're probably right. I'll keep working on it."

DI Adams tucked her phone back in her jacket pocket and rubbed Dandy's ears as he leaned against her leg. Campbell was taller than 170 cm, but not so much that he was outside the margin of error. Jean-Claude was around the right height. So they remained firmly in the possible suspects pool, as far as she was concerned, even if neither of them exactly screamed guilty. They'd both do anything for Rose, that was clear. Whether that extended to helping her stash a body in a freezer, or offing someone they considered competition, remained to be seen. As far as the hair went, it might be relevant or it might not – they could belong to the joyrider, or they could simply be transferred from Rose's house, if the killer had been less than careful.

Or they could be from Rose herself.

"What do you think?" she asked Dandy. "Can you tell who it is? Go point your nose at someone guilty."

Dandy flopped onto his back, offering her his belly, and she stooped to rub it just as two boys in their teens came around the corner. She immediately pretended to be inspecting her boot, while Dandy caught her hand in his teeth delicately and tugged, almost pulling her off balance. One of the boys snickered as they went past, and she barely resisted the urge to ask them why they weren't in class. It was a college, not a school. The boys were probably older than they looked.

The office door opened as she retrieved her hand from a disappointed Dandy.

"I'm finished here," DI Collins said, looking at her curiously. "Do you have any more questions for Mr Jones?"

She could see the teacher behind him, worrying at his thinning hair with one hand. "Did you get anything else?"

"Not really. He hasn't seen anything unusual, they were at a lecture given by the deceased the evening before he died, and Rose went home alone late that night."

"So Rose had seen our vic rather more recently than January, then." DI Adams scratched her jaw, trying to ignore the unhappy twist in her belly. "Can anyone vouch for the fact that Campbell didn't accompany her home?"

"No – no alibi until the following morning, when he got to school."

DI Adams looked around Collins' bulk, examining Campbell. He was scratching his arm, his shoulders hunched and his chin sticking out, making him look much more like Rose's contemporary than her toy boy. "Right, well. Lucas had a bit of new info – we should get a move on, although doubtless the Gateau Gang have already beaten us to the assistant's house."

"The who?" Collins asked.

"Never mind." She raised her voice as Collins joined her in the hall. "Mr Jones, please keep us updated if you hear from Rose, okay?"

"Of course." He waved DI Adams' card at her. "Right away. But she can't call – she doesn't have her phone, you know? Her friends have it."

"So we've gathered," DI Adams said.

Campbell blinked, his eyes watering behind his glasses. "They wanted the code for it."

"And did you give it to them?"

"I don't know it. I just told them Bethany's address."

"How helpful of you."

He blinked harder. "Shouldn't I have done that? They were looking for Rose, so I thought I was helping, but they wouldn't let me go with them, which is really unfair—"

"Sensible," DI Adams said. "It's really *sensible,* because otherwise you'd be interfering in a police investigation, wouldn't you?"

"Would I?" He sounded equal parts intrigued and horrified, like a child considering the delights of rule-breaking, and for the first time DI Adams realised what Rose might actually like about him.

"You would."

"Well, I wouldn't want *that.*"

DI Adams squinted at him. "No, you wouldn't, Mr Jones." She nudged Dandy with her knee, trying to suggest he go in and have a sniff around the teacher's office, like a good canine sidekick should. He just panted at her, his dark tongue lolling out of his mouth and a little drool splatting on her boots. She swallowed a sigh, and examined Campbell, who had stopped scratching his arms and was staring into space. "Can you think of anything else that might help us?"

"*Mmm?* Oh. No, nothing."

DI Adams looked at Collins, who shrugged, and said, "We'll be in touch, Mr Jones."

He refocused on them, and nodded. "Of course. Thank you. Good luck?"

"Right. Thanks," Collins said, and pulled the door shut behind him. He raised his eyebrows at her as they headed back down the hall. "Good luck?"

"Bit weird, that."

"Well, we've got the whole W.I. interfering in police business. What's one more science teacher?"

She sighed, pinching the bridge of her nose. "I can't believe they're ahead of us on this. We should have sent a unit to the assistant's address to head them off. Who knows what they've stirred up there."

"Well, they *wouldn't* be ahead of us if Alice hadn't told you last night that Rose was still married to Jean-Claude, and that he might still be in her will. We'd have started with the boyfriend if we hadn't known that."

DI Adams dropped her hand, staring at him. "That—" She couldn't think of a word that quite expressed her feelings regarding Alice, so she just growled and shoved her hands in her pockets.

Collins grinned. "Don't be too miffed, Adams. She's got a good couple of decades practice on you when it comes to being sneaky."

"I'm not miffed, I'm … I'm in need of coffee, is what I am. A large one."

"That we can probably manage. Off to talk to the assistant, then?"

"Yes. And quick about it, too. They'll be there already, causing the usual carnage. I'd quite like to get there in time to arrest them for interfering in a police investigation."

"Haven't you already tried that once?"

"It got Alice to talk."

"It got a dragon claw stuck in your DC's tyre, if I recall the story correctly," Collins said, giving his visitor pass to the receptionist with a smile. "Thanks very much. Have a good afternoon."

"You too," the receptionist said, and smiled at them both. DI Adams tried to return the smile, but it evidently didn't work too well, since he flinched back. She slapped her pass on the desk and stalked toward the doors as her phone rang again.

She pulled it out of her pocket, frowned, and waited until she was outside to answer. The display read, *PS Harrison, Graham?*

She hit answer. "PS Harrison?"

Collins glanced at her, eyebrows raised. She shrugged, although unease twisted in her belly.

"Graham." Ah, so it *was* Graham.

"Sorry, Graham. Still getting used to the first name thing."

"Just because you refuse to use yours." He sounded momentarily amused, but his tone changed as he said, "Someone's been into the crime scene."

"What? Who?" Although she had a fairly good suspicion. It couldn't be Alice and Miriam, but that still left eight members of the W.I. unaccounted for. Plus dragons. "And aren't you watching Miriam— Ms Ellis' house?"

"I am. PC Ben Shaw called me. He's on duty at Professor Howard's house, and he reckons he's rumbled someone either trying to get into the house, or they've already been in it."

DI Adams said something that the W.I. wouldn't have approved of. "Are you there now?"

"No, that's why I'm calling. He wanted backup, and I'm the only other person handy. I've just knocked on the door at Ms Ellis', but there's no reply. I haven't seen her since this morning, and I've seen no sign at all of Professor Howard."

"It's fine. Professor Howard isn't there. She's missing. We just found out." DI Adams opened the car door as Collins beeped the unlock. "Has Ben found anything at the crime scene?"

"Nowt. That damn garden is so thick, though, that you can't search it on your own effectively. But Ben says he heard multiple voices, and the door to the house was unlocked."

"Dammit." She rubbed her forehead. "He didn't leave it unlocked? I asked him to look for some evidence for me."

"He was on his way to start when he heard voices."

"Right." It could be Rose sneaking back, or the W.I. up to something. Or anyone else, judging by how many keys Rose seemed to have given out.

"Am I good to head over there, then?" Graham asked. "Seems pointless me waiting at Ms Ellis' now."

"Yeah, do that. There should be a team on the way out to look for Professor Howard, so they'll be in the area. We'll follow as soon as we can. Sit tight, and call if anything else happens."

"Will do." The phone went dead and she shoved it into her pocket.

"Change of plan?" Collins asked, as he started the car.

DI Adams considered it. "I don't think so. We're still a good hour away from Toot Hansell anyway. And we need to check out the assistant. The odds are it's just the bloody W.I. again."

"It's amazing how quickly that's become merely a hazard of the job."

"Horrifying. It's *horrifying.*"

"That's a little harsh," Collins said, swinging them out of the car park and onto the road. "They have proved themselves quite handy."

"That's entirely beside the point. They're not meant to be *handy*. They're meant to be having bake sales and making jam. Not being *handy* in police investigations."

He gave her an amused look. "Shall we go and stop them, then?"

She sighed. "No. Let's go and find out if the assistant knows anything, preferably *before* the mobile faction of the W.I. sends her on the run along with Rose."

"I doubt they sent Rose on the run. They're more likely to be hiding her."

DI Adams stared at him. "But they're … oh, *bloody hell.* You think they've got her stashed somewhere and are using it as a ruse to give them carte blanche to poke around in our investigation?"

Collins gave her an amused look, then accelerated to overtake a lorry. "Doesn't it seem rather more likely than Rose running *away* from the W.I.?"

DI Adams fell back in her seat, looking up at the roof of the car. Sometimes London, even with its bridges (and the things that happened under those bridges), seemed quite logical and inviting and even *sensible* when one compared it to small town policing in Yorkshire. Well, the policing of one small town, anyway. "Can I drive?" she asked. "We need to get there *now.*"

"No, you can't drive. You *always* drive, and it's my car besides." He flicked the lights on, giving the siren a polite little blip as the stolid green Citroen ahead stuck firmly to the centre of the lane. "I can drive fast too, you know."

"Well, get on with it, then."

DI ADAMS SUPPOSED that Collins could drive at a decent pace when he wanted, and it wasn't long before the city had fallen far enough behind them that the country was starting to take on rough, untamed edges, the shoulders of the hills hulking higher as they hinted at wider spaces beyond. They took the tree-lined back roads into Skipton, past the grey stone of bigger houses watching them severely over stone walls, and wound their way into the tighter coils of buildings toward the centre of town and the assistant's address. They were scooting past the rows of parked cars, looking for a space, when Collins said, "Is that Alice's car?"

DI Adams leaned forward, following his pointing finger. "I think so. Right model, anyway."

"Still here, then."

"Oh, wonderful. Just what we need. Let's get in there."

"I am, I am." He pulled them into the loading bay in front of the newsagent's and stuck his pass in the window.

DI Adams swung out of the car, checking the street each way. It was quiet, only a few shoppers hurrying past, hunched inside their coats. The newsagent's had tall, wheeled racks of bedding plants lined up outside, mostly pansies splashing their colour about the place, and there was a black and white cat sitting on top of one of the racks, its eyes narrowed as it watched Dandy sniffing his way along the pavement. She frowned at it, wondering if it was a Thompson sort of cat, observing and sneaking and taking tales back to mysterious councils, or if it were just an everyday sort of observant, sneaky cat. It yawned, displaying a wide pink mouth and sharp white teeth, then turned its flat green gaze on her, and winked. She winked back, without thinking – it had become a habit since meeting Thompson, in case that wink was fraught with meaning and it was dangerous to ignore it. The cat regarded her for a moment, then got up and stretched, revealing the dull gleam of a brass-toned bell on its collar.

"Dandy chatting to the neighbourhood contacts?" Collins asked, joining her, and she glanced at him, then looked for the cat again. It had vanished.

"He doesn't seem too interested."

"Different divisions, I suppose. Cats and invisible dogs. Never the twain shall meet and all that."

DI Adams sighed. "Let's go and see if the assistant's survived a vigorous questioning by the W.I."

"The horror," Collins said, with a theatrical shudder. "It probably involves cake forks and tea strainers used in an ingenious manner."

DI Adams rang the bell for the flat above the shops. "I do worry about your imagination at times, Collins."

He rocked back on his heels, looking at the window above them. "But who's to say I'm wrong?"

"That worries me, too," DI Adams said, and raised her hand to try the bell again. There was a scuffle behind the door before she could. "Hello?"

The door opened without warning, and she stepped back quickly, but it only revealed Alice, her cardigan neatly buttoned and a small, polite smile curving her lips. Miriam and Jasmine hovered behind her, looking distinctly less comfortable.

"Hello, Inspectors," Alice said. "You were quick."

"I didn't realise you were timing us," DI Adams said. "Although sending us off chasing Jean-Claude must have given you plenty of space for interfering."

"I don't know what you mean, Inspector. He seemed a very viable suspect to me."

"So why are you here instead of there?"

"We're looking for Rose. As you were there when we spoke to Jean-Claude, it was a natural assumption that if he knew about Rose, you would have got that information from him." Alice gave DI Adams a look that made the inspector feel that she'd somehow failed in not doing so.

She folded her arms. "Really. So you're running around Yorkshire talking to *suspects*, when the most logical place to find Rose would be in a W.I. house, which is probably more secure than witness protection?"

Alice raised her eyebrows. "She ran away, Inspector. We've all been looking for her, and we have no idea where she went. We're desperately worried, as it happens. We had hoped she'd called someone to pick her up, but we seem to have run out of candidates for that."

"No relatives?" Collins asked, frowning at the women. "Friends that aren't suspects?"

"None that occurred to us immediately."

"Of course not," DI Adams said.

"She might be in danger," Jasmine said. "The murderer could be after her!"

Collins sighed. "You should have called us. Not gone off mounting search parties on your own."

"We thought we might have better luck than the police, considering Rose fears you may doubt her innocence." There was that reproving tone again, and DI Adams felt absurdly as if she needed to show her workings to prove she was behaving reasonably.

"And has that got you anywhere?" she asked aloud.

"Not with Rose, as it happens. Regarding the poor man in the freezer, however ... well, Miriam made the breakthrough on that." Alice stepped onto the street, smiling at Miriam, who looked as if she wanted to flee back up the stairs.

"What's this?" DI Adams asked, and Miriam took a step back, both shaking her head and waving her hands in a very clear *don't ask me.*

"Aunty Miriam?" Collins asked, his voice gentle. "Are you alright?"

"Not really," she managed, still not emerging from the stairwell. Jasmine had come out to join Alice, tugging her coat more firmly around her and frowning at DI Adams. Wonderful. That was all she needed. Alice version two.

Collins fumbled in his jacket pocket and found a small, square tin. "Mint?" he suggested, shaking it at Miriam.

Miriam peered out of the door, as if afraid someone was waiting to grab her, and DI Adams checked for the cat. It hadn't reappeared, and she couldn't decide if that made her feel more relieved or unsettled. It wasn't as though this was Folk business. She looked for Dandy, and spotted him sampling a tray of pansies. She sighed, and turned back in time to see Miriam accept a mint from Collins.

"So, what's this about breakthroughs?" Collins asked, offering the tin around. Jasmine took one, but Alice shook her head.

"It wasn't really a *breakthrough,*" Miriam said. "I just saw a photo."

"And then she tackled Bethany," Jasmine said around her mint. "It was quite impressive."

"As in a literal tackle?" DI Adams asked. "Not figurative?"

"Oh, quite literal," Alice said. "Bethany was running for the door at the time."

DI Adams swallowed the urge to use unsuitable language and just said, "Why?"

"She's a wrestler," Miriam said, as if that explained everything.

After a pause, DI Adams said, "I hope you had more to go on than that when you tackled her."

"She was *running,*" Jasmine said, and DI Adams looked at Collins. He was rocking on his heels as he sucked thoughtfully on his mint and gazed up at the windows above them.

She took a deep breath. "Was she perhaps running because three women had come into her house acting like Neighbourhood Watch extremists?"

"She's a *wrestler,*" Miriam almost whispered, and Alice patted her on the arm.

"She confessed, inspector," she said, and Collins choked on his mint. DI Adams pounded him absently on the back, trying to rearrange her face into something that wasn't outright disbelief.

"She confessed to the murder?"

"No. Just to putting the body in the freezer. I'm sure she'll tell you all about it. Apparently she was only waiting to talk to Rose before she went to the police."

"Because that's exactly the right order in which to do things."

"Adams, stop," Collins said. "I'm more in danger of a bruised lung than choking at this point."

"Sorry." She dropped her hand, started to say something, then just stared at Alice. Alice returned her gaze, her eyes level, but there was an unfamiliar tightness in her jaw, and lines pulled into the soft skin of her cheeks. "Go home," DI Adams said. She didn't even bother threatening to arrest them. It was obvious that never worked. "If you actually know where Rose is, just stay with her and look after her, and get her to call me and tell me she's safe. I'm not even asking about that at this point. But *stay out* of this investigation. This is too much now."

"It is," Collins said. "I'll be looking into rest homes myself if this keeps up."

"Of course," Alice said. "We shall go home directly. One mustn't get in the way of the police in their duties."

"Of course," DI Adams said, looking at Collins with her eyebrows raised.

"Of course," he agreed gravely, crossing his arms over his broad chest.

They watched the three women head to the car, having a moment of argument over who should go in the front passenger seat, and waited until they pulled away, heading serenely down the road.

"What do you think?" DI Adams asked.

"If they're hiding Rose, they're covering it well."

"That's what I'm afraid of, too."

"Call McLeod and tell him to get another team out to Toot Hansell. We need more feet on the ground."

"Can't you?"

Collins grunted and took his phone out. "I'm doing this for him, not you. I can't be having a constable quitting over a terrifying inspector."

"I'm not terrifying," she said, heading up the stairs.

"You are somewhat unsettling, though. I think it's the invisible dog that does it."

DI Adams looked at Dandy, climbing the stairs next to her. He had a pansy stuck between his teeth. "I see what you mean."

18
MORTIMER

Mortimer stared at Angelus, and wondered where, exactly, he'd gone wrong. Surely he must have done something wrong, at some point, if his life now involved trying to rescue monstrous dogs who didn't want to be rescued.

"Good boy," Gilbert said. "Sit." He clapped his paws encouragingly, and Angelus howled.

"Gods," Mortimer muttered. "Why's he so *loud?*"

"He's upset," Gilbert said. "We have to be nice to him. He's lost Rose."

Mortimer thought that *he* was also upset, and wished someone would be nice to *him*. But until they could be reunited with the W.I., he supposed he was stuck herding dogs. He sighed.

It hadn't taken them long to track down Angelus. The big dog had been howling so mournfully that they had heard him almost as soon as they got into the woods. They had followed the sound through the mossy trunks of old trees, around bluebells and foxgloves and the pungent, crushed leaves of wild garlic, and found him half-crouched in the shelter of an old tree that had fallen to form a clearing in the leafy canopy above. Its trunk was heavy and broad, and one of its stubby, shattered branches had slid neatly under Angelus' collar, holding the dog in place.

"Good boy," Gilbert said again, and started forward to free him. Angelus' howls turned into panicked yelps that were quickly strangled as he twisted and flailed, eyes rolling as he tried to free himself.

"Gil, no!" Mortimer exclaimed. "Come back."

The younger dragon backed up, and the dog settled a little, panting harshly.

"He's hurting himself," Gilbert said. "We have to get him free."

"We can't. If we go near him he's just going to struggle more. He'll strangle himself."

Angelus whined, and wriggled against the collar, trying to back out of it, but it fitted too well, and the branch was too strong to break.

"We have to get help," Gilbert said. "*Human* help."

Mortimer found himself briefly agreeing with Walter's thoughts on dogs, then said, "Alright. Miriam may be home by now, and if not we'll try one of the other ladies."

"Should I stay?" Gilbert asked. "In case Walter comes back?"

Mortimer considered it, then nodded, although he wasn't sure Gilbert would be able to stop the old dragon on his own if he really had his mind set on dog for dinner. But Gilbert probably stood a better chance than Mortimer did, so he just said, "Good idea. I'll be back as quick as I can." He turned and hurried in the direction of the village, following his own quiet internal compass that swung with the magic of the world, Toot Hansell burning bright as a harbour marker on a stormy night as he ran.

It didn't take him long to reach Miriam's, and he paused on the edge of the woods for a moment, looking for movement in the garden. It was hard to tell if anyone was there among the riot of spring growth, and in the end he just scuttled across the footbridge and over the little gate, curling himself into the shelter of the nearest rose bush as soon as he was inside the fence. Still no movement, and in the shifting, travelling scents of the wind he couldn't pick up any markers other than the steady, deep earth comfort of Miriam's house. He repeated a few of Walter's dog-related curses, then crept up the path toward the house, hoping someone was home. Surely they couldn't *still* be out?

He made it to the flowerbed under the kitchen window, listened carefully, then raised himself onto his hindquarters with his taloned paws against the wall and peered inside, hoping to spot Miriam. He caught a flash of movement, and raised one paw in greeting before the colours registered. Black and faded jeans, hurrying toward the door. He froze, his scales clattering with sudden fright. It wasn't Miriam. Miriam wore a myriad of luminous colours, as bright and varied as Gilbert's talons, but she almost never wore jeans. And she *certainly* didn't wear black.

He dropped back to the ground, gathering himself to flee, and the door flew open. A woman charged out, a video camera in one hand and her gaze sharp as she jumped the step to the ground. She came to a staggering halt, staring at Mortimer, and the man following almost crashed into her.

"*There* you are," she breathed, and Mortimer stared back at her, eyes wide and panic-stricken, and all he could think was that Walter had been right about more than dogs.

MORTIMER COULDN'T SEEM to move, and he didn't even know if he should. The woman – Katherine the Terrifying – was still staring at him, but she kept rubbing her eyes and blinking furiously.

"Damn, it's hard to focus on it," she said, and her companion leaned over her shoulder.

"It's … a lizard?" he offered doubtfully.

"No, it's got … look, there's wings," Katherine said, pointing vaguely. She sounded unsure, and Mortimer held his position, hunched up and on the verge of leaping away. He wasn't even breathing, and his chest was starting to hurt. He felt very much like a lizard, as it happened. One hoping for a moment's inattentiveness from a crow.

"Is it alive?" the man asked. "It's not moving."

It. This was awful. This was worse than he could've imagined, and all because of that silly, panicked dog! If only he hadn't agreed to help Gilbert track him. If only Walter hadn't been trying to eat the horrible thing. And Angelus wasn't a *puppy*, or some silly creature like Primrose. He could probably have fended for himself just fine, but no. Mortimer had had to get involved, and now here he was, stuck in a flowerbed with two humans staring at him.

And if they stared long enough, they were going to see him. *Really* see him, and then not even Thompson would be able to fix this with his *suggestions* that made humans think they'd seen nothing stranger than an escaped iguana. The next thing, the Watch would be involved, and their methods of fixing things were rather more final for humans, and more problematic for dragons who wanted to spend time with humans. And that was if The Government didn't get hold of them first. Mortimer still wasn't entirely sure what The Government might want with dragons, but he'd watched enough movies on Miriam's TV to know they couldn't be trusted.

"Can we catch it?" the man asked.

"Try and get some photos," Katherine said, handing him her camera without looking away from Mortimer. "I'll keep an eye on it. We might not see it again if we lose sight of it."

Mortimer had the brief, uncharitable thought that he should have let Walter carry on with his dragon hunter crusade undisturbed.

"Right." The man took the camera, and in the bird-filled half-silence Mortimer heard the beep and click of his image being captured, evidence of dragons being burned into the world. He wanted to close his eyes, to look away from the horror of it all, but he stayed still. He wasn't sure why. It wasn't helping anything.

"Huh," the man said.

"What?"

He leaned over, holding the camera screen toward Katherine. "It's not showing up."

She didn't take her eyes off Mortimer. "Try again."

There was the snap of the camera shutter a few more times, then the man said, "No. Just the same. It doesn't show up."

"Try the video."

The man lifted his video camera, and Mortimer heard the whirr of the lens. Then the man shook his head. "No."

"What— Bloody hell, just give it here, alright?" She reached for the camera, finally looking away from Mortimer, and Mortimer bolted. He was still in his half-crouch, just as he had been when the journalists had emerged from the house, and he launched himself into the garden, wings tucked close and heart hammering in fright.

"*Dammit!* Get him, Lloyd!" Katherine sprinted after him, the man cursing as he fumbled to catch hold of the camera, and there was a nasty-sounding crunch as it hit the steps. Mortimer didn't turn back. He was thundering for the corner of the house simply because that was the direction he was pointed in, and somewhere in the back of his mind was the thought that he couldn't go into the woods, not with Gilbert – friendly, non-flying Gilbert – still out there. Not when it might give them an idea of where to start searching for dragons. Maybe he could get into another garden and hide until they left. Or make it to the village green and get the sprite to set some geese on them, but that was really too far to go for now, so maybe—

He almost hit a pair of legs as their owner ran around from the front of the house, and he stopped so hard that he lost his footing and rolled into the peony bushes, scattering petals like a bright pink snowstorm. He peered out at the owner of the legs, half-expecting them to be armed with nets and tranquilliser guns and rope. Lots and lots of rope. Instead, he saw DI Adams' least favourite journalist looking back at him, a finger to his lips.

"What the hell's going on?" Ervin demanded, dropping his hand and stepping in front of the peonies as the journalists came racing around the house and staggered to a halt. "What're you two up to?"

"Same as you," Katherine retorted. "Looking for a story."

"I didn't know the Monster Mag covered village murders."

"Not the *murder,* you pillock," she said. "There's more going on here than that. Not that I'd expect some mainstream muppet like you to see it. Too busy sniffing around the police to see what's *really* going on."

"And what's that, then?" Ervin asked. "Alien abductions? Demonic possession? Lizard people taking over the town hall?"

"Funny you should say that," Lloyd started, and Katherine waved at him impatiently. "What? We had that story on lizard people being in charge of the planning permissions department just last month!"

"Quality journalism," Ervin said.

"These are the kind of stories *your* lot are scared to tell," Lloyd said, stabbing a finger at Ervin.

"Less scared, more interested in finding, you know, *facts.*"

"We had an eyewitness! They *saw—*"

"Lloyd, shut up," Katherine said. "He's just winding you up."

"No, I'm quite serious about the facts," Ervin said, crossing his arms over his chest. "Also quite serious about the fact that you're trespassing."

"So're you."

"I came to see what all the shouting was about. *Unlike* you, I was waiting for the homeowner to get back before I started wandering about her veggie garden."

Mortimer wanted to shout that they'd actually been *inside* the house, but as everyone seemed to have forgotten about him he just concentrated on trying to look like a peony bush.

Katherine glared at Ervin for a moment, then looked at Lloyd. "Let's go."

"But what about—"

"Let's go," she repeated, shaking her head sharply.

"What about what?" Ervin asked. "Did you spot some faeries at the end of the garden you need to go back for?" He gave an almost imperceptible shudder as soon as he'd said it, and Mortimer was fairly sure he was thinking about the faeries from the Christmas market. No one would ever hope for faeries at the bottom of the garden if they actually knew what they were like.

"Nothing," Katherine said. "Good luck on your murder story. It sounds *fascinating."*

"I'm sure it's nothing compared to the alien abductions," Ervin said. "Have you connected them to the cow tipping in Hellifield yet?"

Lloyd started to say something, but Katherine grabbed his arm, tugging him back toward to the road. Ervin followed them, and Mortimer stayed exactly where he was. He wasn't sure he was actually capable of movement. He wasn't even sure if he was breathing. His head was buzzing so loudly he could barely even think. So he just looked at his talons and waited for something to happen. Hopefully something that involved tea and cake and Miriam coming home.

HE WAS STILL SITTING THERE when Ervin came back around the house, his hands in his pockets, and leaned down to examine him.

"You okay?" the journalist asked.

Mortimer tried to say something, but he could barely think for the buzzing. He wondered if he was going to pass out. Could dragons pass out? He wasn't sure he'd ever heard of it before.

Ervin crouched, reaching out a hand, and Mortimer flinched back in fright. Suddenly the buzzing was gone, and he shook his head, startled.

"Did you know you had a bee in your ear?" Ervin asked.

Mortimer squawked and launched himself out of the bushes, sending the journalist falling backward with a matching yelp.

Ervin caught himself on his hands and stared at the dragon, his eyes wide. "I was only asking!"

"Is it off?" Mortimer asked, shaking his head as hard as he could. "Is it gone? *Is it gone?*"

"It's fine, it's gone." Ervin sat down on the path, brushing his hands off. "Are you okay?"

"I might be allergic."

"Allergic?"

"To the bees. I could go into shock!"

"Dragons have allergies?"

"I don't know," Mortimer almost wailed, then rocked back onto his haunches and clamped his paws over his snout. "Have *they* gone? Do you think they heard me?"

Ervin looked at him as if unsure whether to pat his shoulder or to get up and walk away, then said, "I watched until they drove off. Doesn't mean they won't come back, of course."

"They tried to take photos," Mortimer whispered. "They wanted to *catch* me."

"Well, they didn't catch you, and I can tell you from personal experience that photos don't come out."

"You tried to take photos?"

"Of course I tried to take photos. You're *dragons.*"

Mortimer looked at him suspiciously. "Were you going to show them to The Government?"

"Why would I show them to the government?"

"I'm not sure," Mortimer admitted. "But you might be working for them. Or think there was a story in it."

"A good journalist is never too cosy with the government," Ervin said firmly. "And I have no intentions of telling anyone about *any* of this, because I don't want to end up discredited, fired, and working for a cryptid rag like that lot." He got up, brushing the seat of his jeans off. "But you need to keep clear of the village while they're around."

"I know that," Mortimer said. "Only I was trying to find Miriam. Rose's dog is stuck."

"Stuck?"

"He's caught on a tree, and we can't get close enough to release him, and Walter was chasing him and will probably eat him if we can't get him home."

"Walter. He's the grumpy old one with the ..." Ervin indicated the corner of his mouth, as if a trail of drool should be there, and Mortimer nodded.

"He mostly only drools around humans."

"Well, that's reassuring." They looked at each other for a moment, then Ervin sighed. "I suppose I could come and get the dog. It'll get me some brownie points, anyway."

Mortimer blinked. "Actual house brownies or chocolate ones?"

Ervin opened his mouth, shut it again, then said, "Figure of speech."

"Oh. I like the chocolate ones. Not the actual ones so much."

"Good to know. Shall we get this dog, then?"

Mortimer looked up at him, wishing he were Miriam or Alice or even DI Adams, with her terrifying Dandy. Wishing he were someone Mortimer knew he could trust, someone he could be sure wasn't going to start writing articles about dragons, or trying to take more photos, or just simply exposing them with careless talk to the wrong people. But he was here, and no one else was. And he had seen off the other journalists. Plus proved himself quite handy at getting rid of feral Santas. So he sighed, nodded, and said. "Those journalists were in the house. We should see if we can lock the door."

"Sneaky sods," Ervin said, and followed Mortimer through the garden.

MORTIMER HAD SEEN where Miriam hid her spare key, under a rusting pink metal flowerpot, and Ervin checked inside then locked the door, pocketing the key.

"They got in somehow," he explained to Mortimer. "It wouldn't be hard to find that key."

Mortimer supposed that was right, but he decided he'd make sure Ervin gave the key back as soon as Miriam returned. He turned and headed toward the bottom of the garden, leading the way through the little gate and over the bridge, the beck chattering just as happily as if the village wasn't suddenly overrun by nosy journalists. They ducked into the trees, Ervin swearing as he stumbled into a spiderweb and flailed about wildly.

"Shh," Mortimer said. "They might be watching!"

"You *shh,*" Ervin grumbled, but wiped his face and followed Mortimer as the dragon wound his way through the trees, quick and unerring. "Can't you slow down?"

"No," Mortimer said. "If Walter comes back for Angelus, Gilbert won't be able to stop him."

"You think he might come back?" Ervin sounded worried.

"He was *very* determined to catch him. I think he was upset that I stopped him eating that cryptic journalist."

"Oh, good. So I'm stealing a hungry dragon's dinner? Is that the situation here?"

"I suppose," Mortimer said, ducking under a fallen tree and pausing while Ervin clambered over it.

"Are we sure he won't decide *I'm* dinner? What with the drooling and all?"

Mortimer thought about it. "He's never shown any indication that he'd eat the W.I. He just thought those journalists were dragon hunters."

"How good is he at distinguishing between journalists?"

"I'm almost certain he won't eat you," Mortimer said, and picked up the pace before Ervin could ask any more questions.

By the time they reached Gilbert, who was keeping an eye on Angelus from atop a comfortable-looking, mossy tree stump, Ervin had walked into three more spiderwebs, torn his jeans clambering through some rocks, and hit his head on a low-hanging tree branch. He looked unimpressed.

"*There* you are," Gilbert said, sitting up, and Angelus burst into a volley of barking. "I was starting to think you weren't coming!"

"There were complications," Mortimer said.

"There were *trees,*" Ervin said, examining his jeans. Mortimer thought he might not be the rambling sort.

"Well, you need to get Angelus out of here," Gilbert said. "He keeps howling, and I've heard wings. Walter must be hunting for him still, and he's going to find him if this keeps up." Angelus illustrated his point obligingly, lifting his nose and wailing hopelessly. *"Shh!"*

Ervin checked the sky, frowning. "I'm definitely having second thoughts about this."

"You said you'd help," Mortimer said. "He's not going to eat you!"

"Probably," Gilbert said, and Mortimer glared at him. "What? He's unpredictable."

"Just grab Angelus," Mortimer said to Ervin. "If you can keep him quiet, Walter won't find him."

"Alright, alright," Ervin said, and scrambled across the rough ground to the dog. "Come on, boy. You're okay." Angelus wagged his tail, shoving his nose into Ervin's hands, then howled again. "Quiet!"

"He's coming back!" Gilbert hissed, and Mortimer caught the faintest whisper of wingbeats.

He waved at Ervin. "Duck!"

Ervin gave him a horrified look and dropped into the shadow of the tree, pulling Angelus with him. Angelus whined, licking the journalist's face as a shadow slipped across the clearing accompanied by the creak of leathery wings. Mortimer pressed himself against the rocks, holding to their greys, and a moment later the sky was clear again. He waved at Ervin. "Hurry! You need to get Angelus back to the village."

"Ew," Ervin said, sitting up and wiping his face with a grimace. "Okay. You're coming, right?"

"We can't. Those other journalists might still be around."

Ervin stared at him. "You can't just leave me here! I'll never find my way back – and there's a dragon *hunting* up there!"

"You just go back the same way," Mortimer said.

"*What* way?" Ervin waved at the trees wildly. "I'm not a bloody Boy Scout!"

Mortimer hesitated. He didn't want to risk heading back to the village, but it'd all be for nothing if Ervin got lost. And he really wasn't sure if Walter *would* be picky about which journalists he tried to eat. "Alright," he said, gathering himself up. "Come on, Gilbert."

"Yes," Gilbert said, and took off at a run. At least someone was enjoying themselves.

THEY PLUNGED INTO THE UNDERGROWTH, Ervin with a firm hold on Angelus' collar despite the dog's determination to tear himself free. Mortimer led the way back toward Miriam's, trying to find slightly more open ground for easier passage. Gilbert fell back to bring up the rear, and they moved as fast as the journalist could manage. At one point the young dragon hissed, *"Stop!"* and they cowered in the cover of the thickest bushes like rabbits as heavy wingbeats swept the trees above them. They were getting too close to the village, Mortimer thought. Walter was taking a terrible risk, flying here. What was he *doing?* Was it just because they'd taken the dog from him? Was he really that single-minded?

"Clear," Gilbert called, his voice low, and they hurried off again. Ervin was sweating, the sleeves of his jumper pushed up to his elbows and his hair sticking to his neck, smelling of salted liquorice frustration and cinnamon twists of fright. Mortimer glanced back to check on him as the journalist looked up at the glimpses of sky above them, his face tight with concern. Mortimer started to call a warning, but Ervin had already hooked his foot on a protruding root. He stumbled, and Angelus jerked forward, twisting and surging against his collar. Ervin fell to one knee with a yelp of protest, his grip slipping, and Angelus tore himself free.

"No!" Mortimer lunged for the dog as Ervin flung himself after the creature, one hand sliding off his hindquarters. "Gilbert, stop him!"

Gilbert was already charging after Angelus, who howled in alarm, and Ervin scrambled to his feet and crashed off in pursuit, one arm raised to protect his face. Mortimer rushed after them, and as he did he heard the wings coming back, low over the trees. "Oh, no," he whispered, as Angelus howled again. The silly creature! And how were they going to explain *that* to Rose? That they'd let Walter *eat* him?

The wings swept above them, nothing more than a shadow through the treetops, then there was a crash overhead as a heavy body plunged into the foliage.

"Walter, no!" Mortimer yelled. "Stop! *Stop!*" He pushed himself faster, overtaking Ervin and thundering into a tiny clearing shoulder to shoulder with Gilbert, who was shouting about greed and rabbits and nasty old wyrms. Camouflaged scales flashed ahead of them, Angelus howled again, and Mortimer came to a stumbling halt, bracing himself for the sight of the dog pinned to the ground. Or worse.

Beaufort looked up, one heavy paw resting lightly on Angelus' trembling back. "Oh, there you are, lad. What on earth is going on? You vanished, and when I came back to look for you all I saw was Walter crashing off through the trees in the direction of the village. I lost him, but I heard the dog, and I've been trying to find you ever since."

Mortimer sagged to the ground. "We thought you were Walter, still hunting for Angelus."

"He was going to *eat* him," Gilbert said.

"Or me," Ervin added, sitting down on the nearest bit of open ground. He was panting.

"Nonsense," Beaufort said. "Well, the dog bit, anyway. This is Rose's dog. Walter would *never* eat Rose's dog."

"Why was he chasing him, then?" Gilbert asked. "He'd have had him if I hadn't stepped in! And Mortimer, of course."

"Walter was chasing Mortimer?" Beaufort asked.

"No, Mortimer was chasing Walter."

"That seems foolish," the High Lord said, and looked at Mortimer expectantly, but Mortimer wasn't listening. *Walter would never eat Rose's dog.*

"So the eating *me* bit isn't nonsense?" Ervin asked. "This isn't great news."

"You haven't been rude to him, have you?" Beaufort asked. "One doesn't want to be rude to Walter."

"I haven't been rude to anyone! I was trying to help!"

Walter was crashing off in the direction of the village. Walter would never eat Rose's dog. Walter had been in Rose's garden right before they'd lost her. He'd run off, just as she had. He— "Walter has Rose," he said.

"What, lad?" Beaufort asked.

"Walter has Rose. He helped her get away when she ran. That's why he was trying to catch Angelus – for Rose." Everyone was staring at him, and he stared back at them, his scales suddenly hot.

"But why's he going to the village?" Gilbert asked. "You just said Rose was running away from it."

"She was running from the police, not the village," Mortimer said. "What if Walter found that scent? The one I almost had? And he and Rose are going after the murderer?"

"What's this?" Ervin asked. "There's definitely a murderer? The police didn't seem so sure."

"The police don't have Mortimer's nose," Beaufort said. "But even I can tell Rose smells as much like a murderer as she does a kelpie."

Ervin frowned, evidently wondering what a kelpie smelled like.

"I didn't have time to trace the scent, though," Mortimer said.

"Walter always had an excellent nose for such things," Beaufort said. "If he found it ..."

"Oh, no," Gilbert said. "Oh, *no*. We have to stop him!"

Ervin pulled a twig out of his hair. "Isn't catching a murderer a good thing?"

"Not with Walter in his current mindset," Beaufort said, which Mortimer thought was generous. Walter was always in the exact same mindset, as far as he was concerned.

"Well, go on, then," Ervin said. "I'll look after the dog."

"Those journalists might still be around," Mortimer said.

Ervin stared at him for a moment, then got to his feet and grabbed Angelus. "Bloody hell. Fine. But I expect one of you to stop Walter from eating me."

"Well done, lad," Beaufort said, and turned his nose toward the village. "I'm sure it won't come to that."

"It had better not come to well done *or* rare," Ervin muttered, scowling at the High Lord's back, and Mortimer gave him a sympathetic look.

Beaufort led the charge through the trees, the three dragons, the human and the dog plunging through the undergrowth, secrecy forgotten, until they found one of the hidden paths that ran toward the village. Then they broke into mismatched versions of an all-out sprint, the birds screaming alarm above them and the world sharp with fright.

Mortimer hoped they were going to be in time. Eating a murderer might feel morally superior to eating a journalist, but he was fairly sure the Watch would still frown on it. As would The Government.

He ran harder.

19
ALICE

The air on the street tasted clear and cold after the incense-tinted oiliness inside, and Alice led the way to the car, feeling the inspectors' gaze on her back. Miriam was lingering on the pavement, as if she couldn't decide whether to be more worried about the drive back or the prospect of further lectures regarding interfering in investigations.

"Come along, Miriam," Alice said, leaning against the driver's door as she waited for a car to pass. "Almost home."

"One moment. I really don't feel so good, you know."

"You take the front seat," Jasmine said, already climbing in the back. "I don't get carsick."

"Oh, no," Miriam started, but Jasmine was already pulling her door shut. "Oh no," she repeated, almost in a whisper.

"Honestly, Miriam," Alice said. "I'm a very safe driver, you know. It's not like you're in the car with Rose."

Miriam gave an involuntary shudder, which Alice sympathised with. She had been in a car with Rose before, and although Rose had driven them to lunch, Alice had insisted on driving home. It hadn't saved them any time, as Rose seemed to be more aligned with Alice's views on speed limits than Miriam's, but they'd stayed on their own side of the road the whole way, which had made for a far more enjoyable trip.

"It was really very hot in there," Miriam said. "Or was that just me again?"

"No, it was," Alice said. "Far too warm for comfort. And, of course, you exerted yourself rather admirably."

Miriam made a small, doubtful noise, and Alice smiled at her, then got in and started the engine. Miriam followed, clambering into the front seat reluctantly and double-checking her seatbelt. The inspectors watched them in the rear-view mirror while they pulled away, and Alice tapped her fingers on the wheel as she wound her way through the narrow streets with their ranks of stone houses.

"We are no further forward on Rose, ladies."

"No messages from anyone?" Miriam asked.

Alice shook her head. "Nothing. It's most concerning." She thought of her sudden fear last night, that Rose had become lost to herself on the streets of Toot Hansell, and hoped she hadn't had a Miriam-like moment of intuition. But then, was it worse to wonder if Rose was running because she was a murderer than it was to imagine her adrift somewhere? Or to imagine that a murderer had spirited her away from Alice's own door? She rubbed the soft skin of her forehead. "Are we sure there are no family or friends she might have gone to? What about the sister Priya mentioned?"

"I think she's down south somewhere," Miriam said. "Rose never really talks about her."

"We should try and track her down anyway," Alice said, but without much hope. Rose wouldn't have gone that far. She was almost sure of it.

Jasmine leaned between the seats. "Look at this," she said, and held out Rose's phone.

"Oh, well done," Alice said. "You got into it."

"Yes. But look. The texts are from *Monster Man,* but I'm sure it's … you know. Him." She tipped the phone toward Miriam. There was a catch in her voice that suggested she didn't want to read it alone, and Alice made her fingers ease their grip on the wheel. They were starting to hurt.

"Rose, good to see you tonight, but it was all too brief and busy. I'm taking you up on that invite. See you soon!" Miriam read. "That was on … that was late Friday night."

"After the lecture," Jasmine said, scrolling down. "Then he says, *Alright, my Yorkshire dragon—"*

"Ugh," Alice said. Pet names were just so demeaning. Although, if one were to have one, she supposed *Yorkshire dragon* wasn't terrible.

"*—leaving now.* Then the last message says, *Is this even the right number still? Rose, I'm going through Skipton now, so I'll come by anyway. I have some papers that might interest you – new evidence on Yeti! See you soon."*

No one spoke for a moment, then Miriam said, "She never replied. And Campbell said she didn't have her phone, so she probably didn't even know he was coming." Her voice was shaky.

"He says he's taking her up on the invite, though," Jasmine said.

"Is the invitation there?" Alice asked.

Jasmine scrolled up through the messages. "No – wait. Yes, it's here, but it's from last month. He asks her about meeting up, and she says, *Monster Man, come by any time. I'll be happy to explain the flaws in your logic to you!"*

"Last month," Alice said. "So she wasn't expecting him on Friday. And the time on his last text—"

"Just after nine p.m.," Miriam said. "He must have left right after the lecture. He'd have been there by eleven."

Alice nodded. "Earlier, if he drove a little more quickly. And it sounds like he'd been before, so he might have simply let himself in to wait. Rose could have had her late dinner with Campbell, come home, then walked in on what she assumed to be an intruder in her kitchen."

"And then what?" Miriam asked. "She messaged Campbell at one, telling him everything was fine, but Bethany found the body *after* that, and Rose wasn't even there."

"And then who knows?" Alice's voice was quiet, and she adjusted the vents. She was feeling unaccountably cold. "We need to find Rose, ladies. And before the police get any closer."

"She wouldn't have," Jasmine whispered. "Bethany's lying, or someone else did it. Rose *wouldn't!*"

"She knew the body was there all day before she told me," Miriam said. She was staring blankly out of the windscreen, her hands limp in her lap. "All *day.*"

"She wouldn't," Jasmine repeated, staring at the phone.

Alice tucked hair behind her ears with stiff fingers. "We shall go home. Maybe the others have found her by now and just haven't had a chance to call."

Neither Jasmine nor Miriam replied to that, and Alice accelerated out of town, heading back into the familiar, half-wild lands of fells and valleys.

For the first time she could remember, they felt forbidding rather than welcoming.

THEY WERE quiet on the drive back to Toot Hansell, and Alice had to admit that outing Bethany as, if not the murderer, at least as a part of the puzzle, didn't feel as satisfying as she might have liked. They were no further forward on who had done the actual deed, or on finding Rose, or even on proving Rose wasn't so impaired that she could be termed a risk to herself and others. It was all just so *frustrating*. Everything seemed to lead them to dead ends and more questions.

She glanced at Miriam, sitting in the passenger seat with her fingers twisted together in her lap. For once, the younger woman wasn't clinging to the door handle or squeezing her eyes closed dramatically. She just frowned at the scenery outside as the houses fell away behind them and the fields filled in, green and rich and pocked with the grey of ruined barns and the white and black of grazing sheep. Alice turned her attention back to the road and her own thoughts.

"You don't think someone *is* hiding Rose, do you?" Miriam asked finally, as they joined a queue behind a rust-stained green tractor that was jouncing down the road on giant, chunky tyres.

"Other than one of us? I doubt it," Alice said. "I can't imagine who else she'd have trusted to keep her hidden."

"Unless she's embarrassed," Miriam pointed out. "If things really are ... if she's not herself." Her voice was soft. "I'm not sure I'd want everyone knowing that, if it was me."

Alice frowned. "But we wouldn't judge her. Age comes for us all. There's no shame in that."

Miriam made a thoughtful noise and looked over at Alice. "That's an easy thing to say when it's not you."

Alice didn't answer for a moment, trying to imagine what it would be like to find oneself reaching for a memory, or a thought, and finding it simply *not there*. To know connections existed, but being unable to make them. For every face to be that of a stranger, their stories lost. The idea was intolerable. And the idea of others *knowing* ... She shook her head. "Oh, Miriam. You may be right. But who else would she go to? I don't even know where to start."

"Meena," Jasmine said from the back seat.

"Well, she wouldn't go to *her*," Miriam said. "She was the one Rose was running from!"

"No. *Meena*." Jasmine leaned between the seats, still clutching

Rose's phone. "I found … I mean, I know I'm snooping, but …" She trailed off, staring at the phone, and Alice glanced at her. The younger woman's face was pinched and pale and anxious.

"I think a little snooping is more than justified, in the circumstances," Alice said, thinking of the file tucked away in her reading room. "I didn't want to say this is front of everyone, but I found something in Rose's office."

"What was it?" Miriam asked.

Alice sighed. "Someone has been reporting Rose's house as not fit for habitation, and a case was filed with social services, suggesting she couldn't look after herself."

"What?" Jasmine demanded. "Ooh, I bet it's that Meena! That—"

"How *dare* she?" Miriam's hands were in fists on her lap. "She's trying to force her into a home!"

"We don't know that," Alice said. "Anyone could have filed those. But it suggests that Rose's problems are not new."

"Or someone setting her up isn't new," Miriam said.

Alice nodded. "Perhaps. What have you found, Jasmine?"

"Some emails and text messages from *her*."

"Meena?" Miriam demanded.

"Yes. The emails are discussing organising the cognitive tests," Jasmine said. "There's a whole chain of them, going back to January. Some of them are just Meena asking questions, but in others she's setting dates and telling Rose to meet her in Manchester for the consultation. Rose doesn't reply to any of them, and from Meena's responses it looks like she never attended the appointments. But then in the last few, Meena says she has one organised for Tuesday."

Miriam frowned. "But it's Monday. Why was she here today?"

"This is Rose," Alice said. "Even for an event she wants to go to, one has to tell her a time at least an hour before one actually needs to leave."

"That's true," Miriam said. "Do you remember the medieval

medicine event last year? I agreed to go with her, since no one else would, and we only ended up seeing the last lecture of a three-day series. It was on tapeworms." She shuddered. "But we just kept missing all the others. We didn't get there until the end of the first day because we left so late, and then the second day she kept getting distracted by people selling herbal tinctures—"

"*Rose* wanted to buy herbal tinctures?" That seemed out of character. Alice rather admired the fact that Rose refused to buy anything that couldn't back up its claims with scientific research. Could this be another sign that things weren't right?

"No, she wanted to shout at people selling herbal tinctures, and lecture people buying them."

"Ah."

"But still, a day ahead?" Miriam added.

"Or four days, if you two are quite finished," Jasmine said.

"I'm sorry?" Alice watched a car at the head of the queue try to overtake the tractor, then dive back into line as another vehicle came over the next hill. There just wasn't a lot of room for such manoeuvres around here.

"Four days. There's a couple of missed calls on Friday, then a text in the evening just after ten, saying, *Rose, answer your phone.* Then another ten minutes later, which says, *I'm here, and I'm not leaving until you talk to me.* Then nothing."

"Just after ten?" Alice said.

"Yes."

"Does Meena actually say she's at the house?"

"No, it just says 'here', but where else would it be? Rose was in York, and I'm sure she wasn't planning to meet Meena there."

"Unless she'd agreed to meet Meena elsewhere, and then either forgot or decided to ignore it. There's nothing conclusive there, Jasmine. Maybe Meena did come up early, to run through things with Rose or to make sure she couldn't avoid her. But there's no way of telling if she was actually at the house that night."

Jasmine made an uncertain noise, and Miriam said, "*Cameras.*"

Alice swallowed a sigh. "What cameras, dear?"

"Bethany said that Dougal had her on camera, when he thought she was a trespasser. Maybe he has Meena on camera." She gasped, and grabbed Alice's arm, jerking her hand on the steering wheel. "*Maybe he filmed the murderer!*"

Alice shook her off gently. "Well. Let's not have an accident over it." But she eased her foot down on the accelerator, overtaking two cars while they had a relatively straight stretch of road in front of them.

Perhaps there might be a use for nosy neighbours after all.

❧

THEY SKIMMED into the village with Miriam clinging to the door handle once again, but this time looking less nauseous and more excited, her nose and cheeks pink. Alice skirted the village centre with its cobbled market square and slate-roofed well, instead following the side roads lined with little cottages and semi-detached houses mired in their blossoming gardens, and rows of terraces with contrasting doors. She drove slowly, both Miriam and Jasmine craning to see into the yards as they passed, as if they might spot Rose talking to a neighbour or hiding among someone's hydrangeas. But no one was out in the gardens today, with the wind still carrying the tail edge of winter, and before long they were driving casually past Rose's front gate, where two police cars were parked in the shade of an overhanging bird cherry tree. There was no sign of the occupants, but Jasmine ducked anyway. Alice kept going, heading around the corner and pulling into the little parking area in front of the village hall.

"Why didn't we stop?" Miriam asked. "We're not going to Rose's."

"I feel the police may take a dim view of us being anywhere near their crime scene," Alice said.

"And I think Ben's there," Jasmine said. "I'd rather he didn't see me. He doesn't like me getting involved with investigations. He says you're a bad influence."

"How rude," Miriam said.

"Although possibly quite accurate," Alice said. "But we would hate to cause marital strife, Jasmine."

"So we're not going to see Dougal?" Miriam asked.

"Oh, we're going to see him. We'll just go through the bottom of Rose's garden and into his, so as to avoid any police issues."

"*I* can't avoid them entirely," Jasmine said, and sighed. "Ben'll find out, even if he doesn't see us. He's going to be very put out with me."

"You don't have to *tell* him," Miriam said.

"Quite," Alice agreed. "And we shall just pop over to Dougal's and ask him about his cameras, and if we are spotted we can say, quite honestly, that we have no intention of disturbing the crime scene, and we were merely passing through on our own business."

"That's only half honest," Jasmine said, but she was already climbing out of the car. "We're still interfering with the *case*. You are a bad influence, you know."

"All the best friends are," Alice said, and took her cane from the back seat.

"Is that necessary?" Miriam asked, eyeing it.

Alice swished it a couple of times, the silver dragon's head handle glinting in the sun. "My hip is a little stiff today."

"Right," Miriam said, and Alice didn't miss the glance she exchanged with Jasmine. But they both fell into step with her as she crossed the road and headed for the village green, Rose's garden visible as a wilderness beyond the sweep of grass.

Rose's garden was quiet as they made their way through the bottom gate, and Alice found a winding path that took them along the inside of the wall toward Dougal's property. The path was as well-worn as any of the small trails that curled through the garden, which was to say that she was glad she was wearing trousers. There were more than a few clumps of nettles encroaching on the clearer ground, and she heard Miriam hiss behind her as one caught her hand.

"Are you alright, Miriam?" she asked, her voice low.

"Yes. I just need a dock leaf."

"Here," Jasmine whispered. Alice didn't pause to watch them administer the rudimentary first aid. She kept going, scanning the thicket of undergrowth that made up the bottom of the garden. She knew Rose let this side grow up deliberately wilder, both as wildlife habitat and to give the house some privacy from the village green, and it was impossible to see much through it. Which was helpful when it came to keeping them hidden, but also meant that she couldn't tell if there was activity at the house. She wondered where the police officers were. Simply patrolling the garden, perhaps? Or had something happened to draw them away?

She reached the boundary wall between Rose and Dougal's property without seeing anyone lurking in the undergrowth, and found an old stile built into the stone. At a cursory glance it looked unused, brambles crowding around it on this side and a shed backed up to it on the other, but the thick green moss that crowned the dry-stone wall to either side was scuffed away, and there was just enough room to slip between the reaching, thorny arms of the bramble shoots without being caught. Alice inspected them curiously. Yes, some had been cut back with secateurs. She hadn't thought Rose was *that* friendly with Dougal, but perhaps he used the trail as a shortcut to the village green himself.

"Can we get over?" Jasmine asked. She was still holding a handful of dock leaves.

"It's a little tight behind the shed, but I think so," Alice replied, and they all stood there for a moment, regarding the stile dubiously. The heavy grey stone of the wall was stark against the luminous yellow paint of the wooden shed, and Alice wondered why anyone would choose such a colour. It was less reminiscent of sunshine than of those hideous yellow jellies one always seemed to have as a child, that purported to be lemon but tasted of nothing but sugar.

"It's so *quiet,*" Miriam said, rubbing her hand where the nettle had stung her. "Where are all the birds?"

Alice lifted her head, listening. "You're quite right. We must've disturbed them."

"They normally chatter *more,* in that case," Jasmine pointed out.

No one spoke for a moment, and Alice could hear someone shouting joyfully on the village green. Finally she said, "Well, the mystery of the birds will have to wait. Let's see if Dougal has any cameras we can look at, shall we?"

"I don't like it," Miriam said, and shivered. "It feels like something's going to happen."

"Something's always going to happen, dear. It's called life."

THE GARDEN beyond the shed was neat, well-trimmed lawn laid between the defined edges of carefully arranged flowerbeds, all cut through with curving gravel paths. A sundial stood amid a circle of pansies, the flowers divided by colour to give six segments. Alice supposed twelve would have been a little messy. There was a small wooden bridge arching over a koi pond, and a water feature of stacked, smooth grey stones chuckling to itself softly at one end. There were also a number of trellis arches crowned with roses, and a white summer house with a gabled roof and cane furniture stacked inside. At the bottom of the garden, to their right, tall, tightly packed boxwood bushes trimmed to look like crenelations lined the boundary and blocked the view of the village green, offering no way past. All through the flowerbeds were scattered mysterious metal sculptures that twisted in the wind, and giant stained-glass dragonflies, and Picasso-coloured, glossy-curved porcelain creations that looked like they required regular cleaning, along with more traditional statues of women with water jugs and chubby cherubs and so on. There were no bird feeders or bird houses, though, and the whole place had the feel of somewhere that was meant to be looked at, not lived in.

Alice stopped by the side of the shed, turning to look back at Rose's. She felt like she'd stepped into some foreign country. The yellow shed stood at the bottom corner of the garden, and running from it along Rose's border wall was a high, well-kept wooden fence, hanging baskets fixed to it at regular intervals and the wooden panels painted in alternating pastels that made her think the colour of the shed really might have been a mistake. It was terribly bright.

"I feel like I should take my shoes off," Miriam said.

"It's extraordinary," Alice agreed. All she could see of Rose's house beyond the wall were the scraggly tops of wild trees, and she wondered why Dougal had left the stile unblocked. This was a garden where aesthetics trumped function, and she rather thought Dougal would have preferred a longer walk to the green than to have a glimpse of unruly nature intruding.

"It's *excessive,*" Jasmine said. "The front's fairly normal. This is ..." Her voice trailed off as she stared at a marble sculpture of a woman with one bare breast, reclining among the agapanthus. "Excessive," she repeated.

Alice nodded. It did feel rather as if someone had attempted to recreate numerous formal manor gardens of varying styles within the confines of one decent but not overly large bungalow back yard. "To each their own, I suppose," she said. "Maybe that's why he's so keen to keep an eye on things." The shed had a window on the side, and she cupped one hand to the glass, peering into the dim interior. Just in case of large dogs, really. One never knew.

There appeared to be curtains of some sort on the inside of the glass, which seemed as excessive as the garden. Was he worried about the sun damaging his lawnmower? She blinked at the dark, folded material, which looked more like bin bags than cloth, then said, "Miriam?"

"Yes?" Miriam had a soft sheen of sweat on her forehead as she frowned at the garden.

"Do you remember the golf clubs in Rose's utility?"

"Um. I suppose?"

"Was the set missing one?"

"I don't really know. I don't play golf."

Alice supposed that there were many reasons why one might keep a golf club on the shelf below the window of a curtained garden shed, the head well-wrapped in a plastic bag, but for the life of her she couldn't think of one right now.

"What's that next to it?" Miriam asked, leaning in beside her and peering at the shadowy interior.

"A tool bag, perhaps?" Alice said. There was some grey gaffer tape sticking out of it, and some heavy gloves, and—

"Why's it got a hairbrush in it?" Jasmine asked. There was a wobble to her voice. "And why does it look like *Rose's* hairbrush?"

No one spoke for a moment. Alice's eyes kept coming back to the gaffer tape. Rose had left the house this morning accompanied only by Angelus, yes, but what had happened after that? Where had she gone?

Suddenly she thought she might know why the stile was open, and who had kept it that way. And who had filed the cases with the council, for that matter. Not *why* he had, not yet, but sometimes one had to be prepared to step aside and let those better equipped handle certain situations. Especially when missing ladies of a certain age were concerned.

"Back the way we came, ladies. I think we will call on the police officer at the gate, after all." She took a last look, attempting to see deeper into the shed, but the bin bags – and she had a horrible suspicion that they *were* bin bags – stopped her seeing any further. They were moving faintly, though, and she said, "Miriam, do you see this?"

"Um," Miriam said, the word almost a whisper.

Alice stayed where she was for a moment, her hand tight on her cane as she watched the bin bags ripple, then she turned around and faced the garden. The garden, and the man standing there with a taser in one hand.

"Ah. Mr Brown," she said, her voice level. "Our kidnapper and murderer, I presume?"

20
DI ADAMS

DI Adams scratched her jaw, looking around Bethany's stuffy, oil-scented flat, searching for signs that she might be a murderer as well as the sort of person who puts bodies in freezers. Bethany was crying, quietly and undramatically, and had been since they walked in the door, and Collins was making sympathetic noises as he guided her to the squishy sofa. DI Adams wondered if she should offer to make tea. It seemed like that sort of situation, but that was only going to slow things up, and she wanted to get back to Toot Hansell. Something about Alice heading off so dutifully was niggling at her, as was the continued absence of Rose. She felt as though she were missing something.

So when her phone rang, she pointed at it and stepped out into the hall, only checking the display once she was outside. *PS Harrison, Graham?*, it read. She needed to remember to remove the question mark.

She hit reply and said, "Ser— Graham. Any progress there?"

"It's pronounced *sir*, not *sar*. Not that I'm actually a knight, of course, but I accept the honorific if you're offering."

DI Adams looked at the ceiling. How could they be *in the middle of an investigation*, and these men still wanted to chatter away like five-year-olds? "I'll keep it in mind," she said. "Did you find who was in the garden?"

"We haven't. It's all gone quiet again, but we're both in the garden now. Figured it was better to keep circulating in here. More likely to stumble across something."

"Sounds good." She waited, and when he didn't say anything else she added, "Was there more?"

"Maybe." He sounded uncertain, and she could see him, a familiar figure around the station, tall and lean, but with a comfortable softness around the middle, his big hands tucked behind his stab vest, telling terrible jokes or sitting next to complainants in the cracked plastic chairs at the front of the station, his head bent gravely toward them. There was nothing uncertain about him.

"What is it?" she asked.

"It might be nothing."

"Doesn't matter if it is. Rather say it and it be nothing than say nothing and it be everything."

She expected him to snort and tell her that her southern cop thinking didn't work up here, but all he said was, "I suppose. And it's probably nowt, but like you say – it might be everything." He paused again, then said, "Did you think the neighbour looked familiar?"

"Dougal Brown? No. Should he?"

"I'm not sure. Ben didn't think so, but he's only been on the force for five, six years. And you might not have noted the case so much, being London and all." He hesitated. "Did Colin not say anything?"

"Collins didn't interview him. I don't think he's even seen him."

"Ah." Graham exhaled the sound. "Okay. Look, there was a case here about ten years back. Colin was a PS in Leeds at the time, and it was his inspector in the middle of it. Inspector Donny Cooper. It was a big thing – he had his fingers in a lot of pies, and a journalist almost brought the whole thing down. He wriggled out somehow – the journalist's house burned down, a lawyer ended up in a car accident, and a bunch of potential witnesses had painful accidents. That sort of wriggling out."

"Bloody hell. I do remember something about that. He retired, didn't he? Full pension, the lot." She peeked in the door to the flat. Collins was sitting on a wooden chair opposite the sofa, his elbows on his knees and his smile warm and understanding while Bethany nibbled on some sort of nuts with no evidence of enjoyment. She was still crying.

"That's him. Not that he needed it – as well as running all sorts of protection rackets, rumour has it that he basically had a property empire going on in Leeds and the golden triangle, all acquired through persuasive means. He was meant to have moved to Spain."

"Meant to have?"

"Dougal Brown bears a striking resemblance to Donny Cooper, if you ask me. *Striking.* And do you know how much a property the size of Professor Howard's would go for?"

"I hate to think."

"Exactly. Like I said, Donny was persuasive when it came to property. Places burned down. Crime rates went up. Homeowners found themselves in possession of incriminating evidence that they claimed no knowledge of."

DI Adams stared at Dandy, who'd joined her in the hall. He had apparently eaten the pansy, or lost it somewhere, and was staring at her steadily. She wished he wouldn't. It was unnerving. He should be staring at murderers, not her. Rather like he'd stared at Dougal, both nights in the garden. She pressed her palm to her forehead. "Is he there now?" she asked.

"Pretty sure. His car's there, and I saw him in the front garden about ten minutes ago."

"Good. Keep an eye on him. We've got to get a person of interest to the station, but we'll be there as soon as we can."

"So don't engage?"

"No. Sit tight."

"Alright." The relief in his voice was unmistakable, and she wondered just how bad Donny Cooper's reputation had been. And how much time they might have to find Rose.

❧

DI Adams turned back to the door, then paused and unlocked her phone again, scrolling down to find Lucas' number.

Anything on those vids?

She didn't wait for an answer, just let herself back into the tight confines of the apartment.

Collins raised his eyebrows at her as she let herself back into the room, and she gave a little one-shouldered shrug that she hoped indicated that she had a lead but couldn't say much right now.

"Bethany was just telling me about finding the body," he said. "She's very happy to come down to the station and have someone take the statement formally."

"That's wonderful," DI Adams said, then when Bethany gave her a startled look she added, "I mean, not wonderful about the body. But very good of you to cooperate. Sensible, you know."

Bethany nodded. "I didn't mean to keep it a secret. I just didn't want to get Rose in trouble, and by the time I was able to go back to talk to her, you were all there, and, well, it was too late. I didn't know what to do."

DI Adams thought it was pretty bloody obvious what one did in such a situation, but she just said, "Of course. Tell me, did you ever meet the neighbour? Dougal Brown?"

"Yes. He comes over to Rose's sometimes."

"Is he friendly?"

"He's alright. He's a bit funny about stuff – he's always offering to help Rose with her garden, but not really *offering,* you know. Like he wants to just do it himself. And he's always asking how she is, or if she shouldn't be thinking about downsizing for her health. I think he's lonely, really."

"So they didn't have any altercations? Nothing like that?"

Bethany shook her head. "Not that I know of. Rose used to make Angelus chase him if he came over too often." She frowned. "I remember him walking into the office once when Rose was out and I was there on my own. He was really surprised to see me. I thought that was weird, that he'd just walk in and not shout or anything."

"Weird," DI Adams agreed. "And, the night you found the body – did you see a strange car outside?"

Bethany thought about it. "I parked behind one, but I thought it belonged to the holiday let across the street. They always seem to see Rose parked there and think they have to park in the same place."

"Was it still there when you left?"

"I don't know. It was really late, and—" She stopped. "No, it can't have been. I don't remember having to go around it when I turned the car to leave."

DI Adams wondered if the idea had been to frame Rose as competent enough to dispose of the body while also being dotty enough to kill them in the first place – and inefficient enough to get caught. It made a horrible sort of sense. If Rose didn't end up in jail, she'd be in a very secure home of the sort that was only one step removed. "One last thing, Bethany. Did you clean up the blood?"

She looked puzzled. "There wasn't any. I thought … I thought he'd just had a heart attack or something, until I saw his head." She thought about it. "It did smell really clean in there, though. Bleach-

y. I thought maybe Angelus had had an accident earlier and Rose had scrubbed the floor."

DI Adams looked at Collins, who rocked back in the sofa with his hands clasped over his belly. "Bethany, we're going to take you to the station and get someone to take your statement, alright?"

"Alright," she said, wiping her mouth. "Are you arresting me? Should I call my mum?"

"We're just going to get your statement first," Collins said. "But yes, you might want to call your mum so you have some support." He hesitated. "And a lawyer, if you want one present."

She gave him a horrified look. "Do I need one?"

DI Adams managed not to say, *Well, you did put the body in the freezer,* and instead just said, "That's up to you."

"I'll ask Mum," she said. "She'll know what to do."

"That's fine," DI Adams said. "We'll wait for you outside." She inclined her head to Collins. He hauled himself out of the sofa and followed her.

"What set that off?" he asked her.

"Do you recognise the name Donny Cooper?"

He frowned. "Sure. He was in Leeds. Got forced out about ten years ago when a journalist started uncovering some of the stuff he'd been up to. It was pretty bad – extortion, protection money, lots of evidence tampering. Half the city was in his pocket. The only reason it never came out properly was the force closed ranks."

DI Adams watched him for a long moment, then said, "Were you in Leeds then?"

"Yes." He gave her a thoughtful look. "What's all this, Adams?"

"Did you know he was in Toot Hansell?"

"*What?* No, I heard he went to Spain."

She examined him, waiting. She wanted him to be the first to speak, but at the same time she dreaded it. Because what if it tasted of an untruth?

Collins put his hands in his pockets. "I had suspicions. We all did. But Donny picked his ... *associates* well. They were mostly older, had been in the force long enough for the charm to wear off. They just wanted an easy life and a bit of extra to pad the nest." His mouth twisted. "I should have done more when I did see things. But all I did was say no if he approached me offering extra hours, or a few extra pounds."

DI Adams still didn't speak. Dandy nosed her hand, but she didn't look away from Collins.

Collins sighed. "I moved back to Skipton after he left, and started again as a DC. I couldn't stand knowing it had all been going on for so long and no one did anything to stop it. That they just let him walk away. That *I* didn't do more."

They looked at each other for a long moment, Collins' face calm as he waited. She couldn't decide if she did believe him, or just wanted to. A little of both, perhaps. But finally she said, "Did you ever see Rose's neighbour?"

"No. You think it's him?"

"Graham thinks it could be. I don't see why he'd kill a cryptozoologist, though."

"No," Collins said, already taking his keys from his pocket. "But we always said the cryptozoologist might not have been the target." He leaned back in the door. "Bethany? We're going now. Hurry up."

DI Adams looked at him, eyebrows raised, as he turned back into the hall.

"I didn't do anything back then," he said. "I wanted to keep my job. But I *knew*. Not really any excuse for it, is there?" He didn't wait for an answer, just headed down the stairs, and DI Adams looked at Dandy. He offered her a pansy plant, still trailing roots and dirt.

"Thanks," she said.

THEY LEFT Bethany at the station, clutching a tattered tissue and snuffling steadily. DC Genny Smythe had looked horrified as they handed the young woman over, which DI Adams rather sympathised with. But that was why you worked your way up. So someone else could deal with sobbing suspects. And also why you got yourself an approachable work partner.

They'd stopped at the garage for fuel and drinks as they sped out of Skipton, and DI Adams risked a mouthful of coffee while they were on a fairly straight stretch of road, then scowled at the takeaway mug. It wasn't coffee. Coffee should be smooth and rich and muscular, with just a touch of bitterness, and this was … This was not. This tasted like it had been made by someone who had heard of coffee, once, from a third cousin twice removed.

"Problem, Adams? Has that coffee personally insulted you?" Collins asked. He was driving, taking the wider sweeps of road fast, barely slowing for the bends even as the afternoon light grew low and heavy.

"It's certainly insulting the good name of coffee everywhere," she said, not really thinking about it. Her head was still with Donny/Dougal and the question of where Rose was. A text had dinged in from Lucas while she was getting their terrible drinks, and it seemed to suggest that Graham's suspicions were right.

Jules taking her time on vids. Date stamps messed with, and she's certain it's old footage. Not an accident. How about Pork Pie Posse?

"You should try hot chocolate," Collins said, taking a swig from his own drink. "Even the garage can manage hot chocolate."

"I'm not twelve," DI Adams said, bracing herself as they slid into another corner. "Caravan ahead."

"I can see that, Adams." He glanced at her. "Any news from anyone?"

DI Adams had called Graham before they left the station. He had reported that everything was still quiet. She told him to keep her updated, then tried calling Alice and Miriam. There was no answer from either.

"Should we just get Graham and PC Shaw – Ben – to bring Donny in?" she asked Collins now, as the country opened up around them.

"No," he said. "We'll be there soon enough. And we're going to have to be careful – we need to be sure it's going to stick. He'll have got rid of all the evidence, if he did it, and the last thing we need is him claiming police harassment."

"We don't know for sure it's him."

"If there's even a chance it is, we need to get this right. He can't get away with this again." Collins' knuckles were white on the wheel, and he was driving fast enough that DI Adams kept finding herself trying to brake on the passenger side. "Are Graham and Ben watching for the W.I., too?"

"For anyone. It sounds like they're lurking around Rose's garden like commandos."

"Why do I think they might be enjoying that?"

"Because they will be. I'll put money on Ben Shaw having mud stripes painted on his face by now."

Collins *tsk*ed. "He is a professional, Adams."

"He plays Dungeons and Dragons with Lucas."

"Who is also a professional. Hobbies are hobbies."

"Like cheese?"

"Like cheese." His hands were tight on the wheel as they spun around a corner, but he lifted one casually enough to take another slurp of hot chocolate. DI Adams would have thought he was entirely unaffected by the latest developments, if not for a small, unfamiliar twitch at the corner of his jaw. He put the cup back, glanced at her and said, "Are we good, Adams?"

"We?"

"Do you suspect me of nefarious dealings with a disgraced former superior?"

"I'm not sure I'd have put it like that, even if I did."

His voice was serious as he said, "I can call the DCI and get her to come in. I'll step out of this case, and once it's cleared up you can consider if you're still happy working with me."

DI Adams stared at her to-go mug. It was a souvenir one that Collins had bought her when she first arrived, and it had Yorkshire sheep all over it, big cartoonish eyes staring back at her. "That's not necessary."

"It is if you have doubts."

She considered it, watching the dry-stone walls rendered gold by the low afternoon light, and the fields washed with sun. In it, the sheep were almost as white as the ones on her mug. "No," she said finally. "We all take the easy road sometimes."

He nodded, and took one hand off the wheel, holding it out to her. She took it and they shook, solemnly. "Good," he said. "Now you know my deepest, darkest secret. So, since we're deepening our partnership through the sharing of meaningful experiences, what happened in London that sent you up here? Was that your easy road?"

"I'm going to call Graham and warn him about the W.I. again. They're so damn sneaky that they could still get past him."

"I'm starting to suspect you're avoiding the subject."

"I have no idea why. This is important. They should include W.I. wrangling in modern policing courses," she said, as she pulled up Graham's number again.

"And dragon wrangling?" Collins suggested.

"That'd be just for specialists." The phone rang in her hand before she could hit dial, and she blinked at the display. "Oh, bloody journalist." She refused the call and took a sip of fake coffee, and the phone rang again. "Ugh." She hit *reject call.*

"Can't fault his persistence."

"Why not?"

Collins' phone rang, and the display on the dashboard lit up with *E. Giles, Craven Chronicle.* "It seems urgent."

"I'm sure he thinks so," she said, but didn't protest as Collins answered.

"DI Collins," he said. "DI Adams is also here."

"Adams! Bloody hell – did you not get my message?" Ervin shouted, and Collins turned the volume down. The journalist sounded as if he were running, and DI Adams frowned.

"I've been slightly busy. Giving statements to journalists isn't exactly high—"

"Never mind that!" He was panting, and now he yelped, and she heard the crack of branches.

"What's going on?"

"We may have a situation here."

"We? Who's we?" Collins demanded.

"Ah, the dragons and me. We're in the woods. I— hang on. Angelus! Angelus, *stop!*"

"Ervin!" DI Adams snapped. "*What's going on?* What's the situation?"

"Um— Bloody hell, what was *that?*" There was the rumble of an answer somewhere, and Ervin's voice went up slightly. "*Just* an adder? Why's there an adder? We *have* adders?" Another rumble. *"How is that better than standing on a pixie?"*

"Ervin!" DI Adams managed not to shout, barely. "What is your situation?"

"Um— did you know a pixie bite is worse than an adder? Oh, wait – no, not worse, they're just more likely to bite you. And have bad dental hygiene."

DI Adams looked at Collins. He shrugged, and said, "Have you been eating any strange mushrooms in those woods, Ervin?"

"No." DI Adams could almost see the journalist collecting himself, then he said, "We think Walter might know where Rose is,

and who the murderer is. And apparently there's a more than even chance that he might eat them."

"What?" DI Adams demanded.

"And how did you come to this conclusion?" Collins asked.

"Because he was chasing Rose's dog, and we thought he was going to eat it, but apparently he'd never hurt her dog."

DI Adams looked at Collins, who shook his head. "Are you sure about those mushrooms?"

"Look, I don't have time to explain!" Ervin's voice went up at the end into a yelp, and there was a crack that sounded like he'd run into something. "*Dammit!* I could really use some help here. Apparently Walter has a good nose, so may have been able to track the murderer. So now we somehow have to stop him eating said murderer, which is something I'd rather leave in the capable hands – sorry, paws – of dragons, but those journalists are back in the village. I just got Mortimer away from them."

There was another rumble of a deep voice just out of earshot, and DI Adams squeezed her temples with one hand.

"What the hell was Mortimer doing in the village? We *knew* those damn journalists were there!"

"He was trying to save Rose's bloody dog, who I now have, and is currently trying to dislocate my arm, and can you not say *damn journalists* like I'm just as bad as them?"

"So you've got the dog? The one Walter was chasing?" Collins said. "So Walter's there? Can't Beaufort deal with him *before* you get to the village?"

"Yes, yes, no, and I'm sure he could if we could find him." There was a crash and Ervin swore. "This is *not* territory for anything taller than the bloody dog."

"So where's Walter now?"

"Hunting the murderer, I assume. The dragon consensus seems to be that he stashed Rose somewhere, came out to get Angelus for her, and they'll now be going after the murderer together before anyone rumbles them."

"Bloody hell," Collins said, and looked at DI Adams. "Wasn't Walter the one that got all drooly over the humans that first Christmas?"

DI Adams squeezed the bridge of her nose. "That's the one."

"That sounds less than promising."

"How's this for promising?" Ervin asked. "Walter would also like to eat the journalists. There seems to be some disagreement as to whether he actually *will,* but I think the safe assumption right now is that we have the first rogue dragon on our hands since the days of Saint— What?" His voice grew fainter as he addressed someone else. "Why can't I say Sai— Oh. I see."

DI Adams just stared at the dashboard display until Ervin said, "Adams? Collins? Are you there?"

"Um, yes." She'd pinched the skin of her forehead hard enough to hurt, and she rubbed it gently as she said, "Ervin, we're on the way. Just keep the rest of the dragons away from the d— the journalists, okay? You don't know for sure that's where Walter's going, and the last thing we need is anyone catching a whiff of dragons."

"I'll try," he said, not sounding too sure of himself, then yelped again. "*Ow!* Is there not a proper bloody path anywhere in this place?"

Collins hung up without waiting to hear any more, and DI Adams looked at him. "Do you think Walter might actually have figured it out? Or Rose?"

"I wouldn't put it past her," he said, and revved a little harder. "Some things about Donny made it into the news, so it's possible she might have stumbled across something that made her suspicious. And if Walter has a *good nose* …"

DI Adams clung to the door as they slid around a corner. "How do you write up *dragon ate suspect* in a report, then?"

"Hopefully, you won't have to figure that out."

She wished she felt quite as confident.

THEY CHARGED into the village with the lights flashing, although Collins didn't put the sirens on. Not that they needed to – the streets were quiet, and the few cars they passed pulled obligingly onto the pavements to allow them to pass unimpeded. Heads popped out of front doors to watch them go, and curtains twitched in a trail behind them.

"We've still not completely exhausted the possibility that the W.I. are hiding Rose," Collins said, turning onto the street that ran past Rose's toward the village hall. "We're going to feel a bit bloody silly if we turn up to find the W.I. at tea with her, and she's just been hiding out in someone's spare room."

"How likely do you think that is?" DI Adams asked. "Considering I still can't get Alice or Miriam on the phone. And, you know, the whole dragon situation."

"Not very," Collins admitted, and they rounded the corner to find two empty police cars in front of Rose's house, the driver's door hanging open on one of them, as if they'd left in a hurry. "Not at all, actually."

He braked hard, DI Adams already unbuckling her seatbelt. She scrambled out, Dandy arriving on the pavement next to her and cocking his head curiously. Shouts were coming from various directions in Rose's big, overgrown garden, but from here all she could really see was the front of the house, staring back at her blandly over the early blooms of the pocket-sized wildflower meadow and the low stone wall. Dandy leaped the gate easily and headed left, his dreadlocked hair flopping as he ran.

"Good enough," she said, and sprinted after him, listening for roars. So far all she could hear were human shouts, and she hoped it stayed that way.

Rogue dragon was not something she wanted to have to write up either.

21
MIRIAM

Miriam, who'd been feeling uncomfortably warm after hurrying through Rose's garden and scrambling over the stile, what with the assorted threats of arrest and lurking murderers and journalists, had the distinct impression that a hefty cloud had just moved in front of the sun. She shivered, blinking away black spots in her vision, and tried to stop looking at the taser. She couldn't. It drew her eye horribly, some impossible combination of bland and chunky and vicious.

"That's illegal," Jasmine said, her voice wobbly. "You can't have one of those."

"Trespassing's also illegal," Dougal said. His pursed little smile was gone, the twirled corners of his moustache abandoned to droop into his beard. "So I suppose that makes us equal."

"And just what do you propose to do with that?" Alice asked, her eyebrows arched. She examined Dougal as if *she* were the one discovering a trespasser. "You can only use it once."

"I'm not intending to use it at all, if it can be helped."

"That's hardly a threat, then, is it?" Alice hadn't moved from by the shed, and Miriam could see her hands tightening on her cane.

She hoped Alice wasn't going to try to attack him. He might *say* he wasn't going to use it, but the odds were high that he'd change his mind if confronted with the chair of the W.I. wielding her own weapon.

"It's merely to ensure cooperation. I'd hate to tase any of you. You're all old enough to have a heart attack over it."

"*Excuse* me?" Jasmine said, crossing her arms over her chest.

Dougal ignored her, still looking at Alice. "I don't need any unnecessary complications, but I'll be making a citizen's arrest."

"I see," Alice said.

"That's ridiculous," Jasmine snapped. Her face was very pink. "There's a police officer right next door. Why don't you just call *him* to come and arrest us?"

Dougal smoothed his moustache with one hand. "I need to make sure this is dealt with properly. I can't just hand you over to any old plod."

Jasmine took half a step forward, and Dougal swung the taster in her direction. "He's not an *old plod.* He's my husband, and he's very good at his job!"

"Sure he is. Some village copper, moving to it as a second career? School teacher, wasn't he? For the littlies? I'm sure he's just lighting up the ranks."

Jasmine stared at him, her mouth open, and Alice said, "My. You do take an interest in the local police, Mr Brown."

"One likes to know who's patrolling one's neighbourhood."

Miriam thought Dougal sounded odd, as if the soft lilt that accented his voice was fading, giving way to something broader and harder, something that belonged to a rougher side of Yorkshire than Toot Hansell.

"I think *we* should call the police," she managed, flinching as he turned his gaze on her.

"Excellent idea," Alice said. "Don't you agree, Jasmine? Why don't you call Ben? Let them come and sort all this out."

"*Yes.*" Jasmine fumbled for her mobile, glaring at Dougal. "He'll show you *old plod*."

"Put that down," Dougal said, raising the taser slightly. "The only person calling the police will be me."

"Why's that, Mr Brown?" Alice asked. "Is it because you don't want us telling them about the golf club in your shed?"

"I find it very handy for dealing with pests," he said, not taking his gaze from Jasmine. "Phone back in your pocket. Now."

Jasmine let go of her phone, her face so pink that Miriam wasn't sure if she was about to cry or start shouting.

"Why don't we just go into the shed and have a look at your golf club, then?" Alice asked, and Miriam's legs almost gave way. Go into a *shed* in a *murderer's garden?* Had Alice gone quite potty? "Since we'll be telling the police about it anyway," Alice continued. "Let's have a look inside and get the full story." She tapped her cane firmly against the shed, leaving marks on the bright yellow paint, and Miriam thought she heard two knocks come back, but it could have been in her own head. The heat was making her dizzy. Or something was.

Dougal sighed, as if his patience were being tested but he was holding on as well as he could, and deserved some respect for that fact. "You are trespassers. You don't get to choose what happens now." He examined them, his gaze lingering on Alice's cane. "Although, I can see that you're more than just trespassers, aren't you? I think you may be accomplices to the terrible murder next door."

"*What?*" Jasmine demanded. "That was you! It had to be you! You killed that poor man with Rose's golf club, and you're framing her! I bet you took her hairbrush to plant hairs somewhere!"

"In the car," Alice said. "Eric's car wasn't here. I imagine that once the police find it, there will be some of Rose's hairs in it."

"Oh, what scheming." He laughed, pressing his free hand to his chest. "How ridiculous. *I'm* not a murderer. Poor, dotty *Rose* is a murderer, and you've been helping her cover it up."

Dotty. Miriam took a shaky breath. "You *have* been doing it. You've been moving stuff around. Making her think she's forgetting things. It was you."

"Surely not. At her age, it's pretty much expected that she's going to start losing the plot."

Miriam just stared at him, her heart too loud in her ears, and Alice nodded. "I assume you also reported her to social services."

"Just doing my neighbourly duty. Too late to save her poor visitor, alas. But look – I caught you trying to sneak into my garden to plant the evidence!" He pointed at Alice's cane, and smiled at her. "Looks rather similar to a golf club, doesn't it?"

"If somewhat lacking in forensic evidence," she said.

"Oh, that won't be a problem." He nodded at the house. "My security cameras are rather good, but not good enough to tell the difference from here. I merely have to present the golf club to the police as the murder weapon that *you* brought into the garden with you."

"In my bare hands?" Alice asked.

"I'm sure we shall find you were wearing thin latex gloves. I have some inside."

And Alice smiled. Miriam blinked at her, wondering if she'd missed something, if this was all some elaborate joke and no one had ever been in Rose's freezer, and there was no murder weapon in the shed right next to them, and the taser was nothing more than a pound store toy. "You have thought this through," Alice said. "One could almost admire it. I'm starting to see that the whole situation is rather more premeditated than we imagined."

Miriam had been trying very hard not to imagine the murder at all, let alone the question of if it was premeditated or not. She was also still seeing spots in her vision, and her mouth had gone very dry. She wondered if Dougal would tase her if she sat down.

"Let's go inside," Dougal said. "I'd rather not have some second-rate PC stumble in until I have everything set up just right." He stepped to the side and waved them toward the house, where a folding door stood partly open onto a patio. And it really was a patio, Miriam noticed. There were terracotta tiles on the ground and open beams above, from which a few vines hung in a manner which suggested they felt they were in the wrong climate. "Please use the paths," he added. "The grass is very delicate at this time of year."

❧

MIRIAM WAS the closest to Dougal, and she regarded the ground in front of her with more concentration than was normally required. Everything was off, the sun so bright it made her squint, but the garden somehow dank and cold at the same time. The dearth of birdsong was a screaming void that made her heartbeat far too loud in her ears, and she thought she'd heard more thumps from the shed, but that could have just been inside her head. She wondered if one could actually die of fright. She supposed it would technically be via a heart attack, and her heart had always been terribly healthy, but it would really be fright that got you.

"Hurry up," Dougal said, waving the taser at her.

"Miriam?" Alice said, moving to Miriam's side as she bent over and rested her hands on her knees, breathing hard.

"No! Back off!" Dougal snapped, waving the taser at her. "No games."

"Miriam is very sensitive," Alice said, her voice cool. "I think she's feeling a little overwhelmed by it all."

"Well, she can be overwhelmed inside. Get moving, Ms Ellis. I'm sure the village can manage without its resident herbalist fraudster if I have to tase you. And it'll bloody save me having to see you wafting about the place like some super-sized Joni

Mitchell wannabe." Alice's phone started ringing, interrupting him, and he snapped, "Don't even *think* about answering that."

"I rather assumed that would be your stance on it."

Fraudster? And *Joni Mitchell?* Miriam had never *once* made a single claim about her tinctures or herbal teas or Tarot reading that wasn't entirely true. *Entirely.* She'd never have slept at night otherwise. She *helped* people! She never pretended to have any medical cures, or that she could see the future – she merely made things that smelled nice, or tasted good, and that people enjoyed. And as for her Tarot readings – well, people went to therapists, didn't they? And no one ever accused *them* of being fraudsters!

Alice was saying something sharp and pointed to Dougal, who was replying equally sharply, and Miriam looked at Alice's cane, grasped lightly in the older woman's hand, the silver tip denting the soft ground through the grass. Then she reached out and grabbed it, feeling Alice stumble but recover herself, and whipped the stick as hard as she could at Dougal. He swore, jumping back and firing the taser, and Miriam squawked in alarm, letting go of the cane as she flung her arms wide, trying to protect Alice and bracing herself for the shock.

The darts shot forward, and Jasmine hit Miriam in a tackle that was almost as impressive as Miriam's own had been earlier. They crashed to the ground together as the cane swiped through the trailing wires of the taser darts, sending them still further off course, and they plinked neatly into the ground near where Miriam's feet had been. She was almost certain she could hear the fizz of electricity on them.

Dougal swore again and lunged forward, reaching for the walking stick. Miriam rolled away from Jasmine and lashed out with one leg, not bothering to try to get up. She caught Dougal just below the knee and he sprawled to the ground, biting down on a howl of pain, but he was still scrabbling to reach the cane. She belly-flopped after him, reaching desperately to grab him before he got to the walking stick, then he gave an unexpected shriek and rolled away, fetching up against the shed with both hands clutching his leg.

"You cow!" he managed, his eyes bright with tears.

Alice looked down at the taser in her hand. "Well, how about that," she said. "You *can* use it twice, after a fashion."

Miriam blinked at the darts, still lying innocuously on the grass, and then at the twin scorch marks on the man's bare leg, where he must've been lying on top of them. Then she scrambled up and grabbed the cane. "I don't even *like* Joni Mitchell," she shouted, pointing the end of the cane at him.

"Miriam, step back," Alice started, but Dougal had already launched himself forward. Miriam swung the cane hard, but he was too close, and he grabbed it, trying to wrestle it away from her. Jasmine rushed over, joining Miriam, and he shoved forward suddenly, sending them both stumbling backward like contestants winning a tug o'war. Then he hauled back again, while they were still off balance, managing to tear the cane away from Jasmine, and Alice swung a stained-glass dragonfly with neat, almost surgical precision at the back of his head.

Dougal gave a small, startled sound of protest, and crumpled softly to the ground. Miriam sprawled onto her bottom, the cane clutched to her chest, and for a moment all was silent.

Then someone started hammering wildly on the shed door, and from the garden next door someone else screamed. It was a full-throated, horrified scream, and they all spun toward it.

"Ben!" Jasmine gasped, and grabbed the dragonfly off Alice, bolting for the stile.

"Jasmine, wait!" Alice called, but the younger woman was already over the wall and vanishing into the garden beyond.

Miriam froze where she was. Dougal was already moaning and twitching, and whoever was in the shed was still trying to beat the door down, and more shouts were going up next door, and

Jasmine had run off armed with nothing but a stained-glass dragonfly. She knew one was meant to do some sort of triage in such situations, but how did one know which was most important?

"Miriam, quickly," Alice said, hurrying to the shed door. "It has to be Rose."

Miriam rushed to help her, relieved that someone else was better at triage than she was, then saw the heavy-duty padlock on the door. "We can't get through that," she said, then stepped back as Rose – if it was her – hit the door again. The sound was coming from around knee-height.

Alice sighed. "No, we can't." She glanced at Dougal, who had stopped twitching. "He might have the key in his pocket."

Miriam gave the man a horrified look. "I don't want to get that close to him. Can't we just break a window?"

Alice peered at them. "Yes, but they're a bit small and high for climbing through. And Rose is probably tied up, so one of us needs to get in and free her."

"If we get the gaffer tape out, we can tie him up and *then* check his pockets." A heavy thump accompanied that, so it seemed that Rose agreed with her.

"Oh, well done, Miriam," Alice said, and nodded at the cane, which Miriam had almost forgotten she was holding. "Whenever you're ready."

Miriam thrust the cane at Alice. "You do it. I'll only make a mess of things."

"Of course you won't. Go on. You've earned it."

Miriam was about to argue that she didn't think one *earned* the right to break windows, as if it were some sort of reward, but another volley of shouting went up next door, accompanied by a yell of *"Stop! North Yorkshire Police!"*, so she just hurried to the side of the shed, shouted, "Cover your eyes, Rose!" and swung wildly at the window with her head turned away.

The cane connected solidly, and the glass shattered with a

sound that was both horrifying and delightful. Miriam opened her eyes and stared at the shards still clinging to the frame. "*Ooh,*" she said, and jabbed gleefully at the remaining pieces, sending them tumbling into the darkness beyond.

Alice's phone was ringing again, and she waved at Miriam to keep going as she answered it. "Ervin?"

Miriam couldn't hear what the journalist was saying, but she paused with her hand on the gaffer tape as Alice said, "Why are you with the dragons? And no, I don't think Walter has Rose at all. I think we've found her."

Miriam grabbed a handful of the bin bag curtains and ripped them away, peering down into the depths of the shed. She was blocking most of the light from this window, and the other was similarly covered, but she could just make out a small form on the floor, curled on its side. As she looked, it raised its legs and kicked the door again, a little wearily.

"Ervin, where are you?" Alice asked. "You're not letting the dragons come to the village, are you?"

There was a squawk from the phone that Miriam thought likely had to do with the question of young journalists *letting* dragons do anything. She cleared the last of the glass away and called, "Rose, we're here. We'll have you out in a jiffy."

The bound figure kicked the door a few more times, and made some muffled noises.

"They absolutely *cannot* come here!" Alice exclaimed. "You have to stop them!" A pause, and Miriam looked at her as she said, "I don't care if Walter wants to eat a journalist." Another squawk, then, "Well, it's not you in particular, is it?"

Miriam picked up the gaffer tape and went to kneel by Dougal, wondering if Katherine was still around. The cheek of her, coming right into the garden! Not that Miriam would condone Walter eating anyone, of course, but a small scare wouldn't hurt. Although, seeing as she was a cryptid journalist, that would probably only make her more determined.

She set the cane down, still half-listening to Alice as she said, "Ervin, if you don't keep those dragons away from the village, I will personally make sure Rose gives her story to your competitors."

The gaffer tape was proving very tricky to unroll. It kept coming away in strips, rather than the whole width at once, and she was scraping at it with her newly trimmed fingernails when Alice shouted, "Miriam, *move!*"

Miriam dropped the tape with a yelp and flung herself back as Alice rushed forward, grabbing for the cane. But Dougal already had a hand on it, rolling to his feet and towering over Miriam, his lips pulled back from his teeth.

"Look at that," he said. "You *attacked* me. I was merely defending myself when I hit you back. And it's not my fault at all that one blow was all it took." He raised the cane, and Miriam scrabbled back along the grass until her spine hit the shed, barely feeling the impact, her eyes fixed on him.

"You'll never make that stick," Alice said. She still had her phone clutched in one hand. "You've murdered a man. Imprisoned Rose. And now you're threatening us. You can't get away with that."

"It's all about who you know," Dougal said, and took a step toward Miriam. She raised one arm, bracing herself for the attack, and Alice rushed forward. Dougal pivoted on his heel, bringing the cane up in a swing so fast and hard that Alice had no chance of deflecting it.

"*No!*" Miriam shouted, and a shadow plummeted straight out of the sunny sky. The cane vanished, leaving Dougal stumbling forward, pulled off balance as it was torn away from him. Alice grabbed him, trying to push him all the way to the ground, and Miriam scrambled up, rushing to join her.

"What—" Dougal shoved Alice away, sending her staggering,

and jumped back, one hand out to Miriam as if telling her to stop. He peered around. "What the hell was that?"

Miriam ignored the outstretched hand and rushed him, hoping that her success with tackling was down to some innate talent, and that she could bring him to the floor as easily as she had Bethany. Dougal sidestepped, his hands balling into fists, and she realised she was too late to change her trajectory, that she was going to go sailing straight past him, and he was going to make it hurt while she did so. But there was no chance of stopping now, so she threw herself sideways in the hope that would catch him off guard.

It shouldn't have worked, of course, but at that moment his gaze flicked skywards. "What—" he started again, the words breathless, and Miriam hit him in a clumsy shoulder charge that sent him stumbling back into an intricate bed of azaleas, the delicate stems and petals crumpling under their weight as Miriam bounced off him and ended up on her hands and knees.

"What the *hell* is that?" he managed, and the words were a shriek.

The only answer he got was a roar, one so full-throated and primal that Miriam almost shrieked herself. She looked around in time to see Walter raise himself on his hind quarters, his saggy chest swelling with fire and rage as he lifted his snout to the sky and roared once more, then lowered his gaze to Dougal.

"Oh, no," she said, and scrambled out of the way as the old dragon dropped his forepaws to the roof and released a blast of fire into the garden. Dougal screamed, lost on the other side of the inferno, and Miriam raised an arm to protect herself, the heat searing the skin.

"Walter, *no,*" Alice said. "That's very unhelpful."

Walter swung his head to glare at her, growling deep in his chest.

"No," Alice said again. "This is not how civilised creatures resolve things."

Miriam looked at the cane, and thought that was maybe a little inaccurate.

Walter jumped to the ground, wings flaring, and stalked toward Dougal. Miriam could see his chest glowing with contained flames, and his tail coiled and flicked behind him in agitated fury.

"Where's Rose?" he rumbled. "I smell her, false friend. Where is she?"

Dougal made some wordless sound. His beard was blackened and distinctly shorter, and Miriam could smell the acrid stench of burned hair.

"Where is Rose?" Walter raised one heavy paw, talons hooked and gleaming. "Tell me, or I shall boil your eyes in their sockets and decorate the fells with your teeth. Magpies will hunt the streams for your vertebrae. Your toe bones will become chew toys for hatchlings. Your ribs will be crafted into—"

"Walter, *really,*" Alice said, and he looked around at her. "We've found Rose. She's in here." She pointed at the shed.

"What? Why haven't you let her out?" he demanded.

"It's locked," Miriam whispered. She was still wondering what one's ribs could be crafted into.

Walter leaped away from Dougal, the movement fluid and so swift that Miriam had to hold a yelp in. He was at the door in an instant, seizing the lock and ripping it away effortlessly. The door came with it, one hinge tearing free and leaving it sagging over the garden, and Miriam was dimly aware of Dougal scrambling to his feet and bolting for the stile. She didn't stop him. He was heading in the direction she'd heard the shouts of police coming from, and she had no desire to see anyone be fried by a furious dragon, no matter how justified it might feel.

"Rose!" Walter roared, and Miriam spotted two small, booted feet waving in what appeared to be a celebratory manner. She rolled to her feet and rushed over with Alice, while the old dragon

patted Rose's legs heavily. "There you are," he said. "There you are, you silly human. There you are."

Miriam leaned against the shed door, her eyes prickling unexpectedly.

The birds were singing again.

And then someone screamed from the next garden, *"Help! Monsters!"*

"Oh dear," Alice said, and crouched a little stiffly next to Walter. "I think our assistance may be required."

Miriam sighed and had to admit to herself that she rather hoped not.

22
ALICE

Alice used the little Swiss army knife on her key ring to saw through the gaffer tape binding Rose's hands, knees, and ankles. As soon as her hands were free Rose grabbed the tape that was over her mouth and prised it off, already talking.

"Where is he? Where is that horrible man? I'm going to—"

"*I'll* do it," Walter declared. He was sitting just outside the shed, watching Alice as if he suspected her of putting the knife to some dastardly work if she weren't properly supervised. "I almost had him, but your *friends* here called me off."

"I rather think an incinerated murderer might be stretching even DI Collins' patience," Alice said, folding the knife and popping her keyring back in her jacket pocket. "Never mind DI Adams. Are you alright, Rose?"

Rose nodded, rubbing the back of her head carefully. "I've got an awful bump. He jumped me in my own garden, you know."

"But what were you doing in your garden? You were quite safe at mine, then you had to run off putting yourself in the way of murderers."

Rose touched her lips, a small, painful movement. "I saw

Meena. And I thought, well, I just can't take it. Maybe I *am* going dotty, leaving haddock in my glovebox and my glasses in the ice cream. But I was sure I didn't kill Eric. And if Meena had got me to that appointment, maybe I'd never have had a chance to prove that a little dotty isn't the same as losing one's way completely."

Alice patted her shoulder lightly, aware that she should say something, but not sure what. That being eighty-three and still independent was a wonderful thing? That one must count one's blessings? As true as both statements were, they had the flat, stale taste of platitudes. Plus she was aware that there were still shouts rising from next door. It was hardly the time for this sort of thing.

Miriam squeezed past Walter and crouched down next to them, putting a hand on Rose's leg. "We'd never have let Meena take you away."

"We wouldn't," Alice agreed. That, at least, was true. "That's just not how things are done."

Rose smiled, her mouth still looking red and raw from the tape, and said, "Does how things are done include bagging ourselves a murderer?"

"Yes," Walter said immediately.

"Not you," Alice said firmly. "This is human business."

Walter growled, and Miriam tried to jump away from him, still in a crouch, and fell back on the shed floor.

"Stop that," Rose said. "Alice is quite right. There are those cryptid journalists about the place still, and explaining a half-eaten murderer would be quite tricky."

Walter reared back, one paw on his chest. "I wouldn't *eat* him."

Alice thought the little thread of drool currently hanging from one of Walter's worn but still impressive canines ruined his protestations somewhat.

More shouts went up beyond the pastel fence, and Miriam said, "Jasmine's out there."

"She is." Alice pushed herself up to standing, ignoring a twinge in her hip, and offered a hand to Rose, but she was already scrambling to her feet. "If everyone promises to refrain from biting, eating, or setting fire to anyone, perhaps we shall all go, then."

"I only bite in extremis," Rose said, looking around the shed. "Best not use the golf club, although I know he's put my fingerprints on it already."

"Best not," Alice agreed, and went to collect her cane while Miriam and Rose armed themselves with a hoe and a rake, respectively. "Ladies? And dragon?"

"Ready," Rose and Miriam said, and Walter blew a restrained little puff of flame that scorched the yellow paint of the shed. Alice thought it was an improvement.

"Onward," she said, and clambered over the stile, into the rich green depths of Rose's garden and toward the shouts and crashes that were coming from it.

It was rather less frightening than talking of dementia on a shed floor.

ALICE HAD ALWAYS KNOWN that Rose took delight in the overgrown nature of her garden, and the lawn to the front of the house (such as it was, between the rowan trees that had once lived in pots by the door but now almost blocked it, and the pine trees that had once been Christmas trees and now towered over the little house) was always left to be a wildflower meadow, growing and fading on its own natural cycle. She also knew that, other than the vegetable patch, Rose preferred to leave the rest of the garden to grow as wild as it needed.

But, until now, she had never appreciated just how impenetrable that made it. She could hear DI Adams shouting somewhere, her voice clear and hard-edged. "Stop! Police!" Someone else was shouting that they were the police, too, and a third person was yelling, "Rose! *Rose!*" in constantly rising register. Yet another was shrieking wordlessly, and there was an awful lot of crashing going on, as though a large proportion of the current occupants of the garden were attempting to force their way across it without using paths.

"Where do we start?" Miriam asked, clutching the hoe to her chest. "Should we go to the front and see if the police are there?"

"No," Rose said, before Alice could answer. "Let's catch that bloody Dougal. Walter?"

Walter growled, low and delighted, his scales flushing in shades of orange and red.

"No," Alice started, but Walter surged forward so fast that all she could do was stumble out of the way before he barged her off the narrow path. Rose sprinted after him, far too quickly for someone who'd been tied up all afternoon, let alone someone of her age, waving the rake over her head like a javelin. Alice shook her hand irritably where the nettles had got her, stepping back onto the trail. "Rose!" she shouted, but the only response was someone else shouting back, "Rose? Rose!" It was like some absurd game of Marco Polo.

"Rose!" Miriam shouted, rushing after the woman and the dragon. *"Rose!"*

"Rose!" the unseen person shouted, and a third voice joined in. "Rose! *Chérie!*"

"Jean-Claude?" the first voice yelled. "Is that you?"

"Ah, *putain,*" Jean-Claude said, loudly enough that it carried. "Is that you, schoolboy?"

"Bloody Frenchie," Campbell yelled.

"You come here and say this to me!"

"Police!" A familiar voice rose over them. Colin. "Clear the garden, lads. *Now!*"

Alice shook her head and broke into a jog. Colin and DI Adams had been very quick to follow them, which was rather a good thing if they had two of Rose's men friends rattling helplessly around the garden. But the inspectors didn't know about Dougal, and the two men didn't know about dragons, and somewhere in here were two more police officers who also weren't going to expect large, enraged mythical beasts charging through the undergrowth. This was all going to come together in a terribly messy way if they weren't careful.

She was just skirting the compost bin, following the path toward the vegetable patch in the hope that some more open ground would help her ascertain what was happening, when someone burst out of the bushes from the direction of the house. She stumbled to a stop, sweeping the cane up to protect herself, and a man swerved to avoid her, tripped over a tree stump covered with mushrooms, and rolled to the ground with a yelp, grabbing his shin.

"Are you alright?" Alice asked, not lowering the cane. For all she knew, Dougal had called in reinforcements.

"Run!" the man screamed at her. "There are *monsters* in here!" And he scrambled to his feet and sprinted down the path in the direction of the gate to the village green, injured leg forgotten. Someone else was crashing through the bush where he'd emerged, and Alice spun to face them as Jasmine popped into view, dragging Ben with her.

"Alice!" she exclaimed. "Did a man go past?"

"That way," Alice said, pointing. She assumed the man hadn't been talking about Jasmine and her bewildered-looking husband when he'd mentioned monsters.

"Hurry, Ben!" Jasmine exclaimed. "We need to get him before he reaches the green!"

"You really can't be here," Ben started, although Alice wasn't sure if he was addressing her or Jasmine.

"Come *on,*" Jasmine insisted. "Quick! He was trespassing!"

"Jasmine, I'm looking for a murderer—"

"DI Adams has that covered. Hurry!" And Jasmine let go of him, sprinting down the path toward the green. Alice watched her go, and looked at Ben.

He rubbed the back of his head. "There seems to be a dog in here somewhere."

"Angelus, I imagine," Alice said.

"No …"

"Jasmine is going to catch up to that man, you know. She's rather quick."

Ben swore and sprinted off, yelling Jasmine's name as more shouts of "Rose!" bounced around the garden.

Alice considered it, then took the rough path they'd appeared from, emerging from the worst of the undergrowth and threading her way through a haphazard orchard of leafy apple and pear trees and blossoming stone fruit trees. The shouting was mostly ahead of her now, although she could hear some off to the side somewhere, toward the front of the house. She ignored that and hurried on, just as something *roared* ahead of her, and every small, primal instinct screamed at her to flee.

"Oh, dear," she muttered, and broke into a run.

"Rose!"

"*Chérie!*"

"Rose, I'm here, where are you?"

"*Chérie,* it is okay, a grown man is here too—"

"Bloody hell, it's hardly the time—"

The voices were coming from somewhere around the house, but Alice kept going, jogging gently in the direction of the roars. She almost collided with the tall police officer who'd been watching Miriam's house as he emerged out of one of the other paths that fed into the orchard, his face red and his hair dishevelled.

"Ms Martin?" he said, blinking at her. "What are you— Never mind. You need to clear the area. There's a, uh … dog? Dog. There's a dog in here." He peered uncertainly through the trees. There hadn't been any more roaring, but there was a lot of growling drifting to them, as well as some screeches that sounded vaguely human.

Alice started to answer, but Colin appeared at a run from further down the garden. "Graham!" he shouted. "Get to the bloody road and make sure that—" He hesitated, glancing at Alice. "Secure the perimeter. *Move!*"

"On it." Graham turned and ran for the house, and Colin paused next to Alice.

"Are you alright?" he asked her.

"Yes. I'm a little concerned that our murderer might get himself eaten, though."

"That's in hand," Colin said. "Well, sort of." He pivoted on his heel as the sounds of Campbell and Jean-Claude swapping insults drifted to him. "Oh, bloody hell. I better get them out of here."

"Best do," Alice agreed, and headed for the vegetable patch again before he could insist she went with him. *Sort of* sounded as if assistance might still be required. And she certainly wasn't going to miss out on that.

ALICE EMERGED from the little orchard area to find the surprisingly uniform beds of Rose's vegetable garden ahead of her, half-hidden behind a trellis of climbing beans and crowded with companion plants and sprawling rhubarb and the fluffy heads of carrots. Walter was crouched among the potatoes, his talons digging divots out of the soil and his wings flung wide. His yellow teeth were bared and his eyes were narrowed to slits of green fire. Rose stood beside him, one hand on his flank, and Dougal sprawled on the ground among the parsnips, looking more bewildered than frightened. Between him and the dragon was a huge dog sporting matted locks of dark grey hair, as big as the dragon himself and growling in a low rumble that Alice could feel in her bones. She had an idea that the dog had its hackles raised, too, but as it mostly resembled a walking carpet it was hard to tell.

"Down, dog," Walter snarled. "Rose wants that one."

"Dandy, stay," DI Adams said. She was standing over Dougal, handcuffs in one hand, but her eyes were on Walter.

Dandy gave her a glance which clearly conveyed that he didn't need to be told what to do.

"Rose?" DI Adams called. "I need to arrest him now."

Walter swung his head toward her, drool dripping from one fang, and Alice was rather impressed that the inspector managed not to flinch.

"Well, the thing is," Rose said, "We caught him, didn't we, Walter? So we should get to decide what to do."

"Not how it works," DI Adams said.

Alice looked around for Miriam, but she didn't seem to be here. Other than Dougal, there were just the three of them, plus the dragon and the dandy, and she wasn't quite sure how one stopped a furious dragon. And while Dandy in his large angry form was really exceptionally large and toothy, he wasn't as toothy or as armoured as Walter.

"It should," Rose said. "He's more than just a murderer, aren't you, Dougal?"

Dougal blinked at her, then said, "What, you think you can scare me with your … your *dogs?* Just some stupid old—"

"Shut up," DI Adams said, her voice flat, and Dougal turned his glare on her.

"I'll have you, too. Police bloody harassment, this is! I recognised that Collins. Still hanging round, is he? Lucky he even made inspector. Herding dotty old ladies is about his level."

"Seriously, shut up," DI Adams said, still with her eyes on Rose.

"He's been sneaking into my house," Rose said. "He's been moving all my stuff." Her hands were clenched into fists, and she was shaking. *"He's been making me think I'm going dotty."*

"You *are* dotty, you old—" He broke off as both Walter and Dandy growled, the chorus making the birds screech in fright.

"Rose," Alice said, and both she and DI Adams turned to look at her.

"Oh, hello, Alice," Rose said. "Sorry to leave you back there. I thought you might not approve."

Alice made her way around the trellis and regarded Dougal. "It's not that I don't approve. It's just that this really isn't right. You must let the police deal with this."

"Like you let them deal with your unsatisfactory husband?" Rose asked, and DI Adams raised her eyebrows.

"How I dealt with my husband is neither here nor there. And I certainly didn't get *dragons* involved."

"*Huh.* Well, that's something, I suppose," DI Adams said, almost to herself.

"But he tried to make me think I should be locked up," Rose said. "Like my sister."

Alice raised her eyebrows slightly. The mysterious sister. "You never talk about her."

"She's been in a home since she was in her sixties."

"I'm sorry," Alice said. "I didn't know."

"*Meena* knows. It's why she was so keen for me to get checked. I've always been waiting for it to catch me up, somehow."

"It's not a sure thing, Rose," DI Adams said. "Everyone's different."

Rose's jaw was set in a hard line. "He did all of it. The chicken in my bedside table. My glasses in the flour. *All of it.* He was trying to send me mad. *And* he killed poor Eric, who never hurt anyone!"

DI Adams looked at Dougal. "Is this true?"

He glanced at her, then said, "I can see interrogation techniques have really come a long way. You think you can scare me with ... with ..." He waved at Dandy and Walter vaguely. "With your dogs in silly costumes?"

Alice wondered how he thought one of the "dogs" was talking, as well as breathing fire. But people can be very convinced of their own realities when their minds are made up enough.

DI Adams snorted. "Well, we've got you for murder. You may as well tell me the rest as well."

"You don't have me for anything. There's nothing to incriminate me."

"Not even the murder weapon in your shed?" Alice asked.

"With *her* prints on it," Dougal said, nodding at Rose. "She planted it there. Can't prove she didn't."

"Not even with your cameras? The ones that will show us freeing Rose, who you'd *imprisoned* in your shed?"

"It's a set up."

DI Adams rubbed her jaw, looking at Dandy as if considering telling him to just step back and let Walter at the man. But all she said was, "We're surprisingly good at what we do, Donny Cooper. And your track record will count against you."

Dougal didn't flinch when DI Adams used a different name, but his eyes narrowed. Not much, but enough for Alice to know that the name was right.

"Track record?" Rose asked. "You've done this *before?*"

Walter lowered his head still further, moving forward with the low-slung intensity of a stalking cat.

"No," DI Adams said. "Walter, *stop."*

Walter ignored her, and Dandy lowered his own head, baring

his teeth. He'd grown to the size of a small horse, but he looked rangy and insubstantial against the bulk and length of the dragon.

"Walter!" Alice snapped. "Stop this right now!"

Walter gathered himself and launched into a leap, sweeping his hind legs under him with the talons aimed at Dandy as the dog rose to meet him. Dandy twisted aside, slipping out from under Walter as he came down then slamming into the dragon's shoulder, driving him sideways.

"No!" DI Adams shouted. She wrestled a length of bamboo stake out of the garden and lunged forward, whipping the bamboo across Walter's snout as he snapped at Dandy. "Back off! *Back off!*"

Walter flung one tatty wing out almost lazily, hitting the inspector hard enough to knock her off her feet, but she rolled straight back up and chased the dragon and the dandy as they tumbled through the vegetables, Dandy somehow avoiding the dragon's talons. He moved with astonishing, fluid grace, but Walter was dribbling steam from his jaws as well as drool, and his chest was starting to glow with fire. Dandy couldn't escape that, no matter how fast he was, and DI Adams showed no signs of giving up her assault with the bamboo stick.

"Rose, we have to stop Walter," Alice said. "This has gone too far now. He's quite out of control."

"He was only helping me. That man was making me think I needed to go into a *home!*"

"So you think he deserves to be eaten?"

"Walter was never going *eat* him," Rose said, and Alice frowned at her. "He wouldn't! He was just going to scare him!"

"I think that's worked," Alice said, and they turned to look at Dougal just in time to see him scramble to his feet while DI Adams' attention was on Dandy and Walter. The inspector caught the movement and spun to face him, ducking a punch that he feinted at her head but not avoiding the one he landed in her belly.

She doubled over, and he turned to sprint back into the depths of the garden.

"Oh, really?" Rose asked, as DI Adams sank to her knees, gasping.

"Really," Alice said. Dandy had abandoned Walter, leaping away from the dragon with his teeth bared. Dougal barely made it two metres before the massive dog pulled him to the ground, two paws on his back and his teeth gripping the back of the man's neck.

Dougal screeched, flailing wildly, and DI Adams called a little breathlessly, "Easy, Dandy."

Dandy lifted his gaze to her, his stature diminishing, as if he was dissolving in the cool air, and then he was suddenly gone. DI Adams gave him a thumbs up. Well, Alice assumed it was for Dandy. It seemed unlikely to be for Dougal. The inspector pressed a hand to her belly, took a deep breath, then nodded and climbed to her feet.

"Donny Cooper, I'm arresting you on suspicion of murder," she started, picking her handcuffs up from where she'd dropped them to chase the dragon. She glanced around, as if suddenly reminded that Dougal wasn't the only one she had to worry about. "Oh, for—Walter, *no!*"

Walter was loping back across the garden with his teeth bared and his growl rattling in his chest. "I told you, didn't I?" he rumbled, his eyes glinting green as he narrowed them at Dougal. "I'll line my nest with your bones. I'll feed your eyes to the fish. I'll—"

"You will not," DI Adams snapped, stepping in front of Dougal. "You'll stop this right now."

"Rose, make Walter stop! *Hurry!*" Alice couldn't decide if the inspector was extraordinarily brave or just foolhardy, but Walter was showing no signs of relinquishing his claim to the murderer.

"Walter!" Rose shouted. "Walter, no, it's all okay! You can stop now!"

The old dragon ignored her entirely, and Dandy shimmered back into sight, shouldering DI Adams out of the way as he bounded forward, leaping for Walter. Walter didn't even hesitate. He rose onto his hindquarters and met Dandy with both front paws, spinning with surprising grace and using the dog's speed to fling him the length of the garden. Dandy landed with a crash, rolling wildly through some fledgling climbing beans on their supports, and Walter turned back to DI Adams.

"Behave!" she snapped. She'd reclaimed her position, standing between the dragon and the man on the ground, and she waved the piece of bamboo at Walter as if he were a recalcitrant dog. He made to lunge forward, and she caught him a smart blow across the snout. He snarled, rearing back and lifting one paw to knock her away. On the other side of the vegetable garden Dandy leaped to his feet and came charging back. He was too far away, though, even with his huge, terrifying bounds eating up the ground. DI Adams braced herself, not moving. *"No."*

"Walter!" Alice shouted, Rose's protest rising in a chorus with hers.

DI Adams swished the bamboo, and Walter snarled again, a terrifying sound that made even Dougal curl into an instinctive fetal position, his arms over his head. Alice could feel the hair on her arms straining away from the skin.

"Don't," the inspector said.

Alice felt a most unfamiliar urge to look away as the inspector lifted her puny weapon to meet the dragon, her jaw set, and Walter brought his paw down in a heavy, vicious sweep.

23
MORTIMER

The three dragons raced back to the village without even bothering to try and conceal themselves, Ervin trailing them with his jumper strung through Angelus' collar as a makeshift leash, his arms scratched and his hair looking a different sort of unruly to usual.

"Stop!" he managed, as they crashed out of the trees and onto the path that bordered the stream. "We can't just go running around the village. Or you lot can't, anyway, and I'm knackered." He pressed a hand to his side and gulped air.

"We have to find Walter," Beaufort said. "He won't hesitate to hurt anyone who's threatening Rose. He'll see it as his duty."

Ervin wiped sweat from his neck. "What, does he think she's some sort of princess needing rescuing, or something? Because I can guarantee you—"

"Don't be ridiculous," Beaufort said. "The damsel in distress is a human creation, based merely on the fact that certain male humans like to think of themselves as superior to female ones simply because they're physically larger. Which is patently ridiculous. But Rose is Walter's friend, and humans are rather fragile, compared to dragons."

"Fragile isn't the word I'd use for Rose," Ervin said. "But whatever – you can't go crashing around the village."

"He's right," Mortimer said. "It won't help anything if the journalists see us again."

"Then how do we find Walter?" Beaufort asked. "And we *must* find him. This could be a disaster."

"We find Rose," Ervin said. "Can't you lot track her or something?"

"Not without a trail to start from," Beaufort said. "And even then, it's a delicate art."

"What about Angelus?" Gilbert asked. He'd been drinking from the stream, and now he rejoined them, water dripping from his jaws. "I bet he could find her."

They all looked at the dog, panting unhappily and straining at his collar. "Maybe?" Ervin said doubtfully.

"But Walter was chasing him all over the fells," Mortimer said. "Rose isn't out there, surely?"

"I'd run all over the fells if Walter was chasing me, too," Ervin said. "Let's try it." He crouched down next to Angelus and patted the big dog's head. Angelus glanced at him, then went back to staring down the track. "Where's Rose?" Ervin asked, his voice high-pitched and encouraging. "Where's Rose? Can you find Rose, boy?"

Angelus whined, taking a step down the path.

"He's doing it!" Gilbert exclaimed.

"Or he's just trying to get away from dragons," Ervin said.

"We may as well try," Beaufort said. "Lead on, lad."

"Joy," Ervin muttered, but he started jogging down the track, letting Angelus lead him.

Angelus was soon running as fast as Ervin would allow, the journalist leaping roots and stray rocks in the path and fending off low-hanging bushes with one hand as he went. The dragons loped behind, keeping a little distance between them, although Mortimer still wasn't sure if Angelus was actually running *to* Rose or simply *away* from them. But before long they were scrambling over the stile into the churchyard and sprinting through the dappled shade of the trees.

"He's going to Rose's," Beaufort said.

"He might just be going home," Mortimer pointed out, as Ervin opened the gate from the churchyard to the village hall, Angelus straining to pull them through.

"I don't think so," Gilbert said.

Mortimer glanced at him. "Why not?"

"Can't you hear it?"

Mortimer started to ask *hear what,* then he caught the sound. It rose faint but clear and unmistakable. It was the roar of a dragon, coming from the direction of Rose's house.

"Oh, no," he said quietly, and the three dragons washed around Ervin and Angelus, leaving them behind as they sprinted over the road and dived into the green cover of Rose's garden, following the roars to their source.

"Walter!"

Beaufort was in the lead as the dragons burst from the trees, and he leaped over the man cowering on the ground, passing DI Adams and meeting Walter with a clash of talons and scales that sounded like lightning exploding into a rockslide.

Walter roared his fury, tumbling sideways as Beaufort drove him back with his bulk, and Dandy, who was of such an enormous size that Mortimer almost tripped over his own paws in fright, slid around the dragons and came to a skidding stop just a little too late. His massive, dreadlocked form crashed into DI Adams and sent her to the ground, both of them giving matching yelps of alarm, then the dandy promptly shrank to a more manageable size, looking slightly apologetic. Behind them, the cowering man had rolled onto his belly, arms covering his head.

Meanwhile, tails and wings were going everywhere among the vegetables, punctuated by snarls and the crack of teeth and claws meeting.

"*Stand down,* Walter!" Beaufort bellowed.

"It's for Rose!"

"Don't be such a hatchling!"

"I'll give you hatchling—" The words fell into a roar, and the dragons rolled straight over the rhubarb, flattening all the stems.

Mortimer looked around wildly, seeing Alice pulling Rose out of the way as Beaufort and Walter rolled past again, spitting flames.

"Stop them!" Gilbert shouted. "Stop them, they're too old for this!" He hesitated as Alice and Rose glared at him. "They'll hurt themselves!" he insisted, and ran after the old dragons, shouting for them to stop. Mortimer wondered if he should follow. He wasn't at all sure he could be any help out there.

"Walter!" Rose shouted. "Walter, we've got him! You can stop now."

There was no response, just more roars and snarls and half-caught snatches of inventive cursing as the two old dragons flung themselves and each other furiously across the garden, colliding with trees and flattening everything in their path. Puffs of fiery breath scorched what little vegetation remained standing, and scales glittered as they fell in their wake.

"I don't think he's listening," Rose said.

Alice looked at Mortimer. "How do we stop them?" she asked.

"I don't know," he whispered, his eyes wide. "I'm not even sure we can, now."

DI Adams walked over with one hand pressed to her belly,

leaving Dandy sitting next to the man on the ground with both forepaws resting on the man's back. The dandy was about the size of Pearl's Labrador, but the man gave no sign that he might try to throw him off. Mortimer assumed the man had been able to see Dandy when he was fighting size. It would rather put one off trying to throw the dog anywhere.

DI Adams looked from the brawling dragons, with Gilbert bouncing around them pleading them to stop, to Rose and Alice, and said, "I don't know what I expected. Honestly, I *should* expect this by now. But you're just ..." she paused, looking for words, then shook her head and jogged after the dragons, shouting and flicking her bamboo switch in the air enthusiastically. "Stop! Stop it, both of you! What are you, dogs? Sorry," she added, glancing back at Dandy. He tilted his head. The dragons ignored her.

Alice looked at Rose. Rose folded her arms. "For the record, I regret nothing," she said, then followed DI Adams, yelling for Walter.

Alice turned back to Mortimer, and he braced himself to be ordered into the fight. "You haven't seen Miriam, have you?" she asked. "I seem to have lost her."

"Lost her?" Mortimer asked, and glanced at the man on the ground. There was a nasty stink coming from him, all closed rooms and lives turned inward, suspicious green and milky, unfocused anger. "Is that the murderer?"

"Yes. We followed him in here from his garden. Miriam was a little ahead of me – she must have been distracted elsewhere. There seem to be a lot of people in this garden."

Mortimer nodded as Collins emerged from the trees, looking a little pink. Thompson stalked in behind him, and stopped short. Collins blinked at DI Adams, who was making liberal use of her bamboo stick, then looked at the man on the ground and grunted. He took his handcuffs out and knelt by the man, giving no sign of seeing Dandy, who panted in his ear happily.

"You're under arrest," Collins announced, with evident pleasure, and the man made some irritated noise.

"Gods," Thompson said, still watching the dragons. Then, when that didn't seem to be enough, he sat down and added in a conversational tone, "May you all end up with pixies in your beds, you mangey bloody lizards. *And* humans. Old Ones take you." Then he started grooming a paw.

"Well, things seem to be in hand," Alice said. "Shall we go and find Miriam?"

Mortimer let out a little sigh of relief. "That would be good. I can't help here. I'm not much of a fighter."

Alice patted his shoulder. "That's something to be proud of, Mortimer. The world needs more people who use their brains before their fists. Or teeth." She thought about it. "Or words, for that matter."

Mortimer thought that there were far too many ways to cause violence in the world, when one thought about it.

❧

He led the way into the thicket of the garden, his ears twitching with the fighting going on behind them, as well as the sound of more altercations ahead. He wasn't sure how guilty he should feel about leaving Beaufort to battle Walter alone, but they really did need to find Miriam. Who knew if the murderer had accomplices.

Shouting from near the woodshed caught his ear, and he turned toward it, breaking into a trot.

"Is that her?" Alice asked, jogging behind him.

"I think so," he said, and a moment later they emerged onto the clear path by the shed. Ervin and Katherine were sparring with a hoe and a garden broom while Miriam stood next to the woodshed holding Angelus.

"Let me *through!*" Katherine shouted. "This is *my* story!"

"It's a murder!" he yelled back. "That's *my* story!"

"Freedom of press!"

"I *am* the press! You're a bloody tabloid hack! And a fake monster one at that!"

"You call those fake?"

"It's a dog!" Ervin waved wildly at Angelus, who whined and tried to hide behind Miriam. She patted his head, then spotted Mortimer and Alice. She waved brightly, and Mortimer lifted a paw in return. Miriam had some twigs in her hair, and the hem of her skirt was torn. Judging by the look of Katherine, Miriam and Ervin had formed some sort of tag team.

"He's not making those noises!" Katherine jabbed at Ervin with the broom. He parried, and for a moment there was nothing but the angry crack of wood on wood, and their panting breath. Alice took a couple of steps forward, picked up Katherine's camera from where she'd dropped it on the ground, and looked back at Mortimer.

"I think you should stay there."

"I rather think you're right," he agreed, and Alice handed him the camera then turned to face the scrapping journalists. Mortimer took the camera and retreated into the bushes. This was more his level, he felt. Let Beaufort handle Walter, and let Alice handle the journalists. He'd handle the camera.

It seemed a dreadfully long time before everything calmed down. Mortimer gathered that Jasmine and Ben had caught Lloyd, the cryptid photographer, and Jasmine had insisted that they bring him to the front of Rose's house and that Ben had to guard him and not go back into the garden. Which had been made slightly easier by Collins and the other tall police officer appearing with Campbell and Jean-Claude. Collins had left the two officers guarding the men and gone back to help DI Adams. Which had left only Katherine the Terrifying still roaming about, at risk of seeing dragons. Until Miriam caught her, at least. From what Mortimer could understand, because she was still a bit excited, she'd been doing rather a lot of tackling people today.

Campbell and Jean-Claude were forbidden to leave their cars, which had worked until they saw Rose coming up the garden with DI Adams. Then they'd both rushed out and tried to be the first to hug her, but were forced back by Angelus, who had decided he must protect Rose at all costs now that they were reunited. Rose waved them both away and told them they really did make such an extraordinary fuss, and how was one supposed to think?

The cryptid journalists were sent packing with a warning that they'd be charged with trespassing if they came back. No one knew where their cameras were, so they left empty-handed, Katherine glaring at Ervin and threatening him with a plagiarism suit if he wrote anything about cryptids in Toot Hansell. He informed her that he had all the story he needed, looking hopefully at DI Adams. She just dabbed blood from a scrape on her cheek and asked if anyone had any coffee.

Which was how they ended up in Alice's kitchen, surrounded by the scents of coffee brewing and bread warming in the oven, the table heaped with cakes removed from the Tupperware containers left behind by the ladies of the Woman's Institute. Mortimer currently had a slice of plum cake in one paw and a wedge of lemon drizzle in the other.

"Dandy, stop it," DI Adams said, holding a piece of ginger cake out of reach of the drooling dog. "You've already had my coffee."

"Maybe he wants a little something to take the taste away," Beaufort suggested. "I felt rather the same when I tried coffee."

DI Adams scowled at him. "Coffee is what stops me throwing things at you. All of you. Heavy things. Or possibly arrest warrants."

Beaufort nodded. "One must find one's own methods to make life tolerable, I suppose. I favour some good midnight flights, myself. Fast ones. Windy nights are best." He considered it. "Bluebells are also nice."

DI Adams blinked at him. "What, to eat?"

He returned her puzzled look. "No, to lie among." Mortimer could hear the *obviously* at the end, and took another piece of ginger cake, swallowing it quickly before Dandy noticed.

"Bluebells," Walter said. *"Flowers.* What sort of dragon are you?"

"One that …" Beaufort paused. "What's the word, Mortimer? For when you beat someone roundly in a fight?"

"I have no idea," Mortimer said around his ginger cake. It was very warm and soft, tasting of hot days and salt seas.

"Owned him," Gilbert suggested.

"You did not own me," Walter thundered, and Miriam clapped her hands over her ears. Beaufort grinned.

"Stop that, you two," Collins said, leaning back in his chair. His feet were crossed at the ankles and he was resting a mug of tea on the smooth rise of his belly. He looked rather more composed than DI Adams, who looked exactly as if she'd been rolling in the dirt fighting criminals. "I think you wiped out Rose's veggie garden entirely."

"Not entirely," Rose said, helping herself to some more shortbread. "And what are a few strawberries between friends?"

"It looked like it was going to be more than strawberries," Alice said. "What *were* you thinking with Walter, Rose?"

Walter lifted his head from his tea, frowning at them all, and Mortimer scooted a little closer to Miriam's chair.

Rose *hmm*ed thoughtfully. "I wasn't, really. I was just so *angry* at that Dougal. I wanted him good and scared."

"I rather think that worked," Collins said.

"And the running away?" DI Adams asked. "Did you really think we'd arrest you?"

Rose screwed up her face. "I don't know. I just panicked when I saw Meena. As I said, my sister's been in a home for years, and I was scared I was heading the same way. That's where I went on Friday night. After I left Campbell. I sneaked into her room at the home and sat with her until just before the carers started doing their rounds on Saturday morning. I was trying to see how it would feel, you know. To be there."

No one spoke for a moment, and Walter put a heavy paw on her knee, making the chair creak. "Silly human," he said, and gave her a toothy grin. Rose grinned back, and Angelus stared up at them with the whites of his eyes showing.

"What happened then?" DI Adams asked, her voice softer. "After you ran away from Alice's?"

"Oh. Well, I thought maybe I'd find some clues at home, something to make me feel sure I wasn't really going dotty, but just after I got inside the door blew shut in the wind and Ben heard it. So I ran back down the garden to hide and saw those bloody journalists lurking about the place. I knew I had to scare them off before they saw Mortimer or Walter."

"They wouldn't have seen *me,*" Walter said. "Some young dragons are no good at hiding, though."

Mortimer took a bit of lemon drizzle cake, his chest hot.

"Tosh," Rose said. "You were the one *drooling* on her, not Mortimer."

"But how did you end up in Dougal's shed?" Miriam asked.

"Oh, I ducked into his garden to hide, because I'd lost Angelus what with the dragons and all, so I didn't want to leave. I spotted my golf club in his damn shed, and was just about to run and find Ben, then *bam*. Lights out." She shrugged.

"You were very lucky," Collins said. "He could easily have killed you."

Walter growled. "I'd have had that bloody murderer if you hadn't all interfered."

"Not how it works," DI Adams said.

"It used to."

"It doesn't anymore."

"And you call that progress?"

"Walter," Beaufort said, the word a low rumble. Walter gave him a sulky look. He appeared to have lost a lot of scales, but the High Lord looked as if he'd enjoyed himself almost as much as he might a midnight flight. Or some bluebells.

"You were damn lucky I was looking for Rose," Walter said. "You'd have been too late."

"That's true," Alice said. "Your timing was excellent."

"Even if that bloody dog was my best lead and *you* chased me off," Walter said, baring his teeth at Gilbert. Gilbert looked indignant.

"I thought you were going to eat him!"

"Rubbish. You think I'm going to eat *everything.* I'm not a damn goblin."

"I almost wish you had eaten Dougal," Rose said, frowning. "I really thought I was going dotty."

Miriam put her hand on Rose's arm, and Rose gave her an uncertain smile. Those threads of concerned scent were still there, sharp and acrid as a lemon gone to rot.

"Can we do an interview?" Ervin asked, leaning forward and flashing his dimples at Rose. He had put his jumper back on, but it was torn at the neck and one sleeve was stretched longer than the other. "It'll add such a wonderful human dimension to the story."

"Absolutely not," Rose snapped. "I'm not having people think I'm old enough to doubt myself like that."

"But you did," Ervin started, and Alice cleared her throat firmly.

"Must you still be here?"

"Hey, I was key in keeping Katherine out of the way. *And* I got Rose's dog back."

"It was all very close," Colin said. "I thought for sure we were going to have Thompson running about hypnotising people again."

"It's *suggestion,*" the cat said from the windowsill. "I'm not some pub night Houdini."

"Wasn't he an escapologist?" Miriam asked.

"Whatever. You get the drift," the cat said. "And I'm going to have to do *something* about those journalists. Too risky to leave them poking about out there. You could've kept them for me rather than just letting them wander off."

"What were we meant to do, tie them up in Rose's woodshed?" Alice asked.

"You've got two detectives here. Surely you could've arrested them for something."

"Crimes against journalism," Ervin suggested.

"He's got the idea," Thompson said, and Ervin grinned.

"Don't encourage him," DI Adams said, glancing at her watch. Mortimer wasn't sure if she was referring to the journalist or the cat. "We need to get going. We've still got to interview Donny and maybe talk to Bethany again."

"Poor Bethany, " Rose said. "She really must have thought she was helping me."

"She did," DI Adams agreed. "But she obstructed an investigation and tampered with evidence. There has to be consequences for that."

Rose sighed, and Miriam patted her hand.

"So what happens now?" Alice asked. "Has this Dougal/Donny person confessed?"

"He's a little tougher than that," Collins said. "But he's done this sort of thing before. One that came out when his schemes came to light the first time was that he had three connecting properties in Chelsea. One he bought straight up, and one he got cheap after it had an unexpected attack of spontaneous combustion. The third was owned by an elderly gentleman who went into a sudden cognitive decline. I mean, according to his family, he was just fine, but the council social worker *Donny*, in his role as a concerned neighbour, called in, agreed that the only place for the poor old boy was a home. Which the house then had to be sold cheap to pay for. Oddly, the social worker came into a bit of money shortly afterward."

"Sudden cognitive decline?" Rose asked.

"Things turning up in strange places. His car parked on playgrounds. That sort of thing."

"I would very much have liked Walter to singe him, at least."

"Please tell me I'm getting an exclusive on this," Ervin said. "I will chase dogs and joust with cryptid journalists any time it's required."

"Do you think Eric disturbed Dougal when he was moving things around, then?" Alice asked.

"Quite likely," DI Adams said. "And framing Rose for it probably presented itself as a good nudge forward on getting her off the property."

"Definitely a singe," Rose said. "Maybe even a small nibble to the extremities."

Walter growled agreement. Dandy growled back, and Angelus howled, but didn't move from Rose's side. Mortimer backed up until he hit Miriam's legs.

She patted his shoulder and said, "Does this explain all the memory lapses, Rose?"

"I think so," she said slowly. "I think maybe I should do those tests after all, though. You know, just to be sure." She looked at her cup as she spoke, and for a long moment no one spoke.

Then Gilbert said, "While we're all here, can I just have a word about hedgehogs?"

DI Adams looked from him to Collins, then said, "Well. Things seem back to normal."

"Quite," Collins said, and took a piece of bread as Alice laid the board on the table, smelling of rosemary and garlic and the fresh days of spring. "Let's go before Jasmine arrives with the rest of the W.I."

"Oh, bloody hell," DI Adams said, and got up. "That would just be too much."

"That's a little rude," Alice said. "We've been very helpful."

DI Adams squinted at her, as if trying to decide if she were serious. "We've got a murderer to interview."

"We do at that," Collins said. "And Lucas to apologise to regarding the state of the crime scene." He got up, taking another piece of bread, and looked at Mortimer. "Did you get all the scales?"

"Please, small gods of worthless things, please tell me you got all the scales," Thompson said.

"I think so," Mortimer said, although he couldn't be sure. There had been an awful lot of them, all ground into the devastated garden.

"We did," Gilbert said. "I went over the whole place twice."

"Let's hope so," DI Adams said, and headed for the door. "I do not want that on my report."

"It'd be Lucas' report," Collins said, following her. "Found, one mysterious and possibly magical scale."

"He wouldn't put that, would he?"

"Depends how much D&D he's been playing."

DI Adams groaned as the door swung shut behind them.

"Hedgehogs," Gilbert said to Ervin. "Now *there's* a crime. Mass murder!"

EPILOGUE

MIRIAM

Spring had decided that a corner had been turned. The skies grew high and blue, the clouds turning into filmy white things with no strength to steal the heat of the sun. Gardens turned to growing in earnest, sprouting vines and shoots and blossom and buds, and Miriam gave up fighting to keep the weeds out of her vegetable garden. Some of them were quite pretty, anyway.

Now she rested against the low wall in front of Rose's house, the sun warm through the soft cloth of her blouse, and listened to a car purring up the road. Alice leaned next to her, her legs crossed at the ankles and her feet clad in some very summery sandals that looked at least as impractical as Miriam's flip-flops for Investigating.

"Is that her?" Teresa asked, peering down the road.

"I don't think you can tell by the sound of the car," Pearl said.

"I wasn't asking you," Teresa replied, and petted Angelus on his heavy head. His tail was going wildly, shaking his whole body. "*He* can tell."

It had been almost a week since the showdown in the garden, and Rose's house had only been released by the police a day ago. She'd been staying with Meena while she did the cognitive tests down in Manchester, so the W.I. had descended on the house immediately, scrubbing it clean of every trace of fingerprint dust and the footsteps of the police, and Miriam thought the whole place was likely cleaner than it had been in decades. She was actually mildly worried that Rose might have been cultivating spider colonies in the rafters, and that they'd vacuumed away years of research.

But the worn kitchen counters were spotless, the old tiles in the bathroom scrubbed to a startled shine, and Angelus had hit his head on the living room windows twice when he tried to put his head through them, evidently believing them to be open. Stray letters and research papers were stacked neatly in boxes fetched from the utility, and the kitchen table was crowded with chairs and laden with food, and Gert's sister's best friend's niece's step-brother had turned out to live not far away and to "have a way" with locks. He had been very efficient, and not even Alice had commented on the fact that none of the locks he fitted were new or matched at all, or that his prices were suspiciously reasonable. Miriam supposed it didn't matter. Rose was unlikely to start actually using them anyhow.

Rose's car came around the corner, and the nine ladies of the Toot Hansell Women's Institute got up and started to cheer. Angelus bounced on his lead, unsure whether to flee or join in, and a moment later Rose parked in front of them and climbed out, smiling her same Rose smile, her hair a particularly vivid electric blue. She folded her arms and leaned against the car. "What are you lot up to, then?"

No one spoke for a moment, then Alice said, "Well?"

Rose looked up at the sky, then back at them, her smile wider than ever. "The consultant says that she knows thirty-year-olds with more memory issues than me."

There was a pause, then Gert said, "Well, she does deal in cognitive decline, so is that a good thing or not?"

Rose laughed, and Miriam's heart lifted with the sound of it, shaking off all the fright and the worry and the endless, creeping concern of the weeks before. "It's a good thing," she said. "There's nothing wrong with my head. You're stuck with me."

The W.I. surged forward, arms open, hugging each other as much as Rose, creating a tangle of warmth and love and laughter that Miriam knew would have held Rose up no matter what the answer had been. It was both a vessel to carry them through the rough seas of the world and an embracing of all the complicated, painful, beautiful things that comprised it. She looked up at the sky, not bothering to blink away the hot tears in the corners of her eyes, and surrendered herself to the simple, glorious magic of friendship and sunlight and sweet spring days, and thought her heart could never hold all of it.

But no heart was designed to. Some things are boundless.

And that was exactly as it should be.

THANK YOU

Lovely reader, thank you so much for coming along on the Beaufort Scales journey. So many of you have emailed me, or chatted with me on the social medias, to let me know how Beaufort and the world of Toot Hansell have touched you, and it's the most wonderful thing. It makes this writer's heart so incredibly full and happy.

And all of you, whether you're quietly reading in a corner or reaching out to chat, you are all what makes this whole writing thing so entirely magical from a writer's point of view. Without your support for modern dragons and formidable women of a certain age, there would be no scaly sleuths and exasperated DIs, no snarky cats and invisible dogs. So thank you so, so much. You are all entirely wonderful.

And in order to spread the word about these slightly unorthodox sleuths, I'd appreciate it immensely if you could take the time to pop a quick review up at the webs of your choice. More readers means more dragons!

And if you'd like to send me a copy of your review, chat about dragons and baked goods, or anything else, drop me a message at kim@kmwatt.com. I'd love to hear from you!

Until next time,

Read on!

PS - head over the page to discover snarky cats and claim your free recipe collection!

SOMETHING'S STRANGE IN YORKSHIRE …

A missing dragon. A mysterious Beast.
A strange abduction …

DI Adams' missing person is a human, not a dragon. But the trails for both lead straight to the village of Eldmere, where glimpses of a mysterious Beast have drawn the attention of the nation's monster hunters.

Some of whom are more serious - and more dangerous - than DI Adams ever imagined ...

***Beast-Laid Plans* is out now!**

Scan the code to pre-order your copy in ebook (paperbacks coming soon), or use the link: https://readerlinks.com/l/2642212

RECIPES FOR ALL OCCASIONS

Rose's shortbread included!

One of these recipes includes frozen berries in the ingredients list, but if you're eyeing your chest freezer with suspicion then fresh will do just fine. But don't forget to stock up on frozen peas in case of invisible dogs ...

Head to the link to download a selection of Toot Hansell recipes for grey days and strange nights, spring mornings and autumn evenings. For always, really, because baked goods suit every occasion.

Plus, if this is your first visit to Toot Hansell and my newsletter, I'm also going to send you some story collections - including one about how that whole barbecue thing started ...

Your free recipe collection is waiting - grab it now!

Happy baking!

Scan above or head to https://readerlinks.com/l/2369430/curpb to claim your recipes todaY!

ACKNOWLEDGEMENTS

To you, lovely reader, who, whether for the first time or the sixth, have picked up a book about tea-drinking, crime-solving dragons. You are my people. Thank you so much.

No book grows in a vacuum (cat hair does, though, judging from what I find every time I do the floor), and as well as you lovely readers, there are some others without whom none of these stories would exist.

My wonderful beta readers are some of the best people I know. They are unfailingly supportive, critical in all the right ways, and my books would be in terrible shape without them. They're all, every single one, amazing friends and supporters. And fonts of information, especially when it comes to anything to do with gardens and entomologists. Tina, I will never not be grateful for the fact that I can ask you such pressing questions as, "can a pig roll their eyes ...?" and you will not only have the answer – you'll teach me weird and wonderful things at the same time.

And, every time, thank you Lynda Dietz at Easy Reader Editing. Every time I work with you I learn new things, and every time you work with me you must wonder how it's *still* possible that I'm misnaming characters, despite the many times that you have pointed out we have a character file to help us avoid just this situation. I couldn't ask for a better editor and friend. Please don't fire me.

ABOUT THE AUTHOR

Hello, lovely person. I'm Kim, and in addition to the Beaufort Scales stories I write other funny, magical books that offer a little escape from the serious stuff in the world and hopefully leave you a wee bit happier than you were when you started. Because happiness, like friendship, matters.

I write about baking-obsessed reapers setting up baby ghoul petting cafes, and ladies of a certain age joining the Apocalypse on their Vespas. I write about friendship, and loyalty, and lifting each other up, and the importance of tea and cake.

But mostly I write about how wonderful people (of all species) can really be.

If you'd like to find out the latest on new books in *The Beaufort Scales* series, as well as discover other books and series, giveaways, extra reading, and more, jump on over to www.kmwatt.com and check everything out there.

Read on!

amazon.com/Kim-M-Watt/e/B07JMHRBMC
goodreads.com/kimmwatt
bookbub.com/authors/kim-m-watt
facebook.com/KimMWatt
instagram.com/kimmwatt

ALSO BY KIM M. WATT

The Beaufort Scales Series (cozy mysteries with dragons)

"The addition of covert dragons to a cozy mystery is perfect ... and the dragons are as quirky and entertaining as the rest of the slightly eccentric residents of Toot Hansell."

– Goodreads reviewer

The Gobbelino London, PI series

"This series is a wonderful combination of humor and suspense that won't let you stop until you've finished the book. Fair warning, don't plan on doing anything else until you're done ..."

– Goodreads reviewer

The DI Adams Mysteries

"... will grip you within its story and not let go so be prepared going in with snacks and caffeine because you won't want to put it down."

– Goodreads reviewer

The Hollowbeck Paranormal Cozy Mysteries

(With Amelia Ash)

"It's a no-brainer to recommend this one to anyone who enjoys cozies. Or laughing. Or paranormal stuff. Or sarcastic wit. Or great writing in any form."

- Amazon reviewer

Short Story Collections

Oddly Enough: Tales of the Unordinary, Volume One

"The stories are quirky, charming, hilarious, and some are all of the above without a dud amongst the bunch ..."

– Goodreads reviewer

Need more stories?

Join the Ko-fi membership site for monthly, member-exclusive short stories, behind-the scenes content, early access to ebooks, and more!

Free stories!

The Cat Did It

Of course the cat did it. Sneaky, snarky, and up to no good – that's the cats in this feline collection, which you can grab free by signing up to the newsletter. Just remember – if the cat winks, always wink back ...

The Tales of Beaufort Scales

Modern dragons are a little different these days. There's the barbecue fixation, for starters ... You'll get these tales free once you've signed up for the newsletter!

Printed in Dunstable, United Kingdom

84137421R00204